D0998692

NEBULA AWARD STORIES TWO

NEBULA AWARD STORIES
☆☆TWO☆☆

EDITED BY BRIAN W. ALDISS
AND HARRY HARRISON

DOUBLEDAY AND COMPANY, INC.
GARDEN CITY, NEW YORK
1967

ALL OF THE CHARACTERS IN THIS BOOK ARE FICTITIOUS, AND ANY RESEMBLANCE TO ACTUAL PERSONS, LIVING OR DEAD, IS PURELY COINCIDENTAL.

LIBRARY OF CONGRESS CATALOG CARD NUMBER 66-20974

PRINTED IN THE UNITED STATES OF AMERICA
FIRST EDITION

CONTENTS

INTRODUCTION

This book is the second in a series that shows promise of continuing far into the very future which science fiction authors so lovingly write about. It is a creature born of inspiration, the product of the writers who are members of the organization known as the Science Fiction Writers of America.

SFWA is a new group, possibly the newest organization of professional writers in the world, an honor that surely matches the material it deals with. The first SFWA bulletin is dated January 1965; by January of 1967 the membership list stood at 266. All of them working, selling writers, since the requirements for membership specify just that.

Each year the members of SFWA nominate and vote for the stories and books that they consider the best produced during that year. In the spring, in simultaneous banquets in California and New York, the Nebula awards are presented. These handsome objects are more than just physical prizes, being tokens of achievement and worth from their associates to the deserving authors.

Because of length, the award-winning novel cannot be presented here, but that is the only exception. Here are the prize winning novella, novelette and short story, as well as a hand-picked selection from among the runners-up. Here is good fiction, by writers chosen by writers.

This volume closes with a panoramic look at the year in science fiction, at the books and stories and the books about science fiction that are slowly beginning to make their presence felt.

We, the editors, enjoyed our work, and our hope is to pass some of that enjoyment on to you, the reader.

Brian W. Aldiss

Harry Harrison

Though best known to the world as the author of The Sand Pebbles, *Richard McKenna had an earlier and most enthusiastic reception as a writer of first quality science fiction. It is therefore most fitting that this story, one of a half dozen found among his papers after his death, should receive the Nebula Award as the Best Short Story of the year. It is a sensitive piece of writing, a perfect example of second generation science fiction, the retelling and reexamination of a theme that originated in the pulp years of this medium.*

THE SECRET PLACE

Richard McKenna

This morning my son asked me what I did in the war. He's fifteen and I don't know why he never asked me before. I don't know why I never anticipated the question.

He was just leaving for camp, and I was able to put him off by saying I did government work. He'll be two weeks at camp. As long as the counselors keep pressure on him, he'll do well enough at group activities. The moment they relax it, he'll be off studying an ant colony or reading one of his books. He's on astronomy now. The moment he comes home, he'll ask me again just what I did in the war, and I'll have to tell him.

Nebula Award, Best Short Story 1966

But I don't understand just what I did in the war. Sometimes I think my group fought a death fight with a local myth and only Colonel Lewis realized it. I don't know who won. All I know is that war demands of some men risks more obscure and ignoble than death in battle. I know it did of me.

It began in 1931, when a local boy was found dead in the desert near Barker, Oregon. He had with him a sack of gold ore and one thumb-sized crystal of uranium oxide. The crystal ended as a curiosity in a Salt Lake City assay office until, in 1942, it became of strangely great importance. Army agents traced its probable origin to a hundred-square-mile area near Barker. Dr. Lewis was called to duty as a reserve colonel and ordered to find the vein. But the whole area was overlain by thousands of feet of Miocene lava flows and of course it was geological insanity to look there for a pegmatite vein. The area had no drainage pattern and had never been glaciated. Dr. Lewis protested that the crystal could have gotten there only by prior human agency.

It did him no good. He was told he's not to reason why. People very high up would not be placated until much money and scientific effort had been spent in a search. The army sent him young geology graduates, including me, and demanded progress reports. For the sake of morale, in a kind of frustrated desperation, Dr. Lewis decided to make the project a model textbook exercise in mapping the number and thickness of the basalt beds over the search area all the way down to the prevolcanic Miocene surface. That would at least be a useful addition to Columbia Plateau lithology. It would also be proof positive that no uranium ore existed there, so it was not really cheating.

That Oregon countryside was a dreary place. The search area was flat, featureless country with black lava outcropping everywhere through scanty gray soil in which sagebrush grew hardly knee high. It was hot and dry in summer and dismal with thin snow in winter. Winds howled across it at all seasons. Barker was about a hundred wooden houses on dusty streets, and some hay farms along a canal. All the young people were away at war or war jobs, and the old people seemed to resent us. There were twenty of us, apart from the contract drill crews who lived in their own trailer camps, and we were gown against town, in a way. We slept and ate at Colthorpe House, a block down the street from our headquarters. We had our own "gown" table there, and we might as well have been men from Mars.

I enjoyed it, just the same. Dr. Lewis treated us like students, with lectures and quizzes and assigned reading. He was a fine teacher and a brilliant scientist, and we loved him. He gave us all a turn at each phase of the work. I started on surface mapping and then worked with the drill crews, who were taking cores through the basalt and into the granite thousands of feet beneath. Then I worked on taking gravimetric and seismic readings. We had fine team spirit and we all knew we were getting priceless training in field geophysics. I decided privately that after the war I would take my doctorate in geophysics. Under Dr. Lewis, of course.

In early summer of 1944 the field phase ended. The contract drillers left. We packed tons of well logs and many boxes of gravimetric data sheets and seismic tapes for a move to Dr. Lewis's Midwestern university. There we would get more months of valuable training while we worked our data into a set of structure contour maps. We were all excited and talked a lot about being with girls again and going to parties. Then the army said part of the staff had to continue the field search. For technical compliance, Dr. Lewis decided to leave one man, and he chose me.

It hit me hard. It was like being flunked out unfairly. I thought he was heartlessly brusque about it.

"Take a jeep run through the area with a Geiger once a day," he said. "Then sit in the office and answer the phone."

"What if the army calls when I'm away?" I asked sullenly.

"Hire a secretary," he said. "You've an allowance for that."

So off they went and left me, with the title of field chief and only myself to boss. I felt betrayed to the hostile town. I decided I hated Colonel Lewis and wished I could get revenge. A few days later old Dave Gentry told me how.

He was a lean, leathery old man with a white mustache and I sat next to him in my new place at the "town" table. Those were grim meals. I heard remarks about healthy young men skulking out of uniform and wasting tax money. One night I slammed my fork into my half-emptied plate and stood up.

"The army sent me here and the army keeps me here," I told the dozen old men and women at the table. "I'd like to go overseas and cut Japanese throats for you kind hearts and gentle people, I really would! Why don't you all write your Congressman?"

I stamped outside and stood at one end of the veranda, boiling. Old Dave followed me out.

"Hold your horses, son," he said. "They hate the government, not you. But government's like the weather, and you're a man they can get aholt of."

"With their teeth," I said bitterly.

"They got reasons," Dave said. "Lost mines ain't supposed to be found the way you people are going at it. Besides that, the Crazy Kid mine belongs to us here in Barker."

He was past seventy and he looked after horses in the local feed-yard. He wore a shabby, open vest over faded suspenders and gray flannel shirts and nobody would ever have looked for wisdom in that old man. But it was there.

"This is big, new, lonesome country and it's hard on people," he said. "Every town's got a story about a lost mine or a lost gold cache. Only kids go looking for it. It's enough for most folks just to know it's there. It helps 'em to stand the country."

"I see," I said. Something stirred in the back of my mind.

"Barker never got its lost mine until thirteen years ago," Dave said. "Folks just naturally can't stand to see you people find it this way, by main force and so soon after."

"We know there isn't any mine," I said. "We're just proving it isn't there."

"If you could prove that, it'd be worse yet," he said. "Only you can't. We all saw and handled that ore. It was quartz, just rotten with gold in wires and flakes. The boy went on foot from his house to get it. The lode's got to be right close by out there."

He waved toward our search area. The air above it was luminous with twilight and I felt a curious surge of interest. Colonel Lewis had always discouraged us from speculating on that story. If one of us brought it up, I was usually the one who led the hooting and we all suggested he go over the search area with a dowsing rod. It was an article of faith with us that the vein did not exist. But now I was all alone and my own field boss.

We each put up one foot on the veranda rail and rested our arms on our knees. Dave bit off a chew of tobacco and told me about Owen Price.

"He was always a crazy kid and I guess he read every book in town," Dave said. "He had a curious heart, that boy."

I'm no folklorist, but even I could see how myth elements were already creeping into the story. For one thing, Dave insisted the boy's shirt was torn off and he had lacerations on his back.

"Like a cougar clawed him," Dave said. "Only they ain't never been cougars in that desert. We backtracked that boy till his trail crossed itself so many times it was no use, but we never found one cougar track."

I could discount that stuff, of course, but still the story gripped me. Maybe it was Dave's slow, sure voice; perhaps the queer twilight; possibly my own wounded pride. I thought of how great lava upwellings sometimes tear loose and carry along huge masses of the country rock. Maybe such an erratic mass lay out there, perhaps only a few hundred feet across and so missed by our drill cores, but rotten with uranium. If I could find it, I would make a fool of Colonel Lewis. I would discredit the whole science of geology. I, Duard Campbell, the despised and rejected one, could do that. The front of my mind shouted that it was nonsense, but something far back in my mind began composing a devastating letter to Colonel Lewis and comfort flowed into me.

"There's some say the boy's youngest sister could tell where he found it, if she wanted," Dave said. "She used to go into that desert with him a lot. She took on pretty wild when it happened and then was struck dumb, but I hear she talks again now." He shook his head. "Poor little Helen. She promised to be a pretty girl."

"Where does she live?" I asked.

"With her mother in Salem," Dave said. "She went to business school and I hear she works for a lawyer there."

Mrs. Price was a flinty old woman who seemed to control her

daughter absolutely. She agreed Helen would be my secretary as soon as I told her the salary. I got Helen's security clearance with one phone call; she had already been investigated as part of tracing that uranium crystal. Mrs. Price arranged for Helen to stay with a family she knew in Barker, to protect her reputation. It was in no danger. I meant to make love to her, if I had to, to charm her out of her secret, if she had one, but I would not harm her. I knew perfectly well that I was only playing a game called "The Revenge of Duard Campbell." I knew I would not find any uranium.

Helen was a plain little girl and she was made of frightened ice. She wore low-heeled shoes and cotton stockings and plain dresses with white cuffs and collars. Her one good feature was her flawless fair skin against which her peaked, black Welsh eyebrows and smoky blue eyes gave her an elfin look at times. She liked to sit neatly tucked into herself, feet together, elbows in, eyes cast down, voice hardly audible, as smoothly self-contained as an egg. The desk I gave her faced mine and she sat like that across from me and did the busy work I gave her and I could not get through to her at all.

I tried joking and I tried polite little gifts and attentions, and I tried being sad and needing sympathy. She listened and worked and stayed as far away as the moon. It was only after two weeks and by pure accident that I found the key to her.

I was trying the sympathy gambit. I said it was not so bad, being exiled from friends and family, but what I could not stand was the dreary sameness of that search area. Every spot was like every other spot and there was no single, recognizable *place* in the whole expanse. It sparked something in her and she roused up at me.

"It's full of just wonderful places," she said.

"Come out with me in the jeep and show me one," I challenged.

She was reluctant, but I hustled her along regardless. I guided the jeep between outcrops, jouncing and lurching. I had our map photographed on my mind and I knew where we were every minute, but only by map coordinates. The desert had our marks on it: well sites, seismic blast holes, wooden stakes, cans, bottles and papers blowing in that everlasting wind, and it was all dismally the same anyway.

"Tell me when we pass a 'place' and I'll stop," I said.

"It's all places," she said. "Right here's a place."

I stopped the jeep and looked at her in surprise. Her voice was strong and throaty. She opened her eyes wide and smiled; I had never seen her look like that.

"What's special, that makes it a place?" I asked.

She did not answer. She got out and walked a few steps. Her whole posture was changed. She almost danced along. I followed and touched her shoulder.

"Tell me what's special," I said.

She faced around and stared right past me. She had a new grace and vitality and she was a very pretty girl.

"It's where all the dogs are," she said.

"Dogs?"

I looked around at the scrubby sagebrush and thin soil and ugly black rock and back at Helen. Something was wrong.

"Big, stupid dogs that go in herds and eat grass," she said. She kept turning and gazing. "Big cats chase the dogs and eat them. The dogs scream and scream. Can't you hear them?"

"That's crazy!" I said. "What's the matter with you?"

I might as well have slugged her. She crumpled instantly back into herself and I could hardly hear her answer.

"I'm sorry. My brother and I used to play out fairy tales here. All this was a kind of fairyland to us." Tears formed in her eyes. "I haven't been here since . . . I forgot myself. I'm sorry."

I had to swear I needed to dictate "field notes" to force Helen into that desert again. She sat stiffly with pad and pencil in the jeep while I put on my act with the Geiger and rattled off jargon. Her lips were pale and compressed and I could see her fighting against the spell the desert had for her, and I could see her slowly losing.

She finally broke down into that strange mood and I took good care not to break it. It was weird but wonderful, and I got a lot of data. I made her go out for "field notes" every morning and each time it was easier to break her down. Back in the office she always froze again and I marveled at how two such different persons could inhabit the same body. I called her two phases "Office Helen" and "Desert Helen."

I often talked with old Dave on the veranda after dinner. One night he cautioned me.

"Folks here think Helen ain't been right in the head since her brother died," he said. "They're worrying about you and her."

"I feel like a big brother to her," I said. "I'd never hurt her, Dave. If we find the lode, I'll stake the best claim for her."

He shook his head. I wished I could explain to him how it was only a harmless game I was playing and no one would ever find gold out there. Yet, as a game, it fascinated me.

Desert Helen charmed me when, helplessly, she had to uncover her secret life. She was a little girl in a woman's body. Her voice became strong and breathless with excitement and she touched me with the same wonder that turned her own face vivid and elfin. She ran laughing through the black rocks and scrubby sagebrush and momentarily she made them beautiful. She would pull me along by the hand and sometimes we ran as much as a mile away from the jeep. She treated me as if I were a blind or foolish child.

"No, no, Duard, that's a cliff!" she would say, pulling me back.

She would go first, so I could find the stepping stones across streams. I played up. She pointed out woods and streams and cliffs and castles. There were shaggy horses with claws, golden birds, camels, witches, elephants and many other creatures. I pretended to see them all, and it made her trust me. She talked and acted out the fairy tales she had once played with Owen. Sometimes he was enchanted and sometimes she, and the one had to dare the evil magic of a witch or giant to rescue the other. Sometimes I was Duard and other times I almost thought I was Owen.

Helen and I crept into sleeping castles, and we hid with pounding hearts while the giant grumbled in search of us and we fled, hand in hand, before his wrath.

Well, I had her now. I played Helen's game, but I never lost sight of my own. Every night I sketched in on my map whatever I had learned that day of the fairyland topography. Its geomorphology was remarkably consistent.

When we played, I often hinted about the giant's treasure. Helen never denied it existed, but she seemed troubled and evasive about it. She would put her finger to her lips and look at me with solemn, round eyes.

"You only take the things nobody cares about," she would say. "If you take the gold or jewels, it brings you terrible bad luck."

"I got a charm against bad luck and I'll let you have it too," I said once. "It's the biggest, strongest charm in the whole world."

"No. It all turns into trash. It turns into goat beans and dead snakes and things," she said crossly. "Owen told me. It's a rule, in fairyland."

Another time we talked about it as we sat in a gloomy ravine near a waterfall. We had to keep our voices low or we would wake up the giant. The waterfall was really the giant snoring and it was also the wind that blew forever across that desert.

"Doesn't Owen ever take anything?" I asked.

I had learned by then that I must always speak of Owen in the present tense.

"Sometimes he has to," she said. "Once right here the witch had me enchanted into an ugly toad. Owen put a flower on my head and that made me be Helen again."

"A really truly flower? That you could take home with you?"

"A red and yellow flower bigger than my two hands," she said. "I tried to take it home, but all the petals came off."

"Does Owen ever take anything home?"

"Rocks, sometimes," she said. "We keep them in a secret nest in the shed. We think they might be magic eggs."

I stood up. "Come and show me."

She shook her head vigorously and drew back. "I don't want to go home," she said. "Not ever."

She squirmed and pouted, but I pulled her to her feet.

"Please, Helen, for me," I said. "Just for one little minute."

I pulled her back to the jeep and we drove to the old Price place. I had never seen her look at it when we passed it and she did not look now. She was freezing fast back into Office Helen. But she led me around the sagging old house with its broken windows and into a tumbledown shed. She scratched away some straw in one corner, and there were the rocks. I did not realize how excited I was until disappointment hit me like a blow in the stomach.

They were worthless waterworn pebbles of quartz and rosy granite. The only thing special about them was that they could never have originated on that basalt desert.

After a few weeks we dropped the pretense of field notes and simply went into the desert to play. I had Helen's fairyland almost completely mapped. It seemed to be a recent fault block mountain with a river parallel to its base and a gently sloping plain across the river. The scarp face was wooded and cut by deep ravines and it had castles perched on its truncated spurs. I kept checking Helen on it and never found her inconsistent. Several times when she was in doubt I was able to tell her where she was, and that let me even more deeply into her secret life. One morning I discovered just how deeply.

She was sitting on a log in the forest and plaiting a little basket out of fern fronds. I stood beside her. She looked up at me and smiled.

"What shall we play today, Owen?" she asked.

I had not expected that, and I was proud of how quickly I rose to it. I capered and bounded away and then back to her and crouched at her feet.

"Little sister, little sister, I'm enchanted," I said. "Only you in all the world can uncharm me."

"I'll uncharm you," she said, in that little girl voice. "What are you, brother?"

"A big, black dog," I said. "A wicked giant named Lewis Rawbones keeps me chained up behind his castle while he takes all the other dogs out hunting."

She smoothed her gray skirt over her knees. Her mouth drooped.

"You're lonesome and you howl all day and you howl all night," she said. "Poor doggie."

I threw back my head and howled.

"He's a terrible, wicked giant and he's got all kinds of terrible magic," I said. "You mustn't be afraid, little sister. As soon as you uncharm me I'll be a handsome prince and I'll cut off his head."

"I'm not afraid." Her eyes sparkled. "I'm not afraid of fire or snakes or pins or needles or anything."

"I'll take you away to my kingdom and we'll live happily ever afterward. You'll be the most beautiful queen in the world and everybody will love you."

I wagged my tail and laid my head on her knees. She stroked my silky head and pulled my long black ears.

"Everybody will love me." She was very serious now. "Will magic water uncharm you, poor old doggie?"

"You have to touch my forehead with a piece of the giant's treasure," I said. "That's the only onliest way to uncharm me."

I felt her shrink away from me. She stood up, her face suddenly crumpled with grief and anger.

"You're not Owen, you're just a man! Owen's enchanted and I'm enchanted too and nobody will ever uncharm us!"

She ran away from me and she was already Office Helen by the time she reached the jeep.

After that day she refused flatly to go into the desert with me. It looked as if my game was played out. But I gambled that Desert Helen could still hear me, underneath somewhere, and I tried a new strategy. The office was an upstairs room over the old dance hall and, I suppose, in frontier days skirmishing had gone on there between men and women. I doubt anything went on as strange as my new game with Helen.

I always had paced and talked while Helen worked. Now I began mixing common-sense talk with fairyland talk and I kept coming back to the wicked giant, Lewis Rawbones. Office Helen tried not to pay attention, but now and then I caught Desert Helen peeping at me out of her eyes. I spoke of my blighted career as a geologist and how it would be restored to me if I found the lode. I mused on how I would live and work in exotic places and how I would need a wife to keep house for me and help with my paper work. It disturbed Office Helen. She made typing mistakes and dropped things. I kept it up for days, trying for just the right mixture of fact and fantasy, and it was hard on Office Helen.

One night old Dave warned me again.

"Helen's looking peaked, and there's talk around. Miz Fowler says Helen don't sleep and she cries at night and she won't tell Miz Fowler what's wrong. You don't happen to know what's bothering her, do you?"

"I only talk business stuff to her," I said. "Maybe she's homesick. I'll ask her if she wants a vacation." I did not like the way Dave looked at me. "I haven't hurt her. I don't mean her any harm, Dave," I said.

"People get killed for what they do, not for what they mean," he said. "Son, there's men in this here town would kill you quick as a coyote, if you hurt Helen Price."

I worked on Helen all the next day and in the afternoon I hit just the right note and I broke her defenses. I was not prepared for the way it worked out. I had just said, "All life is a kind of playing. If you think about it right, everything we do is a game." She poised her pencil and looked straight at me, as she had never done in that office, and I felt my heart speed up.

"You taught me how to play, Helen. I was so serious that I didn't know how to play."

"Owen taught me to play. He had magic. My sisters couldn't play anything but dolls and rich husbands and I hated them."

Her eyes opened wide and her lips trembled and she was almost Desert Helen right there in the office.

"There's magic and enchantment in regular life, if you look at it right," I said. "Don't you think so, Helen?"

"I know it!" she said. She turned pale and dropped her pencil. "Owen was enchanted into having a wife and three daughters and he was just a boy. But he was the only man we had and all of them but me hated him because we were so poor." She began to tremble and her voice went flat. "He couldn't stand it. He took the treasure and it killed him." Tears ran down her cheeks. "I tried to think he was only enchanted into play-dead and if I didn't speak or laugh for seven years, I'd uncharm him."

She dropped her head on her hands. I was alarmed. I came over and put my hand on her shoulder.

"I did speak." Her shoulders heaved with sobs. "They made me speak, and now Owen won't ever come back."

I bent and put my arm across her shoulders.

"Don't cry, Helen. He'll come back," I said. "There are other magics to bring him back."

I hardly knew what I was saying. I was afraid of what I had done, and I wanted to comfort her. She jumped up and threw off my arm.

"I can't stand it! I'm going home!"

She ran out into the hall and down the stairs and from the window I saw her run down the street, still crying. All of a sudden my game seemed cruel and stupid to me and right that moment I stopped it. I tore up my map of fairyland and my letters to Colonel Lewis and I wondered how in the world I could ever have done all that.

After dinner that night old Dave motioned me out to one end of the veranda. His face looked carved out of wood.

"I don't know what happened in your office today, and for your sake I better not find out. But you send Helen back to her mother on the morning stage, you hear me?"

"All right, if she wants to go," I said. "I can't just fire her."

"I'm speaking for the boys. You better put her on that morning stage, or we'll be around to talk to you."

"All right, I will, Dave."

I wanted to tell him how the game was stopped now and how I wanted a chance to make things up with Helen, but I thought I had better not. Dave's voice was flat and savage with contempt and, old as he was, he frightened me.

Helen did not come to work in the morning. At nine o'clock I went out myself for the mail. I brought a large mailing tube and some letters back to the office. The first letter I opened was from Dr. Lewis, and almost like magic it solved all my problems.

On the basis of his preliminary structure contour maps Dr. Lewis had gotten permission to close out the field phase. Copies of the maps were in the mailing tube, for my information. I was to hold an inventory and be ready to turn everything over to an army quartermaster team coming in a few days. There was still a great mass of data to be worked up in refining the maps. I was to join the group again and I would have a chance at the lab work after all.

I felt pretty good. I paced and whistled and snapped my fingers. I wished Helen would come, to help on the inventory. Then I opened the tube and looked idly at the maps. There were a lot of them, featureless bed after bed of basalt, like layers of a cake ten miles across. But when I came to the bottom map, of the prevolcanic Miocene landscape, the hair on my neck stood up.

I had made that map myself. It was Helen's fairyland. The topography was point by point the same.

I clenched my fists and stopped breathing. Then it hit me a second time, and the skin crawled up my back.

The game was real. I couldn't end it. All the time the game had been playing me. It was still playing me.

I ran out and down the street and overtook old Dave hurrying toward the feedyard. He had a holstered gun on each hip.

"Dave, I've got to find Helen," I said.

"Somebody seen her hiking into the desert just at daylight," he said. "I'm on my way for a horse." He did not slow his stride. "You better get out there in your stinkwagon. If you don't find her before we do, you better just keep on going, son."

I ran back and got the jeep and roared it out across the scrubby sagebrush. I hit rocks and I do not know why I did not break something. I knew where to go and feared what I would find there. I knew I loved Helen Price more than my own life and I knew I had driven her to her death.

I saw her far off, running and dodging. I headed the jeep to intercept her and I shouted, but she neither saw me nor heard me. I stopped and jumped out and ran after her and the world darkened. Helen was all I could see, and I could not catch up with her.

"Wait for me, little sister!" I screamed after her. "I love you, Helen! Wait for me!"

She stopped and crouched and I almost ran over her. I knelt and put my arms around her and then it was on us.

They say in an earthquake, when the direction of up and down tilts and wobbles, people feel a fear that drives them mad if they can not forget it afterward. This was worse. Up and down and here and there and now and then all rushed together. The wind roared through the rock beneath us and the air thickened crushingly above our heads. I know we clung to each other, and we were there for each other while nothing else was and that is all I know, until we were in the jeep and I was guiding it back toward town as headlong as I had come.

Then the world had shape again under a bright sun. I saw a knot of horsemen on the horizon. They were heading for where Owen had been found. That boy had run a long way, alone and hurt and burdened.

I got Helen up to the office. She sat at her desk with her head down on her hands and she quivered violently. I kept my arm around her.

"It was only a storm inside our two heads, Helen," I said, over and over. "Something black blew away out of us. The game is finished and we're free and I love you."

Over and over I said that, for my sake as well as hers. I meant and believed it. I said she was my wife and we would marry and go a thousand miles away from that desert to raise our children. She quieted to a trembling, but she would not speak. Then I heard hoofbeats and the creak of leather in the street below and then I heard slow footsteps on the stairs.

Old Dave stood in the doorway. His two guns looked as natural on him as hands and feet. He looked at Helen, bowed over the desk, and then at me, standing beside her.

"Come on down, son. The boys want to talk to you," he said.

I followed him into the hall and stopped.

"She isn't hurt," I said. "The lode is really out there, Dave, but nobody is ever going to find it."

"Tell that to the boys."

"We're closing out the project in a few more days," I said. "I'm going to marry Helen and take her away with me."

"Come down or we'll drag you down!" he said harshly. "We'll send Helen back to her mother."

I was afraid. I did not know what to do.

"No, you won't send me back to my mother!"

It was Helen beside me in the hall. She was Desert Helen, but grown up and wonderful. She was pale, pretty, aware and sure of herself.

"I'm going with Duard," she said. "Nobody in the world is ever going to send me around like a package again."

Dave rubbed his jaw and squinted his eyes at her.

"I love her, Dave," I said. "I'll take care of her all my life."

I put my left arm around her and she nestled against me. The tautness went out of old Dave and he smiled. He kept his eyes on Helen.

"Little Helen Price," he said, wonderingly. "Who ever would've thought it?" He reached out and shook us both gently. "Bless you youngsters," he said, and blinked his eyes. "I'll tell the boys it's all right."

He turned and went slowly down the stairs. Helen and I looked at each other, and I think she saw a new face too.

That was sixteen years ago. I am a professor myself now, graying a bit at the temples. I am as positivistic a scientist as you will find anywhere in the Mississippi drainage basin. When I tell a seminar student "That assertion is operationally meaningless," I can make it sound downright obscene. The students blush and hate me, but it is for their own good. Science is the only safe game, and it's safe only if it is kept pure. I work hard at that, I have yet to meet the student I can not handle.

My son is another matter. We named him Owen Lewis, and he has Helen's eyes and hair and complexion. He learned to read on the modern sane and sterile children's books. We haven't a fairy tale in the house—but I have a science library. And Owen makes fairy tales out of science. He is taking the measure of space and time now, with Jeans and Eddington. He cannot possibly understand a tenth of what he reads, in the way I understand it. But he understands all of it in some other way privately his own.

Not long ago he said to me, "You know, Dad, it isn't only space that's expanding. Time's expanding too, and that's what makes us keep getting farther away from when we used to be."

And I have to tell him just what I did in the war. I know I found manhood and a wife. The how and why of it I think and hope I am incapable of fully understanding. But Owen has, through Helen, that strangely curious heart. I'm afraid. I'm afraid he will understand.

"Light of Other Days" is one of the three short stories that tied for first place in the penultimate ballot. Its author, Bob Shaw, is a newspaper reporter who has sold a small but steady stream of tales to the science fiction magazines. He confesses he is addicted to puns and whiskey—and the "e" in that "whiskey" goes toward revealing something of his origins; for Bob Shaw is a sturdy Irishman in his mid-thirties, Belfast born and bred. He is married and has three children. He says he admires the writing of Lawrence Durrell; the only science fiction writer he will commit himself to naming is Anthony Burgess. Though by no means as prolific a writer as Burgess, Shaw is now working on his first novel, which has been contracted for by Avon.

LIGHT OF OTHER DAYS

Bob Shaw

Leaving the village behind, we followed the heady sweeps of the road up into a land of slow glass.

I had never seen one of the farms before and at first found them slightly eerie—an effect heightened by imagination and circumstance. The car's turbine was pulling smoothly and quietly in the damp air so that we seemed to be carried over the convolutions of the road in a kind of supernatural silence. On our right the mountain sifted down into an incredibly perfect valley of timeless pine, and everywhere stood the great frames of slow glass, drinking light. An occasional flash of afternoon sunlight on their wind bracing created an illusion of movement, but in fact the frames were deserted. The rows of windows had been standing on the hillside for years, staring into the valley, and men only cleaned them in the middle of the night when their human presence would not matter to the thirsty glass.

They were fascinating, but Selina and I didn't mention the windows. I think we hated each other so much we both were reluctant to sully anything new by drawing it into the nexus of our emotions. The holiday, I had begun to realize, was a stupid idea in the first place. I had thought it would cure everything, but, of course, it didn't stop Selina being pregnant and, worse still, it didn't even stop her being angry about being pregnant.

Rationalizing our dismay over her condition, we had circulated the usual statements to the effect that we would have *liked* having children—but later on, at the proper time. Selina's pregnancy had cost us her well-paid job and with it the new house we had been negotiating and which was far beyond the reach of my income from poetry. But the real source of our annoyance was that we were face to face with the realization that people who say they want children later always mean they want children never. Our nerves were thrumming with the knowledge that we, who had thought ourselves so unique, had fallen into the same biological trap as every mindless rutting creature which ever existed.

The road took us along the southern slopes of Ben Cruachan until we began to catch glimpses of the gray Atlantic far ahead. I had just cut our speed to absorb the view better when I noticed the sign spiked to a gatepost. It said: "SLOW GLASS—Quality High, Prices Low—J. R. Hagan." On an impulse I stopped the car on the verge, wincing slightly as tough grasses whipped noisily at the bodywork.

"Why have we stopped?" Selina's neat, smoke-silver head turned in surprise.

"Look at that sign. Let's go up and see what there is. The stuff might be reasonably priced out here."

Selina's voice was pitched high with scorn as she refused, but I was too taken with my idea to listen. I had an illogical conviction that doing something extravagant and crazy would set us right again.

"Come on," I said, "the exercise might do us some good. We've been driving too long anyway."

She shrugged in a way that hurt me and got out of the car. We walked up a path made of irregular, packed clay steps nosed with short lengths of sapling. The path curved through trees which clothed the edge of the hill and at its end we found a low farmhouse. Beyond the little stone building tall frames of slow glass gazed out towards the voice-stilling sight of Cruachan's ponderous descent towards the waters of Loch Linnhe. Most of the panes were perfectly transparent but a few were dark, like panels of polished ebony.

As we approached the house through a neat cobbled yard a tall middle-aged man in ash-colored tweeds arose and waved to us. He had been sitting on the low rubble wall which bounded the yard, smoking a pipe and staring towards the house. At the front window of the cottage a young woman in a tangerine dress stood with a small boy in her arms, but she turned disinterestedly and moved out of sight as we drew near.

"Mr. Hagan?" I guessed.

"Correct. Come to see some glass, have you? Well, you've come to the right place." Hagan spoke crisply, with traces of the pure highland which sounds so much like Irish to the unaccustomed ear. He had one of those calmly dismayed faces one finds on elderly road-menders and philosophers.

"Yes," I said. "We're on holiday. We saw your sign."

Selina, who usually has a natural fluency with strangers, said nothing. She was looking towards the now empty window with what I thought was a slightly puzzled expression.

"Up from London, are you? Well, as I said, you've come to the right place—and at the right time, too. My wife and I don't see many people this early in the season."

I laughed. "Does that mean we might be able to buy a little glass without mortgaging our home?"

"Look at that now," Hagan said, smiling helplessly. "I've thrown away any advantage I might have had in the transaction. Rose, that's my wife, says I never learn. Still, let's sit down and talk it over." He pointed at the rubble wall then glanced doubtfully at Selina's immaculate blue skirt. "Wait till I fetch a rug from the house." Hagan limped quickly into the cottage, closing the door behind him.

"Perhaps it wasn't such a marvelous idea to come up here," I whispered to Selina, "but you might at least be pleasant to the man. I think I can smell a bargain."

"Some hope," she said with deliberate coarseness. "Surely even you must have noticed that ancient dress his wife is wearing? He won't give much away to strangers."

"Was that his wife?"

"Of course that was his wife."

"Well, well," I said, surprised. "Anyway, try to be civil with him. I don't want to be embarrassed."

Selina snorted, but she smiled whitely when Hagan reappeared and I relaxed a little. Strange how a man can love a woman and yet at the same time pray for her to fall under a train.

Hagan spread a tartan blanket on the wall and we sat down, feeling slightly self-conscious at having been translated from our city-oriented lives into a rural tableau. On the distant slate of the Loch, beyond the watchful frames of slow glass, a slow-moving steamer drew a white line towards the south. The boisterous mountain air seemed almost to invade our lungs, giving us more oxygen than we required.

"Some of the glass farmers around here," Hagan began, "give strangers, such as yourselves, a sales talk about how beautiful the autumn is in this part of Argyll. Or it might be the spring, or the winter. I don't do that—any fool knows that a place which doesn't look right in summer never looks right. What do you say?"

I nodded compliantly.

"I want you just to take a good look out towards Mull, Mr. . . ."

"Garland."

". . . Garland. That's what you're buying if you buy my glass, and it never looks better than it does at this minute. The glass is in perfect phase, none of it is less than ten years thick—and a four-foot window will cost you two hundred pounds."

"*Two hundred!*" Selina was shocked. "That's as much as they charge at the Scenedow shop in Bond Street."

Hagan smiled patiently, then looked closely at me to see if I knew enough about slow glass to appreciate what he had been saying. His price had been much higher than I had hoped—but *ten years thick!*

The cheap glass one found in places like the Vistaplex and Pane-o-rama stores usually consisted of a quarter of an inch of ordinary glass faced with a veneer of slow glass perhaps only ten or twelve months thick.

"You don't understand, darling," I said, already determined to buy. "This glass will last ten years and it's in phase."

"Doesn't that only mean it keeps time?"

Hagan smiled at her again, realizing he had no further necessity to bother with me. "Only, you say! Pardon me, Mrs. Garland, but you don't seem to appreciate the miracle, the genuine honest-to-goodness miracle, of engineering precision needed to produce a piece of glass in phase. When I say the glass is ten years thick it means it takes light ten years to pass through it. In effect, each one of those panes is ten light-years thick—more than twice the distance to the nearest star—so a variation in actual thickness of only a millionth of an inch would . . ."

He stopped talking for a moment and sat quietly looking towards the house. I turned my head from the view of the Loch and saw the young woman standing at the window again. Hagan's eyes were filled with a kind of greedy reverence which made me feel uncomfortable and at the same time convinced me Selina had been wrong. In my experience husbands never looked at wives that way, at least, not at their own.

The girl remained in view for a few seconds, dress glowing warmly, then moved back into the room. Suddenly I received a distinct, though inexplicable, impression she was blind. My feeling was that Selina and I were perhaps blundering through an emotional interplay as violent as our own.

"I'm sorry," Hagan continued, "I thought Rose was going to call me for something. Now, where was I, Mrs. Garland? Ten light-years compressed into a quarter of an inch means . . ."

I ceased to listen, partly because I was already sold, partly because I had heard the story of slow glass many times before and had never yet understood the principles involved. An acquaintance with scientific training had once tried to be helpful by telling me to visualize a pane of slow glass as a hologram which did not need coherent light from a laser for the reconstitution of its visual information, and in which every photon of ordinary light passed through a spiral tunnel coiled outside the radius of capture of each atom in the glass. This gem of, to me, incomprehensibility not only told me nothing, it convinced me once again that a mind as nontechnical as mine should concern itself less with causes than effects.

The most important effect, in the eyes of the average individual, was that light took a long time to pass through a sheet of slow glass. A new piece was always jet black because nothing had yet come through, but one could stand the glass beside, say, a woodland lake until the scene emerged, perhaps a year later. If the glass was then removed and installed in a dismal city flat, the flat would—for that year—appear to overlook the woodland lake. During the year it wouldn't be merely a very realistic but still picture—the water would ripple in sunlight, silent animals would come to drink, birds would cross the sky, night would follow day, season would follow season. Until one day, a year later, the beauty held in the subatomic pipelines would be exhausted and the familiar gray cityscape would reappear.

Apart from its stupendous novelty value, the commercial success of slow glass was founded on the fact that having a scenedow was the exact emotional equivalent of owning land. The meanest cave dweller could look out on misty parks—and who was to say they weren't his? A man who really owns tailored gardens and estates doesn't spend his time proving his ownership by crawling on his ground, feeling, smelling, tasting it. All he receives from the land are light patterns, and with scenedows those patterns could be taken into coal mines, submarines, prison cells.

On several occasions I have tried to write short pieces about the enchanted crystal but, to me, the theme is so ineffably poetic as to be, paradoxically, beyond the reach of poetry—mine at any rate. Besides, the best songs and verse had already been written, with prescient inspiration, by men who had died long before slow glass was discovered. I had no hope of equaling, for example, Moore with his:

Oft in the stilly night,
Ere slumber's chain has bound me,
Fond Memory brings the light,
Of other days around me . . .

It took only a few years for slow glass to develop from a scientific curiosity to a sizable industry. And much to the astonishment of we poets—those of us who remain convinced that beauty lives though lilies die—the trappings of that industry were no different from those of any other. There were good scenedows which cost a lot of money, and there were inferior scenedows which cost rather less. The thickness, measured in years, was an important factor in the cost but there was also the question of *actual* thickness, or phase.

Even with the most sophisticated engineering techniques available thickness control was something of a hit-and-miss affair. A coarse discrepancy could mean that a pane intended to be five years thick might be five and a half, so that light which entered in summer emerged in winter; a fine discrepancy could mean that noon sunshine emerged at midnight. These incompatibilities had their peculiar charm—many night workers, for example, liked having their own private time zones—but, in general, it cost more to buy scenedows which kept closely in step with real time.

Selina still looked unconvinced when Hagan had finished speaking. She shook her head almost imperceptibly and I knew he had been using the wrong approach. Quite suddenly the pewter helmet of her hair was disturbed by a cool gust of wind, and huge clean tumbling drops of rain began to spang round us from an almost cloudless sky.

"I'll give you a check now," I said abruptly, and saw Selina's green eyes triangulate angrily on my face. "You can arrange delivery?"

"Aye, delivery's no problem," Hagan said, getting to his feet. "But wouldn't you rather take the glass with you?"

"Well, yes—if you don't mind." I was shamed by his readiness to trust my scrip.

"I'll unclip a pane for you. Wait here. It won't take long to slip it into a carrying frame." Hagan limped down the slope towards the seriate windows, through some of which the view towards Linnhe was sunny, while others were cloudy and a few pure black.

Selina drew the collar of her blouse closed at her throat. "The least he could have done was invite us inside. There can't be so many fools passing through that he can afford to neglect them."

I tried to ignore the insult and concentrated on writing the check. One of the outsize drops broke across my knuckles, splattering the pink paper.

"All right," I said, "let's move in under the eaves till he gets back." You worm, I thought as I felt the whole thing go completely wrong. I just had to be a fool to marry you. A prize fool, a fool's fool—and now that you've trapped part of me inside you I'll never ever, never ever, *never ever* get away.

Feeling my stomach clench itself painfully, I ran behind Selina to the side of the cottage. Beyond the window the neat living room, with its coal fire, was empty but the child's toys were scattered on the floor. Alphabet blocks and a wheelbarrow the exact color of freshly pared carrots. As I stared in, the boy came running from the other room and began kicking the blocks. He didn't notice me. A few moments later the young woman entered the room and lifted him, laughing easily and whole-heartedly as she swung the boy under her arm. She came to the window as she had done earlier. I smiled self-consciously, but neither she nor the child responded.

My forehead prickled icily. *Could they both be blind?* I sidled away.

Selina gave a little scream and I spun towards her.

"The rug!" she said. "It's getting soaked."

She ran across the yard in the rain, snatched the reddish square from the dappling wall and ran back, towards the cottage door. Something heaved convulsively in my subconscious.

"Selina," I shouted. "Don't open it!"

But I was too late. She had pushed open the latched wooden door and was standing, hand over mouth, looking into the cottage. I moved close to her and took the rug from her unresisting fingers.

As I was closing the door I let my eyes traverse the cottage's interior. The neat living room in which I had just seen the woman and child was, in reality, a sickening clutter of shabby furniture, old newspapers, cast-off clothing and smeared dishes. It was damp, stinking and utterly deserted. The only object I recognized from my view through the window was the little wheelbarrow, paintless and broken.

I latched the door firmly and ordered myself to forget what I had seen. Some men who live alone are good housekeepers; others just don't know how.

Selina's face was white. "I don't understand. I don't understand it."

"Slow glass works both ways," I said gently. "Light passes out of a house, as well as in."

"You mean . . . ?"

"I don't know. It isn't our business. Now steady up—Hagan's coming back with our glass." The churning in my stomach was beginning to subside.

Hagan came into the yard carrying an oblong, plastic-covered frame. I held the check out to him, but he was staring at Selina's face. He seemed to know immediately that our uncomprehending fingers had rummaged through his soul. Selina avoided his gaze. She was old and ill-looking, and her eyes stared determinedly towards the nearing horizon.

"I'll take the rug from you, Mr. Garland," Hagan finally said. "You shouldn't have troubled yourself over it."

"No trouble. Here's the check."

"Thank you." He was still looking at Selina with a strange kind of supplication. "It's been a pleasure to do business with you."

"The pleasure was mine," I said with equal, senseless formality. I picked up the heavy frame and guided Selina towards the path which led to the road. Just as we reached the head of the now slippery steps Hagan spoke again.

"Mr. Garland!"

I turned unwillingly.

"It wasn't my fault," he said steadily. "A hit-and-run driver got them both, down on the Oban road six years ago. My boy was only seven when it happened. I'm entitled to keep something."

I nodded wordlessly and moved down the path, holding my wife close to me, treasuring the feel of her arms locked around me. At the bend I looked back through the rain and saw Hagan sitting with squared shoulders on the wall where we had first seen him.

He was looking at the house, but I was unable to tell if there was anyone at the window.

Insurance is of course a form of gambling, with the odds carefully calculated so that the house always wins—since the insurance companies always make a profit no matter how much they pay out during the year. If we could read the future and discover when we were going to die—or when our homes might burn down—the insurance companies would be out of business within a day. Another thing that might cause the companies trouble would be a safety-prone, a man who would be the opposite of an accident-prone, an individual who never *got into trouble. With realistic appraisal Mr. Scott examines just this interesting problem.*

WHO NEEDS INSURANCE?

Robin S. Scott

I've always been a pretty lucky guy. I don't mean at cards or even—before Marty—with women. Just lucky in the sense that my ration of ill fortune has always been slight. All my life I seem to have walked dry through the shower of vicissitude which seems to be the normal human lot. I never broke a bone as a kid or had more than the usual run of childhood diseases. I never piled up a car, or had appendicitis, or suffered food poisoning, or got cleated by that vicious fullback who played for Carrolsville before they threw him out in 1941, the year I graduated from Mumford Junction.

And because there are lots of others I've known who seemed lucky in this way, I never suspected my luck was any different—more than just plain "luck"—even after the Ploesti raid. It wasn't until Vietnam that I became convinced that my luck was really out of the ordinary, and even then I didn't really understand it. I never would have known what it really amounted to if it weren't for Marty. But I'm getting ahead of myself.

Ploesti was a simple enough thing. That I survived the raid was good luck indeed, but not *unusual* good luck. Lots of others survived, too. The unusual part was the *way* I survived.

I was copilot of a pretty rickety B-24 attached to the 389th Bomber Group, which, we discovered later, had somehow slipped through its last maintenance check without being checked. Anyway, we'd come in from the southwest, over the rolling foothills of the Transylvanian Alps, made our bomb-run on "White One" without taking many hits, and slid weaving out through smokestacks of the refineries at about sixty feet. We were just beginning to congratulate ourselves on getting through what was obviously one of the hairiest raids of the war. I had just turned a little in my seat to see if George wanted me to take it when an 88 mm shell popped in through the nose canopy, through the bombardier, and exploded somewhere above and behind us, knocking out both inboard engines.

Funny how suddenly aware you can be at a time like that. My whole life did not pass before my eyes; I was much too busy watching the curious, almost slow-motion effect of eight pounds of high-explosive and fine German steel. There was light, of course, like a hundred flashbulbs going off at once, and there was heat and blast. George simply disappeared. So did his yoke and several feet of fuselage. The nose canopy was gone and the sudden drag and the blast threw me forward against my yoke. I grabbed it, surprised that I could still grab, and looked to see if I had any feet left. All I could see was gore, but it wasn't mine. It was the bombardier's. He was a young kid, a year younger than my ancient twenty, and I can't even remember his name.

My being thrown against the yoke nosed us down enough so that we didn't stall out then and there, and I was able to get us a little flying speed before we ran out of air and joined the Rumanian underground. I went to full power on Number One and Number Four and we got on out of there. Major Ericks, the Squadron Intelligence Officer, was riding observer and doubling at one of the waist guns. He stuck his head in through the hatch, took one look at the mess, and went back to the waist, praying—as he told me later—all the way.

So that was the first miracle of the Ploesti trip—that I had survived that 88. When we got back to base at Benghazi, no one could believe what they saw in the cockpit of the *Goldbrick*. One half—the pilot's—completely torn apart; the other—mine—almost untouched.

But it wasn't all that easy getting back to Benghazi, and that's the second miracle—real unusual stroke of luck if you will—of my visit to Ploesti, the oil capital of Rumania. We'd clawed our way on two engines up to thirty-five hundred feet, and I was beginning to breathe easier when whacko! Oil pressure on Number Four dropped to zilch in about ten seconds. I could see the black gold streaming out through the cooler flaps. I pulled off power and feathered, and we were lucky again: no fire. But that is usual luck, although very good luck indeed. What was unusual was this: a B-24 can, if you are very lucky and not heavily loaded, maintain altitude on one engine. But not with most of the front end of the airplane missing. No sir. It ruins the streamlining, and as they used to kid us at Randolph Field, "that which draggeth, falleth." So I fiddled along without much real hope, trying to coax the maximum thrust out of that poor, tortured Number One engine, and calculating how far we had to go in order to jump into that part of Yugoslavia controlled by Tito.

I boosted the mixture to rich and increased pitch slowly, trying to keep manifold pressure somewhere in the neighborhood of the red line. And then I discovered it. *I could pull the propeller to full high pitch and the RPM's didn't drop!* The prop was roaring like an insane lion and chewing great chunks of air with each revolution, but it didn't slow. It took all my strength with both feet on the left rudder pedal to keep us from crabbing around into a flat turn. I figured out later that strange engine had an effective power boost equivalent to an extra eight hundred horsepower, and that in a twelve hundred horsepower engine! Right then, though, twenty-five hundred feet over Yugoslavia, I didn't do any figuring. I was just too shook to be anything but properly grateful.

So we went bucketing and yawing down across the Balkans, down through the Ionian Sea and across the Mediterranean to Libya. I was into the slot for an upwind approach when both outboard engines went bang, and I mean exploded. I could understand Number One going. It had roared long enough and had earned the honor of a decent burial. But old Number Four had been loafing on full feather and hadn't turned a lick for almost five hours. Anyway, both went bang, Number One deserting us entirely, whistling down to bury itself in the sand off the end of the Four-Five runway, while Number Four burned merrily in its cowling, although with no oil and only a carburetor full of gas, without much real malice.

Despite everything, it was a satisfactory landing, and like the rest of the slobs who had visited sunny Rumania that day, I was too thankful to be back in one piece to speculate much about the nature of my good luck. It wasn't until a couple of days later, after a very alcoholic evening in Major Ericks' tent, that I began to get really curious about that Number One engine and its evident ability to do full RPM's at full high pitch.

I can't stand being curious. It's like an itch, a painful irritation somewhere deep inside, and I have to scratch. I went to see Mcdougal, the Chief of Maintenance for the 389th. Like me, Mcdougal had been pulled into the Army Air Corps from college. But, while I had put in only two years at Indiana, Mac was doing graduate work in Fluid Mechanics when he was offered a choice between civilian work on some highly classified project in a little Tennessee town named Oak Ridge or a direct commission in the Air Corps. Mac is a little unconventional and a little nuts, and he thought he'd have a better time in the war if he could smell gunpowder. He was the sort of Maintenance Chief who used to sneak rides as gunner, radioman, flight engineer, what-have-you. He could even fly passably well.

It was after ten in the evening when I caught up with Mac. The desert heat had been sucked off into a series of towering thunderheads which instead of shedding their favors on Libyan soil would undoubtedly move out into the Mediterranean and kick hell out of some poor Greek sponge fishermen. It was cool even inside the silver corrugations of the R & M hangar, and Mac was relaxing with one of those thin little books on mathematics which have no numbers in them, just alphabets, and which cost about twelve dollars a running inch. I went to see Mac because I had to scratch my curiosity itch, and because besides being a first-rate technical mind, Mac had been a friend since we had been boys together in Mumford Junction.

Mac offered me a beer from the avgas compressed air beer cooler in the corner of his office and set me at ease with the back-home southern Indiana drawl he affected. I'd lost mine at Bloomington, in college. MIT and the sophistication of Boston had intensified Mac's.

"How's it goin', Ace," he drawled. Mac called everybody "Ace." Everybody he liked, that is.

"Like a hawg with both feet in the trough," I answered, slipping back into Mumford Junction to make Mac feel good.

Mac took a long pull on his beer. "Just about creamed yourself on that Ploesti party, didn't you?" He looked out from under his bushy red eyebrows and down his long arched nose at me, and his eyes twinkled. "I'm glad you made it, Ace."

"Thanks, Mac." His pleasure was sincere, and I was touched. "Have you seen what's left of the *Goldbrick*?"

"Yeah, I seen it, and I seen better lookin' junk spreadin' fertilizer on your old man's back forty. You could just as well have left it for the Krauts in Ploesti. I ain't gonna be able to fix it up none."

"D'you check it out before you scrapped it? Go over the engines or anything?"

"What I wanna do that for? I had a crew pull out what we could use for spares and then tow the carcass over to the boneyard. Anyway," he exclaimed, sitting up from his moribund slouch, "one of them engines is all burned up, two is shot to pieces, and I b'lieve you buried the other with full military honors out there off'n the end of Four-Five runway."

I explained about flying all the way home from Rumania on one engine and about the extra eight hundred horsepower. This really sat him up. He uncurled his six-foot-four and went over to the beer cooler, eyeing me all the time. He knew me too well, however, to go into the "you must be nuts."

"Full RPM at full high pitch, eh?" he muttered as he opened a can for himself and one for me. His can opener was a tool steel die set into an unpowered drill press.

I didn't answer his mutter. He paced a moment, the foam from his beer can dripping to the concrete floor, and then: "Come on, Ace. Let's go dig that baby up."

He called for a crash truck, and beckoning to the duty crew chief, he swung behind the wheel and we sped off through the cool desert night, bumping over the low dunes at the end of Four-Five. Even with the blackout lights, it didn't take long to find the crater. There'd been plenty of oil pressure in that engine when it blew loose from the *Goldbrick*, which meant the reservoir in the oil cooler had been pretty full, and the sand around the crater looked like the backyard of a filling station.

We cleared sand away from the corpse with shovels, and then while the crew chief was loading up with the crash truck's A-frame, Mac and I walked around like a couple of whitewings, picking up the bits and pieces. When we had pretty well policed up the area, we ploughed back to the R & M hangar, unloaded our booty on the oil-stained concrete floor, and Mac went to work. I had a beer and went to bed. I had to fly the next day.

It was a milkrun—the courier flight to Gibraltar; likewise the day after that. Then another hairy one came along, this time up in Sicily, but the Group had to stand down two days in a row because of bad weather over the target area. When the weather finally broke, my plane had to abort when we couldn't get a decent magneto check. I taxied back to the hangar, sore at the world. I didn't like aborts. A runner met me as I swung down through the hatch. "Lieutenant Albers, sir, Lieutenant Mcdougal says he would like to see you at your convenience." I acknowledged the message and shuffled over to the R & M shop, still sore at those magnetos.

Major Ericks was sitting in Mac's tiny office, his feet up on the beer cooler, a white moustache of foam on his upper lip. The cooler, carefully vented to allow the evaporating gasoline to escape safely, kept the small office a few degrees cooler than the sweltering hangar which surrounded it. Major Ericks is a fat little bird with sleepy eyes, and he was obviously enjoying the coolness of the beer and the office. He is a deceptive man with those eyes. He looks like a retarded Santa Claus, but I saw him fracture a Berber's skull with the side of his hand one time in a barroom brawl in Tripoli. He talks like a college professor, which is not surprising since that is what he was before the Great Unpleasantness—as he called it—broke out in 1941.

"Peter!" he exclaimed when I walked in. "I've not had a chance to properly thank you for your magnificent performance last Sunday. You had me praying, and the unaccustomed exercise did my fat soul good."

I grinned and accepted the beer from Mac. "It must have been the prayers that did it, Major. By all rights we ought to be walking across Transylvania at this moment, dodging Germans and werewolves."

The major chuckled. "I hadn't thought of it, Pete, but I suppose you've a point. Perhaps we should include a silver spike in the escape and evasion kit for Ploesti-bound fliers."

Mac, who never read a book unless it was one of those twelve dollars a running-inch types, looked mystified and turned the conversation to business. He is an inarticulate man, and when he has to address more than one man at a time, he gets a little nervous.

"Major, I asked you an' Ace here to come over on account of I got a problem I can't handle and maybe you can gimme an idea." He stopped abruptly, not sure where to begin.

"Is it the business with the Number One engine from *Goldbrick?*" I asked.

"Yeah," said Mac, and I explained the problem to the major.

"Ah tore it down," continued Mac, "and there wasn't a thing unusual about her. She was a fine, healthy engine before she blew, but I couldn't figure out for the longest time where she was gettin' all that extra power. Then I found this." Mac pulled a wheeled dolly over to the two of us. On it was a square box, about ten inches on a side and maybe five inches thick. Its surface was featureless except for a series of bolt holes along a flange on one end and a helical gear extending from a short shaft on the other. "This was bolted in and geared to the flywheel, and it don't belong there."

"Doesn't belong?" queried the major. "What do you mean?"

"Look, Major," said Mac, "we get maybe six . . . seven modifications a month in these here airplanes. Maybe two a month in the engines. Every one of these mods go through me. I'd know for sure if we was to install little boxes like this geared to the flywheel." Mac's voice carried an injured tone, almost as if his honor had been slurred. "And more'n that, Major, it don't *do* nothin', this little box. It don't take power in and it don't put power out, least not so's you can tell."

We were silent for a minute. Then I said: "Why don't you open her up, Mac, and see what's inside. Maybe you can figure out what it's for when you see the guts."

Mac gave me a pitying look. "You think I ain't *tried*? I've tried everything but a cuttin' torch on her, and no luck."

The major peered at the box intently. "Get your torch, Mac. Let's see what's inside."

Mac left wordlessly and returned a moment later with two gas bottles on a cart. He pulled goggles down over his eyes, lit the gas with a pop, and adjusted the valves until he had a good flame. I watched the box as he heated one end with the flame. The term "black box" had not yet come into currency, and this utterly mysterious, completely unknowable box was not black at all. I watched as its gray-green exterior began to glow cherry red, watched as Mac thumbed the oxygen valve for a cutting flame. I watched as the entire box suddenly turned to grayish powder and melted and formed a hard little ball and danced and sizzled on the steel top of the dolly. And I saw Mac cut off the gas and push his goggles slowly up onto his forehead, and I saw Major Ericks sigh and look at me with a strange glint in his eyes, and I began to suspect then that I had had unusual luck at Ploesti—more than the sort of extra-special good luck that almost everyone experiences now and again.

So we had a mystery on our hands, Major Ericks, Mac, and I. But we didn't particularly relate the mystery to me, Lieutenant Peter Albers. Having had my very personal bacon saved by the mystery led me to relate it to myself—to wonder "why *me*? why *my* airplane?" —and maybe Major Ericks was feeling the same way about himself. But as a group, sitting around as we did for weeks afterwards, drinking beer in Mac's cool little office and speculating about the golfball-sized chunk of glassy slag that sat on Mac's desk, we didn't relate the mystery to me. And after a while we began to forget about it and talk of other things. We were all pretty close by then. Bill Ericks had flown with me a good deal, explaining in his offhand way that he wanted to share what he called my "flair for Providence." And he and Mac came to respect each other in the abstruse world of mathematics. Mac even began to call him "Ace."

And we stuck together this way, sitting in one R & M hangar after another, talking politics and girls and airplanes and girls and the world series and girls, until the war was over. After Ploesti a lot of little things conspired to keep me in good shape. I flew plenty, but it seemed like there was always a shot magneto, or a leaky hydraulic line or a cracked de-icing boot that kept me on the ground when the bad ones came along. It was only much later that I saw how these many tiny things added up to be a bit more, in aggregate, than ordinary circumstance. Like shooting seventeen straight passes or drawing to an inside straight two or three times consecutively.

After the war, we drifted apart, despite our protestations to the contrary. Bill Ericks got an Associate Professorship at some eastern college, married a girl from Smith, and wound up finally as a wheel in one of those Government outfits which are too secret even to have alphabetical names. We exchanged Christmas cards for a while, and I ran into him once in 1955 coming out of the Dorchester in New York. Mac went back to MIT to finish his degree, married a girl from back home in Mumford Junction, and took her out to California with him in '52 when he went to work for one of the big R & D outfits out there that were springing up like weeds on the rich diet of Federal money following the outbreak of the Korean War. Mac never wrote, but his parents lived on in Mumford Junction, as did mine, and I followed his travels through them.

As for me? I finished up at Bloomington with an MS in Aeronautical Engineering in 1949 and went to work for one of the big airframe manufacturers in Kansas. After a year on the board copying other men's ideas, I was glad to be rescued by the Korean War. I was retreaded as a captain and learned to fly A-26s, but the same combination of hydraulic lines, fouled-up radio gear, and erratic magnetos—speaking metaphorically—kept me out of serious action, and I flew two combat tours without a scratch. I left Korea as Major Peter Albers, the "lucky Pierre" of the 2731st Recon Squadron, and after two wars and over four thousand hours of flight time, I figured I'd just as well stay in the Air Force and make it a career.

My luck—as I explained before—didn't extend to the realm of women: A. I hadn't met many girls who were prepared to put up with a rather tired-looking caricature of Lindbergh with a rapidly-receding hairline and too much length to stuff into a standard bed. And B, the ones I had met who were willing to accept the material described in A. (above) seemed to consider marriage a kind of Inertial Navigation System with which they could accurately plot my course for all the years to come. And if there is one thing about me, it is that I like to at least pretend that I am the Captain of My Own Soul and the Master of My Own Fate (to paraphrase Henley).

You might think it strange that lucky Pierre Albers, by his own admission an independent sort of bird, would choose a military career, with all its traditional restraints. Well, I suppose it's the same in Big Business and Big Government, and even Big Labor: you learn the ground rules, the taboos and the angles, and then if you can produce you're left pretty much to yourself. I knew the rules in the Air Force—I'd had (by 1953, when I finally decided to make a career of it) seven years of practical experience, and I figured I could have a fairly satisfactory life, doing what I most enjoyed, with a minimum of interference from outside sources. And I had my luck. By this time I had come to count on it. Not that I got sloppy in my flying or anything; I just always knew it was there. And this made what is otherwise a career hard to insure—not many people realize that most military pilots in those days had to pay as much as fifty per cent more for insurance—even more attractive. All that flight pay and nothing to lose.

So the years rolled by. I was often lonely, all bachelors—despite their claims to the contrary—are. And sometimes, in lonely moments on a long flight at very high altitude or in the middle of the night in the BOQ, I'd think about the Ploesti raid and about that gray-green "blackbox." But this was mostly middle-of-the-night stuff, and

I had long since given up bringing up the story in bull sessions. Too damaging to the reputation, and pointless anyway.

I rolled along, piling up safe hours in all types of aircraft. In 1955 I was promoted to light Colonel and shifted to flight test duties—the degree in Engineering did it—and I rolled and twisted hundreds without incident. In 1961 I got my eagles, and in mid '63 I was given command of a helicopter squadron in Vietnam. And then, a few weeks before I was due to be relieved in the Spring of '64, I found out some more about my unusual luck, my "chicken sandwich" luck: Mac used to say in Libya, way back when, that with luck like mine, I could reach into an Arab privy and come up with a chicken sandwich.

We were working our way up the Mekong River in H-34s—Choctaws, the Army called them—dropping supplies here and there in friendly villages, setting down to drop off squads of replacements, and generally doing our bit to hold together the whirli-bird lifeline of the miserable Vietnamese war. I had been loaned to the Army because I had worked with H-34s a good deal and the Army was rapidly growing short of trained chopper jockeys on the command level. I'd been actually leading the squadron in combat for nearly a year, and had I not been so convinced of my own invincible good luck, I'd have realized I'd just about outlived the statistical odds for survival in that unhappy part of the world.

On this day in particular, the great muddy Mekong lay spread out some five hundred feet beneath us, swollen and fat from the spring rains. There were spots of early morning mist obscuring the banks and the horizon was a purple band of dampness no more than two miles away. The Viet Cong held a strong point on the west side of the river and they had developed a new trick. They would anchor a small boat or a raft out in the middle of the river and zero in on it with their little dinky 3" mortars. Then, knowing we used the river to navigate by when we were flying resupply, they calculated a series of trajectories for various altitudes, and when we came flying by, they would fill the air with big, lazy mortar shells with timed fuses.

Well, we caught one. And it was Ploesti all over again. No gore this time, although the crew chief back in the cargo compartment had a pretty lively fire on his hands for a few minutes. Otherwise the damage was slight. The rotor blades were nicked and vibrated like hell; there was rice and "C" rations plastered all over the interior of the cargo compartment; and there was a hole about the size of the southern tip of Florida in the main fuel tank. I got us stable again and headed back to base, pulling off power to conserve gas. The main tank was soon empty—without fire, thank my usual, everyday, run-of-the-mill luck—and I started nursing throttle and mixture control to stretch the two reserve tanks for the two-hundred mile flight back to base.

By all rights and the laws of aerodynamics we should never have made it. But I found I could throttle way down and still keep a steady thirty-five knots and full stability, and as we flew along, the engines barely turning over, I began to realize that my unusual, more-than-run-of-the-mill luck had taken hold. And sure enough, some five hours later when we began to windmill in over the base, there was a loud report, as if someone had dropped a grenade into the engine, and we came flopping like a wounded bird into a safe but destructive no-power landing.

We all walked away from it, and after debriefing the other members of the squadron and reporting in to Operations, I borrowed a tool kit from one of the mechs and headed for the boneyard where they had towed the remains of the Choctaw. I had a good idea what to look for and where to look for it, and it took only a few minutes with a flashlight and a set of sockets to get the gray-green box loose from its mounting next to the flywheel.

Twenty years is a long time, but that strange box, identical with the one I had seen in Benghazi, except for the cut of the teeth on the spur gear, brought back my memory with detailed precision. I sat and stared at it where it lay on my bed in the BOQ, and then I stuffed it into the bottom of my foot locker while I thought the whole thing over.

A month later, in June 1963, I rotated out of Vietnam with reassignment to the Air Force War College at Maxwell AFB in Montgomery. For a professional warrior, such an assignment is to be treasured: it is one of the most essential elements in the construction of a general officer, and to have made it at forty-one—and not as an Academy graduate—made me feel doubly-blessed. As a consequence, I rapidly lost interest in the mystery posed by the gray-green "blackbox." It knocked around with me in the bottom of my foot locker on the trip from Saigon to Washington and then on to Mumford Junction. I thought about it occasionally, and I couldn't help but be intrigued by the long recurrent thought, "Why me?" During my six weeks leave in Indiana, there were too many other things to do and to talk about, too many sea stories to swap with old friends, and too much to do helping Dad with the farm and enjoying the simplicity of a midwestern summer to fret about what was obviously—to me, then—unknowable. After a while, just before I left for Montgomery, I packed the strange device carefully in a crate, determined Mac's address from his mother, and shipped it off to him with a brief letter describing the circumstances under which I had found it.

By the end of October I had been at the War College a couple of months and was doing well. Thus it came as a bolt from the blue when I received sudden orders detaching me from the War College and instructing me to report to the Pentagon, room such-and-such, Colonel so-and-so. Colonel so-and-so wasn't much help in clearing up the mystery. Instead he handed me the address of an apartment house over in the District and told me to report back to his office once a month to get paid. Otherwise, he wasn't interested in seeing me anymore. I was sore; I didn't welcome missing out on the opportunity presented by the War College, and I didn't like the Mickey Mouse mystery I was being handed. But Colonel so-and-so accepted my indignation with bland indifference, and if you've ever seen two colonels trying to pull rank on each other, you can imagine how comical the scene in room such-and-such was.

As I said, I had been in the Air Force long enough to recognize the fact that there are times when You Can't Fight City Hall, and just then, Colonel so-and-so represented City Hall. There were the initials of the Secretary of the Air Force on my orders to prove it. So I swallowed my anger, hailed a cab, and went to the address on Connecticut Avenue I'd been given. It can be hot in Washington in

October, and the air-conditioning in the Grover Apartments did nothing to cool me off. Suite 8334 was high in the building and I had to wait a long time for the elevator. But my frustration and anger died in puzzlement when the door was opened to my impatient buzz by none other than friend Mcdougal, older, his face wrinkling, his red hair salted with white, but indubitably Mac.

"Howdy, Ace," he grinned. "Ah hope you ain't too put out at bein' drug up here like this."

Before I could answer, my surprise was compounded by the appearance of Bill Ericks, feet up on the suite's expensive upholstery, a can of cold beer in his hand. Suddenly twenty years dropped off me. The jumbled events of the past few hours shifted into neat rows, all in perfect alignment, and I knew what it was all about. I shook Ericks' hand and took the proffered beer from Mac. "What is this, Libyan Reunion Week?" I said, as if I didn't know better.

Ericks chuckled. "Better call it the organization meeting of the Pete Albers Little Green Box and Marching Society." He turned to the entryway leading to the rest of the suite and called: "Marty, our rabbit's foot is here!"

"Marty" came in and we were introduced. If you have ever noticed, it is exceedingly difficult to form a clear mental picture of someone you love, but I can remember with photographic clarity how Marty looked then, in that instant, standing in the doorway. She is a small woman, and she looked even more diminutive standing next to Mac's six feet four. Her auburn hair was done up in a severe knot which somehow did nothing to detract from her complete femininity: a small heart-shaped face, shining green eyes set wide apart under heavy, almost masculine brows, full lips and a straight nose, a bit too long for perfection perhaps. Altogether a thoroughly beautiful woman, but a woman whose expression—and subsequent words—made you realize that she was used to dealing with men on a level of equality, without being militant about it—a woman whose abilities were such that she had no need to use her obvious good looks and lithe young figure to make her way in a man's world.

Unlike Mac, I am not an inarticulate man. But I stuttered as I acknowledged the introduction. When I could tear my eyes away, I turned questioningly to Ericks to ask him what was up.

He anticipated my question. "Martha Perkins is a Chief Programmer at the Aerospace Center, *and* probably the best programmer in the general field of variant probability in the country. She's part of the 'green box' team."

"The what?" I said.

"Sit down, Pete," said Ericks. "Let me fill you in."

So I sat down, and Ericks—with an occasional assist from Mac or Marty—filled me in. It seems that when my parcel from Mumford Junction got to Mac, he was so excited he couldn't see straight. He'd felt for twenty years that he'd muffed a good chance back in Libya, and it was like having an opportunity to undo a bad error. He set to work immediately on the box, and since he was Chief of Research and Development for his firm, he got all the help and equipment he needed. There was no nonsense with a cutting torch this time. They didn't even risk X-raying the box for fear of setting off the reaction which had destroyed the first one. Instead they did a careful closed-systems check, looking for any sign of input or output, anywhere in the electromagnetic spectrum. They found nothing. Then they bolted the box to an H-34 engine on a test stand with the spur gear meshing with the flywheel, just as it had in Vietnam. No results. They ran the engine up to full power and dropped it back to idle with no discernible effect from the green box, except for the obvious fact that the spur was being driven at a merry clip by the flywheel.

Mac had just about decided that the box was a one-shot affair and that it had had its one shot when he thought of one other test condition. He had the engine trundled into a pressure chamber, evacuated the air to a simulated altitude of a thousand feet and tried the full-power run-up again. This time it took. When he cut the throttle back, engine speed dropped off to a little more than 3,000 RPM and would drop no lower, even under a heavy dynamometer load. Only when the air came whistling back into the chamber, approximating sea-level pressure, did the engine speed drop off to the comfortable idle indicated by the power settings.

"So that was it," continued Ericks. "Mac still didn't know what he had, but he knew what it took to make it perform, and it was enough for him to call for more help."

"Ah figgered it was no job for a country boy like me," chipped in Mac, "so I got on the phone to old Ace here and he come out to Bakersfield on the next plane. Since then I ain't seen my wife an' kids for more'n about two days, an' we been more hush-hush than a moonshine cooker."

"And what *that* amounts to," added Ericks, "is that we're a project now. Our own funds and our own mission."

"We?" I asked, getting a little of my earlier anger back.

"We," said Ericks emphatically. "Me and Mac and Marty and *you.*"

"Now just a minute," I said. "I'm a military officer, not a scientist. Anyway, I've got plans of my own."

Ericks gave me a queer look. "I'm sorry Pete. I know about the War College. But look . . ."

"But look hell!" I said, my anger really showing for the first time. "You've known me long enough to know I won't hold still to be pushed around by you two slide-rulers and Miss Variant Probability of 1964 over here!" The minute I'd said it I was sorry. "I'm sorry, Miss Perkins, I . . . uh . . ." Marty was wearing one of those white lab coats, but it did little to conceal her striking figure. And those green eyes looked genuinely sympathetic, and kind of smoldering, and—let's face it—sexy.

Marty opened her mouth for the first time in a long while. "I know how you must feel, Colonel Albers, and you must hear us out. Hear the rest of the story." She looked at Ericks, and he nodded slightly. "I came into the picture when it was decided to approach the problem of the green box from a causal and motivational point of view."

I looked blank, which was better than the leer I was about to display.

"All that means is that we couldn't find out how the box did what it did, so we decided to try to find out *why* it did what it did. That is, why the box was installed in two aircraft piloted by you, who installed the boxes, what *his* motives were for doing so, and so forth. You see, causality and motivation."

"I see," I said. "You can't figure out what's in this Chinese puzzle, so you're hunting for the Chinaman who put it together in the first place so you can ask *him.*"

"Precisely," said Ericks. "And that's where Marty came in. Marty and her pet 2703 computer."

I'm not entirely stupid and I began to see where the explanation was leading. My anger drained away in front of those brilliant green eyes, and I smiled at the idea of Marty having a 2703 as a pet.

"Beauty and the beast, eh?" I said gallantly.

The green eyes twinkled at me. "Oh, I wouldn't call my 2703 exactly beautiful," she said. "Anyway, Colonel Albers, that's where I came in, me and my pet. It was clear from the very modest information we had about the circumstantial existence of the box—apart from its physical nature—that you were an essential element. But statistically, so were B-24s and H-34s. We ran every scrap of information about the two aircraft, and about you, into the 2703. We poured most of the records of the units to which you were attached during both occurrences into the tank, and then we added what physical information about the green box we had. Then we took the personnel records for all individuals who had had access to the two aircraft, from factory to scrap heap, and fed them to my pet, and for dessert, we sent field investigators to your home town, to your former commanding officers, to everyone we could find who had ever known you well, and we poured a pretty full biography of Colonel Peter Canfield Albers down the 2703's gullet. Then we started asking questions."

"And?" I asked, my voice unpleasant. My mother had written about investigators, but I had assumed it was simply a security check in connection with my assignment to the War College. I didn't like the idea of strangers poking around in my life like this.

"And," said Ericks, "we got a few answers. Just enough to tantalize. We know why you are known throughout the Air Force as 'Lucky Pierre' Albers. You've flown for eighty-five hundred hours, a lot of it in combat, and you've never been scratched."

My irritation grew. "Did it ever occur to you big domes that I might just be a pretty good airplane driver? Isn't that explanation enough?"

"Of course you are, Pete," said Ericks, his voice apologetic. "It's just that in that much flying you're bound to have some close ones, some near accidents. Even commercial airline pilots may experience hundreds of 'near collisions' in the course of a few years flying. But not you. The only times you've come close to piling in—both times—there's been that green box. Do you see why we're interested in every fact about Pete Albers we can find?"

I saw. I'd known my luck was something special, but I guess I'd wanted someone else to say it, someone with some backing, like that hungry 2703 of Marty's. "O.K., Bill, I see your point. Any other answers?"

"A lot of negatives and one positive. The box is clearly not of American manufacture; no one has ever even dreamed of such a device. Obvious, perhaps, but we did a lot of checking just to make sure. Second, it is highly unlikely that the green box is of terrestrial manufacture. From scrapings, Mac determined that the box is made of a very queer metal indeed, a kind of expanded steel with silicon instead of carbon locking the Fe into a molecule that just doesn't exist in nature, and is far beyond anything our technology knows of right now."

My mouth was really open on that one. "Not of terrestrial origin?" I parroted. "You mean it wasn't made here on Earth? But how do you know? Maybe some little guy makes these things for kicks in his basement, some undiscovered genius . . ."

"Ah b'lieve it'd take a helluva lot more'n genius," chimed in Mac. "It'd take pressure, gangs of it. And it'd take heat, like on the order of fusion temperatures. Son, it just ain't in the state of the art, as we say."

I walked over to the window and looked up at the smoky blue of the October sky. "You all are trying to tell me that someone up there likes old lucky Pierre Albers and has gone to great expense and pressure and heat and stuff to save old lucky Pierre's neck on a couple of occasions, and maybe keep him out of trouble on a lot of others."

Nobody said anything. After a few seconds Marty began to nod her head up and down like a solemn child. I wanted to say something smart, or make a wisecrack. But I didn't have it in me. That "not of terrestrial origin" bit had me scared.

After a bit I said: "Bill, you said several negatives and a positive. What did the 2703 deliver on the positive side?"

"A name. Or rather two names. Corporal Frazer Lorenz Thompson and Mr. Edwin Michael Conners. Thompson was assigned as an Aviation Mechanic to the 389th Bomber Group at Benghazi in mid-July 1943. He only signed one payroll there, but there is a record that he was billeted at Benghazi for two weeks in July. Orders transferring him to Blackbushe in England were cut that same month, and he apparently shipped out without attracting any attention."

"July '43," I said. "The Ploesti raid . . ."

Ericks nodded and went on. "Edwin Michael Conners was shipped to Saigon in March 1964 as a civilian technician attached to your squadron. The day of your last flight, he announced to his supervisor that he was quitting, paying his own passage back to the States, and he moved out of his room at the BOQ that night. There is an airline manifest that shows him on a flight from Saigon to Hong Kong on that date. Nothing after that."

"So what's the connection?" I asked.

"According to the FBI—and this is how we got on to it in the first place—Conners and Thompson are the same man, or at least they have the same fingerprints."

"Oh," I said.

"Furthermore, so far as we—or the FBI—can tell, neither man legally exists. There is no record of Thompson, except the paybook with his fingerprint. His enlistment was false, and apparently so were his orders to the 389th BG. Likewise, Conners left prints aplenty in his BOQ—that's where we got 'em, but otherwise no record. His passport, contract with the Army—everything—must have been phony. There is no Edwin Conners matching his description in the United States."

I got up for the beer Marty handed me and stared thoughtfully at the foam for a minute or so. Then Marty said: "Mr. Ericks, tell Colonel Albers about the ages. Maybe he'll have an idea."

"It's simple enough, Pete," said Ericks. "Unlike the case with Thompson, we've been able to talk to quite a few people who remember Conners from Saigon, people whose memories are still fresh. They all agree he couldn't have been more than thirty at the outside. Most estimated his age at around twenty-five."

"B-but," I spluttered, "if he and Thompson are the same guy, Thompson would have to have been, uh, between five and ten years old at Benghazi!"

"Yeah," said Mac dryly, "and ah b'lieve I woulda remembered a ten year old corporal if'n he'd a worked for me then."

Marty's green eyes flashed at me and now it was her quiet smile which was part sympathy, part unconscious sexiness. "We've an idea who our Chinaman is now, Colonel Albers, but he's a puzzle too, isn't he?"

Her question was rhetorical and I didn't bother to answer it. I was too busy absorbing the suddenly confirmed notion that my luck —my unusual, chicken-sandwich luck—was no blind hiccup in the laws of probability, no impersonal cast of the die by one of the Fatal Sisters, but rather the conscious work of a specific individual: Corporal Thompson/Mr. Conners. Who was he? And, *why me?* Bill Ericks seemed to read my mind, to anticipate any unspoken questions.

"So you see why we had to bring you up from the War College, Pete," he said quietly. "The FBI has done everything they could to get a line on this man, and they've not been able to get much of anything. Every lead they've turned up on Conners/Thompson has petered out, and they've admitted confidentially that they don't have much hope of digging up anything more. Now the only opening left to us is you. We can't solve the Chinese puzzle; we can't find the Chinaman; all we can do now is to try to figure out why the Chinaman chose you, and apparently only you, to work his magic on."

"It may not get us anywhere," said Marty, "but you're our last hope." The green eyes were at work again, and my high dudgeon was losing altitude rapidly.

"O.K.! O.K.!" I said. "But I'm just a poor country boy who makes a living driving airplanes and frightening junior officers. How can I help?"

"By letting us get down on tape everything that has ever happened to you, everyone you've ever known," said Marty. "We'll need tape-code descriptions of the minutest details of your life, examples of the writing of all your correspondents, your flight logs, conversations you can remember . . ."

"Now wait a minute . . ." I started. The invasion of privacy all this would entail was putting my ego back into orbit. Then the green eyes attracted my attention and the thought crossed my mind that Marty would be the one who had to tape all this junk, which would mean days and days, if not weeks or months, of more green eyes. And then I thought of the Air Force Undersecretary's initials on my orders, and I thought again of "why me?" and I looked at the green eyes, and my resistance collapsed. My ego went into hibernation for the winter.

"When do we start," I said.

Marty looked questioningly at Ericks, who said: "What's wrong with now?"

So we started in. Not right then, but the next morning. I had to move in first, and send off for the box of personal papers—the detritus of my adult life—which had grown larger and larger with old canceled checks, letters from forgotten friends, memorabilia from a thousand weekends, copies of old orders, college graduation pictures, and a few scented love letters. I'm a lazy man, and it had always seemed easier to ship my collections of personal junk home periodically for storage in my parents' capacious attic than to go to the trouble of sorting through it and purging the vast quantity of useless stuff. Marty was delighted when the boxes arrived, and she put two technicians to work on it right away.

In the meantime, life was not entirely unpleasant. No one at heart really minds talking about himself, and I was doing it ten hours a day. The suite in the Grover was spacious. Besides my living quarters there was a room full of tape-cutting equipment manned by a middleaged woman named Madge who sat from 8:30 in the morning until 5:00 in the evening reducing Marty's handwritten notes to various combinations of holes on paper tapes. Then there was the room in which the technicians worked over the written remains of Pete Albers, sorting and analyzing and occasionally chuckling at some choice bit. It was a real temptation some evenings to flip a lighted cigarette into their room.

There was still another room in which I was subjected to a series of interviews—sometimes with drugs, most of the time without—conducted by a depth-psychologist with heavy black eyebrows growing straight across his forehead. He was a nice enough guy—Dr. Nagy—but I didn't care much for his line of questioning. Even his most innocent questions left me feeling vaguely guilty, as if I were somehow at fault for having benefited from the magic of our mysterious Chinaman. But then when he had pumped me dry—and I really felt that way some evenings—Madge put it all down on tape and I felt better. The little holes punched through the paper seemed to make all that information, some of it deeply personal, impersonal again.

And as the weeks rolled by my prediction to myself about the green eyes came true. Marty began to stay after the others had left, and we got to going out to dinner together. At first I think she felt a little sorry for me, at the opportunity I had been forced to miss, at the ordeal of confession I had to go through. Then it was something else. One cold night just before Christmas she left early, but returned with a bird and a bottle, the second of which we drank and the first she cooked to a golden brown. I won't go into the details of *that* evening, but about a month later she stopped going away at all in the evening, and late in February 1965 we drove to West Virginia and were married by a sleepy Justice of the Peace in Moorefield, just across the Virginia border.

When we got back, by way of Mumford Junction and Cleveland—where Marty's mother lived—Ericks was hopping mad, saying things to Marty about "lack of objectivity" and "the impersonality of scientific endeavor," but she just grinned at him and held my hand a bit tighter, and after he cooled down he offered his congratulations, which weren't at all necessary because we both knew just how lucky we were.

Even operating at high speed, it takes a computer a while to digest so much varied and unconnected information, but old 2703 finally came through. There was a letter from an obscure insurance agency signed in the same handwriting identified as that of "Thompson" in his 1943 paybook. The signature was that of one "Atchison," but the similarity in script was unmistakable, even to me. And thus we had another name for our Chinaman. The letter he had signed was an offer of a twenty-five thousand dollar life insurance policy at a ridiculously low rate, and a canceled check dated in April 1950 showed I had sent him one hundred nineteen dollars and fifty cents for five years' premiums. I was flying in the Air National Guard then and insurance had been hard to get. And while I didn't really need any—no wife and kids—I thought it might be a good idea to leave a little bundle for Mom and Dad if one of those rusty P-51s we were flying then decided it had had the course. There had been renewals in '55 and '60 followed by letters bearing the same signature and copies of ornate policies issued by one of the major underwriters and endorsed by the same "H. L. Atchison."

And more than just another name for our Chinaman, we had an address. All correspondence from Atchison had been mailed from Houston, and although I couldn't recall—even under Dr. Nagy's most extreme ministrations—to what address I had written my renewals, enclosing of course the stub of the bill with the address, an FBI check of Houston post offices turned up a box in a branch just off Jensen Road which had been rented under the name H. L. Atchison since 1950. After several days of monumental work, the Bureau located an affable real-estate agent who readily admitted making the quarterly payments for the postoffice box and explained that Atchison had long paid him a handsome retainer for looking after his sparse affairs in Houston and seeing to the rent payments for the modest apartment he had procured for Atchison there. I still have a copy of the Bureau report because I'm still lazy about sorting through my papers and throwing things away:

> "SUBJECT (Bureau jargon for the real estate man) asserted that his files reflect the information that T-27 (more FBI jargon for Atchison) first came to him in February 1950 in order to

procure a domicile. An apartment satisfactory to T-27 was procured in the Bennington Arms Apartments, 3345 Alamo Road, Houston 6, Texas, and T-27 paid for extensive alterations, explaining to SUBJECT that he desired to redecorate the premises as a shrine to his deceased spouse and had no plans or intentions of living in or otherwise occupying the premises except during occasional visits to Houston, Texas.

"SUBJECT further asserted that T-27 informed him that he was an oil geologist and since he would often be in areas where contact by mail would not be possible, he preferred that SUBJECT handle all his affairs in Houston, Texas, on a five-year basis.

"SUBJECT's deposition (attached) describes his single visit to the above-mentioned premises in the Bennington Arms Apartments, 3345 Alamo Road, Houston 6, Texas, which occurred in April 1950. He avers that his impression of the interior of these premises, while striking him as eccentric, seemed to correspond to the avowed intentions of his client to convert the premises into a religious shrine in memory of the deceased spouse."

"It's obvious," said Ericks, when we had all read the FBI report, "that Thompson/Conners/Atchison—oh hell, let's call him the 'Chinaman'—pulled into Houston and established an address in 1950 with the idea of returning only often enough to handle his insurance business with you, Pete."

"But why?" I asked. "Surely not just to bilk me out of one hundred nineteen dollars and fifty cents every five years."

"And why this funny business with a dead wife?" said Marty. "It's certainly touching, a tribute like that, but somehow it seems more than just eccentric." She cast a speculative green eye at me. "I can't imagine *you* doing anything so sweet, Peter."

"Spouse, if you decease, I have every plan and intention of erecting a shrine to you constructed of heart-shaped memory drums and magnetic tape in the premises located at 2762 Connecticut Avenue N. W., Washington 5, D. C."

"It must be sheer cover," said Ericks, ignoring the horseplay. "Just an excuse for keeping up an uninhabited apartment without arousing suspicion. And it seems to have worked." Ericks pulled his plump bulk up from the couch and walked to the window. "As to why, Pete, suppose we go to Houston and find out."

Our plane was met in Houston by the chief of the local FBI Field Office, a gray little man named Pollock who looked a great deal more like a shoe salesman than an FBI man. He drove us to the address on Alamo Drive, where we were met by a plainclothes cop from the Houston Detective Bureau armed with a search warrant and an immense bundle of keys and lock picks. It was only a moment before he had us out of the glare of a Texas March and into the dry mustiness of the long unoccupied apartment.

The description in the real estate man's deposition had been accurate. The living room was hung about with heavy dark drapes. Except for a broad black buffet and two small chairs in one corner of the room, there was no furniture, but the floor was covered with thick, dark carpeting. Atop the buffet was the faded photograph of a handsome young woman in her twenties, a nondescript woman, beautiful in an impersonal sort of way, the kind of face that smiles up at you from a thousand magazine covers and chewing-gum advertisements. Tall candles stood on either side of the photograph, and the wall behind the buffet was almost covered with a vast clutter of religious ornaments of one sort or another, as if Atchison had gone to one of those shops where they sell plaster crucifixes and cheap reproductions of *The Last Supper* and bought one of everything.

Leading off to the right from this dismal room, a corridor ran first past a small kitchen, dust covered, a rusty streak in the sink, and then past a minuscule bathroom to the stoutly locked door leading to a single bedroom. The detective with the keys and lock picks didn't have so much luck with this one, and he finally resorted to two blasts from his service revolver, a most effective key indeed.

But there was no bed there, and the real estate agent had quite obviously never penetrated that far. A broad bench ran down one side of the room and supported a tangle of electrical wiring and strange looking devices and instruments whose purpose I couldn't even guess. Across the end of the room, crammed into the narrow space, were a precision lathe, a shaper, a drill press, and a small but efficient arc furnace. Thick power cables terminated in a heavy-duty fuse panel mounted on the wall behind the machine tools.

Ericks whistled at the sight. "Mac ought to see this. I bet this is where the green boxes were made."

"Not the first one," I said. "Atchison hasn't had this place that long."

"Yes, of course. He must have had another place before this one. I'll get the Bureau on it."

We went back into the somber shrine. Pollock was methodically sorting through the contents of the black buffet. He handed a fat billfold to Ericks. "Your friend Atchison is pretty careless with his money, whatever else he is. There's something over twenty thousand dollars here." He flipped the card case open. "And look, he's left his driver's license, Social Security card, draft card, and so forth behind him."

I peered over Ericks' pudgy shoulder at the cards. Even to my untrained eyes there could be no doubt: the signatures were familiar and we had definitely found our Chinaman. Ericks stared at the cards, turning the card case over and over in his hand. "I'll bet they're phony," he said finally. Pollock nodded wordlessly, took the proffered case from Ericks and slipped it into his coat pocket. "We'll check," he said.

There was nothing more to be learned. Ericks left instructions with Pollock to keep the apartment under twenty-four hour watch, and we headed back for the airport. On the way Ericks stopped to put in a call to Mac in California, to tell him of our discovery. But Mac was off somewhere in the Pacific Missile Impact Range, and he was not to be reached. But with the apartment under tight surveillance there didn't appear to be any hurry. It could wait, we thought.

Back in Washington, we spent a couple of days, chewing over bits of evidence, trying to put together a cohesive picture of the Chinaman and his motives. But none of it made any sense. We knew who he was and where he had lived from time to time over the past fifteen years, but we still had no answers to any major parts of the mystery. We still didn't know how he had done what he had done. Or why. Or why to *me*.

And I was getting tired of the whole business. I've always been impatient with puzzles and games like chess. I haven't got the patience for it. And I was bored with the inactivity of sitting around Washington waiting for someone else to sort out this particular can of worms. My curiosity itch still needed scratching, but I could live with it, and I was anxious to get back to the War College, to pull Marty away from her work and spend a week or two with her in the little shack I had down at Cape Hatteras where there would be no black-shrouded apartments, no stilted FBI reports, no mysteries except the delightful one of how it was a lanky, balding, forty-two-year-old airplane driver, long past thoughts of marriage, could have been so fortunate as to latch on to someone like Marty.

But that was not to be for a while. The FBI had done some more digging and had come up with the fact that the Houston Power and Light Company had recorded sudden increases in power consumption on the transformer leg servicing the Bennington Arms Apartments between the fourth and seventh of April in 1950, 1955, and 1960. In those years I had received my billings from Atchison sometime around the end of April, the time we had figured for a concentrated stakeout if we were to get a glimpse of our Chinaman. Now, however, it looked like a real good bet that he'd be showing up in Houston considerably earlier, sometime in the next week, and a small army of surveillants were ordered into position around the Bennington Arms. On the off-chance that I might be able to spot Atchison—either from my Libyan days or from the more recent period in Vietnam—the Bureau asked that I fly down to join in the watch.

So Ericks and I flew down to Houston again on the second of April. Marty wanted to come along, but she was now pregnant two months with Ethan, and felt too lousy to make the trip. Since it was apparent we might have a long wait, and since Atchison could approach the apartment house from any of four directions—east or west on Alamo, or north or south on Richards—it was decided that I should occupy the apartment itself. We moved a cot into the crowded machine shop—I couldn't bring myself to sleep in that grisly shrine of a bedroom—and I tried to make myself comfortable. Ericks, comfort-loving slob that he is, registered in the Sam Houston, and from the luxury of his room kept in touch with me and the ten or fifteen thousand cops, FBI agents, and boy scouts who seemed to be standing silently around on the street beneath my window. One agent was even disguised as an ice-cream vendor, which was all right during the day, although he had to keep shaking his head at disappointed kids, but at night he presented a somewhat implausible figure.

I sat around for two days—the third and fourth of April—reading paperbacks, smoking too many cigarettes, and missing Marty. Now and again my transceiver would crackle a warning, and I would peer carefully out the front windows at some bird who was roughly the same height, build and age we presumed our Chinaman to be. I recognized no one, and none turned into the Bennington Arms and headed for the second floor apartment where I waited. The last of these came a little after midnight on the fourth. I had been long asleep when the buzz and crackle of the transceiver awakened me from dreams of Hatteras. I responded and stumbled down the hall to peer through the shrouded front windows as I had been bid. But the young man who was idling by was no one I recognized and he idled with undiminished slouch on past the building entrance and around the corner on Richards. I yawned mightily and headed on bare feet back toward the bedroom. There was a faint, keening whine behind me and the narrow corridor down which I was padding sleepily was suddenly illuminated with an eerie greenish glow. I came full awake instantly—one of the tricks you learn from dozing on autopilot when a trouble light comes on—and turned back toward the living room to see the damndest thing I have ever seen.

There in the center of that macabre shrine was a bright mass of shimmering light, coalescing into solidity as I watched, and dimming steadily as it coalesced. It was roughly egg-shaped, a couple of yards long and maybe four feet through the middle, like an old model Link trainer without the silly little tail empennage they used to stick on them. But I wasn't thinking of Link trainers. All I could think of was Ericks' theory that the green box was of extraterrestrial origin, and I was scared to death. The quintessence of all the old B movies I'd seen in a hundred ready-rooms, movies with Hollywood electronics, flashes of green lightning, and little green men with big green death-rays went whipping through my mind. Boy, was I scared.

But I didn't run to the transceiver, or jump out the window. My curiosity was itching at maximum ferocity, and despite my better instincts, I edged gingerly into the room and flicked on the overhead lights to counter the gloom that had supplanted the dying fluorescence of the egg. I stood there for maybe thirty seconds, my knees trembling, all kinds of wild thoughts going through my head. I remember thinking, finally, that I might see things more clearly with a cigarette, and I was about to head for the bedroom to get one when a hatchway in the top of the egg snapped inward and the head and shoulders of a dark young man appeared. He had braced both hands on the side of the hatch to hoist himself the rest of the way out before he noticed me. He made a swift motion as if to duck back inside and then caught himself, gave a visible shrug, rose again, and with a single well-muscled movement, pushed himself out of the egg and dropped lightly to the floor. He was naked as a jaybird.

"Hello!" he said, peering intently at me from under heavy dark brows.

I said "Hi."

"Sorry I beed so . . . so—" he indicated his nudity with a wave of the hand. "The probe willn't transmit anything but living protoplasm."

"That's all right," I said. "I used to swim at the YMCA."

He looked mystified at this. I didn't blame him; the conversation was getting pretty inane considering the circumstances. The funny thing was, I recognized him right away. I thought I could remember him from the R & M shack at Benghazi; I was sure I'd had a drink with him once in the Officers' Club in Saigon.

He fumbled in a closet for clothing and I headed for the bedroom and my cigarettes. When I got back I offered him one and lit it for him as he buttoned his shirt. My knees were weak and I sat down in one of the two chairs. When I get good and scared, my first reaction is always a sort of light-headed jolliness. I get flippant and want to crack jokes, I guess to cover up any signs of fear I might show. Then when the initial shock is over I get weak in the knees.

I took a nervous puff on my cigarette. "You, Atchison?" I asked.

"Yo, in a manner of speaking. My real name is Timmons. Ethan Timmons."

I lit a new cigarette from the butt of the old one. "You the guy who saved my bacon at Ploesti and in the chopper last year?"

"Yo. I be the guy." He pronounced "guy" almost like "gooey". I couldn't place the accent. "I haved to protect the insurance company, Colonel Albers." He grinned at this, his eyes wrinkling in good humor, his young face taking on a mischievous, we-share-a-secret look.

"Why?" I asked. "Will you tell me?" I made a wide gesture with my cigarette, sweeping in the egg, the apartment, and my blue pajama'd self.

"Yo, I will tell you. It willn't make any difference. But first you tell me how you finded me."

I told him. About the boxes and Mac, about the FBI work, about Ericks' theory that the boxes were of extraterrestrial origin. I even told him about Mac's plans to inspect the machine shop in the bedroom, and that stopped him for a minute before he grinned and said something about fixing *that.*

When I was done he bummed another cigarette from me and lit it. "Yo. You telled me your story, now I will tell you mine." Then more to himself than to me, "It willn't make any difference. I will have to rerun it all from Saigon on." He rolled his eyes up toward the ceiling, obviously searching for a starting point. He was a very young man and clearly enjoying his role as a revealer of the astonishing.

After a bit he leaned forward in his chair and said: "You, Colonel Albers, be a latent Espy."

"How about that," I said. "Here all this time I thought I was an Episcopalian."

He looked mystified again but went on with his explanation. He was a volatile young man, and from time to time he rose from his chair, borrowed another cigarette, and paced up and down the black carpet alongside the egg, punctuating his words with quick thrusts of the lighted cigarette. He spoke with broad vowels and clipped consonants, somewhat like a Yorkshireman I had served with in Korea. And he had trouble with verbs. "Thought" was "thinked," "ran" was "runned," and so forth.

His story was complicated and I'm not sure even now how much of it I have straight. The essence: Timmons was—is—will be (the tenses get confusing) a time traveler. "Prober" is the word he used. His home time is about a hundred and fifty years from now, 2107 to be precise, and he is one of a group of highly trained men who poke around in the past to do one chore or another, mostly to retrieve objets d'art—paintings, books, curios of one kind or another—which for one reason or another have not survived down to the probers' own time.

He spoke at some length of something he called "temporal momentum," and while I didn't begin to grasp all his explanation, I gather it involves the problem of just how much the past can be altered without *significantly* affecting the future. As well as I could get it, there was a dividing line, an uncertain and dangerous boundary beyond which the probers dared not pass: little things they did, things which remained unknown or which made no real impact on the public consciousness in the time in question, were swallowed up in the momentum of events and had no significant effect on the future. On the other hand the principle of "for want of a nail the shoe was lost, for want of a shoe . . ." could apply disastrously, and he made his point by asking me to speculate on the results if he were to journey to 1910 Vienna and offer gainful employment to frustrated painter Adolf Hitler. "It will'd be, for me and my time, a kind of suicide," he said. "I might still exist, yo. But my times will'd be very different indeed, and I willdn't exist as *me*."

He went on to explain about Espys and Pete Albers' luck. In 2106 there was—will be?—a major military threat against Earth posed by a rapacious horde of beings from without the solar system, the first sentient life detected by man outside his own system. All the resources of Earth and her three struggling planetary colonies had been mobilized to stand off the would-be invaders. At immense cost in men and materiel, the invaders' thrust had been parried, but the invaders themselves lay undamaged just outside the maximum range of Terran weapons systems, and their constant thrusts and probes were quickly exhausting the Earth.

Then, explained Timmons, had come the discovery of *Corticon*, which—if I understood what he was talking about—is some sort of a gizmo for stimulating and tremendously amplifying some sort of psychic force. At first the Corticon was employed simply as a superior guidance system in conjunction with conventional weapons equipped with biological on-board computers—which, I gather, are some sort of doctored-up animal brains—but then they had discovered more or less by accident that a Corticon beam which swept over an invader ship sometimes stimulated it either to mindless apathy or spectacular self-destruction.

But there was a catch in all this: they had been able to turn up only something over two hundred telekinetic adepts—that was Timmons' phrase—in the entire population, and they were simply not enough to give the invaders a decisive blow. However, after a good deal of genealogical research, they had traced a fair number of these adepts—although by no means all—to the offspring of one Harold Gruber Schindhorst, himself not traceable further back than 1916 when he started up in the grocery business in Indianapolis. Schindhorst's sister, Ellen, married Robert Ethan Albers of Mumford Junction, Indiana, and it seemed more than just possible that she had shared her brother's latent Espy potentialities. But the Albers' only child, old lucky Pierre Pete Albers, had died in an airplane crash at Strumica, Yugoslavia, on August 1, 1943, on his return from the Great Ploesti raid of that date. With him, according to Timmons, died some six generations of potential Espys, the genes he might have transmitted to two or three hundred telekinetic adepts—depending upon luck and fecundity—scattered broadly on the fallow soil of Macedonia.

It's an interesting experience to hear your own death described in such matter-of-fact, history-book style. But I don't recommend it. It is unsettling. Still, a lot of pieces began to fall into place, and there was an answer to the question: "But why Pete Albers? Why *me*?" I was sore at first at the thought of all the meddling in my affairs that had gone on. And then I was grateful. I'm glad I didn't die in the Ploesti raid. I wished I could haul out my chromosomes and give them a loving pat. Forty-six good luck pieces, they were.

"So you see, Colonel Albers, I goed back through time to 1943, set up shop in London, and when I had made the power source I goed on to Libya and installed it in your aircraft. Then I comed back to 1950, getted this dwelling as a base, and comed on up to 1980, stopping off every five years to mail you a bill for your insurance. Back I goed again to 1950 about three weeks after I mailed the first bill, and I comed up again every five years and looked for the answers. No one hundred nineteen dollars and fifty, no Peter Albers, and I had to go all the way out to Mumford Junction, find out what happened, where, when and how you'd beed killed. Then I had to do something about it. Rupture a hydraulic line, get the brakes repaired on your old MG, or install another power source. Each time, then, I comed up to the next five-year check to see if a letter from you will'd indicate that the steps I had tooked had beed effective." He sighed deeply. "You've beed a problem, Colonel."

"Sorry," I said. "I'll try to be more careful in the future."

"No. It been't that." There was a faint blush high on his young forehead. "I don't want to get personal, Colonel, but I have beed working on your case for almost four months now, and it beed just wasted effort if you doon't . . . ah—" He stopped in embarrassment and then tried a different tack. "Colonel, I keep waiting for you to change the beneficiary of your insurance policy from your parents to a wife." Then, impatiently, "I can keep you alive, Colonel, but I can't make you marry, *and we need those genes!*"

"Take 'em," I said. "They're yours." I was overcome with reaction to the strange evening. And to the humor of my position. I began to chuckle uncontrollably.

Timmons, of course, didn't see the humor. "Colonel, this beed deadly serious to me. While I will erase any trace of this evening's conversation by going back to Saigon, tell me now if we be wasting our hopes on you." He leaned forward, the flush on his forehead spreading downward to his cheeks. "Tell me, Colonel, be you a homosexual?"

At this question, which I would normally answer with a dose of knuckles, I could contain myself no longer and laughed uncontrollably. "Timmons," I chortled, "relax. I was married almost three months ago and my wife is pregnant."

A broad grin replaced the blush of embarrassment and anger on the young man's face. "Wonderful, Colonel. Congratulations! Wonderful! There be nothing left, then, but to get back to Saigon and erase this unfortunate business. I wish you long life, sir, and"—his voice dropping into sincerity—"best wishes to you in your marriage."

"Back to Saigon?" I said. "Erase *what* business?"

"No cause for alarm, Colonel. It be the law of temporal momentum. With all you know now, and all that your friends Ericks and Mcdougal know, or soon will—well, I can't take the chance. If a wide circle of people beed to learn the existence of time-probing, that alone will'd produce significant change. And then there beed all that your friend Mcdougal can'd get out of the shop back there." He nodded toward the bedroom.

"I'll never tell," I said. "And I like the things the way they are."

Timmons started to take his clothes off, hanging each piece carefully back in the closet for use five years hence. "I will'd like to take your word for it," he said, "but I can't take the chance." He smiled brightly at me from the far side of the egg. "Anyway, it willn't hurt a bit. We'll just wipe out the last . . . let me see . . . eleven months. I'll find a better way to get you out of that helicopter over the Mekong, and you, of course, will never know the difference."

"But wait a minute," I said. "I'll keep quiet and Ericks and Mac will shut up, too. Mac hasn't made any headway with the green box, and Ericks has no proof for his theories. Anyway, they're the wrong theories. He thinks you're some man from Mars."

"Can't take the chance," said Timmons stubbornly. "Try to understand, Colonel. I have to do it. And doon't worry, you'll never know."

Maybe he was right, I guess he was. I would never know, and what you don't know never hurts you. But maybe that was the trouble. All the Indiana hick stubbornness welled up in me. I *liked* things the way they were. Sure, I was grateful that my bacon had been saved a number of times in the past—how often I still have no idea—but I do like to think I'm the master of my own fate and the captain of my own soul, and I couldn't bear the idea of this young squirt zipping around time, altering things that had already happened to me, "erasing" everything that had happened in the last eleven months.

And then it hit me. Martha! *My Lord I wouldn't meet Martha!*

Timmons was once again nude and he had both legs in the egg, about to lower himself in. "Wait! Timmons," I shouted. "You've forgotten something!"

He paused. "What?"

"My wife! I met my wife on the green box project! You cancel out the last eleven months and you cancel out my marriage!"

His face whitened and he froze in the hatchway. You could almost hear the wheel spinning in his head, and I knew I had him. In a mixture of panic and exultation, I drove the lance deeper. "Genes! Timmons, Genes! No wife, no genes! At least none that'll do you any good. Come on back out, Timmons! I'm forty-two, Timmons, and a man forty-two doesn't have many opportunities to marry!"

Timmons pulled himself up and sat on the egg, his legs dangling into the open hatch. "Yo," he said. And then he was silent for a time, calculating. I was beginning to estimate my chances for clobbering him when he swung down to the carpet and headed for the bedroom. He had twenty pounds and the best part of twenty years on me, and I decided my chances were slim. Instead I followed him down the hall.

Over his shoulder he asked: "When do you expect your friend Mcdougal?"

"Sometime in the next couple of days. Not before day after tomorrow."

He did something to one of the thick cables feeding the apparatus on the long bench. "What time be it now?" he asked, his hands very busy.

I looked at my watch. "Four twenty-seven."

He finished whatever he was doing and I trailed him back into the living room. "You'd better be out of that room," he said, hoisting himself back into the egg, "by twelve twenty-seven tomorrow. It willn't be very violent, but there might be some flying glass." With just his head and shoulders protruding from the egg, he turned for a last look at me. "Yo, Colonel Albers. It be a stand-off, and we'll give it a try. I will find a new place for my shop, and your friend Mcdougal will get nowhere with the green box without this shop." He lowered himself a bit further. "Doon't forget one thing, Colonel Albers."

"Yo?" I said politely.

"Doon't forget to forget all this. I'll be around from time to time to check up."

"I'll keep quiet." I said. "But don't you forget."

"What?" he said, his voice muffled by the closing hatch.

"Genes! Timmons, Genes!" I shouted. And then there was the green phosphorescence and the whine, and nothing at all. I went back to bed.

At seven-thirty, the transceiver buzzed and crackled and I got up to peek out at a young, dark-haired meter-reader trying to buy a popsicle from the FBI man in the Good Humor truck.

And so, boys, you now know why I've left you this rather long account of some matters that occurred before you were born. As I write this I have no idea how much longer I will be around. I will be careful, though, and not depend very much on my luck. The fact that you three are healthy, lively youngsters—I hear you, Timmy, shouting for that last glass of water that is always the youngest's prerogative—would suggest to me that Timmons is not going to be overly concerned about *my* welfare from now on. However, he *is* going to be concerned about yours. And could any father ask more?

Maybe this will reach you when you, too, are middle-aged and graying. I hope so. Maybe some lawyer—or your mother—will hand it to each of you when you reach twenty-one. However it happens, keep the contents to yourselves. No one would believe the story anyway. But if you want to prove it to yourselves, get a couple of small pith balls, put them on a smooth surface, concentrate as hard as you can, and *will* them to move. It's the best proof I can offer, but there is something else. Look back in my household files to this month, April 1970. You'll find a carbon of my last letter to Mr. Atchison. It reads:

Dear Mr. Atchison;

Inclosed please find my check for $119.50 for another five years premium.

I don't know why I bother. After all, who needs insurance?

Peter L. Albers, Brig. USAF.

This is an allegory that contains a good deal of subtlety. It is an entertaining and fanciful story by a writer who, although a relative newcomer to science fiction, has developed a unique understanding of his craft. Incidentally, Mr. Lafferty prefers the title "A Pride of Children" for this story.

AMONG THE HAIRY EARTHMEN

R. A. Lafferty

There is one period of our World History that has aspects so different from anything that went before and after that we can only gaze back on those several hundred years and ask:

"Was that *ourselves* who behaved so?"

Well, no, as a matter of fact, it wasn't. It was beings of another sort who visited us briefly and who acted so gloriously and abominably.

This is the way it was:

The Children had a Long Afternoon free. They could go to any of a dozen wonderful places, but they were already in one.

Seven of them—full to the craw of wonderful places—decided to go to Eretz.

"Children are attracted to the oddest and most shambling things," said the Mothers. "Why should they want to go to Eretz?"

"Let them go," said the Fathers. "Let them see—before they be gone—one of the few simple peoples left. We ourselves have become a contrived and compromized people. Let the Children be children for half a day."

Eretz was the Planet of the Offense, and therefore it was to be (perhaps it recently had been) the Planet of the Restitution also. But in no other way was it distinguished. The Children had received the tradition of Eretz as children receive all traditions—like lightning.

Hobble, Michael Goodgrind, Ralpha, Lonnie, Laurie, Bea and Joan they called themselves as they came down on Eretz—for these were their idea of Eretzi names. But they could have as many names as they wished in their games.

An anomalous intrusion of great heat and force! The rocks ran like water where they came down, and there was formed a scarp-pebble enclave.

It was all shanty country and shanty towns on Eretz—clumsy hills, badly done plains and piedmonts, ragged fields, uncleansed rivers, whole weedpatches of provinces—not at all like Home. And the Towns! Firenze, Praha, Venezia, Londra, Colonia, Gant, Roma—why, they were nothing but towns made out of stone and wood! And these were the greatest of the towns of Eretz, not the meanest.

The Children exploded into action. Like children of the less transcendent races running wild on an ocean beach for an afternoon, they ran wild over continents. They scattered. And they took whatever forms first came into their minds.

Hobble—dark and smoldering like crippled Vulcan.

Michael Goodgrind—a broken-nosed bull of a man. How they all howled when he invented that first form!

Ralpha—like young Mercury.

And Lonnie—a tall giant with a golden beard.

Laurie was fire, Bea was light, Joan was moon-darkness.

But in these, or in any other forms they took, you'd always know that they were cousins or brethren.

Lonnie went pure Gothic. He had come onto it at the tail end of the thing and he fell in love with it.

"I am the Emperor!" he told the people like giant thunder. He pushed the Emperor Wenceslas off the throne and became Emperor.

"I am the true son of Charles, and you had thought me dead," he told the people. "I am Sigismund." Sigismund was really dead, but Lonnie became Sigismund and reigned, taking the wife and all the castles of Wenceslas. He grabbed off gangling old forts and mountain-rooks and raised howling Eretzi armies to make war. He made new castles. He loved the tall sweeping things and raised them to a new height. Have you never wondered that the last of those castles—in the late afternoon of the Gothic—were the tallest and oddest?

One day the deposed Wenceslas came back, and he was possessed of a new power.

"Now we will see who is the real Emperor!" the new Wenceslas cried like a rising storm.

They clashed their two forces and broke down each other's bridges and towns and stole the high ladies from each other's strongholds. They wrestled like boys. But they wrestled with a continent.

Lonnie (who was Sigismund) learned that the Wenceslas he battled was Michael Goodgrind wearing a contrived Emperor body. So they fought harder.

There came a new man out of an old royal line.

"I am Jobst," the new man cried. "I will show you two princelings who is the real Emperor!"

He fought the two of them with overwhelming verve. He raised fast-striking Eretzi armies, and used tricks that only a young Mercury would know. He was Ralpha, entering the game as the third Emperor. But the two combined against him and broke him at Constance.

They smashed Germany and France and Italy like a clutch of eggs. Never had there been such spirited conflict. The Eretzi were amazed by it all, but they were swept into it; it was the Eretzi who made up the armies.

Even today the Eretzi or Earthers haven't the details of it right in their histories. When the King of Aragon, for an example, mixed into it, they treated him as a separate person. They did not know that Michael Goodgrind was often the King of Aragon, just as Lonnie was often the Duke of Flanders. But, played for itself, the Emperor game would be quite a limited one. Too limited for the children.

The girls played their own roles. Laurie claimed to be thirteen different queens. She was consort of all three Emperors in every one of their guises, and she also dabbled with the Eretzi. She was the wanton of the group.

Bea liked the Grande Dame part and the Lady Bountiful bit. She was very good on Great Renunciations. In her different characters, she beat paths from thrones to nunneries and back again; and she is now known as five different saints. Every time you turn to the Common of the Mass of Holy Women who are Neither Virgins nor Martyrs, you are likely to meet her.

And Joan was the dreamer who may have enjoyed the Afternoon more than any of them.

Laurie made up a melodrama—Lucrezia Borgia and the Poison Ring. There is an advantage in doing these little melodramas on Eretzi. You can have as many characters as you wish—they come free. You can have them act as extravagantly as you desire—who is there to object to it? Lucrezia was very well done, as children's burlesques go, and the bodies were strewn from Napoli to Vienne. The Eretzi play with great eagerness any convincing part offered them, and they go to their deaths quite willingly if the part calls for it.

Lonnie made one up called The Pawn-Broker and the Pope. It was in the grand manner, all about the Medici family, and had some very funny episodes in the fourth act. Lonnie, who was vain of his acting ability, played Medici parts in five succeeding generations. The drama left more corpses than did the Lucrezia piece, but the killings weren't so sudden or showy; the girls had a better touch at the bloody stuff.

Ralpha did a Think Piece called One, Two, Three—Infinity. In its presentation he put all the rest of the Children to roast grandly in Hell; he filled up Purgatory with Eretzi-type people—the dullards; and for the Paradise he did a burlesque of Home. The Eretzi use a cropped version of Ralpha's piece and call it the Divine Comedy, leaving out a lot of fun.

Bea did a poetic one named the Witches' Bonfire. All the Children spent many a happy evening with that one, and they burnt twenty thousand witches. There was something satisfying about those Eretzi autumnal twilights with the scarlet sky and the frosty fields and the kine lowing in the meadows and the evening smell of witches burning. Bea's was really a pastoral piece.

All the Children ranged far except Hobble. Hobble (who was Vulcan) played with his sick toys. He played at Ateliers and Smithies, at Furnaces and Carousels. And often the other Children came and watched his work, and joined in for a while.

They played with the glass from the furnaces. They made gold-toned goblets, iridescent glass poems, figured spheres, goblin pitchers, glass music boxes, gargoyle heads, dragon chargers, princess salieras, figurines of lovers. So many things to make of glass! To make, and to smash when made!

But some of the things they exchanged as gifts instead of smashing them—glass birds and horses, fortune-telling globes that showed changing people and scenes within, tuned chiming balls that rang like bells, glass cats that sparked when stroked, wolves and bears, witches that flew.

The Eretzi found some of these things that the Children discarded. They studied them and imitated them.

And again, in the interludes of their other games, the Children came back to Hobble's shops where he sometimes worked with looms. They made costumes of wool and linen and silk. They made trains and cloaks and mantles, all the things for their grand masquerades. They fabricated tapestries and rugs and wove in all sorts of scenes: vistas of Home and of Eretz, people and peacocks, fish and cranes, dingles and dromedaries, larks and lovers. They set their creations in the strange ragged scenery of Eretz and in the rich contrived gardens of Home. A spark went from the Children to their weaving so that none could tell where they left off and their creations began.

Then they left poor Hobble and went on to their more vital games.

There were seven of them (six, not counting the backward Hobble), but they seemed a thousand. They built themselves Castles in Spain and Gardes in Languedoc. The girls played always at Intrigue, for the high pleasure of it, and to give a causus for the wars. And the wars were the things that the boys seldom tired of. It is fun to play at armies with live warriors; and the Eretzi were live . . . in a sense.

The Eretzi had had wars and armies and sieges long before this, but they had been aimless things. Oh, this was one field where the Eretzi needed the Children. Consider the battles that the Children engineered that afternoon:

Gallipoli—how they managed the ships in that one! The Fathers could not have maneuvered more intricately in their four-dimension chess at Home.

Adrianople, Kunovitza, Dibra, Varna, Hexamilion! It's fun just to call out the bloody names of battles.

Constantinople! That was the one where they first used the big cannon. But who cast the big cannon for the Turks there? In their histories the Eretzi say that it was a man named Orban or Urban, and that he was Dacian, or he was Hungarian, or he was Danish. How many places did you tell them that you came from, Michael Goodgrind?

Belgrad, Trebizond, Morat, Blackheath, Napoli, Dornach!

Cupua and Taranto—Ralpha's armies beat Michael's at both of those.

Carignola—Lonnie foxed both Michael and Ralpha there, and nearly foxed himself. (You didn't intend it all that way, Lonnie. It was seven-cornered luck and you know it!)

Garigliano where the sea was red with blood and the ships were like broken twigs on the water!

Brescia! Ravenna! Who would have believed that such things could be done with a device known as Spanish infantry?

Villalar, Milan, Pavia! Best of all, the sack of Rome! There was a dozen different games blended into that one. The Eretzi discovered new emotions in themselves there—a deeper depravity and a higher heroism.

Siege of Florence! That one called out the Children's every trick. A wonderfully well played game!

Turin, San Quentin, Moncontour, Mookerhide!

Lepanto! The great sea-siege where the castled ships broke asunder and the tall Turk Ochiali Pasha perished with all his fleet and was drowned forever. But it wasn't so forever as you might suppose, for he was Michael Goodgrind who had more bodies than one. The fish still remember Lepanto. Never had there been such feastings.

Alcazar-Quivar! That was the last of the excellent ones—the end of the litany. The Children left off the game. They remembered (but conveniently, and after they had worn out the fun of it) that they were forbidden to play Warfare with live soldiers. The Eretzi, left to themselves again, once more conducted their battles as dull and uninspired affairs.

You can put it to a test, now, tonight. Study the conflicts of the earlier times, of this high period, and of the time that followed. You will see the difference. For a short two or three centuries you will find really well contrived battles. And before and after there is only ineptitude.

Often the Children played at Jealousies and raised up all the black passions in themselves. They played at Immoralities, for there is an abiding evil in all children.

Maskings and water-carnivals and balls, and forever the emotional intrigue!

Ralpha walked down a valley, playing a lute and wearing the body of somebody else. He luted the birds out of the trees and worked a charm on the whole countryside.

An old crone followed him and called, "Love me when I'm old."

"*Sempremai, tuttavia,*" sang Ralpha in Eretzi or Earthian. "For Ever, For Always."

A small girl followed and called, "Love me when I'm young."

"Forever, for always," sang Ralpha.

The weirdest witch in the world followed him and called, "Love me when I'm ugly."

"For always, forever," sang Ralpha, and pulled her down on the grass. He knew that all the creatures had been Laurie playing Bodies.

But a peculiar thing happened: the prelude became more important than the play. Ralpha fell in love with his own song, and forgot Laurie who had inspired it. He made all manner of music and poem—aubade, madrigal, chanson; and he topped it off with one hundred sonnets. He made them in Eretzi words, Italy words, Languedoc words, and they were excellent. And the Eretzi still copy them.

Ralpha discovered there that poetry and song are Passion Deferred. But Laurie would rather have deferred the song. She was long gone away and taking up with others before Ralpha had finished singing his love for her, but he never noticed that she had left him. After Hobble, Ralpha was the most peculiar of them all.

In the meanwhile, Michael Goodgrind invented another game of Bodies. He made them of marble—an Eretzi limestone that cuts easily without faulting. And he painted them on canvas. He made the People of Home, and the Eretzi. He said that he would make angels.

"But you cannot make angels," said Joan.

"We know that," said Michael, "but do the Eretzi know that I cannot? I will make angels for the Eretzi."

He made them grotesque, like chicken men, like bird men, with an impossible duplication of humeral function. And the Children laughed at the carven jokes.

But Michael had sudden inspiration. He touched his creations up and added an element of nobility. So an iconography was born.

All the Children did it then, and they carried it into other mediums. They made the Eretzi, and they made themselves. You can still see their deep features on some of those statues, that family look that was on them no matter what faces they wore or copied.

Bronze is fun! Bronze horses are the best. Big bronze doors can be an orgy of delight, or bronze bells whose shape is their tone.

The Children went to larger things. They played at Realms and Constitutions, and Banks and Ships and Provinces. Then they came down to smaller things again and played at Books, for Hobble had just invented the printing thing.

Of them all, Hobble had the least imagination. He didn't range wide like the others. He didn't outrage the Eretzi. He spent all his time with his sick toys as though he were a child of much younger years.

The only new body he acquired was another one just like his own. Even this he didn't acquire as did the other Children theirs. He made it laboriously in his shop, and animated it. Hobble and the Hobble Creature worked together thereafter, and you could not tell them apart. One was as dull and laboring as the other.

The Eretzi had no effect whatsoever on the Children, but the Children had great effect on the Eretzi. The Children had the faculty of making whatever little things they needed or wanted, and the Eretzi began to copy them. In this manner the Eretzi came onto many tools, processes, devices and arts that they had never known before. Out of ten thousand, there were these:

The Astrolabe, Equatorium, Quadrant, Lathes and Traversing Tools, Ball-Bearings, Gudgeons, Gig-Mills, Barometers, Range-Finders, Cantilever Construction, Machine-Saws, Screw-Jacks, Hammer-Forges and Drop-Forges, Printing, Steel that was more than puddled Iron, Logarithms, Hydraulic Rams, Screw-Dies, Spanner-Wrenches, Flux-Solder, Telescopes, Microscopes, Mortising Machines, Wire-Drawing, Stanches (Navigation-Locks), Gear Trains, Paper Making, Magnetic Compass and Wind-Rhumb, Portulan Charts and Projection Maps, Pinnule-Sights, Spirit-Levels, Fine Micrometers, Porcelain, Fire-Lock Guns, Music Notation and Music Printing, Complex Pulleys and Snatch-Blocks, the Seed-Drill, Playing Cards (the Children's masquerade faces may still be seen on them), Tobacco, the Violin, Whisky, the Mechanical Clock.

They were forbidden, of course, to display any second-aspect powers or machines, as these would disrupt things. But they disrupted accidently in building, in tooling, in armies and navies, in harbors and canals, in towns and bridges, in ways of thinking and recording. They started a thing that couldn't be reversed. It was only the One Afternoon they were here, only two or three Eretzi Centuries, but they set a trend. They overwhelmed by the very number of their new devices, and it could never be simple on Eretz again.

There were many thousands of Eretz days and nights in that Long Afternoon. The Children had begun to tire of it, and the hour was growing late. For the last time they wandered off, this time all Seven of them together.

In the bodies of Kings and their Ladies, they strode down a High Road in the Levant. They were wondering what last thing they could contrive, when they found their way blocked by a Pilgrim with a staff.

"Let's tumble the hairy Eretzi," shouted Ralpha. "Let him not stand in the way of Kings!" For Ralpha was King of Bulgaria that day.

But they did *not* tumble the Pilgrim. That man knew how to handle his staff, and he laid the bunch of them low. It was nothing to him that they were the high people of the World who ordered Nations. He flogged them flat.

"Bleak Children!" that Pilgrim cried out as he beat them into the ground. "Unfledged little oafs! Is it so that you waste your Afternoon on Earth? I'll give you what your Fathers forgot."

Seven-colored thunder, how he could use that staff! He smashed the gaudy bodies of the Children and broke many of their damnable bones. Did he know that it didn't matter? Did he understand that the bodies they wore were only for an antic?

"Lay off, old Father!" begged Michael Goodgrind, bleeding and half beaten into the earth. "Stay your bloody bludgeon. You do not know who we are."

"I know you," maintained the Pilgrim mountainously. "You are ignorant Children who have abused the Afternoon given you on Earth. You have marred and ruined and warped everything you have touched."

"No, no," Ralpha protested—as he set in new bones for his old damaged ones— "You do not understand. We have advanced you a thousand of your years in one of our afternoons. Consider the Centuries we have saved you! It's as though we had increased your life by that thousand years."

"We have all the time there is," said the Pilgrim solidly. "We were well and seriously along our road, and it was not so crooked as the one you have brought us over. You have broken our sequence with your meddling. You've set us back more ways than you've advanced us. You've shattered our Unity."

"Pigs have unity!" Joan shouted. "We've brought you diversity. Think deep. Consider all the machines we have showed you, the building and the technique. I can name you a thousand things we've given you. You will never be the same again."

"True. We will never be the same," said the Pilgrim. "You may not be an unmixed curse. I'm a plain man and I don't know. Surety is one of the things you've lost us. But you befouled us. You played the game of Immoralities and taught it to us earthlings."

"You had it already," Laurie insisted. "We only brought elegance instead of piggishness to its practice." Immoralities was Laurie's own game, and she didn't like to hear it slighted.

"You have killed many thousands of us in your battles," said the Pilgrim. "You're a bitter fruit—sweet at the first taste only."

"You would yourselves have killed the same numbers in battles, and the battles wouldn't have been so good," said Michael. "Do you not realize that we are the higher race? We have roots of great antiquity."

"We have roots older than antiquity," averred the Pilgrim. "You are wicked Children without compassion."

"Compassion? For the Eretzi?" shouted Lonnie in disbelief.

"Do you have compassion for mice?" demanded Ralpha.

"Yes. I have compassion for mice," the Pilgrim said softly.

"I make a guess," Ralpha shot in shrewdly after they had all repaired their damaged bodies. "You travel as a Pilgrim, and Pilgrims sometimes come from very far away. You are not Eretzi. You are one of the Fathers from Home going in the guise of an Eretzi Pilgrim. You have this routine so that sometimes one of you comes to this world—and to every world—to see how it goes. You may have come to investigate an event said to have happened on Eretz a day ago."

Ralpha did not mean an Eretzi day ago, but a day ago at Home. The High Road they were on was in Coele-Syria not far from where the Event was thought to have happened, and Ralpha pursued his point:

"You are no Eretzi, or you would not dare to confront us, knowing what we are."

"You guess wrong in this and in everything," said the Pilgrim. "I am of this Earth, earthy. And I will not be intimidated by a gangle of children of whatever species! You're a weaker flesh than ourselves. You hide in other bodies, and you get earthlings to do your slaughter. And you cannot stand up to my staff!

"Go home, you witless weanlings!" and he raised his terrible staff again.

"Our time is nearly up. We will be gone soon," said Joan softly.

The last game they played? They played Saints—for the Evil they had done in playing Bodies wrongly, and in playing Wars with live soldiers. But they repented of the things only after they had enjoyed them for the Long Afternoon. They played Saints in hairshirt and ashes, and revived that affair among the Eretzi.

And finally they all assembled and took off from the high hill between Prato and Firenze in Italy. The rocks flowed like water where they left, and now there would be a double scarp formation.

They were gone, and that was the end of them here.

There is a theory, however, that one of the Hobbles remained and is with us yet. Hobble and his creature could not be told apart and could not finally tell themselves apart. They flipped an Eretzi coin, Emperors or Shields, to see which one would go and which one would stay. One went and one stayed. One is still here.

But, after all, Hobble was only concerned with the sick toys, the mechanical things, the material inventions. Would it have been better if Ralpha or Joan stayed with us? They'd have burned us crisp by now! They were damnable and irresponsible children.

This short Historical Monograph was not assembled for a distraction or an amusement. We consider the evidence that Children have spent their short vacations here more than once and in both hemispheres. We set out the theses in ordered parallels and we discover that we have begun to tremble unaccountably.

When last came such visitors here? What thing has beset us during the last long Eretzi lifetime?

We consider a new period—and it impinges on the Present—with aspects so different from anything that went before that we can only gasp aghast and gasp in sick wonder:

"Is it *ourselves* who behave so?

"Is it beings of another sort, or have we become those beings?

"Are we ourselves? Are these our deeds?"

There are great deep faces looking over our shoulder, there are cold voices of ancient Children jeering "Compassion? For Earthlings?", there is nasty frozen laughter that does not belong to our species.

Kingsley Amis is one of the more astute critics of science fiction and recently, while speaking about the mainstream writer Anthony Burgess and his occasional forays into SF, Amis said ". . . he's a stylist and that's rare in this field." Quite true. But we do have Jack Vance and his haunting, mood-possessed visions of the distant future, written in a style that stirs the reader to reaction and response. Here, in this award winning story, he once more spins his seductive magic.

THE LAST CASTLE

Jack Vance

Toward the end of a stormy summer afternoon, with the sun finally breaking out under ragged black rain clouds, Castle Janeil was overwhelmed and its population destroyed.

Until almost the last moment the factions among the castle clans were squabbling as to how Destiny properly should be met. The gentlemen of most prestige and account elected to ignore the entire undignified circumstance and went about their normal pursuits, with neither more nor less punctilio than usual. A few cadets, desperate to the point of hysteria, took up weapons and prepared to resist the final assault. Others still, perhaps a quarter of the total

Nebula Award, Best Novella 1966

population, waited passively, ready—almost happy—to expiate the sins of the human race.

In the end death came uniformly to all; and all extracted as much satisfaction in their dying as this essentially graceless process could afford. The proud sat turning the pages of their beautiful books, or discussing the qualities of a century-old essence, or fondling a favorite Phane. They died without deigning to heed the fact. The hot-heads raced up the muddy slope which, outraging all normal rationality, loomed above the parapets of Janeil. Most were buried under sliding rubble, but a few gained the ridge to gun, hack, stab, until they themselves were shot, crushed by the half-alive power-wagons, hacked or stabbed. The contrite waited in the classic posture of expiation, on their knees, heads bowed, and perished, so they believed, by a process in which the Meks were symbols and human sin the reality. In the end all were dead: gentlemen, ladies, Phanes in the pavilions; Peasants in the stables. Of all those who had inhabited Janeil, only the Birds survived, creatures awkward, gauche and raucous, oblivious to pride and faith, more concerned with the wholeness of their hides than the dignity of their castle.

As the Meks swarmed over the parapets, the Birds departed their cotes. They screamed strident insults as they flapped east toward Hagedorn, now the last castle of Earth.

Four months before, the Meks had appeared in the park before Janeil, fresh from the Sea Island massacre.

Climbing to the turrets and balconies, sauntering the Sunset Promenade, from ramparts and parapets, the gentlemen and ladies of Janeil, some two thousand in all, looked down at the brown-gold warriors. Their mood was complex: amused indifference, flippant disdain, over a substratum of doubt and foreboding. All these moods were the product of three basic circumstances: their own exquisitely subtle civilization, the security provided by Janeil's wall and the fact that they could think of nothing to do to alter the circumstances.

The Janeil Meks had long since departed to join the revolt. There only remained Phanes, Peasants and Birds from which to fashion what would have been the travesty of a punitive force.

At the moment there seemed no need for such a force. Janeil was deemed impregnable. The walls, two hundred feet tall, were black rock-melt contained in the meshes of a silver-blue steel alloy. Solar cells provided energy for all the needs of the castle, and in the event of emergency food could be synthesized from carbon dioxide and water vapor, as well as syrup for Phanes, Peasants and Birds. Such a need was not envisaged. Janeil was self-sufficient and secure, though inconveniences might arise when machinery broke down and there were no Meks to repair it. The situation, then, was disturbing but hardly desperate. During the day the gentlemen so inclined brought forth energy-guns and sport-rifles and killed as many Meks as the extreme range allowed.

After dark the Meks brought forward power-wagons and earth-movers, and began to raise a dike around Janeil.

The folk of the castle watched without comprehension until the dike reached a height of fifty feet and dirt began to spill down against the walls. Then the dire purpose of the Meks became apparent, and insouciance gave way to dismal foreboding.

All the gentlemen of Janeil were erudite in at least one realm of knowledge. Certain were mathematical theoreticians, others had made a profound study of the physical sciences. Some of these, with a detail of Peasants to perform the sheer physical exertion, attempted to restore the energy-cannon to functioning condition. Unluckily, the cannon had not been maintained in good order. Various components were obviously corroded or damaged. Conceivably these components might have been replaced from the Mek shops on the second sub-level, but none of the group had any knowledge of the Mek nomenclature or warehousing system. Warrick Madency Arban (which is to say, Arban of the Madency family on the Warrick clan) suggested that a work-force of Peasants search the warehouse. But in view of the limited mental capacity of the Peasants, nothing was done and the whole plan to restore the energy-cannon came to naught.

The gentlefolk of Janeil watched in fascination as the dirt piled higher and higher around them, in a circular mound like a crater. Summer neared its end, and on one stormy day dirt and rubble rose above the parapets, and began to spill over into the courts and piazzas. Janeil must soon be buried and all within suffocated.

It was then that a group of impulsive young cadets, with more elan than dignity, took up weapons and charged up the slope. The Meks dumped dirt and stone upon them, but a handful gained the ridge where they fought in a kind of dreadful exaltation.

Fifteen minutes the fight raged and the earth became sodden with rain and blood. For one glorious moment the cadets swept the ridge clean. Had not most of their fellows been lost under the rubble anything might have occurred. But the Meks regrouped, thrust forward. Ten men were left, then six, then four, then one, then none. The Meks marched down the slope, swarmed over the battlements, and with somber intensity killed all within. Janeil, for seven hundred years the abode of gallant gentlemen and gracious ladies, had become a lifeless hulk.

The Mek, standing as if a specimen in a museum case, was a man-like creature native, in his original version, to a planet of Etamin. His tough rusty-bronze hide glistened metallically as if oiled or waxed. The spines thrusting back from scalp and neck shone like gold, and indeed they were coated with a conductive copper-chrome film. His sense organs were gathered in clusters at the site of a man's ears; his visage—it was often a shock, walking the lower corridors, to come suddenly upon a Mek—was corrugated muscle, not dissimilar to the look of an uncovered human brain. His maw, a vertical irregular cleft at the base of this 'face', was an obsolete organ by reason of the syrup sac which had been introduced under the skin of the shoulders, and the digestive organs, originally used to extract nutrition from decayed swamp vegetation and coelenterates, had atrophied. The Mek typically wore no garment except possibly a work apron or a tool-belt, and in the sunlight his rust-bronze skin made a handsome display. This was the Mek solitary, a creature intrinsically as effective as man—perhaps more by virtue of his superb brain which also functioned as a radio transceiver. Working in the mass, by the teeming thousands, he seemed less admirable, less competent: a hybrid of sub-man and cockroach.

Certain savants, notably Morninglight's D. R. Jardine and Salonson of Tuang, considered the Mek bland and phlegmatic, but the profound Claghorn of Castle Hagedorn asserted otherwise. The emotions of the Mek, said Claghorn, were different from human emotions, and only vaguely comprehensible to man. After diligent research Claghorn isolated over a dozen Mek emotions.

In spite of such research, the Mek revolt came as an utter surprise, no less to Claghorn, D. R. Jardine and Salonson than to anyone else. Why? asked everyone. How could a group so long submissive have contrived so murderous a plot?

The most reasonable conjecture was also the simplest: the Mek resented servitude and hated the Earthmen who had removed him from his natural environment. Those who argued against this theory claimed that it projected human emotions and attitudes into a nonhuman organism, that the Mek had every reason to feel gratitude toward the gentlemen who had liberated him from the conditions of Etamin Nine. To this, the first group would inquire, "Who projects human attitudes now?" And the retort of their opponents was often: "Since no one knows for certain, one projection is no more absurd than another."

II

Castle Hagedorn occupied the crest of a black diorite crag overlooking a wide valley to the south. Larger, more majestic than Janeil, Hagedorn was protected by walls a mile in circumference, three hundred feet tall. The parapets stood a full nine hundred feet above the valley, with towers, turrets and observation eyries raising even higher. Two sides of the crag, at east and west, dropped sheer to the valley. The north and south slopes, a trifle less steep, were terraced and planted with vines, artichokes, pears and pomegranates. An avenue rising from the valley circled the crag and passed through a portal into the central plaza. Opposite stood the great Rotunda, with at either side the tall Houses of the twenty-eight families.

The original castle, constructed immediately after the return of men to Earth, stood on the site now occupied by the plaza. The tenth Hagedorn had assembled an enormous force of Peasants and Meks to build the new walls, after which he demolished the old castle. The twenty-eight Houses dated from this time, five hundred years before.

Below the plaza were three service levels: the stables and garages at the bottom, next the Mek shops and Mek living quarters, then the various storerooms, warehouses and special shops: bakery, brewery, lapidary, arsenal, repository, and the like.

The current Hagedorn, twenty-sixth of the line, was a Claghorn of the Overwheles. His selection had occasioned general surprise, because O. C. Charle, as he had been before his elevation, was a gentleman of no remarkable presence. His elegance, flair, and erudition were only ordinary; he had never been notable for any significant originality of thought. His physical proportions were good; his face was square and bony, with a short straight nose, a benign brow, narrow gray eyes. His expression was normally a trifle abstracted—his detractors used the word 'vacant'. But by a simple lowering of the eyelids, a downward twitch of the coarse blond eyebrows, it at once became stubborn and surly, a fact of which O. C. Charle, or Hagedorn, was unaware.

The office, while exerting little or no formal authority, exerted a pervasive influence, and the style of the gentleman who was Hagedorn affected everyone. For this reason the selection of Hagedorn was a matter of no small importance, subject to hundreds of considerations, and it was the rare candidate who failed to have some old solecism or gaucherie discussed with embarrassing candor. While the candidate might never take overt umbrage, friendships were inevitably sundered, rancors augmented, reputations blasted. O. C. Charle's elevation represented a compromise between two factions among the Overwheles, to which clan the privilege of selection had fallen.

The gentlemen between whom O. C. Charle represented a compromise were both highly respected, but distinguished by basically different attitudes toward existence. The first was the talented Garr of the Zumbeld family. He exemplified the traditional virtues of Castle Hagedorn: he was a notable connoisseur of essences, he dressed with absolute savoir, with never so much as a pleat nor a twist of the characteristic Overwhele rosette awry. He combined insouciance and flair with dignity. His repartee coruscated with brilliant allusions and turns of phrase. When aroused his wit was utterly mordant. He could quote every literary work of consequence; he performed expertly upon the nine-stringed lute, and was thus in constant demand at the Viewing of Antique Tabards. He was an antiquarian of unchallengeable erudition and knew the locale of every major city of Old Earth, and could discourse for hours upon the history of the ancient times. His military expertise was unparallelled at Hagedorn, and challenged only by D. K. Magdah of Castle Delora and perhaps Brusham of Tuang. Faults? Flaws? Few could be cited: over-punctilio which might be construed as waspishness; an intrepid pertinacity which could be considered ruthless.

O. Z. Garr could never be dismissed as insipid or indecisive, and his personal courage was beyond dispute. Two years before a stray band of Nomads had ventured into Lucerne Valley, slaughtering Peasants, stealing cattle, and going so far as to fire an arrow into the chest of an Isseth cadet. O. Z. Garr instantly assembled a punitive company of Meks, loaded them aboard a dozen power-wagons and set forth in pursuit of the Nomads, finally overtaking them near Drene River, by the ruins of Worster Cathedral. The Nomads were unexpectedly strong, unexpectedly crafty, and were not content to turn tail and flee. During the fighting O. Z. Garr displayed the most exemplary demeanor, directing the attack from the seat of his power-wagon, a pair of Meks standing by with shields to ward away arrows.

The conflict ended in a rout of the Nomads. They left twenty-seven lean black-cloaked corpses strewn on the field, while only twenty Meks lost their lives.

O. Z. Garr's opponent in the election was Claghorn, elder of the Claghorn family. As with O. Z. Garr, the exquisite discriminations of Hagedorn society came to Claghorn as easily as swimming to a fish.

He was no less erudite than O. Z. Garr, though hardly so versatile, his principal field of study being the Meks, their physiology, linguistic modes, and social patterns. Claghorn's conversation was more profound, but less entertaining and not so trenchant as that of O. Z. Garr. He seldom employed the extravagant tropes and allusions which characterized Garr's discussions, preferring a style of speech which was almost unadorned. Claghorn kept no Phanes; O. Z. Garr's four matched Gossamer Dainties were marvels of delight, and at the viewing of Antique Tabards Garr's presentations were seldom outshone. The important contrast between the two men lay in their philosophic outlook. O. Z. Garr, a traditionalist, a fervent exemplar of his society, subscribed to its tenets without reservation. He was beset by neither doubt nor guilt; he felt no desire to alter the conditions which afforded more than two thousand gentlemen and ladies lives of great richness. Claghorn, while by no means an Expiationist, was known to feel dissatisfaction with the general tenor of life at Castle Hagedorn, and argued so plausibly that many folk refused to listen to him, on the grounds that they became uncomfortable. But an indefinable malaise ran deep, and Claghorn had many influential supporters.

When the time came for ballots to be cast, neither O. Z. Garr nor Claghorn could muster sufficient support. The office finally was conferred upon a gentleman who never in his most optimistic reckonings had expected it: a gentleman of decorum and dignity but no great depth; without flippancy, but likewise without vivacity; affable but disinclined to force an issue to a disagreeable conclusion: O. C. Charle, the new Hagedorn.

Six months later, during the dark hours before dawn, the Hagedorn Meks evacuated their quarters and departed, taking with them power-wagons, tools, weapons and electrical equipment. The act had clearly been long in the planning, for simultaneously the Meks at each of the eight other castles made a similar departure.

The initial reaction at Castle Hagedorn, as elsewhere, was incredulity, then shocked anger, then—when the implications of the act were pondered—a sense of foreboding and calamity.

The new Hagedorn, the clan chiefs, and certain other notables appointed by Hagedorn met in the formal council chamber to consider the matter. They sat around a great table covered with red velvet: Hagedorn at the head; Xanten and Isseth at his left; Overwhele, Aure and Beaudry at his right; then the others, including O. Z. Garr, I. K. Linus, A. G. Bernal, a mathematical theoretician of great ability, B. F. Wyas, an equally sagacious antiquarian who had identified the sites of many ancient cities: Palmyra, Lubeck, Eridu, Zanesville, Burton-on-Trent, Massilia among others. Certain family elders filled out the council: Marune and Baudune of Aure; Quay, Roseth and Idelsea of Xanten; Uegus of Isseth, Claghorn of Overwhele.

All sat silent for a period of ten minutes, arranging their minds and performing the silent act of psychic accommodation known as 'intression'.

At last Hagedorn spoke. "The castle suddenly is bereft of its Meks. Needless to say, this is an inconvenient condition to be adjusted as swiftly as possible. Here, I am sure, we find ourselves of one mind."

He looked around the table. All thrust forward ivory tablets to signify assent—all save Claghorn, who however did not stand it on end to signify dissent.

Isseth, a stern white-haired gentleman magnificently handsome in spite of his seventy years, spoke in a grim voice. "I see no point in cogitation or delay. What we must do is clear. Admittedly the Peasants are poor material from which to recruit an armed force. Nonetheless, we must assemble them, equip them with sandals, smocks and weapons so that they do not discredit us, and put them under good leadership: O. Z. Garr or Xanten. Birds can locate the vagrants, whereupon we will track them down, order the Peasants to give them a good drubbing and herd them home on the double."

Xanten, thirty-five years old, extraordinarily young to be a clan chief, and a notorious firebrand, shook his head. "The idea is appealing but impractical. Peasants simply could not stand up to the Meks, no matter how we trained them."

The statement was manifestly accurate. The Peasants, small andromorphs originally of Spica Ten, were not so much timid as incapable of performing a vicious act.

A dour silence held the table. O. Z. Garr finally spoke. "The dogs have stolen our power-wagons, otherwise I'd be tempted to ride out and chivvy the rascals home with a whip."*

"A matter of perplexity," said Hagedorn, "is syrup. Naturally they carried away what they could. When this is exhausted—what then? Will they starve? Impossible for them to return to their original diet—what was it, swamp mud? Eh, Claghorn, you're the expert in these matters. Can the Meks return to a diet of mud?"

"No," said Claghorn. "The organs of the adult are atrophied. If a cub were started on the diet, he'd probably survive."

"Just as I assumed." Hagedorn scowled portentously down at his clasped hands to conceal his total lack of any constructive proposal.

A gentleman in the dark blue of the Beaudrys appeared in the doorway: he poised himself, held high his right arm, bowed.

Hagedorn rose to his feet. "Come forward, B. F. Robarth; what is your news?" For this was the significance of the newcomer's genuflection.

"The news is a message broadcast from Halcyon. The Meks have attacked; they have fired the structure and are slaughtering all. The radio went dead one minute ago."

All swung around, some jumped to their feet. "Slaughter?" croaked Claghorn.

"I am certain that by now Halcyon is no more."

Claghorn sat staring with eyes unfocused. The others discussed the dire news in voices heavy with horror.

Hagedorn once more brought the council back to order. "This is clearly an extreme situation; the gravest, perhaps, of our entire history. I am frank to state that I can suggest no decisive counter-act."

* This is only an approximate translation and fails to capture the pungency of the language. Several words have no contemporary equivalents. 'Skirkling', as in 'to send skirkling', denotes a frantic pell-mell flight in all directions accompanied by a vibration or twinkling or a jerking motion. To 'volith' is to toy idly with a matter, the implication being that the person involved is of such Jovian potency that all difficulties dwindle to contemptible triviality. 'Raudelbogs' are the semi-intelligent beings of Etamin Four, who were brought to Earth, trained first as gardeners, then construction laborers, then sent home in disgrace because of certain repulsive habits they refused to forgo.

The statement of O. Z. Garr, therefore, becomes something like this: "Were power-wagons at hand, I'd volith riding forth with a whip to send the raudelbogs skirkling home."

Overwhele inquired, "What of the other castles? Are they secure?"

Hagedorn turned to B. F. Robarth: "Will you be good enough to make general radio contact with all other castles, and inquire as to their condition?"

Xanten said, "Others are as vulnerable as Halcyon: Sea Island and Delora, in particular, and Maraval as well."

Claghorn emerged from his reverie. "The gentlemen and ladies of these places, in my opinion, should consider taking refuge at Janeil or here until the uprising is quelled."

Others around the table looked at him in surprise and puzzlement. O. Z. Garr inquired in the silkiest of voices: "You envision the gentlefolk of these castles scampering to refuge at the cock-a-hoop swaggering of the lower orders?"

"Indeed I do, should they wish to survive," responded Claghorn politely. A gentleman of late middle-age, Claghorn was stocky, strong, with black-gray hair, magnificent green eyes, a manner which suggests great internal force under stern control. "Flight by definition entails a certain diminution of dignity," he went on to say. "If O. Z. Garr can propound an elegant manner of taking to one's heels, I will be glad to learn it, and everyone else should likewise heed, because in the days to come the capability may be of comfort to all."

Hagedorn interposed before O. Z. Garr could reply. "Let us keep to the issues. I confess I cannot see to the end of all this. The Meks have demonstrated themselves to be murderers. How can we take murderers back into our service? But if we don't—well, to say the least, conditions will be austere until we can locate and train a new force of technicians."

"The spaceships!" exclaimed Xanten. "We must see to them at once!"

"What's this?" inquired Beaudry, a gentleman of rock-hard face. "How do you mean: 'see to them'?"

"They must be protected from damage! What else? They are our link to the Home Worlds. The maintenance Meks probably have not deserted the hangars, since, if they propose to exterminate us, they will want to deny us the spaceships."

"Perhaps you care to march with a levy of Peasants to take the hangars under firm control?" suggested O. Z. Garr in a somewhat supercilious voice. A long history of rivalry and mutual detestation existed between himself and Xanten.

"It may be our only hope," said Xanten. "Still—how does one fight with a levy of Peasants? Better that I fly to the hangars and reconnoiter. Meanwhile, perhaps you, and others with military expertise, will take in hand the recruitment and training of a Peasant militia."

"In this regard," stated O. Z. Garr, "I await the outcome of our current deliberations. If it develops that here lies the optimum course, I naturally will apply my competences to the fullest degree. If your own capabilities are best fulfilled by spying out the activities of the Meks, I hope you will be large-hearted enough to do the same."

The two gentlemen glared at each other.

A year previously their enmity had almost culminated in a duel. Xanten, a gentleman tall, clean-limbed, nervously active, was gifted with great natural flair, but likewise evinced a disposition too easy for absolute elegance. The traditionalists considered him 'sthross', indicating a manner flawed by an almost imperceptible slackness and lack of punctilio: not the best possible choice for clan chief.

Xanten's response to O. Z. Garr was blandly polite. "I shall be glad to take this task upon myself. Since haste is of the essence I will risk the accusation of precipitousness and leave at once. Hopefully I return to report tomorrow." He rose, performed a ceremonious bow to Hagedorn, another all-inclusive salute to the council and departed.

III

He crossed to Esledune House where he maintained an apartment on the thirteenth level: four rooms furnished in the style known as Fifth Dynasty, after an epoch in the history of the Altair Home Planets, from which the human race had returned to Earth.

His current consort, Araminta, a lady of the Onwane family, was absent on affairs of her own, which suited Xanten well enough. After plying him with questions she would have discredited his simple explanation, preferring to suspect an assignation at his country place. Truth to tell, he had become bored with Araminta and had reason to believe that she felt similarly—or perhaps his exalted rank had provided her less opportunity to preside at glittering social functions than she had expected. They had bred no children. Araminta's daughter by a previous connection had been tallied to her. Her second child must then be tallied to Xanten, preventing him from siring another child.*

Xanten doffed his yellow council vestments. Assisted by a young Peasant buck, he donned dark yellow hunting-breeches with black trim, a black jacket, black boots. He drew a cap of soft black leather over his head, slung a pouch over his shoulder, into which he loaded weapons: a coiled blade, an energy gun.

Leaving the apartment he summoned the lift and descended to the first level armory, where normally a Mek clerk would have served him. Now Xanten, to his vast disgust, was forced to take himself behind the counter, and rummage here and there. The Meks had removed most of the sporting rifles, all the pellet ejectors and heavy energy-guns. An ominous circumstance, thought Xanten. At last he found a steel sling-whip, spare power-slugs for his gun, a brace of fire grenades, a high-powered monocular.

He returned to the lift, rode to the top level, ruefully considering the long climb when eventually the mechanism broke down, with no Meks at hand to make repairs. He thought of the apoplectic furies of rigid traditionalists such as Beaudry and chuckled. Eventful days lay ahead!

Stopping at the top level he crossed to the parapets, proceeded around to the radio room. Customarily three Mek specialists connected into the apparatus by wires clipped to their quills sat typing messages as they arrived. Now B. F. Robarth stood before the mechanism, uncertainly twisting the dials, his mouth wry with deprecation and distaste for the job.

"Any further news?" Xanten asked.

B. F. Robarth gave him a sour grin. "The folk at the other end

* The population of Castle Hagedorn was fixed; each gentleman and each lady was permitted a single child. If by chance another were born he must either find someone who had not yet sired to sponsor it, or dispose of it another way. The usual procedure was to give the child into the care of the Expiationists.

seem no more familiar with this cursed tangle than I. I hear occasional voices. I believe that the Meks are attacking Castle Delora."

Claghorn had entered the room behind Xanten. "Did I hear you correctly? Delora Castle is gone?"

"Not gone yet, Claghorn. But as good as gone. The Delora walls are little better than a picturesque crumble."

"Sickening situation!" muttered Xanten. "How can sentient creatures perform such evil? After all these centuries, how little we actually knew of them!" As he spoke he recognized the tactlessness of his remark; Claghorn had devoted much time to a study of the Meks.

"The act itself is not astounding," said Claghorn shortly. "It has occurred a thousand times in human history."

Mildly surprised that Claghorn should use human history as referent to a case involving the sub-orders, Xanten asked: "You were never aware of this vicious aspect to the Mek nature?"

"No. Never. Never indeed."

Claghorn seemed unduly sensitive, thought Xanten. Understandable, all in all. Claghorn's basic doctrine as set forth during the Hagedorn selection was by no means simple, and Xanten neither understood it nor completely endorsed what he conceived to be its goals; but it was plain that the revolt of the Meks had cut the ground out from under Claghorn's feet. Probably to the somewhat bitter satisfaction of O. Z. Garr, who must feel vindicated in his traditionalist doctrines.

Claghorn said tersely, "The life we've been leading couldn't last forever. It's a wonder it lasted as long as it did."

"Perhaps so," said Xanten in a soothing voice. "Well, no matter. All things change. Who knows? The Peasants may be planning to poison our food . . . I must go." He bowed to Claghorn, who returned him a crisp nod, and to B. F. Robarth, then departed the room.

He climbed the spiral staircase—almost a ladder—to the cotes, where the Birds lived in an invincible disorder, occupying themselves with gambling at the game of quarrels, a version of chess, with rules incomprehensible to every gentleman who had tried to understand it.

Castle Hagedorn maintained a hundred Birds, tended by a gang of long-suffering Peasants, whom the Birds held in vast disesteem. They were garish garrulous creatures, pigmented red, yellow, blue, with long necks, jerking inquisitive heads, an inherent irreverence which no amount of discipline or tutelage could overcome. Spying Xanten, they emitted a chorus of rude jeers: "Somebody wants a ride! Heavy thing!" "Why don't the self-anointed two-footers grow wings for themselves?" "My friend, never trust a Bird! We'll sky you, then fling you down on your fundament!"

"Quiet!" called Xanten. "I need six fast, silent Birds, upon an important mission. Are any capable of such a task?"

"Are any capable, he asks!" "*A ros ros ros!* When none of us have flown for a week!" "Silence? We'll give you silence, yellow and black!"

"Come then. You. You. You of the wise eye. You there. You with the cocked shoulder. You with the green pompon. To the basket."

The Birds designated, jeering, grumbling, reviling the Peasants, allowed their syrup sacs to be filled, then flapped to the wicker seat where Xanten waited. "To the space depot at Vincenne," he told them. "Fly high and silently. Enemies are abroad. We must learn what harm if any has been done to the spaceships."

"To the depot then!" Each Bird seized a length of rope tied to an overhead framework; the chair was yanked up with a jerk calculated to rattle Xanten's teeth, and off they flew, laughing, cursing each other for not supporting more of the load, but eventually all accommodating themselves to the task and flying with a coordinated flapping of the thirty-six sets of wings. To Xanten's relief, their garrulity lessened; silently they flew south, at a speed of fifty or sixty miles per hour.

The afternoon was already waning. The ancient countryside, scene to so many comings and goings, so much triumph and so much disaster, was laced with long black shadows. Looking down, Xanten reflected that though the human stock was native to this soil, and though his immediate ancestors had maintained their holdings for seven hundred years, Earth still seemed an alien world.

The reason of course was by no means mysterious or rooted in paradox. After the Six-Star War, Earth had lain fallow for three thousand years, unpopulated save for a handful of anguished wretches who somehow had survived the cataclysm and who had become semi-barbaric Nomads. Then seven hundred years ago certain rich lords of Altair, motivated to some extent by political disaffection, but no less by caprice, had decided to return to Earth. Such was the origin of the nine great strongholds, the resident gentlefolk and the staffs of specialized andromorphs.

Xanten flew over an area where an antiquarian had directed excavations, revealing a plaza flagged with white stone, a broken obelisk, a tumbled statue. The sight, by some trick of association, stimulated Xanten's mind to an astonishing vision, so simple and yet so grand that he looked around, in all directions, with new eyes. The vision was Earth re-populated with men, the land cultivated, Nomads driven back into the wilderness.

At the moment the image was far-fetched. And Xanten, watching the soft contours of old Earth slide below, pondered the Mek revolt which had altered his life with such startling abruptness.

Claghorn had long insisted that no human condition endured forever, with the corollary that the more complicated such a condition, the greater its susceptibility to change.

In that case the seven hundred year continuity at Castle Hagedorn—as artificial, extravagant and intricate as life could be—became an astonishing circumstance in itself. Claghorn had pushed his thesis further. Since change was inevitable, he argued that the gentlefolk should soften the impact by anticipating and controlling the changes—a doctrine which had been attacked with great fervor. The traditionalists labeled all of Claghorn's ideas demonstrable fallacy, and cited the very stability of castle life as proof of its viability. Xanten had inclined first one way, then the other, emotionally involved with neither cause. If anything, the fact of O. Z. Garr's traditionalism had nudged him toward Claghorn's views.

Now it seemed as if events had vindicated Claghorn. Change had come, with an impact of the maximum harshness and violence.

There were still questions to be answered, of course. Why had the Meks chosen this particular time to revolt? Conditions had not altered appreciably for five hundred years, and the Meks had never previously hinted dissatisfaction. In fact, they had revealed nothing of their feelings—though no one had ever troubled to ask them—save Claghorn.

The Birds were veering east to avoid the Ballarat Mountains, to the west of which were the ruins of a great city, never satisfactorily identified. Below lay the Lucerne Valley, at one time a fertile farm land. If one looked with great concentration the outline of the various holdings could sometimes be distinguished. Ahead, the spaceship hangars were visible, where Mek technicians maintained four spaceships that were jointly the property of Hagedorn, Janeil, Tuang, Morninglight and Maraval, though, for a variety of reasons, the ships were never used.

The sun was setting. Orange light twinkled and flickered on the metal walls. Xanten called instructions up to the Birds: "Circle down; alight behind that line of trees, but fly low so that none will see."

Down on stiff wings curved the Birds, six ungainly necks stretched toward the ground. Xanten was ready for the impact. The Birds never seemed able to alight easily when they carried a gentleman. When the cargo was something in which they felt a personal concern, dandelion fluff would never have been disturbed by the jar.

Xanten expertly kept his balance, instead of tumbling and rolling in the manner preferred by the Birds. "You all have syrup," he told them. "Rest: make no noise; do not quarrel. By tomorrow's sunset, if I am not here, return to Castle Hagedorn and say that Xanten was killed."

"Never fear!" cried the Birds. "We will wait forever!" "At any rate till tomorrow's sunset!" "If danger threatens, if you are pressed —*a ros ros ros!* Call for the Birds!" *A ros!* We are ferocious when aroused!"

"I wish it were true," said Xanten. "The Birds are arrant cowards, this is well known. Still I value the sentiment. Remember my instructions, and be quiet above all! I do not wish to be set upon and stabbed because of your clamor."

The Birds made indignant sounds. "Injustice, injustice! We are quiet as the dew!"

"Good." Xanten hurriedly moved away lest they should bellow new advice or reassurances after him.

IV

Passing through the forest, he came to an open meadow at the far edge of which, perhaps a hundred yards distant, was the rear of the first hangar. He stopped to consider.

Several factors were involved. First, the maintenance Meks, with the metal structure shielding them from radio contact, might still be unaware of the revolt. Hardly likely, he decided, in view of the otherwise careful planning. Second, the Meks, in continuous communication with their fellows, acted as a collective organism. The aggregate functioned more completely than its parts, and the individual was not prone to initiative. Hence, vigilance was not likely to be extreme. Third, if they expected anyone to attempt a discreet approach, they would necessarily scrutinize most closely the route which he proposed to take.

Xanten decided to wait in the shadows another ten minutes, until the setting sun shining over his shoulder should most effectively blind any who might watch.

Ten minutes passed. The hangars, burnished by the dying sunlight, bulked long, tall, completely quiet. In the intervening meadow long golden grass waved and rippled in a cool breeze.

Xanten took a deep breath, hefted his pouch, arranged his weapons, strode forth. It did not occur to him to crawl through the grass.

He reached the back of the nearest hangar without challenge. Pressing his ear to the metal he heard nothing. He walked to the corner, looked down the side: no sign of life. Xanten shrugged. Very well then; to the door.

He walked beside the hangar, the setting sun casting a long black shadow ahead of him. He came to a door opening into the hangar administrative office. Since there was nothing to be gained by trepidation, Xanten thrust the door aside and entered.

The offices were empty. The desks, where centuries before underlings had sat, calculating invoices and bills of lading, were bare, polished, free of dust. The computers and information banks, black enamel, glass, white and red switches, looked as if they had been installed only the day before.

Xanten crossed to the glass pane overlooking the hangar floor, shadowed under the bulk of the ship.

He saw no Meks. But on the floor of the hangar, arranged in neat rows and heaps, were elements and assemblies of the ship's control mechanism. Service panels gaped wide into the hull to show where the devices had been detached.

Xanten stepped from the office out into the hangar. The spaceship had been disabled, put out of commission. Xanten looked along the neat rows of parts. Certain savants of various castles were expert in the theory of space-time transfer; S. X. Rosenhox of Maraval had even derived a set of equations which, if translated into machinery, eliminated the troublesome Hamus Effect. But not one gentleman, even were he so oblivious to personal honor as to touch a hand to a tool, would know how to replace, connect and tune the mechanisms heaped upon the hangar floor.

When had the malicious work been done? Impossible to say.

Xanten returned to the office, stepped back out into the twilight, walked to the next hangar. Again no Meks; again the spaceship had been gutted of its control mechanisms. Xanten proceeded to the third hangar, where conditions were the same.

At the fourth hangar he discerned the faint sounds of activity. Stepping into the office, looking through the glass wall into the hangar, he found Meks working with their usual economy of motion, in a near silence which was uncanny.

Xanten, already uncomfortable because of skulking through the forest, became enraged by the cool destruction of his property. He strode forth into the hangar. Slapping his thigh to attract attention he called in a harsh voice, "Return the components to place! How dare you vermin act in such a manner?"

The Meks turned about their blank countenances, studied him through black beaded lensclusters at each side of their heads.

"What?" Xanten bellowed. "You hesitate?" He brought forth his steel whip, usually more of a symbolic adjunct than a punitive instrument, and slashed it against the ground. "Obey! This ridiculous revolt is at its end!"

The Meks still hesitated, and events wavered in the balance. None made a sound, though messages were passing among them, appraising the circumstances, establishing a consensus. Xanten could allow them no such leisure. He marched forward, wielding the whip, striking at the only area where the Meks felt pain: the ropy face. "To your duties," he roared. "A fine maintenance crew are you! A destruction crew is more like it!"

The Meks made their soft blowing sound which might mean anything. They fell back, and now Xanten noted one standing at the head of the companionway leading into the ship: a Mek larger than any he had seen before and one in some fashion different. This Mek was aiming a pellet gun at his head. With an unhurried flourish Xanten whipped away a Mek who had leapt forward with a knife, and without deigning to aim fired at and destroyed the Mek who stood on the companionway, even as the slug sang past his head.

The other Meks were nevertheless committed to an attack. All surged forward. Lounging disdainfully against the hull, Xanten shot them as they came, moving his head once to avoid a chunk of metal, again reaching to catch a throw-knife and hurl it into the face of him who had thrown it.

The Meks drew back, and Xanten guessed that they had agreed on a new tactic: either to withdraw for weapons or perhaps to confine him within the hangar. In any event no more could be accomplished here. He made play with the whip and cleared an avenue to the office. With tools, metal bars and forgings striking the glass behind him, he sauntered through the office and out into the night. He did not look behind.

The full moon was rising, a great yellow globe casting a smoky saffron glow, like an antique lamp. Mek eyes were not well adapted for night seeing, and Xanten waited by the door. Presently Meks began to pour forth, and Xanten hacked at their necks as they came.

The Meks drew back inside the hangar. Wiping his blade Xanten strode off the way he had come, looking neither right nor left. He stopped short. The night was young. Something tickled his mind: the recollection of the Mek who had fired the pellet gun. He had been larger, possibly a darker bronze, but, more significantly, he had displayed an indefinable poise, almost authority—though such a word, when used in connection with the Meks, was anomalous. On the other hand, someone must have planned the revolt, or at least originated the concept of a revolt in the first place.

It might be worthwhile to extend the reconnaissance, though his primary information had been secured.

Xanten turned back and crossed the landing area to the barracks and garages. Once more, frowning in discomfort, he felt the need for discretion. What times these were when a gentleman must skulk to avoid such as the Meks! He stole up behind the garages, where a half-dozen power-wagons* lay dozing.

Xanten looked them over. All were of the same sort, a metal frame with four wheels and an earth-moving blade at the front. Nearby must be the syrup stock.

Xanten presently found a bin containing a number of containers. He loaded a dozen on a nearby wagon and slashed the rest with his knife, so that the syrup gushed across the ground. The Meks used a somewhat different formulation; their syrup would be stocked at a different locale, presumably inside the barracks.

Xanten mounted a power-wagon, twisted the 'awake' key, tapped the 'Go' button, pulled a lever which set the wheels into reverse motion. The power-wagon lurched back. Xanten halted it and turned it so that it faced the barracks. He did likewise with three others, then set them all in motion, one after the other.

They trundled forward. The blades cut open the metal wall of the barracks, the roof sagged. The power-wagons continued, pushing the length of the interior, crushing all in their way.

Xanten nodded in profound satisfaction, returned to the power-wagon he had reserved for his own use. Mounting to the seat, he waited. No Meks issued from the barracks. Apparently they were deserted, with the entire crew busy at the hangars. Still, hopefully,

* Power-wagons, like the Meks, were originally swamp-creatures from Etamin 9. They were great rectangular slabs of muscle, slung into a rectangular frame and protected from sunlight, insects and rodents by a synthetic pelt. Syrup sacs communicated with their digestive apparatus, wires led to motor nodes in the rudimentary brain. The muscles were clamped to rocker arms which actuated rotors and drive-wheels. The power-wagons were economical, long-lived and docile, and so they were principally used for heavy cartage, earth-moving, heavy-tillage, and other arduous jobs.

the syrup stocks had been destroyed. Many might perish by starvation.

From the direction of the hangars came a single Mek, evidently attracted by the sounds of destruction. Xanten crouched on the seat and as it passed, coiled his whip around the stocky neck. He heaved; the Mek spun to the ground.

Xanten leapt down, seized its pellet-gun. Here was another of the larger Meks, and now Xanten saw it to be without a syrup sac, a Mek in the original state. Astounding! How did the creature survive? Suddenly there were many new questions to be asked; hopefully a few to be answered. Standing on the creature's head, Xanten hacked away the long antenna quills which protruded from the back of the Mek's scalp. It was now insulated, alone, on its own resources; a situation certain to reduce the most stalwart Mek to apathy.

"Up!" ordered Xanten. "Into the back of the wagon!" He cracked the whip for emphasis.

The Mek at first seemed disposed to defy him, but after a blow or two obeyed. Xanten climbed into the seat, started the power-wagon, directed it to the north. The Birds would be unable to carry both himself and the Mek—or in any event they would cry and complain so raucously that they might as well be believed at first. They might or might not wait until the specified hour of tomorrow's sunset. As likely as not they would sleep the night in a tree, awake in a surly mood and return at once to Castle Hagedorn.

All through the night the power-wagon trundled, with Xanten on the seat and his captive huddled in the rear.

V

The gentlefolk of the castles, for all their assurance, disliked to wander the countryside by night, by reason of what some derided as superstitious fear. Others cited travelers benighted beside mouldering ruins and their subsequent visions: the eldritch music they had heard, or the whimper of moon-mirkins, or the far horns of spectral huntsmen. Others had seen pale lavender and green lights, and wraiths which ran with long strides through the forest; and

Hode Abbey, now a dank tumble, was notorious for the White Hag and the alarming toll she exacted.

A hundred such cases were known. While the hard-headed scoffed, none needlessly traveled the countryside by night. Indeed, if truly ghosts haunt the scenes of tragedy and heartbreak, then the landscape of Old Earth must be home to ghosts and specters beyond all numbering; especially that region across which Xanten rolled in the power-wagon, where every rock, every meadow, every vale and swale was crusted thick with human experience.

The moon rose high. The wagon trundled north along an ancient road, the cracked concrete slabs shining pale in the moonlight. Twice Xanten saw flickering orange lights off to the side, and once, standing in the shade of a cypress tree, he thought to see a tall quiet shape, silently watching him pass. The captive Mek sat plotting mischief, Xanten well knew. Without its quills it must feel depersonified, bewildered, but Xanten told himself that it would not do to doze.

The road led through a town, certain structures of which yet stood. Not even the Nomads took refuge in these old towns, fearing either miasma or perhaps the redolence of grief.

The moon reached the zenith. The landscape spread away in a hundred tones of silver, black and gray. Looking about, Xanten thought that for all the notable pleasures of civilized life, there was yet something to be said for the spaciousness and simplicity of Nomadland . . . The Mek made a stealthy movement. Xanten did not so much as turn his head. He cracked his whip in the air. The Mek became quiet.

All through the night the power-wagon rolled along the old road, with the moon sinking into the west. The eastern horizon glowed green and lemon-yellow, and presently, as the pallid moon disappeared over the distant line of the mountains the sun came up.

At this moment, Xanten spied a drift of smoke off to the right.

He halted the wagon. Standing up on the seat he craned his neck to spy a Nomad encampment about a quarter-mile distant. He could distinguish three or four dozen tents of various sizes, a dozen dilapidated power-wagons. On the hetman's tall tent he thought to see a black ideogram which he thought he recognized. If so, this would be the tribe which not long before had trespassed on the Hagedorn domain, and which O. Z. Garr had repulsed.

Xanten settled himself upon the seat, composed his garments, set the power-wagon in motion and guided it toward the camp.

A hundred black-cloaked men, tall and lean as ferrets, watched his approach. A dozen sprang forward and whipping arrows to bows aimed them at his heart. Xanten turned them a glance of supercilious inquiry, drove the wagon up to the hetman's tent, halted. He rose to his feet. "Hetman," he called. "Are you awake?"

The hetman parted the canvas which closed off his tent, peered out and after a moment came forth. Like the others he wore a garment of limp black cloth, swathing head and body alike. His face thrust through a square opening: narrow blue eyes, a grotesquely long nose, a chin long, skewed and sharp.

Xanten gave him a curt nod. "Observe this." He jerked his thumb toward the Mek in the back of the wagon. The hetman flicked aside his eyes, studied the Mek a tenth-second, returned to a scrutiny of Xanten. "His kind have revolted against the gentlemen," said Xanten. "In fact they massacre all the men of Earth. Hence we of Castle Hagedorn make this offer to the Nomads. Come to Castle Hagedorn! We will feed, clothe and arm you. We will train you to discipline and the arts of formal warfare. We will provide the most expert leadership within our power. We will then annihilate the Meks, expunge them from Earth. After the campaign, we will train you to technical skills, and you may pursue profitable and interesting careers in the service of the castles."

The hetman made no reply for a moment. Then his weathered face split into a ferocious grin and he spoke in a voice which Xanten found surprisingly well-modulated. "So your beasts have finally risen up to rend you! A pity they forebore so long! Well, it is all one to us. You are both alien folk and sooner or later your bones must bleach together."

Xanten pretended incomprehension. "If I understand you aright, you assert that in the face of alien assault, all men must fight a common battle; and then, after the victory, cooperate still to their mutual advantage; am I correct?"

The hetman's grin never wavered. "You are not men. Only we of Earth soil and Earth water are men. You and your weird slaves are strangers together. We wish you success in your mutual slaughter."

"Well then," declared Xanten, "I heard you aright after all. Appeals to your loyalty are ineffectual, so much is clear. What of self-interest then? The Meks, failing to expunge the gentlefolk of the castles, will turn upon the Nomads and kill them as if they were so many ants."

"If they attack us, we will war on them," said the hetman. "Otherwise let them do as they will."

Xanten glanced thoughtfully at the sky. "We might be willing even now, to accept a contingent of Nomads into the service of Castle Hagedorn, this to form a cadre from which a larger and more versatile group may be formed."

From the side another Nomad called in an offensively jeering voice: "You will sew a sac on our backs where you can pour your syrup, hey?"

Xanten replied in an even voice, "The syrup is highly nutritious and supplies all bodily needs."

"Why then do you not consume it yourself?"

Xanten disdained reply.

The hetman spoke. "If you wish to supply us weapons, we will take them, and use them against whomever threatens us. But do not expect us to defend you. If you fear for your lives, desert your castles and become Nomads."

"Fear for our lives?" exclaimed Xanten. "What nonsense! Never! Castle Hagedorn is impregnable, as is Janeil, and most of the other castles as well."

The hetman shook his head. "Any time we choose we could take Hagedorn, and kill all you popinjays in your sleep."

"What?" cried Xanten in outrage. "Are you serious?"

"Certainly. On a black night we would send a man aloft on a great kite and drop him down on the parapets. He would lower a line, haul up ladders and in fifteen minutes the castle is taken."

Xanten pulled at his chin. "Ingenious, but impractical. The Birds would detect such a kite. Or the wind would fail at a critical moment . . . All this is beside the point. The Meks fly no kites. They plan to make a display against Janeil and Hagedorn and then, in their frustration, they will go forth and hunt Nomads."

The hetman moved back a step. "What then? We have survived similar attempts by the men of Hagedorn. Cowards all! Hand to hand, with equal weapons, we would make you eat the dirt like the contemptible dogs you are."

Xanten raised his eyebrows in elegant disdain. "I fear that you forget yourself. You address a clan chief of Castle Hagedorn. Only fatigue and boredom restrain me from punishing you with this whip."

"Bah," said the hetman. He crooked a finger to one of his archers. "Spit this insolent lordling."

The archer discharged his arrow, but Xanten had been expecting some such act. He fired his energy gun, destroying arrow, bow, and the archer's hands. He said, "I see I must teach you common respect for your betters; so it means the whip after all." Seizing the hetman by the scalp, he coiled the whip smartly once, twice, thrice around the narrow shoulders. "Let this suffice. I cannot compel you to fight, but at least I can demand decent respect from scuttling dung beetles." He leapt to the ground and, seizing the hetman, pitched him into the back of the wagon alongside the Mek. Then, backing the power-wagon around, he departed the camp without so much as a glance over his shoulder, the thwart of the seat protecting his back from the arrows of the hetman's stunned subjects.

The hetman scrambled erect, drew his dagger. Xanten turned his head slightly. "Take care! Or I will tie you to the wagon, and you shall run behind in the dust."

The hetman hesitated, made a spitting sound between his teeth, drew back. He looked down at his blade, turned it over, sheathed it with a grunt. "Where do you take me?"

Xanten halted the wagon. "No farther. I merely wished to leave your camp with dignity, without dodging and ducking a hail of arrows. You may alight. I take it you still refuse to bring your men into the service of Castle Hagedorn?"

The hetman once more made the spitting sound between his teeth. "When the Meks have destroyed the castles, we shall destroy the Meks. Then Earth will be cleared of star-things for all time!"

"You are a gang of intractable savages. Very well, alight, return to your encampment. Reflect well before you again show disrespect to a Castle Hagedorn clan chief."

"Bah," muttered the hetman. Leaping down from the wagon, he stalked back down the track toward his camp. He did not look back.

VI

About noon Xanten came to Far Valley, at the edge of the Hagedorn lands.

Nearby was a village of Expiationists: malcontents and neurasthenics in the opinion of castle gentlefolk, and a curious group by any standards. A few had held enviable rank; certain others were savants of recognized erudition; but others yet were persons of neither dignity nor reputation, subscribing to the most bizarre and extreme of philosophies. All now performed toil, no different from that relegated to the Peasants, and all seemed to take a perverse satisfaction in what by castle standards was filth, poverty and degradation.

As might be expected, their creed was by no means homogenous. Some might better have been described as 'nonconformists', and others still, a minority, argued for a dynamic program.

Between castle and village was little intercourse. Occasionally the Expiationists bartered fruit or polished wood for tools, nails, medicaments; or the gentlefolk might make up a party to watch the Expiationists at their dancing and singing. Xanten had visited the village on many such occasions and had been attracted by the artless charm and informality of the folk at their play. Now, passing near the village, Xanten turned aside and followed a lane which wound between tall blackberry hedges and out upon a little common, where goats and cattle grazed. Xanten halted the wagon in the shade, saw that the syrup sac was full. He looked back at his captive. "What of you? If you need syrup, pour yourself full. But no, you have no sac. What then do you feed upon? Mud? Unsavory fare. I fear none here is rank enough for your taste. Ingest syrup or munch grass, as you will; only do not stray overfar from the wagon, for I watch with an intent eye."

The Mek, sitting hunched in a corner, gave no signal that it comprehended. Nor did it move to take advantage of Xanten's offer.

Xanten went to a watering trough. Holding his hands under the trickle which issued from a lead pipe, he rinsed his face, then drank a swallow or two from his cupped hand.

Turning, he found that a dozen folk of the village had approached. One he knew well, a man who might have become Godalming, or even Aure, had he not become infected with expiationism.

Xanten performed a polite salute. "A. G. Philidor. It is I, Xanten."

"Xanten, of course. But here I am A. G. Philidor no longer; merely Philidor."

Xanten bowed. "My apologies. I have neglected the full rigor of your informality."

"Spare me your wit," said Philidor. "Why do you bring us a shorn Mek? For adoption, perhaps?" This last alluded to the gentlefolk practice of bringing over-tally babies to the village.

"Now who flaunts his wit? But you have not heard the news?"

"News arrives here last of all. The Nomads are better informed."

"Prepare yourself for surprise. The Meks have revolted against the castles. Halcyon and Delora are demolished, and all killed; perhaps others by this time."

Philidor shook his head. "I am not surprised."

"Well, then, are you not concerned?"

Philidor considered. "To this extent. Our own plans, never very feasible, become more far-fetched than ever."

"It appears to me," said Xanten, "that you face grave and immediate danger. The Meks surely intend to wipe out every vestige of humanity. You will not escape."

Philidor shrugged. "Conceivably the danger exists . . . We will take counsel and decide what to do."

"I can put forward a proposal which you may find attractive," said Xanten. "Our first concern, of course, is to suppress the revolt. There are at least a dozen Expiationist communities, with an aggregate population of two or three thousand—perhaps more. I propose that we recruit and train a corps of highly disciplined troops, supplied from the Castle Hagedorn armory, led by Hagedorn's most expert military theoreticians."

Philidor stared at him incredulously. "You expect us, the Expiationists, to become your soldiers?"

"Why not?" asked Xanten ingeniously. "Your life is at stake no less than ours."

"No one dies more than once."

Xanten in his turn evinced shock. "What? Can this be a former gentleman of Hagedorn speaking? Is this the face a man of pride and courage turns to danger? Is this the lesson of history? Of course not! I need not instruct you in this; you are as knowledgeable as I."

Philidor nodded. "I know that the history of man is not his technical triumphs, his kills, his victories. It is a composite: a mosaic of a trillion pieces, the account of each man's accommodation with his conscience. This is the true history of the race."

Xanten made an airy gesture. "A. G. Philidor, you over-simplify grievously. Do you consider me obtuse? There are many kinds of history. They interact. You emphasize morality. But the ultimate basis of morality is survival. What promotes survival is good, what induces mortefaction is bad."

"Well spoken!" declared Philidor. "But let me propound a parable. May a nation of a million beings destroy a creature who otherwise will infect all with a fatal disease? Yes, you will say. Once more. Ten starving beasts hunt you, that they may eat. Will you kill them to save your life? Yes, you will say again, though here you destroy more than you save. Once more: a man inhabits a hut in a lonely valley. A hundred spaceships descend from the sky, and attempt to destroy him. May he destroy these ships in self-defense, even though he is one and they are a hundred thousand? Perhaps you say yes. What then if a whole world, a whole race of beings, pits itself against this single man? May he kill all? What if the attackers are as human as himself? What if he were the creature of the first instance, who otherwise will infect a world with disease? You see, there is no area where a simple touchstone avails. We have searched and found none. Hence, at the risk of sinning against Survival, we—I, at least; I can only speak for myself—have chosen a morality that at least allows me calm. I kill—*nothing*. I destroy *nothing*."

"Bah," said Xanten contemptuously. "If a Mek platoon entered this valley and began to kill your children, you would not defend them?"

Philidor compressed his lips, turned away. Another man spoke. "Philidor has defined morality. But who is absolutely moral? Philidor —or I, or you—might in such a case desert his morality."

Philidor said, "Look about you. Is anyone here you recognize?"

Xanten scanned the group. Nearby stood a girl of extraordinary beauty. She wore a white smock and in the dark hair curling to her shoulders she wore a red flower. Xanten nodded. "I see the maiden O. Z. Garr wished to introduce into his menage at the castle."

"Exactly," said Philidor. "Do you recall the circumstances?"

"Very well indeed," said Xanten. "There was vigorous objection from the Council of Notables—if for no other reason than the threat to our laws of population control. O. Z. Garr attempted to sidestep the law in this fashion. 'I keep Phanes,' he said. 'At times I maintain as many as six, or even eight, and no one utters a word of protest. I will call this girl a Phane and keep her among the rest.' I and others protested. There was almost a duel on this matter. O. Z. Garr was forced to relinquish the girl. She was given into my custody and I conveyed her to Far Valley."

Philidor nodded. "All this is correct. Well—we attempted to dissuade Garr. He refused to be dissuaded, and threatened us with his hunting force of perhaps thirty Meks. We stood aside. Are we moral? Are we strong or weak?"

"Sometimes it is better," said Xanten, "to ignore morality. Even though O. Z. Garr is a gentleman and you are but Expiationists . . . Likewise in the case of the Meks. They are destroying the castles, and all the men of earth. If morality means supine acceptance, then morality must be abandoned!"

Philidor gave a sour chuckle. "What a remarkable situation! The Meks are here, likewise Peasants and Birds and Phanes, all altered, transported and enslaved for human pleasure. Indeed, it is this fact that occasions our guilt, for which we must expiate. And now you want us to compound this guilt!"

"It is a mistake to brood overmuch about the past," said Xanten. "Still, if you wish to preserve your option to brood, I suggest that you fight Meks now, or at the very least take refuge in the castle."

"Not I," said Philidor. "Perhaps others may choose to do so."

"You will wait to be killed?"

"No. I and no doubt others will take refuge in the remote mountains."

Xanten clambered back aboard the power-wagon. "If you change your mind, come to Castle Hagedorn."

He departed.

The road continued along the valley, wound up a hillside, crossed a ridge. Far ahead, silhouetted against the sky, stood Castle Hagedorn.

VII

Xanten reported to the council.

"The spaceships cannot be used. The Meks have rendered them inoperative. Any plan to solicit assistance from the Home Worlds is pointless."

"This is sorry news," said Hagedorn with a grimace. "Well then—so much for that."

Xanten continued. "Returning by power-wagon I encountered a tribe of Nomads. I summoned the hetman and explained to him the advantages of serving Castle Hagedorn. The Nomads, I fear, lack both grace and docility. The hetman gave so surly a response that I departed in disgust.

"At Far Valley I visited the Expiationist village, and made a similar proposal, but with no great success. They are as idealistic as the Nomads are churlish. Both are of a fugitive tendency. The Expiationists spoke of taking refuge in the mountains. The Nomads presumably will retreat into the steppes."

Beaudry snorted. "How will flight help them? Perhaps they gain a few years—but eventually the Meks will find every last one of them; such is their methodicity."

"In the meantime," O. Z. Garr declared peevishly, "we might have organized them into an efficient combat corps, to the benefit of all. Well, then, let them perish! We are secure."

"Secure yes," said Hagedorn gloomily. "But what when the power fails? When the lifts break down? When air circulation cuts off so that we either stifle or freeze? What then?"

O. Z. Garr gave his head a grim shake. "We must steel ourselves to undignified expedients, with as good a grace as possible. But the machinery of the castle is sound, and I expect small deterioration or failure for conceivably five or ten years. By that time anything may occur."

Claghorn, who had been leaning indolently back in his seat, spoke at last: "Essentially this is a passive program. Like the defection of the Nomads and Expiationists, it looks very little beyond the immediate moment."

O. Z. Garr spoke in a voice carefully polite. "Claghorn is well aware that I yield to none in courteous candor, as well as optimism and directness: in short, the reverse of passivity. But I refuse to dignify a stupid little inconvenience by extending it serious attention. How can he label this procedure 'passivity'? Does the worthy and honorable head of the Claghorns have a proposal which more effectively maintains our status, our standards, our self-respect?"

Claghorn nodded slowly, with a faint half-smile which O. Z. Garr found odiously complacent. "There is a simple and effective method by which the Meks might be defeated."

"Well then!" cried Hagedorn. "Why hesitate? Let us hear it!"

Claghorn looked around the red velvet-covered table, considered the faces of all: the dispassionate Xanten; Beaudry, with his burly, rigid, face muscles clenched in an habitual expression unpleasantly like a sneer; old Isseth, handsome, erect and vital as the most dashing cadet; Hagedorn troubled, glum, his inward perplexity all too evident; the elegant Garr; Overwhele, thinking savagely of the inconveniences of the future; Aure, toying with his ivory tablet, either bored, morose or defeated; the others displaying various aspects of doubt, foreboding, hauteur, dark resentment, impatience; and in the case of Floy, a quiet smile—or as Isseth later characterized it, an imbecilic smirk—intended to convey his total disassociation from the entire irksome matter.

Claghorn took stock of the faces, and shook his head. "I will not at the moment broach this plan, as I fear it is unworkable. But I must point out that under no circumstances can Castle Hagedorn be as before, even should we survive the Mek attack."

"Bah!" exclaimed Beaudry. "We lose dignity, we become ridiculous, by even so much as discussing the beasts."

Xanten stirred himself. "A distasteful subject, but remember! Halcyon is destroyed, and Delora and who knows what others? Let us not thrust our heads in the sand! The Meks will not waft away merely because we ignore them."

"In any event," said O. Z. Garr, "Janeil is secure and we are secure. The other folk, unless they are already slaughtered, might do well to visit us during the inconvenience, if they can justify the humiliation of flight to themselves. I myself believe that the Meks will soon come to heel, anxious to return to their posts."

Hagedorn shook his head gloomily. "I find this hard to believe. Very well then, we shall adjourn."

The radio communications system was the first of the castle's vast array of electrical and mechanical devices to break down.

The failure occurred so soon and so decisively that certain of the theoreticians, notably I. K. Harde and Uegus, postulated sabotage by the departing Meks. Others remarked that the system had never been absolutely dependable, that the Meks themselves had been forced to tinker continuously with the circuits, that the failure was simply a result of bad engineering. Harde and Uegus inspected the unwieldy apparatus, but the cause of failure was not obvious. After a half-hour of consultation they agreed that any attempt to restore the system would necessitate complete re-design and re-engineering, with consequent construction of testing and calibration devices, and the fabrication of a complete new family of components. "This is manifestly impossible," stated Uegus in his report to the council. "Even the simplest useful system would require several technician-years. There is not even one single technician to hand. We must therefore await the availability of trained and willing labor."

"In retrospect," stated Isseth, the oldest of the clan chiefs, "it is clear that in many ways we have been less than provident. No matter that the men of the Home Worlds are vulgarians! Men of shrewder calculation than our own would have maintained inter-world connection."

"Lack of 'shrewdness' and 'providence' were not the deterring factors," stated Claghorn. "Communication was discouraged simply because the early lords were unwilling that Earth should be over-run with Home-World parvenus. It is as simple as that."

Isseth grunted, and started to make a rejoinder, but Hagedorn said hastily, "Unluckily, as Xanten tells us, the spaceships have been rendered useless. While certain of our number have a profound knowledge of the theoretical considerations, again who is there to perform the toil? Even were the hangars and spaceships themselves under our control."

O. Z. Garr declared, "Give me six platoons of Peasants and six power-wagons equipped with high-energy cannon, and I'll regain the hangars. No difficulties there!"

Beaudry said, "Well, here's a start, at least. I'll assist in the training of the Peasants, and though I know nothing of cannon operation, rely on me for any advice I can give."

Hagedorn looked around the group, frowned, pulled at his chin. "There are difficulties to this program. First, we have at hand only the single power-wagon in which Xanten returned from his reconnaissance. Then what of our energy cannons? Has anyone inspected them? The Meks were entrusted with maintenance, but it is possible, even likely, that they wrought mischief here as well. O. Z. Garr, you are reckoned an expert military theoretician. What can you tell us in this regard?"

"I have made no inspection to date," stated O. Z. Garr. "Today the 'Display of Antique Tabards' will occupy us all until the 'Hour of Sundown Appraisal'."* He looked at his watch. "Perhaps now is as good a time as any to adjourn, until I am able to provide detailed information in regard to the cannons."

Hagedorn nodded his heavy head. "The time indeed grows late. Your Phanes appear today?"

* 'Display of Antique Tabards'; 'Hour of Sundown Appraisal': the literal sense of the first term was yet relevant; that of the second had become lost and the phrase was a mere formalism, connoting that hour of late afternoon when visits were exchanged, wines, liqueurs and essences tasted: in short, a time of relaxation and small talk before the more formal convivialities of dining.

"Only two," replied O. Z. Garr. "The Lazule and the Eleventh Mystery. I can find nothing suitable for the Gossamer Delights nor my little Blue Fay, and the Gloriana still requires tutelage. Today B. Z. Maxelwane's Variflors should repay the most attention."

"Yes," said Hagedorn. "I have heard other remarks to this effect. Very well then, until tomorrow. Eh, Claghorn, you have something to say?"

"Yes, indeed," said Claghorn mildly. "We have all too little time at our disposal. Best that we make the most of it. I seriously doubt the efficacy of Peasant troops; they are like rabbits against wolves. What we need, rather than rabbits, are panthers."

"Ah, yes," said Hagedorn vaguely. "Yes indeed."

"Where, then, are panthers to be found?" Claghorn looked inquiringly around the table. "Can no one suggest a source? A pity. Well then, if panthers fail to appear, I suppose rabbits must do. Let us go about the business of converting rabbits into panthers, and instantly. I suggest that we postpone all fetes and spectacles until the shape of our future is more certain."

Hagedorn raised his eyebrows, opened his mouth to speak, closed it again. He looked intently at Claghorn to ascertain whether or not he joked. Then he looked dubiously around the table.

Beaudry gave a rather brassy laugh. "It seems that erudite Claghorn cries panic."

O. Z. Garr stated: "Surely, in all dignity, we cannot allow the impertinence of our servants to cause us such eye-rolling alarm. I am embarrassed even to bring the matter forward."

"I am not embarrassed," said Claghorn, with the full-faced complacence which so exasperated O. Z. Garr. "I see no reason why you should be. Our lives are threatened, in which case a trifle of embarrassment, or anything else, becomes of secondary importance."

O. Z. Garr rose to his feet, performed a brusque salute in Claghorn's direction, of such a nature as to constitute a calculated affront. Claghorn, rising, performed a similar salute, this so grave and overly complicated as to invest Garr's insult with burlesque overtones. Xanten, who detested O. Z. Garr, laughed aloud.

O. Z. Garr hesitated, then, sensing that under the circumstances taking the matter further would be regarded as poor form, strode from the chamber.

The Viewing of Antique Tabards, an annual pageant of Phanes wearing sumptuous garments took place in the Great Rotunda to the north of the central plaza.

Possibly half of the gentlemen, but less than a quarter of the ladies, kept Phanes. These were creatures native to the caverns of Albireo Seven's moon: a docile race, both playful and affectionate, which after several thousand years of selective breeding had become sylphs of piquant beauty. Clad in a delicate gauze which issued from pores behind their ears, along their upper arms, down their backs, they were the most inoffensive of creatures, anxious always to please, innocently vain. Most gentlemen regarded them with affection, but rumors sometimes told of ladies drenching an especially hated Phane in tincture of ammonia, which matted her pelt and destroyed her gauze forever.

A gentleman besotted by a Phane was considered a figure of fun. The Phane, though so carefully bred as to seem a delicate girl, if used sexually became crumpled and haggard, with gauzes drooping and discolored, and everyone would know that such and such a gentleman had misused his Phane. In this regard, at least, the women of the castles might exert their superiority. They did so by conducting themselves with such extravagant provocation that the Phanes in contrast seemed the most ingenious and fragile of nature sprites. Their life-span was perhaps thirty years, during the last ten of which, after they had lost their beauty, they encased themselves in mantles of gray gauze and performed menial tasks in boudoirs, kitchens, pantries, nurseries and dressing rooms.

The Viewing of Antique Tabards was an occasion more for the viewing of Phanes than the tabards, though these, woven of Phane-gauze, were of intricate beauty in themselves.

The Phane owners sat in a lower tier, tense with hope and pride, exulting when one made an especially splendid display, plunged into black depths when the ritual postures were performed with other than grace and elegance. During each display highly formal music was plucked from a lute by a gentleman from a clan different to that of the Phane owner. The owner never played the lute to the performance of his own Phane. The display was never overtly a competition and no formal acclamation was allowed, but all watching made up their minds as to which was the most entrancing and graceful of the Phanes, and the repute of the owner was thereby exalted.

The current Viewing was delayed almost half an hour by reason of the defection of the Meks, and certain hasty improvisations had been made necessary. But the gentlefolk of Castle Hagedorn were in no mood to be critical and took no heed of the occasional lapses as a dozen young Peasant bucks struggled to perform unfamiliar tasks. The Phanes were as entrancing as ever, bending, twisting, swaying to plangent chords of the lute, fluttering their fingers as if feeling for raindrops, crouching suddenly, gliding, then springing upright straight as wands, finally bowing and skipping from the platform.

Halfway through the program a Peasant sidled awkwardly into the Rotunda, and mumbled in an urgent manner to the cadet who came to inquire his business. The cadet at once made his way to Hagedorn's polished jet booth. Hagedorn listened, nodded, spoke a few terse words and settled calmly back in his seat as if the message had been of no consequence, and the gentlefolk of the audience were reassured.

The entertainment proceeded. O. Z. Garr's delectable pair made a fine show, but it was generally felt that Lirlin, a young Phane belonging to Isseth Floy Gazuneth, for the first time at a formal showing, made the most captivating display.

The Phanes appeared for a last time, moving all together through a half-improvised minuet. Then they performed a final half-gay, half-regretful salute and departed the rotunda. For a few moments more the gentlemen and ladies would remain in their booths, sipping essences, discussing the display, arranging affairs and assignations. Hagedorn sat frowning, twisting his hands.

Suddenly he rose to his feet. The rotunda instantly became silent.

"I dislike intruding an unhappy note at so pleasant an occasion," said Hagedorn. "But news has just been given to me, and it is fitting that all should know. Janeil Castle is under attack. The Meks are there in great force, with hundreds of power-wagons. They have circled the castle with a dike which prevents any effective use of the Janeil energy-cannon.

"There is no immediate danger to Janeil, and it is difficult to comprehend what the Meks hope to achieve, the Janeil walls being all of two hundred feet high.

"The news nevertheless is somber, and it means that eventually we must expect a similar investment—though it is even more difficult to comprehend how Meks could hope to inconvenience us. Our water derives from four wells sunk deep into the earth. We have great stocks of food. Our energy is derived from the sun. If necessary, we could condense water and synthesize food from the air—at least I have been so assured by our great biochemical theoretician X. B. Ladisname. Still—this is the news. Make of it what you will. Tomorrow the Council of Notables will meet."

VIII

"Well, then," said Hagedorn to the council, "for once let us dispense with formality. O. Z. Garr: what of our cannon?"

O. Z. Garr, wearing the magnificent gray and green uniform of the Overwhele Dragoons, carefully placed his morion on the table, so that the panache stood erect. "Of twelve cannon, four appear to be functioning correctly. Four have been sabotaged by excision of the power-leads. Four have been sabotaged by some means undetectable to careful investigation. I have commandeered a half-dozen Peasants who demonstrate a modicum of mechanical ability, and have instructed them in detail. They are currently engaged in splicing the leads. This is the extent of my current information in regard to the cannon."

"Moderately good news," said Hagedorn. "What of the proposed corps of armed Peasants?"

"The project is under way. A. F. Mull and I. A. Berzelius are now inspecting Peasants with a view to recruitment and training. I can make no sanguine projection as to the military effectiveness of such a corps, even if trained and led by such as A. F. Mull, I. A. Berzelius and myself. The Peasants are a mild ineffectual race, admirably suited to the grubbing of weeds, but with no stomach whatever for fighting."

Hagedorn glanced around the council. "Are there any other suggestions?"

Beaudry spoke in a harsh angry voice, "Had the villains but left us our power-wagons, we might have mounted the cannon aboard! The Peasants are equal to this, at least. Then we could roll to Janeil and blast the dogs from the rear."

"These Meks seem utter fiends!" declared Aure. "What conceivably do they have in mind? Why, after these centuries, must they suddenly go mad?"

"We all ask ourselves the same," said Hagedorn. "Xanten, you returned from reconnaissance with a captive: have you attempted to question him?"

"No," said Xanten. "Truth to tell, I haven't thought of him since."

"Why not attempt to question him? Perhaps he can provide a clue or two."

Xanten nodded assent. "I can try. Candidly I expect to learn nothing."

"Claghorn, you are the Mek expert," said Beaudry. "Would you have thought the creatures capable of so intricate a plot? What do they hope to gain? Our castles?"

"They are certainly capable of precise and meticulous planning," said Claghorn. "Their ruthlessness surprises me—more, possibly, than it should. I have never known them to covet our material possessions, and they show no tendency toward what we consider the concomitants of civilization: fine discriminations of sensation and the like. I have often speculated—I won't dignify the conceit with the status of a theory—that the structural logic of a brain is of rather more consequence than we reckon with. Our own brains are remarkable for their utter lack of rational structure. Considering the haphazarded manner in which our thoughts are formed, registered, indexed and recalled, any single rational act becomes a miracle. Perhaps we are incapable of rationality. Perhaps all thought is a set of impulses generated by one emotion, monitored by another, ratified by a third. In contrast the Mek brain is a marvel of what seems careful engineering. It is roughly cubical and consists of microscopic cells interconnected by organic fibrils, each a monofilament molecule of negligible electrical resistance. Within each cell is a film of silica, a fluid of variable conductivity and dielectric properties, a cusp of a complex mixture of metallic oxides. The brain is capable of storing great quantities of information in an orderly pattern. No fact is lost, unless it is purposely forgotten, a capacity which the Meks possess. The brain also functions as a radio transceiver, possibly as a radar transmitter and detector, though this again is speculation.

"Where the Mek brain falls short is in its lack of emotional color. One Mek is precisely like another, without any personality differentiation perceptible to us. This, clearly, is a function of their communicative system. It would be unthinkable for a unique personality to develop under these conditions. They served us efficiently and—so we thought—loyally, because they felt nothing about their condition, neither pride in achievement, nor resentment, nor shame. Nothing whatever. They neither loved us nor hated us. Nor do they now. It is hard for us to conceive this emotional vacuum, when each of us feels something about everything. We live in a welter of emotions. They are as devoid of emotion as an ice-cube. They were fed, housed, maintained in a manner they found satisfactory. Why did they revolt? I have speculated at length, but the single reason which I can formulate seems so grotesque and unreasonable that I refuse to take it seriously. If this after all is the correct explanation . . ." His voice drifted away.

"Well?" demanded O. Z. Garr peremptorily. "What then?"

"Then—it is all the same. They are committed to the destruction of the human race. My speculation alters nothing."

Hagedorn turned to Xanten. "All this should assist you in your inquiries."

"I was about to suggest that Claghorn assist me, if he is so inclined," said Xanten.

"As you like," said Claghorn, "though in my opinion the information, no matter what, is irrelevant. Our single concern should be a means to repel them and to save our lives."

"And—save the force of 'panthers' you mentioned at our previous session—you can conceive of no subtle weapon?" asked Hagedorn wistfully. "A device to set up electrical resonances in their brains, or something similar?"

"Not feasible," said Claghorn. "Certain organs in the creatures' brains function as overload switches. Though it is true that during this time they might not be able to communicate." After a moment's reflection he added thoughtfully: "Who knows? A. G. Bernal and Uegus are theoreticians with a profound knowledge of such projections. Perhaps they might construct such a device, or several, against a possible need."

Hagedorn nodded dubiously, and looked toward Uegus. "Is this possible?"

Uegus frowned. "'Construct'? I can certainly design such an instrument. But the components—where? Scattered through the storerooms helter-skelter, some functioning, others not. To achieve anything meaningful I must become no better than an apprentice, a Mek." He became incensed, and his voice hardened. "I find it hard to believe that I should be forced to point out this fact! Do you hold me and my talents then of such small worth?"

Hagedorn hastened to reassure him. "Of course not! I for one would never think of impugning your dignity."

"Never!" agreed Claghorn. "Nevertheless, during this present emergency, we will find indignities imposed upon us by events, unless now we impose them upon ourselves."

"Very well," said Uegus, a humorless smile trembling at his lips. "You shall come with me to the storeroom. I will point out the components to be brought forth and assembled, you shall perform the toil. What do you say to that?"

"I say yes, gladly, if it will be of real utility. However, I can hardly perform the labor for a dozen different theoreticians. Will any others serve beside myself?"

No one responded. Silence was absolute, as if every gentleman present held his breath.

Hagedorn started to speak, but Claghorn interrupted. "Pardon, Hagedorn, but here, finally, we are stuck upon a basic principle, and it must be settled now."

Hagedorn looked desperately around the council. "Has anyone relevant comment?"

"Claghorn must do as his innate nature compels," declared O. Z. Garr in the silkiest of voices. "I cannot dictate to him. As for myself, I can never demean my status as a gentleman of Hagedorn. This creed is as natural to me as drawing breath; if ever it is compromised I become a travesty of a gentleman, a grotesque mask of myself. This is Castle Hagedorn, and we represent the culmination of human civilization. Any compromise therefore becomes degradation; any expedient diminution of our standards becomes dishonor. I have heard the word 'emergency' used. What a deplorable sentiment! To dignify the rat-like snappings and gnashings of such as the Meks with the word 'emergency' is to my mind unworthy of a gentleman of Hagedorn!"

A murmur of approval went around the council table.

Claghorn leaned far back in his seat, chin on his chest, as if in relaxation. His clear blue eyes went from face to face, then returned to O. Z. Garr whom he studied with dispassionate interest. "Obviously you direct your words to me," he said. "I appreciate their malice. But this is a small matter." He looked away from O. Z. Garr, to stare up at the massive diamond and emerald chandelier. "More important is the fact that the council as a whole, in spite of my earnest persuasion, seems to endorse your viewpoint. I can urge, expostulate, insinuate no longer, and I will now leave Castle Hagedorn. I find the atmosphere stifling. I trust that you survive the attack of the Meks, though I doubt that you will. They are a clever resourceful race, untroubled by qualms or preconceptions, and we have long underestimated their quality."

Claghorn rose from his seat, inserted the ivory tablet into its socket. "I bid you all farewell." Hagedorn hastily jumped to his feet, held forth his arms imploringly. "Do not depart in anger, Claghorn! Reconsider! We need your wisdom, your expertise."

"Assuredly you do," said Claghorn. "But even more you need to act upon the advice I have already extended. Until then we have no common ground, and any further interchange is futile and tiresome." He made a brief all-inclusive salute and departed the chamber.

Hagedorn slowly resumed his seat. The others made uneasy motions, coughed, looked up at the chandelier, studied their ivory tablets. O. Z. Garr muttered something to B. F. Wyas who sat beside him, who nodded solemnly. Hagedorn spoke in a subdued voice: "We will miss the presence of Claghorn, his penetrating if unorthodox insights . . . We have accomplished little. Uegus, perhaps you will give thought to the projector under discussion. Xanten, you were to question the captive Mek. O. Z. Garr, you undoubtedly will see to the repair of the energy cannon . . . Aside from these small matters, it appears that we have evolved no general plan of action, to help either ourselves or Janeil."

Marune spoke. "What of the other castles? Are they still extant? We have had no news. I suggest that we send Birds to each castle, to learn their condition."

Hagedorn nodded. "Yes, this is a wise motion. Perhaps you will see to this, Marune?"

"I will do so."

"Good. We will now adjourn for a time."

The Birds were dispatched by Marune of Aure and one by one returned. Their reports were similar:

"Sea Island is deserted. Marble columns are tumbled along the beach. Pearl Dome is collapsed. Corpses float in the Water Garden."

"Maraval reeks of death. Gentlemen, Peasants, Phane—all dead. Alas! Even the Birds have departed!"

"Delora: *a ros ros ros!* A dismal scene! No sign of life to be found!"

"Alume is desolate. The great wooden door is smashed. The eternal Green Flame is extinguished."

"There is nothing at Halcyon. The Peasants were driven into a pit."

"Tuang: silence."

"Morninglight: death."

IX

Three days later, Xanten constrained six Birds to a lift chair. He directed them first on a wide sweep around the castle, then south to Far Valley.

The Birds aired their usual complaints, then bounded down the deck in great ungainly hops which threatened to throw Xanten immediately to the pavement. At last gaining the air, they flew up in a spiral. Castle Hagedorn became an intricate miniature far below, each House marked by its unique cluster of turrets and eyries, its own eccentric roof line, its long streaming pennon.

The Birds performed the prescribed circle, skimming the crags and pines of North Ridge. Then, setting wings aslant the upstream, they coasted away toward Far Valley.

Over the pleasant Hagedorn domain flew the Birds and Xanten: over orchards, fields, vineyards, Peasant villages. They crossed Lake Maude with its pavilions and docks, the meadows beyond where the Hagedorn cattle and sheep grazed, and presently came to Far Valley, at the limit of Hagedorn lands.

Xanten indicated where he wished to alight. The Birds, who would have preferred a site closer to the village where they could have watched all that transpired, grumbled and cried out in wrath and set Xanten down so roughly that had he not been alert the shock would have pitched him head over heels.

Xanten alighted without elegance but at least remained on his feet. "Await me here!" he ordered. "Do not stray; attempt no flamboyant tricks among the lift-straps. When I return I wish to see six quiet Birds, in neat formation, lift-straps untwisted and untangled. No bickering, mind you! No loud caterwauling, to attract unfavorable comment! Let all be as I have ordered!"

The Birds sulked, stamped their feet, ducked aside their necks, made insulting comments just under the level of Xanten's hearing. Xanten turned with a final glare of admonition and walked down the lane which led to the village.

The vines were heavy with ripe blackberries and a number of the girls of the village filled baskets. Among them was the girl O. Z. Garr had thought to pre-empt for his personal use. As Xanten passed, he halted and performed a courteous salute. "We have met before, if my recollection is correct."

The girl smiled, a half-rueful, half-whimsical smile. "Your recollection serves you well. We met at Hagedorn, where I was taken a captive. And later, when you conveyed me here, after dark, though I could not see your face." She extended her basket. "Are you hungry? Will you eat?"

Xanten took several berries. In the course of the conversation he learned that the girl's name was Glys Meadowsweet, that her parents were not known to her, but were presumably gentlefolk of Castle Hagedorn who had exceeded their birth tally. Xanten examined her even more carefully than before but could see resemblance to none of the Hagedorn families. "You might derive from Castle Delora. If there is any family resemblance I can detect, it is to the Cosanzas of Delora—a family noted for the beauty of its ladies."

"You are not married?" she asked artlessly.

"No," said Xanten, and indeed he had dissolved his relationship with Araminta only the day before. "What of you?"

She shook her head. "I would never be gathering blackberries if I were. It is work reserved for maidens. Why do you come to Far Valley?"

"For two reasons. The first to see you." Xanten heard himself say this with surprise. But it was true, he realized with another small shock of surprise. "I have never spoken with you properly and I have always wondered if you were as charming and gay as you are beautiful."

The girl shrugged and Xanten could not be sure whether she were pleased or not, compliments from gentlemen sometimes setting the stage for a sorry aftermath. "Well, no matter. I came also to speak to Claghorn."

"He is yonder," she said in a voice toneless, even cool, and pointed. "He occupies that cottage." She returned to her blackberry picking. Xanten bowed, proceeded to that cottage the girl had indicated.

Claghorn, wearing loose knee-length breeches of gray homespun, worked with an axe chopping faggots into stove-lengths. At the sight of Xanten he halted his toil, leaned on the axe, mopped his forehead. "Ah, Xanten. I am pleased to see you. How are the folk of Castle Hagedorn?"

"As before. There is little to report, even had I come to bring you news."

"Indeed, indeed?" Claghorn leaned on the axe handle, surveyed Xanten with a bright blue gaze.

"At our last meeting," went on Xanten, "I agreed to question the captive Mek. After doing so I am distressed that you were not at hand to assist, so that you might have resolved certain ambiguities in the responses."

"Speak on," said Claghorn. "Perhaps I shall be able to do so now."

"After the council meeting I descended immediately to the storeroom where the Mek was confined. It lacked nutriment; I gave it syrup and a pail of water, which it sipped sparingly, then evinced a desire for minced clams. I summoned kitchen help and sent them for this commodity and the Mek ingested several pints. As I have indicated, it was an unusual Mek, standing as tall as myself and lacking a syrup sac. I conveyed it to a different chamber, a storeroom for brown plush furniture, and ordered it to a seat.

"I looked at the Mek and it looked at me. The quills which I removed were growing back; probably it could at least receive from Meks elsewhere. It seemed a superior beast, showing neither obsequiousness nor respect, and answered my questions without hesitation.

"First I remarked: 'The gentlefolk of the castles are astounded by the revolt of the Meks. We had assumed that your life was satisfactory. Were we wrong?'

"'Evidently.' I am sure that this was the word signaled, though never had I suspected the Meks of wit of any sort.

"'Very well then,' I said. 'In what manner?'

"'Surely it is obvious. We no longer wished to toil at your behest. We wished to conduct our lives by our own traditional standards.'

"The response surprised me. I was unaware that the Meks possessed standards of any kind, much less traditional standards."

Claghorn nodded. "I have been similarly surprised by the scope of the Mek mentality."

"I reproached the Mek: 'Why kill? Why destroy our lives in order to augment your own?' As soon as I had put the question I realized that it had been unhappily phrased. The Mek, I believe, realized the same; however, in reply he signaled something very rapidly which I believe was: 'We knew we must act with decisiveness. Your own protocol made this necessary. We might have returned to Etamin Nine, but we prefer this world Earth, and will make it our own, with our own great slipways, tubs and basking ramps.'

"This seemed clear enough, but I sensed an adumbration extending yet beyond. I said, 'Comprehensible. But why kill, why destroy? You might have taken yourself to a different region. We could not have molested you.'

"'Infeasible, by your own thinking. A world is too small for two competing races. You intended to send us back to Etamin Nine.'

"'Ridiculous!' I said. 'Fantasy, absurdity. Do you take me for a mooncalf?'

"'No,' the creature insisted. 'Two of Castle Hagedorn's notables were seeking the highest post. One assured us that, if elected, this would become his life's aim.'

"'A grotesque misunderstanding,' I told him. 'One man, a lunatic, can not speak for all men!'

"'No? One Mek speaks for all Meks. We think with one mind. Are not men of a like sort?'

"'Each thinks for himself. The lunatic who assured you of this tomfoolery is an evil man. But at least matters are clear. We do not propose to send you to Etamin Nine. Will you withdraw from Janeil, take yourselves to a far land and leave us in peace?'

"'No. Affairs have proceeded too far. We will now destroy all men. The truth of the statement is clear: one world is too small for two races.'

"'Unluckily then, I must kill you,' I told him. 'Such acts are not to my liking, but, with opportunity, you would kill as many gentlemen as possible.' At this the creature sprang upon me, and I killed it with an easier mind than had it sat staring.

"Now you know all. It seems that either you or O. Z. Garr stimulated the cataclysm. O. Z. Garr? Unlikely. Impossible. Hence, you, Claghorn, you! have this weight upon your soul!"

Claghorn frowned down at the axe. "Weight, yes. Guilt, no. Ingenuousness, yes; wickedness, no."

Xanten stood back. "Claghorn, your coolness astounds me! Before, when rancorous folk like O. Z. Garr conceived you a lunatic—"

"Peace, Xanten!" exclaimed Claghorn irritably. "This extravagant breast-beating becomes maladroit. What have I done wrong? My fault is that I tried too much. Failure is tragic, but a phthisic face hanging over the cup of the future is worse. I meant to become Hagedorn, I would have sent the slaves home. I failed, the slaves revolted. So do not speak another word. I am bored with the subject. You can not imagine how your bulging eyes and your concave spine oppress me."

"Bored you may be," cried Xanten. "You decry my eyes, my spine—but what of the thousands dead?"

"How long would they live in any event? Lives are as cheap as fish in the sea. I suggest that you put by your reproaches and devote a similar energy to saving yourself. Do you realize that a means exists? You stare at me blankly. I assure you that what I say is true, but you will never learn the means from me."

"Claghorn," said Xanten, "I flew to this spot intending to blow your arrogant head from your body—" But Claghorn, no longer heeding, had returned to his wood-chopping.

"Claghorn!" cried Xanten.

"Xanten, take your outcries elsewhere, if you please. Remonstrate with your Birds."

Xanten swung on his heel, marched back down the lane. The girls picking berries looked at him questioningly and moved aside. Xanten halted, looked up and down the lane. Glys Meadowsweet was nowhere to be seen. In a new fury he continued. He stopped short. On a fallen tree a hundred feet from the Birds sat Glys Meadowsweet, examining a blade of grass as if it had been an astonishing artifact of the past. The Birds for a marvel had actually obeyed him and waited in a fair semblance of order.

Xanten looked up toward the heavens, kicked at the turf. He drew a deep breath and approached to Glys Meadowsweet. He noted that she had tucked a flower into her long loose hair.

After a second or two she looked up and searched his face. "Why are you so angry?"

Xanten slapped his thigh, seated himself beside her. "'Angry'?

No. I am out of my mind with frustration. Claghorn is as obstreperous as a sharp rock. He knows how Castle Hagedorn can be saved but he will not divulge his secret."

Glys Meadowsweet laughed—an easy merry sound, like nothing Xanten had ever heard at Castle Hagedorn. "Secret? When even I know it?"

"It must be a secret," said Xanten. "He will not tell me."

"Listen. If you fear the Birds will hear it, I will whisper." She spoke a few words into his ear.

Perhaps the sweet breath befuddled Xanten's mind. But the explicit essence of the revelation failed to strike home into his consciousness. He made a sound of sour amusement. "No secret there. Only what the prehistoric Scythians termed 'bathos'. Dishonor to the gentlemen! Do we dance with the Peasants? Do we serve the Birds essences and discuss with them the sheen of our Phanes?"

"'Dishonor' then?" She jumped to her feet. "Then it is also dishonor for you to talk to me, to sit here with me, to make ridiculous suggestions!"

"I made no suggestions!" protested Xanten. "I sit here in all decorum—"

"Too much decorum, too much honor!" With a display of passion which astounded Xanten, Glys Meadowsweet tore the flower from her hair, hurled it at the ground. "There. Hence!"

"No," said Xanten in sudden humility. He bent, picked up the flower, kissed it, replaced it in her hair. "I am not over-honorable. I will try my best." He put his arms on her shoulders, but she held him away.

"Tell me," she inquired with a very mature severity, "do you own any of those peculiar insect-women?"

"I? Phanes? I own no Phanes."

With this Glys Meadowsweet relaxed and allowed Xanten to embrace her, while the Birds clucked, guffawed and made vulgar scratching sounds with their wings.

X

The summer waned. On June 30 Janeil and Hagedorn celebrated the Fete of Flowers, even though the dike was rising high around Janeil.

Shortly after, Xanten flew six select Birds into Castle Janeil by night and proposed to the council that the population be evacuated by Bird-lift—as many as possible, as many who wished to leave. The council listened with stony faces and without comment passed on.

Xanten returned to Castle Hagedorn. Using the most careful methods, speaking only to trusted comrades, Xanten enlisted thirty or forty cadets and gentlemen to his persuasion, though inevitably he could not keep the doctrinal thesis of his program secret.

The first reaction of the traditionalists was mockery and charges of poltroonery. At Xanten's insistence, challenges were neither issued nor accepted by his hot-blooded associates.

On the evening of September 9 Castle Janeil fell. The news was brought to Castle Hagedorn by excited Birds who told the grim tale again and again in voices ever more hysterical.

Hagedorn, now gaunt and weary, automatically called a council meeting; it took note of the gloomy circumstances. "We then are the last castle! The Meks cannot conceivably do us harm; they can build dikes around our castle walls for twenty years and only work themselves to distraction. We are secure; but yet it is a strange and portentous thought to realize that at last, here at Castle Hagedorn, live the last gentlemen of the race!"

Xanten spoke in a voice strained with earnest conviction: "Twenty years—fifty years—what difference to the Meks? Once they surround us, once they deploy, we are trapped. Do you comprehend that now is our last opportunity to escape the great cage that Castle Hagedorn is to become?"

"'Escape', Xanten? What a word! For shame!" hooted O. Z. Garr. "Take your wretched band, escape! To steppe or swamp or tundra! Go as you like, with your poltroons, but be good enough to give over these incessant alarms!"

"Garr, I have found conviction since I became a 'poltroon'. Survival is good morality: I have this from the mouth of a noted savant."

"Bah! Such as whom?"

"A. G. Philidor, if you must be informed of every detail."

O. Z. Garr clapped his hand to his forehead. "Do you refer to Philidor the Expiationist? He is of the most extreme stripe, an Expiationist to out-expiate all the rest! Xanten, be sensible, if you please!"

"There are years ahead for all of us," said Xanten in a wooden voice, "if we free ourselves from the castle."

"But the castle is our life!" declared Hagedorn. "In essence, Xanten, what would we be without the castle? Wild animals? Nomads?"

"We would be alive."

O. Z. Garr gave a snort of disgust, turned away to inspect a wall-hanging. Hagedorn shook his head in doubt and perplexity. Beaudry threw his hands up into the air. "Xanten, you have the effect of unnerving us all. You come in here, inflict this dreadful sense of urgency, but why? In Castle Hagedorn we are as safe as in our mother's arms. What do we gain by throwing aside all—honor, dignity, comfort, civilized niceties—for no other reason than to slink through the wilderness?"

"Janeil was safe," said Xanten. "Today where is Janeil? Death, mildewed cloth, sour wine. What we gain by 'slinking' is the assurance of survival. And I plan much more than simple 'slinking'."

"I can conceive of a hundred occasions when death is better than life!" snapped Isseth. "Must I die in dishonor and disgrace? Why may my last years not be passed in dignity?"

Into the room came B. F. Robarth. "Councilmen, the Meks approach Castle Hagedorn."

Hagedorn cast a wild look around the chamber. "Is there a consensus? What must we do?"

Xanten threw up his hands. "Everyone must do as he thinks best! I argue no more: I am done. Hagedorn, will you adjourn the council so that we may be about our affairs? I to my 'slinking'?"

"Council is adjourned," said Hagedorn, and all went up to stand on the ramparts.

Up the avenue into the castle trooped Peasants from the surrounding countryside, packets slung over their shoulders. Across the valley, at the edge of Bartholomew Forest, was a clot of power-wagons and an amorphous brown-gold mass: Meks.

Aure pointed west. "Look—there they come, up the Long Swale." He turned, peered east. "And look, there at Bambridge: Meks!"

By common consent, all swung about to scan North Ridge. O. Z. Garr pointed to a quiet line of brown-gold shapes. "There they wait, the vermin! They have penned us in! Well then, let them wait!" He swung away, rode the lift down to the plaza, crossed swiftly to Zumbeld House, where he worked the rest of the afternoon with his Gloriana, of whom he expected great things.

The following day the Meks formalized the investment. Around Castle Hagedorn a great circle of Mek activity made itself apparent: sheds, warehouses, barracks. Within this periphery, just beyond the range of the energy cannon, power-wagons thrust up mounds of dirt.

During the night these mounds lengthened toward the castle; similarly the night after. At last the purpose of the mounds became clear: they were a protective cover above passages or tunnels leading toward the crag on which Castle Hagedorn rested.

The following day several of the mounds reached the base of the crag. Presently from the far end began to flow a succession of power-wagons loaded with rubble. They issued, dumped their loads and once again entered the tunnels.

Eight of these above-ground tunnels had been established. From each trundled endless loads of dirt and rock, gnawed from the crag on which Castle Hagedorn sat. To the gentlefolk who crowded the parapets the meaning of the work at last became clear.

"They make no attempt to bury us," said Hagedorn. "They merely mine out the crag from below us!"

On the sixth day of the siege, a great segment of the hillside shuddered, slumped, and a tall pinnacle of rock reaching almost up to the base of the walls collapsed.

"If this continues," muttered Beaudry, "our time will be less than that of Janeil."

"Come then," called O. Z. Garr in sudden energy. "Let us try our energy cannon. We'll blast open their wretched tunnels, and what will the rascals do then?" He went to the nearest emplacement, shouted down for Peasants to remove the tarpaulin.

Xanten, who happened to stand nearby, said, "Allow me to assist you." He jerked away the tarpaulin. "Shoot now, if you will."

O. Z. Garr stared at him uncomprehendingly, then leapt forward, swiveled the great projector about so that it aimed at a mound. He pulled the switch; the air crackled in front of the ringed snout, rippled, flickered with purple sparks. The target area steamed, became black, then dark red, then slumped into an incandescent crater. But the underlying earth, twenty feet in thickness, afforded too much insulation; the molten puddle became white-hot but failed to spread or deepen. The energy cannon gave a sudden chatter, as electricity short-circuited through corroded insulation. The cannon went dead.

O. Z. Garr inspected the mechanism in anger and disappointment. Then, with a gesture of repugnance, he turned away. The cannons were clearly of limited effectiveness.

Two hours later, on the east side of the crag, another great sheet of rock collapsed, and just before sunset, a similar mass sheared from the western face, where the wall of the castle rose almost in an uninterrupted line from the cliff below.

At midnight Xanten and those of his persuasion, with their children and consorts, departed Castle Hagedorn. Six teams of Birds shuttled from the flight deck to a meadow near Far Valley, and long before dawn had transported the entire group.

There were none to bid them farewell.

XI

A week later another section of the east cliff fell away, taking a length of rock-melt buttress with it. At the tunnel mouths the piles of excavated rubble had become alarmingly large.

The terraced south face of the crag was the least disturbed; the most spectacular damage having occurred to east and west. Suddenly, a month after the initial assault, a great section of the terraces slumped forward, leaving an irregular crevasse which interrupted the avenue and hurled down the statues of former notables emplaced at intervals along the avenue's balustrade.

Hagedorn called a council meeting. "Circumstances," he said in a wan attempt at facetiousness, "have not bettered themselves. Our most pessimistic expectations have been exceeded. A dismal situation! I confess that I do not relish the prospect of toppling to my death among all my smashed belongings."

Aure made a desperate gesture. "A similar thought haunts me! Death—what of that? All must die! But when I think of my precious belongings I become sick. My books trampled! My fragile vases smashed! My tabards ripped! My rugs buried! My Phanes strangled! My heirloom chandeliers flung aside! These are my nightmares."

"Your possessions are no less precious than any others," said Beaudry shortly. "Still they have no life of their own; when we are gone, who cares what happens to them?"

Marune winced. "A year ago I put down eighteen dozen flasks of prime essence; twelve dozen Green Rain; three each of Balthazar and Faidor. Think of these, if you would contemplate tragedy!"

"Had we only known!" groaned Aure. "I would have—I would have . . ." His voice trailed away.

O. Z. Garr stamped his foot in impatience. "Let us avoid lamentation at all costs! We had a choice, remember? Xanten beseeched us to flee; now he and his like go skulking and foraging through the north mountains with the Expiationists. We chose to remain, for better or worse, and unluckily the 'worse' is occurring. We must accept the fact like gentlemen."

To this the council gave melancholy assent. Hagedorn brought forth a flask of priceless Rhadamanth, and poured with a prodigality which previously would have been unthinkable. "Since we have no future—to our glorious past!"

That night disturbances were noted here and there around the ring of Mek investment: flames at four separate points, a faint sound of hoarse shouting. On the following day it seemed that the tempo of activity had lessened a trifle.

But during the afternoon a vast segment of the east cliff fell away. A moment later, as if after majestic deliberation, the tall east wall split off, toppled, leaving the backs of six great houses exposed to the open sky.

An hour after sunset a team of Birds settled to the flight-deck. Xanten jumped from the seat. He ran down the circular staircase to the ramparts, came down to the plaza by Hagedorn's palace.

Hagedorn, summoned by a kinsman, came forth to stare at Xanten in surprise. "What do you do here? We expected you to be safely north with the Expiationists!"

"The Expiationists are not safely north," said Xanten. "They have joined the rest of us. We are fighting."

Hagedorn's jaw dropped. "Fighting? The gentlemen are fighting Meks?"

"As vigorously as possible."

Hagedorn shook his head in wonder. "The Expiationists too? I understood that they had planned to flee north."

"Some have done so, including A. G. Philidor. There are factions among the Expiationists just as here. Most are not ten miles distant. The same with the Nomads. Some have taken their power-wagons and fled. The rest kill Meks with fanatic fervor. Last night you saw our work. We fired four storage warehouses, destroyed syrup tanks, killed a hundred or more Meks, as well as a dozen power-wagons. We suffered losses, which hurt us, because there are few of us and many Meks. This is why I am here. We need more men. Come fight beside us!"

Hagedorn turned, motioned to the great central plaza. "I will call forth the folk from their Houses. Talk to everyone."

The Birds, complaining bitterly at the unprecedented toil, worked all night, transporting gentlemen, who, sobered by the imminent destruction of Castle Hagedorn, were now willing to abandon all scruples and fight for their lives. The staunch traditionalists still refused to compromise their honor, but Xanten gave them cheerful assurance: "Remain here then, prowling the castle like so many furtive rats. Take what comfort you can in the fact that you are being protected; the future holds little else for you."

And many who heard him stalked away in disgust.

Xanten turned to Hagedorn. "What of you? Do you come or do you stay?"

Hagedorn heaved a deep sigh, almost a groan. "Castle Hagedorn is at an end. No matter what the eventuality. I will come with you."

The situation suddenly had altered. The Meks, established in a loose ring around Castle Hagedorn, had calculated upon no resistance from the countryside and little from the castle. They had established their barracks and syrup depots with thought only for convenience and none for defense; raiding parties, consequently, were able to approach, inflict damages and withdraw before sustaining serious losses of their own. Those Meks posted along North Ridge were harassed almost continuously and finally were driven down with many losses. The circle around Castle Hagedorn became a cusp; then two days later, after the destruction of five more syrup depots, the Meks drew back even farther. Throwing up earthworks before the two tunnels leading under the south face of the crag, they established a more or less tenable defensive position, but now instead of beleaguering, they became the beleaguered, though still fighting.

Within the area thus defended the Meks concentrated their remaining syrup stocks, tools, weapons, ammunition. The area outside the earthworks was floodlit after dark and guarded by Meks armed with pellet guns, making any frontal assault impractical.

For a day the raiders kept to the shelter of the surrounding orchards, appraising the new situation. Then a new tactic was attempted. Six light carriages were improvised and loaded with bladders of a light inflammable oil, with a fire grenade attached. To each of these carriages ten Birds were harnessed, and at midnight sent aloft, with a man for each carriage. Flying high, the Birds then glided down through the darkness over the Mek position, where the fire bombs were dropped.

The area instantly seethed with flame. The syrup depot burnt; the power-wagons, awakened by the flames, rolled frantically back and forth, crushing Meks and stores, colliding with each other, adding vastly to the terror of the flames. The Meks who survived took shelter in the tunnels. Certain of the floodlights were extinguished and, taking advantage of the confusion, the men attacked the earthworks.

After a short bitter battle, the men killed all the sentinels and took up positions commanding the mouths of the tunnels, which now contained all that remained of the Mek army. It seemed as if the Mek uprising had been put down.

XII

The flames died. The human warriors—three hundred men from the castle, two hundred Expiationists and about three hundred Nomads—gathered about the tunnel mouth and, during the balance of the night, considered methods to deal with the immured Meks.

At sunrise those men of Castle Hagedorn whose children and consorts were yet within the castle went to bring them forth. With them, upon their return, came a group of castle gentlemen: among them Beaudry, O. Z. Garr, Isseth, and Aure. They greeted their one-time peers, Hagedorn, Xanten, Claghorn and others, crisply, but with a certain austere detachment, which recognized that loss of prestige incurred by those who fought Meks as if they were equals.

"Now what is to happen?" Beaudry inquired of Hagedorn. "The Meks are trapped but you can't bring them forth. Not impossibly they have syrup stored within for the power-wagons. They may well survive for months."

O. Z. Garr, assessing the situation from the standpoint of a military theoretician, came forward with a plan of action. "Fetch down the cannon—or have your underlings do so—and mount them on power-wagons. When the vermin are sufficiently weak, roll the cannon in and wipe out all but a labor force for the castle. We formerly worked four hundred, and this should suffice."

"Ha!" exclaimed Xanten. "It gives me great pleasure to inform you that this will never be. If any Meks survive they will repair the spaceships and instruct us in the maintenance and we will then transport them and Peasants back to their native worlds."

"How then do you expect us to maintain our lives?" demanded Garr coldly.

"You have the syrup generator. Fit yourself with sacs and drink syrup."

Garr tilted back his head, stared coldly down his nose. "This is your voice, yours alone, and your insolent opinion. Others are to be heard from. Hagedorn, is this your philosophy, that civilization should wither?"

"It need not wither," said Hagedorn, "provided that all of us—you as well as we—toil for it. There can be no more slaves. I have become convinced of this."

O. Z. Garr turned on his heel, swept back up the avenue into the castle, followed by the most traditional-minded of his comrades. A few moved aside and talked among themselves in low tones, with one or two black looks for Xanten and Hagedorn.

From the ramparts of the castle came a sudden outcry: "The Meks! They are taking the castle! They swarm up the lower passages! Attack, save us!"

The men below stared up in consternation. Even as they looked the castle portals swung shut.

"How is this possible?" demanded Hagedorn. "I swear all entered the tunnels!"

"It is only too clear," said Xanten bitterly. "While they undermined, they drove a tunnel up to the lower levels!"

Hagedorn started forward as if he would charge up the crag alone, then halted. "We must drive them out! Unthinkable that they pillage our castle!"

"Unfortunately," said Claghorn, "the walls bar us as effectually as they did the Meks."

"We can send up a force by Bird-car! Once we consolidate, we can exterminate them!"

Claghorn shook his head. "They can wait on the ramparts and flight-deck and shoot down the Birds as they approach. Even if we secured a foothold there would be great bloodshed: one of us killed for every one of them. And they still outnumber us three or four to one."

Hagedorn groaned. "The thought of them revelling among my possessions, strutting about in my clothes, swilling my essences—it sickens me!"

"Listen!" said Claghorn. From on high they heard the hoarse yells of men, the crackle of energy-cannon. "Some of them, at least, hold out on the ramparts!"

Xanten went to a nearby group of Birds who were for once awed and subdued by events. "Lift me up above the castle, out of range of the pellets, but where I can see what the Meks do!"

"Care, take care!" croaked one of the Birds. "Ill things occur at the castle."

"Never mind! Convey me up, above the ramparts!"

The Birds lifted him, swung in a great circle around the crag and above the castle, sufficiently distant to be safe from the Mek pellet-guns.

Beside those cannon which yet operated stood thirty men and women. Between the great Houses, the rotunda and the palace, everywhere the cannon could not be brought to bear, swarmed Meks. The plaza was littered with corpses: gentlemen, ladies and their children—all those who had elected to remain at Castle Hagedorn.

At one of the cannon stood O. Z. Garr. Spying Xanten he gave a shout of hysterical rage, swung up the cannon, fired a bolt. The Birds, screaming, tried to swerve aside, but the bolt smashed two. Birds, car, Xanten, fell in a great tangle. By some miracle, the four yet alive caught their balance and a hundred feet from the ground, with a frenzied groaning effort, they slowed their fall, steadied, hovered an instant, sank to the ground.

Xanten staggered free of the tangle. Men came running. "Are you safe?" called Claghorn.

"Safe, yes. Frightened as well!" Xanten took a deep breath, went to sit on an outcrop of rock.

"What's happening up there?" asked Claghorn.

"All dead," said Xanten, "all but a score. Garr has gone mad. He fired on me."

"Look! Meks on the ramparts!" cried A. L. Morgan.

"There!" cried someone else. "Men! They jump! . . . No, they are flung!"

Some were men, some were Meks whom they had dragged with

them; with awful slowness they toppled to their deaths. No more fell. Castle Hagedorn was in the hands of the Meks.

Xanten considered the complex silhouette, at once so familiar and so strange. "They can't hope to hold out. We need only destroy the sun-cells, and they can synthesize no syrup."

"Let us do it now," said Claghorn, "before they think of this and man the cannon! Birds!"

He went off to give the orders, and forty Birds, each clutching two rocks the size of a man's head, flapped up, circled the castle and presently returned to report the sun-cells had been destroyed.

Xanten said, "All that remains is to seal the tunnel entrances against a sudden eruption, which might catch us off guard—then patience."

"What of the Peasants in the stables—and the Phanes?" asked Hagedorn in a forlorn voice.

Xanten gave his head a slow shake. "He who was not an Expiationist before must become one now."

Claghorn muttered, "They can survive two months at most—no more."

But two months passed, and three months, and four months. Then one morning the great portals opened, a haggard Mek stumbled forth.

He signaled: "Men: we starve. We have maintained your treasures. Give us our lives or we destroy all before we die."

Claghorn responded: "These are our terms. We give you your lives. You must clean the castle, remove and bury the corpses. You must repair the spaceships and teach us all you know regarding them. We will then transport you to Etamin Nine."

"The terms you offer are accepted."

Five years later Xanten and Glys Meadowsweet, with their two children, had reason to travel north from their home near Sande River. They took occasion to visit Castle Hagedorn, where now lived only two or three dozen folk, among them Hagedorn.

He had aged, so it seemed to Xanten. His hair was white; his face, once bluff and hearty, had become thin, almost waxen. Xanten could not determine his mood.

They stood in the shade of a walnut tree, with castle and crag looming above them. "This is now a great museum," said Hagedorn. "I am curator, and this will be the function of all the Hagedorns who come after me, for there is incalculable treasure to guard and maintain. Already the feeling of antiquity has come to the castle. The Houses are alive with ghosts. I see them often, especially on the nights of the fetes . . . Ah, those were the times, were they not, Xanten?"

"Yes indeed," said Xanten. He touched the heads of his two children. "Still, I have no wish to return to them. We are men now, on our own world, as we never were before."

Hagedorn gave a somewhat regretful assent. He looked up at the vast structure, as if now were the first occasion he had laid eyes on it. "The folk of the future—what will they think of Castle Hagedorn? Its treasures, its books, its tabards?"

"They will come, they will marvel," said Xanten. "Almost as I do today."

"There is much at which to marvel. Will you come within, Xanten? There are still flasks of noble essence laid by."

"Thank you no," said Xanten. "There is too much to stir old memories. We will go our way, and I think that we will do so immediately."

Hagedorn nodded sadly. "I understand very well. I myself am often given to reverie these days. Well then, good-by, and journey home with pleasure."

"We will do so, Hagedorn. Thank you and good-by," said Xanten, and turned away from Castle Hagedorn, toward the world of men.

Far too many short stories have been tediously strung out as novels, or inflated to novelette length, so that a sharp pang of pleasure can be experienced when a story is written to the proper length—which in this case is jewel-like conciseness. Mr. Pohl, with more years behind him as writer and editor than he cares to remember, draws freely upon his talent and experience to produce a smooth and cool entertainment that conceals a wicked barb of truth.

DAY MILLION

Frederik Pohl

On this day I want to tell you about, which will be about ten thousand years from now, there were a boy, a girl and a love story.

Now, although I haven't said much so far, none of it is true. The boy was not what you and I would normally think of as a boy, because he was a hundred and eighty-seven years old. Nor was the girl a girl, for other reasons. And the love story did not entail that sublimation of the urge to rape, and concurrent postponement of the instinct to submit, which we at present understand in such matters. You won't care much for this story if you don't grasp these facts at once. If, however, you will make the effort you'll likely enough find it jampacked, chockful and tip-top-crammed with laughter, tears and poignant sentiment which may, or may not, be worthwhile. The reason the girl was not a girl was that she was a boy.

How angrily you recoil from the page! You say, who the hell

wants to read about a pair of queers? Calm yourself. Here are no hot-breathing secrets of perversion for the coterie trade. In fact, if you were to see this girl you would not guess that she was in any sense a boy. Breasts, two; reproductive organs, female. Hips, callipygean; face hairless, supra-orbital lobes non-existent. You would term her female on sight, although it is true that you might wonder just what species she was a female of, being confused by the tail, the silky pelt and the gill slits behind each ear.

Now you recoil again. Cripes, man, take my word for it. This is a sweet kid, and if you, as a normal male, spent as much as an hour in a room with her you would bend heaven and Earth to get her in the sack. Dora—We will call her that; her "name" was omicron-Dibase seven-group-totter-oot S Doradus 5314, the last part of which is a colour specification corresponding to a shade of green—Dora, I say, was feminine, charming and cute. I admit she doesn't sound that way. She was, as you might put it, a dancer. Her art involved qualities of intellection and expertise of a very high order, requiring both tremendous natural capacities and endless practice; it was performed in null-gravity and I can best describe it by saying that it was something like the performance of a contortionist and something like classical ballet, maybe resembling Danilova's dying swan. It was also pretty damned sexy. In a symbolic way, to be sure; but face it, most of the things we call "sexy" are symbolic, you know, except perhaps an exhibitionist's open clothing. On Day Million when Dora danced, the people who saw her panted, and you would too.

About this business of her being a boy. It didn't matter to her audiences that genetically she was male. It wouldn't matter to you, if you were among them, because you wouldn't know it—not unless you took a biopsy cutting of her flesh and put it under an electron-microscope to find the XY chromosome—and it didn't matter to them because they didn't care. Through techniques which are not only complex but haven't yet been discovered, these people were able to determine a great deal about the aptitudes and easements of babies quite a long time before they were born—at about the second horizon of cell-division, to be exact, when the segmenting egg is becoming a free blastocyst—and then they naturally helped those aptitudes along. Wouldn't we? If we find a child with an aptitude for music we give him a scholarship to Juilliard. If they found a child whose aptitudes were for being a woman, they made him one. As sex had long been dissociated from reproduction this was relatively easy to do and caused no trouble and no, or at least very little, comment.

How much is "very little"? Oh, about as much as would be caused by our own tampering with Divine Will by filling a tooth. Less than would be caused by wearing a hearing aid. Does it still sound awful? Then look closely at the next busty babe you meet and reflect that she may be a Dora, for adults who are genetically male but somatically female are far from unknown even in our own time. An accident of environment in the womb overwhelms the blueprints of heredity. The difference is that with us it happens only by accident and we don't know about it except rarely, after close study; whereas the people of Day Million did it often, on purpose, because they wanted to.

Well, that's enough to tell you about Dora. It would only confuse you to add that she was seven feet tall and smelled of peanut butter. Let us begin our story.

On Day Million, Dora swam out of her house, entered a transportation tube, was sucked briskly to the surface in its flow of water and ejected in its plume of spray to an elastic platform in front of her—ah—call it her rehearsal hall.

"Oh, hell!" she cried in pretty confusion, reaching out to catch her balance and finding herself tumbled against a total stranger, whom we will call Don.

They met cute. Don was on his way to have his legs renewed. Love was the farthest thing from his mind. But when, absentmindedly taking a shortcut across the landing platform for submarinites and finding himself drenched, he discovered his arms full of the loveliest girl he had ever seen, he knew at once they were meant for each other. "Will you marry me?" he asked. She said softly, "Wednesday," and the promise was like a caress.

Don was tall, muscular, bronze and exciting. His name was no more Don than Dora's was Dora, but the personal part of it was Adonis in tribute to his vibrant maleness, and so we will call him

Don for short. His personality colour-code, in Angstrom units, was 5,290, or only a few degrees bluer than Dora's 5,314—a measure of what they had intuitively discovered at first sight; that they possessed many affinities of taste and interest.

I despair of telling you exactly what it was that Don did for a living—I don't mean for the sake of making money, I mean for the sake of giving purpose and meaning to his life, to keep him from going off his nut with boredom—except to say that it involved a lot of travelling. He travelled in interstellar spaceships. In order to make a spaceship go really fast, about thirty-one male and seven genetically female human beings had to do certain things, and Don was one of the thirty-one. Actually, he contemplated options. This involved a lot of exposure to radiation flux—not so much from his own station in the propulsive system as in the spillover from the next stage, where a genetic female preferred selections, and the sub-nuclear particles making the selections she preferred demolished themselves in a shower of quanta. Well, you don't give a rat's ass for that, but it meant that Don had to be clad at all times in a skin of light, resilient, extremely strong copper-coloured metal. I have already mentioned this, but you probably thought I meant he was sunburned.

More than that, he was a cybernetic man. Most of his ruder parts had been long since replaced with mechanisms of vastly more permanence and use. A cadmium centrifuge, not a heart, pumped his blood. His lungs moved only when he wanted to speak out loud, for a cascade of osmotic filters rebreathed oxygen out of his own wastes. In a way, he probably would have looked peculiar to a man from the 20th century, with his glowing eyes and seven-fingered hands. But to himself, and of course to Dora, he looked mighty manly and grand. In the course of his voyages Don had circled Proxima Centauri, Procyon and the puzzling worlds of Mira Ceti; he had carried agricultural templates to the planets of Canopus and brought back warm, witty pets from the pale companion of Aldebaran. Blue-hot or red-cool, he had seen a thousand stars and their ten thousand planets. He had, in fact, been travelling the starlanes, with only brief leaves on Earth, for pushing two centuries. But you don't care about that, either. It is people who make stories, not the circumstances they find themselves in, and you want to hear about these two people. Well, they made it. The great thing they had for each other grew and flowered and burst into fruition on Wednesday, just as Dora had promised. They met at the encoding room, with a couple of well-wishing friends apiece to cheer them on, and while their identities were being taped and stored they smiled and whispered to each other and bore the jokes of their friends with blushing repartee. Then they exchanged their mathematical analogues and went away, Dora to her dwelling beneath the surface of the sea and Don to his ship.

It was an idyll, really. They lived happily ever after—or anyway, until they decided not to bother any more and died.

Of course, they never set eyes on each other again.

Oh, I can see you now, you eaters of charcoal-broiled steak, scratching an incipient bunion with one hand and holding this story with the other, while the stereo plays d'Indy or Monk. You don't believe a word of it, do you? Not for one minute. People wouldn't live like that, you say with a grunt as you get up to put fresh ice in a drink.

And yet there's Dora, hurrying back through the flushing commuter pipes toward her underwater home (she prefers it there; has had herself somatically altered to breathe the stuff). If I tell you with what sweet fulfilment she fits the recorded analogue of Don into the symbol manipulator, hooks herself in and turns herself on . . . if I try to tell you any of that you will simply stare. Or glare; and grumble, what the hell kind of love-making is this? And yet I assure you, friend, I really do assure you that Dora's ecstasies are as creamy and passionate as any of James Bond's lady spies', and one hell of a lot more so than anything you are going to find in "real life". Go ahead, glare and grumble. Dora doesn't care. If she thinks of you at all, her thirty-times-great-great-grandfather, she thinks you're a pretty primordial sort of brute. You are. Why, Dora is farther removed from you than you are from the australopithecines of five thousand centuries ago. You could not swim a second in the strong currents of her life. You don't think progress goes in a straight line, do you? Do you recognize that it is an ascending, accelerating, maybe even exponential curve? It takes hell's own time to get started, but when it goes it goes like a bomb. And you, you Scotch-drinking steak-eater in your relaxacizing chair, you've just barely lighted the primacord of the fuse. What is it now, the six or seven hundred thousandth day after Christ? Dora lives in Day Million, the millionth day of the Christian Era. Ten thousand years from now. Her body fats are polyunsaturated, like Crisco. Her wastes are haemodialysed out of her bloodstream while she sleeps—that means she doesn't have to go to the bathroom. On whim, to pass a slow half-hour, she can command more energy than the entire nation of Portugal can spend today, and use it to launch a weekend satellite or remould a crater on the Moon. She loves Don very much. She keeps his every gesture, mannerism, nuance, touch of hand, thrill of intercourse, passion of kiss stored in symbolic-mathematical form. And when she wants him, all she has to do is turn the machine on and she has him.

And Don, of course, has Dora. Adrift on a sponson city a few hundred yards over her head, or orbiting Arcturus fifty light-years away, Don has only to command his own symbol-manipulator to rescue Dora from the ferrite files and bring her to life for him, and there she is; and rapturously, tirelessly they love all night. Not in the flesh, of course; but then his flesh has been extensively altered and it wouldn't really be much fun. He doesn't need the flesh for pleasure. Genital organs feel nothing. Neither do hands, nor breasts, nor lips; they are only receptors, accepting and transmitting impulses. It is the brain that feels; it is the interpretation of those impulses that makes agony or orgasm, and Don's symbol manipulator gives him the analogue of cuddling, the analogue of kissing, the analogue of wild, ardent hours with the eternal, exquisite and incorruptible analogue of Dora. Or Diane. Or sweet Rose, or laughing Alicia; for to be sure, they have each of them exchanged analogues before, and will again.

Rats, you say, it looks crazy to me. And you—with your aftershave lotion and your little red car, pushing papers across a desk all day and chasing tail all night—tell me, just how the hell do you think you would look to Tiglath-Pileser, say, or Attila the Hun?

Mrs. Dorman raises Akita dogs, looks after her husband and small daughter, and writes fiction very well and—since all of the capable female writers of science fiction can be counted on one truncated hand, hers is a welcome addition to their ranks. She brings us here a sense of strangeness, more than a hint of human warmth, as well as a good strong whiff of alien chillness.

WHEN I WAS MISS DOW

Sonya Dorman

These hungry, mother-haunted people come and find us living in what they like to call crystal palaces, though really we live in glass places, some of them highly ornamented and others plain as paper. They come first as explorers, and perhaps realize we are a race of one sex only, rather amorphous beings of proteide; and we, even baby I, are Protean, also, being able to take various shapes at will. One sex, one brain lobe, we live in more or less glass bridges over the humanoid chasm, eating, recreating, attending races and playing other games like most living creatures.

Eventually, we're all dumped into the cell banks and reproduced once more.

After the explorers comes the colony of miners and scientists. The warden and some of the other elders put on faces to greet them, agreeing to help with the mining of some ores, even giving them a koota or two as they become interested in our racing dogs. They set up their places of life, pop up their machines, bang-bang, chug-chug; we put on our faces, forms, smiles and costumes; I am old enough to learn to change my shape, too.

The Warden says to me, "It's about time you made a change, yourself. Some of your friends are already working for these people, bringing home credits and sulfas."

My Uncle (by the Warden's fourth conjunction) made himself over at the start, being one of the first to realize how it could profit us.

I protest to the Warden, "I'm educated and trained as a scholar. You always say I must remain deep in my mathematics and other studies."

My Uncle says, "You have to do it. There's only one way for us to get along with them," and he runs his fingers through his long blonde hair. My Uncle's not an educated person, but highly placed, politically, and while Captain Dow is around my Uncle retains this particular shape. The Captain is shipping out soon, then Uncle will find some other features, because he's already warned that it's unseemly for him to be chasing around in the face of a girl after the half-bearded boys from the space ships. I don't want to do this myself, wasting so much time, when the fourteen decimals even now are clicking on my mirrors.

The Warden says, "We have a pattern from a female botanist, she ought to do for you. But before we put you into the pattern tank, you'll have to approximate another brain lobe. They have two."

"I know," I say, sulkily. A botanist. A she!

"Into the tank," the Warden says to me without mercy, and I am his to use as he believes proper.

I spend four days in the tank absorbing the female Terran pattern. When I'm released, the Warden tells me, "Your job is waiting for you. We went to a lot of trouble to arrange it." He sounds brusque, but perhaps this is because he hasn't conjoined for a long time. The responsibilities of being Warden of Mines and Seeds come first, long before any social engagement.

I run my fingers through my brunette curls, and notice my Uncle is looking critically at me. "Haven't you made yourself rather old?" he asks.

"Oh, he's all right," the Warden says. "Thirty-three isn't badly matched to the Doctor, as I understand it."

Dr. Arnold Proctor, the colony's head biologist, is busy making radiograph pictures (with his primitive X-rays) of skeletal structures: murger birds, rodents, and our pets and racers, the kootas—dogs to the Terrans, who are fascinated by them. We breed them primarily for speed and stamina, but some of them carry a gene for an inherited structural defect which cripples them and they have to be destroyed before they are full grown. The Doctor is making a special study of kootas.

He gets up from his chair when I enter his office. "I'm Miss Dow, your new assistant," I say, hoping my long fingernails will stand up to the pressure of punch keys on the computer, since I haven't had much practise in retaining foreign shapes. I'm still in uncertain balance between myself and Martha Dow, who is also myself. But one does not have two lobes for nothing, I discover.

"Good morning. I'm glad you're here," the Doctor says.

He is a nice, pink man, with silver hair, soft-spoken, intelligent. I'm pleased, as we work along, to find he doesn't joke and wisecrack like so many of the Terrans, though I am sometimes whimsical. I like music and banquets as well as my studies.

Though absorbed in his work, Dr. Proctor isn't rude to interrupters. A man of unusual balance, coming as he does from a culture which sends out scientific parties that are ninety per cent of one sex, when their species provides them with two. At first meetings he is dedicated but agreeable, and I'm charmed.

"Dr. Proctor," I ask him one morning. "Is it possible for you to radiograph my koota? She's very fine, from the fastest stock available, and I'd like to breed her."

"Yes, yes, of course," he promises with his quick, often absent, smile. "By all means. You wish to breed only the best." It's typical of him to assume we're all as dedicated as he.

My Uncle's not pleased. "There's nothing wrong with your koota," he says. "What do you want to X-ray her for? Suppose he finds something is wrong? You'll be afraid to race or breed her, and she won't be replaced. Besides, your interest in her may make him suspicious."

"Suspicious of what?" I ask, but my Uncle won't say, so I ask him, "Suppose she's bred and her pups are cripples?"

The Warden says, "You're supposed to have your mind on your work, not on racing. The koota was just to amuse you when you were younger."

I lean down and stroke her head, which is beautiful, and she breathes a deep and gentle breath in response.

"Oh, let him go," my Uncle says wearily. He's getting disgusted because they didn't intend for me to bury myself in a laboratory or a computer room, without making more important contacts. But a scholar is born with a certain temperament, and has an introspective nature, and as I'm destined to eventually replace the Warden, naturally I prefer the life of the mind.

"I must say," my Uncle remarks, "you look the image of a Terran female. Is the work interesting?"

"Oh, yes, fascinating," I reply, and he snorts at my lie, since we both know it's dull and routine, and most of the time is spent working out the connections between my two brain lobes, which still present me with some difficulty.

My koota bitch is subjected to a pelvic radiograph. Afterwards, I stand on my heels in the small, darkened cubicle, looking at the film on the viewing screen. There he stands, too, with his cheekbones emerald in the peculiar light, and his hair, which is silver in daylight, looks phosphorescent. I resist this. I am resisting this Doctor with the X-ray eyes who can examine my marrow with ease. He sees Martha's marrow, every perfect corpuscle of it.

You can't imagine how comforting it is to be so transparent. There's no need to pretend, adjust, advance, retreat or discuss the oddities of my planet. We are looking at the X-ray film of my prized racer and companion to determine the soundness of her hip joints, yet I suspect the Doctor, platinum-green and tall as a tower, is piercing my reality with his educated gaze. He can see the blood flushing my surfaces. I don't need to do a thing but stand up straight so the crease of fat at my waist won't distort my belly button, the center of it all.

"You see?" he says.

I do see, looking at the film in the darkness where perfection or disaster may be viewed, and I'm twined in the paradox which confronts me here. The darker the room, the brighter the screen and the clearer the picture. Less light! and the truth becomes more evident. Either the koota is properly jointed and may be bred without danger of passing the gene on to her young, or she is not properly jointed, and cannot be used. Less light, more truth! And the Doctor is green sculpture—a little darker and he would be a bronze—but his natural color is pink alabaster.

"You see," the Doctor says, and I do try to see. He points his wax pencil at one hip joint on the film, and says, "A certain amount of osteo-arthritic build-up is already evident. The cranial rim is wearing down, she may go lame. She'll certainly pass the defect on to some of her pups, if she's bred."

This koota has been my playmate and friend for a long time. She retains a single form, that of koota, full of love and beautiful speed; she has been a source of pleasure and pride.

Dr. Proctor, of the pewter hair, will discuss the anatomical defects of the koota in a gentle and cultivated voice. I am disturbed. There shouldn't be any need to explain the truth, which is evident. Yet it seems that to comprehend the exposures, I require a special education. It's said that the more you have seen, the quicker you are to sort the eternal verities into one pile and the dismal illusions into another. How is it that sometimes the Doctor wears a head which resembles that of a koota, with a splendid muzzle and noble brow?

Suddenly he gives a little laugh and points the end of the wax pencil at my navel, announcing: "There. There, it is essential that the belly button onto the pelvis, or you'll bear no children." Thoughts of offspring had occurred to me. But weren't we discussing my racer? The radiograph film is still clipped to the view screen, and upon it, spread-eagled, appears the bony Rorschach of my koota bitch, her hip joints expressing doom.

I wish the Doctor would put on the daylight. I come to the conclusion that there's a limit to how much truth I can examine, and the more I submit to the conditions necessary for examining it, the more unhappy I become.

Dr. Proctor is a man of such perfect integrity that he continues to talk about bones and muscles until I'm ready to scream for mercy. He has done something that is unusual and probably prohibited, but he's not aware of it. I mean it must be prohibited in his culture, where it seems they play on each other, but not with each other. I am uneasy, fluctuating.

He snaps two switches. Out goes the film and on goes the sun, making my eyes stream with sensitive and grateful tears, although he's so adjusted to these contrasts he doesn't so much as blink. Floating in the sunshine I've become opaque. He can't see anything but my surface tensions, and I wonder what he does in his spare time. A part of me seems to tilt, or slide.

"There, there, oh dear, Miss Dow," he says, patting my back, rubbing my shoulder blades. His forearms and fingers extend gingerly. "You do want to breed only the best, don't you?" he asks. I begin within me a compulsive ritual of counting the elements; it's all I can do to keep communications open between my brain lobes. I'm suffering from eclipses: one goes dark, the other lights up, that one goes dark, the other goes nova.

"There, there," the Doctor says, distressed because I'm quivering and trying to keep the connections open; I have never felt clogged before. They may have to put me back into the pattern tank.

Profoundly disturbed, I lift my face, and he gives me a kiss. Then I'm all right, balanced again, one lobe composing a concerto for virtix flute, the other one projecting, "Oh Arnie, oh Arnie." Yes, I'm okay for the shape I'm in. He's marking my joints with his wax pencil (the marks of which can be easily erased from the film surface) and he's mumbling, "It's essential, oh yes, it's essential."

Finally he says, "I guess all of us colonists are lonely here," and I say, "Oh yes, aren't we," before I realize the enormity of the Warden's manipulations, and what a lot I have to learn. Evidently the Warden triple-carded me through the Colony Punch Center as a Terran. I lie and say, "Oh, yes. Yes, yes. Oh, Arnie, put out the light," for we may find some more truth.

"Not here," Arnie says, and of course he's right. This is a room for study, for cataloguing obvious facts, not a place for carnival. There are not many places for it, I discover with surprise. Having lived in glass all my life I expect everyone else to be as comfortable there as I am but this isn't so.

Just the same we find his quarters, after dark, to be comfortable and free of embarrassment. You wouldn't think a dedicated man of his age would be so vigorous, but I find out he spends his weekends at the recreation center hitting a ball with his hand. The ball bounces back off a wall and he hits it and hits it. Though he's given that up now because we're together on weekends.

"You're more than an old bachelor like me deserves," he tells me.

"Why are you an old bachelor?" I ask him. I do wonder why, if it's something not to be.

He tries to explain it to me. "I'm not a young man. I wouldn't make a good husband, I'm afraid. I like to work late, to be undisturbed. In my leisure time, I like to make wood carvings. Sometimes I go to bed with the sun and sometimes I'm up working all night. And then children. No. I'm lucky to be an old bachelor," he says.

Arnie carves kaku wood, which has a brilliant grain and is soft enough to permit easy carving. He's working on a figure of a murger bird, whittling lengthwise down the wood so the grain, wavy, full of flowing, wedge-shaped lines, will represent the feathers. The lamp light shines on his hair and the crinkle of his eyelids as he looks down and carves, whittles, turns. He's absorbed in what he doesn't see there but he's projecting what he wants to see. It's the reverse of what he must do in the viewing room. I began to suffer a peculiar pain, located in the nerve cluster between my lungs. He's not talking to me. He's not caressing me. He's forgotten I'm here, and like a false projection, I'm beginning to fade. In another hour perhaps the film will become blank. If he doesn't see me, then am I here?

He's doing just what I do when absorbed in one of my own projects, and I admire the intensity with which he works: it's magnificent. Yes, I'm jealous of it. I burn with rage and jealousy. He has abandoned me to be Martha and I wish I were myself again, free in shape and single in mind. Not this sack of mud clinging to another. Yet he's teaching me that it's good to cling to another. I'm exhausted from strange disciplines. Perhaps he's tired, too; I see that sometimes he kneads the muscles of his stomach with his hands, and closes his eyes.

The Warden sits me down on one of my rare evenings home, and talks angrily. "You're making a mistake," he says. "If the Doctor finds out what you are, you'll lose your job with the colony. Besides, we never supposed you'd have a liaison with only one man. You were supposed to start with the Doctor, and go on from there. We need every credit you can bring in. And by the way, you haven't done well on that score lately. Is he stingy?"

"Of course he isn't."

"But all you bring home in credits is your pay."

I can think of no reply. It's true the Warden has a right to use me in whatever capacity would serve us all best, as I will use others when I'm a Warden, but he and my Uncle spend half the credits from my job on sulfadiazole, to which they've become addicted.

"You've no sense of responsibility," the Warden says. Perhaps he's coming close to time for conjunction again, and this makes him more concerned about my stability.

My Uncle says, "Oh, he's young, leave him alone. As long as he turns over most of those pay credits to us. Though what he uses the remainder for, I'll never know."

I use it for clothes at the Colony Exchange. Sometimes Arnie takes me out for an evening, usually to the Laugh Tree Bar, where the space crews, too, like to relax. The bar is the place to find joy babies; young, pretty, planet-born girls who work at the Colony Punch Center during the day, and spend their evenings here competing for the attention of the officers. Sitting here with Arnie, I can't distinguish a colonist's daughter from one of my friends or relatives. They wouldn't know me, either.

Once, at home, I try to talk with a few of these friends about my feelings. But I discover that whatever female patterns they've borrowed are superficial ones; none of them bother to grow an extra lobe, but merely tuck the Terran pattern into a corner of their own for handy reference. They are most of them on sulfas. Hard and shiny toys, they skip like pebbles over the surface of the colonists' lives.

Then they go home, revert to their own free forms, and enjoy their mathematics, colors, compositions, and seedings.

"Why me?" I demand of the Warden. "Why two lobes? Why me?"

"We felt you'd be more efficient," he answers. "And while you're here, which you seldom are these days, you'd better revert to other shapes. Your particles may be damaged if you hold that woman form too long."

Oh, but you don't know, I want to tell him. You don't know I'll hold it forever. If I'm damaged or dead, you'll put me into the cell banks, and you'll be amazed, astonished, terrified, to discover that I come out complete, all Martha. I can't be changed.

"You little lump of protagon," my Uncle mumbles bitterly. "You'll never amount to anything, you'll never be a Warden. Have you done any of your own work recently?"

I say, "Yes, I've done some crystal divisions, and re-grown them in non-established patterns." My Uncle is in a bad mood, as he's kicking sulfa and his nerve tissue is addled. I'm wise to speak quietly to him, but he still grumbles.

"I can't understand why you like being a two-lobed pack of giggles. I couldn't wait to get out of it. And you were so dead against it to begin with."

"Well, I have learned," I start to say, but can't explain what it is I'm still learning, and close my eyes. Part of it is that on the line between the darkness and the brightness it's easiest to float. I've never wanted to practise only easy things. My balance is damaged. I never had to balance. It's not a term or concept that I understand even now, at home, in free form. Some impress of Martha's pattern lies on my own brain cells. I suspect it's permanent damage, which gives me joy. That's what I mean about not understanding it. I am taught to strive for perfection. How can I be pleased with this, which may be a catastrophe?

Arnie carves on a breadth of kaku wood, bringing out to the surface a seascape. Knots become clots of spray, a flaw becomes wind-blown spume. I want to be Martha. I'd like to go to the Laugh Tree with Arnie, for a good time, I'd like to learn to play cards with him.

You see what happens: Arnie is, in his way, like my original self, and I hate that part of him, since I've given it up to be Martha. Martha makes him happy, she is chocolate to his appetite, pillow for his weariness.

I turn for company to my koota. She's the color of morning, her chest juts out like an axe blade, her ribs spring up and back like wings, her eyes are large and clear as she returns my gaze. Yet she's beyond hope; in a little time, she'll be lame; she cannot race any more, she must not mother a litter. I turn to her and she gazes back into my eyes, dreaming of speed and wind on the sandy beaches where she has run.

"Why don't you read some tapes?" Arnie suggests to me, because I'm restless and I disturb him. The koota lies at my feet. I read tapes. Every evening in his quarters Arnie carves, I read tapes, the broken racer lies at my feet. I pass through Terran history this way. When the clown tumbles into the tub, I laugh. Terran history is full of clowns and tubs; at first it seems that's all there is, but you learn to see beneath the comic costumes.

While I float on the taut line, the horizon between light and dark, where it's so easy, I begin to sense what is under the costumes: staggering down the street dead drunk on a sunny afternoon with everyone laughing at you; hiding under the veranda because you made blood come out of Pa's face; kicking a man when he's in the gutter because you've been kicked and have to pass it on. Tragedy is what one of the Terrans called being a poet in the body of a cockroach.

"Have you heard the rumor?" Arnie asks, putting down the whittling tool. "Have you heard that some of the personnel in Punch Center aren't really humans?"

"Not really?" I ask, putting away the tape. We have no tragedy. In my species, family relationships are based only on related gene patterns; they are finally dumped into the family bank and a new relative is created from the old. It's one form of ancient history multiplying itself, but it isn't tragic. The koota, her utility destroyed by a recessive gene, lies sleeping at my feet. Is this tragedy? But she is a single form, she can't regenerate a lost limb, or exfoliate brain tissue. She can only return my gaze with her steadfast and affectionate one.

"What are they, then?" I ask Arnie. "If they're not human?"

"The story is that the local life forms aren't as we really see them. They've put on faces, like ours, to deal with us. And some of them have filtered into personnel."

Filtered! As if I were a virus.

"But they must be harmless," I say. "No harm has come to anyone."

"We don't know that for a fact," Arnie replies.

"You look tired," I say, and he comes to me, to be soothed, to be loved in his flesh, his single form, his search for the truth in the darkness of the viewing cubicle. At present he's doing studies of murger birds. Their spinal cavities are large, air-filled ovals, and their bone is extremely porous, which permits them to soar to great heights.

The koota no longer races on the wind-blown beaches; she lies at our feet, looking into the distance. The wall must be transparent to her eyes, I feel that beyond it she sees clearly how the racers go, down the long, bright curve of sand in the morning sun. She sighs, and lays her head down on her narrow, delicate paws. I look into the distance too: bright beaches and Arnie, carrying me from his ship. But he will not carry me again.

Arnie says. "I seem to be tired all the time." He puts his head on my breast. "I don't think the food's agreeing with me, lately."

"Do you suffer pains?" I ask him, curiously.

"Suffer," he mutters. "What kind of nonsense is that, with analgesics. No I don't suffer. I just don't feel well."

He's absorbed in murger birds, kaku wood, he descends into the bottom of the darks and rises up like a rocket across the horizon into the thin clarity above, while I float. I no longer dare to breathe I'm afraid of disturbing everything. I do not want anything. His head lies gently on my breast and I will not disturb him.

"Oh. My God," Arnie says, and I know what it's come to, even before he begins to choke, and his muscles leap although I hold him in my arms. I know his heart is choking on massive doses of blood; the brilliance fades from his eyes and they begin to go dark while I tightly hold him. If he doesn't see me as he dies, will I be here?

I can feel, under my fingers, how rapidly his skin cools. I must put him down, here with his carvings and his papers, and I must go home. But I lift Arnie in my arms, and call the koota, who gets up rather stiffly. It's long after dark, and I carry him slowly, carefully, home to what he called a crystal palace, where the Warden and my Uncle are teaching each other to play chess with a set some space captain gave them in exchange for seed crystals. They sit in a bloom of light, sparkling, their old brains bent over the chessmen, as I breathe open the door and carry Arnie in.

First, my Uncle gives me just a glance, but then another glance, and a hard stare. "Is that the Doctor?" he asks.

I put Arnie down and hold one of his cold hands. "Warden," I say, on my knees, on eye level with the chessboard and its carved men. "Warden, can you put him in one of the banks?"

The Warden turns to look at me, as hard as my Uncle. "You've become deranged, trying to maintain two lobes," he says. "You cannot reconstitute or recreate a Terran by our methods, and you must know it."

"Over the edge, over the edge," my Uncle says, now a blond, six-foot, hearty male Terran, often at the Laugh Tree with one of the joy babies. He enjoys life, his own or someone else's. I have, too, I suppose. Am I fading? I am, really, just one of Arnie's projections, a form on a screen in his mind. I am not, really, Martha. Though I tried.

"We can't have him here," the Warden says. "You better get him out of here. You couldn't explain a corpse like that to the colonists, if they come looking for him. They'll think we did something to him. It's nearly time for my next conjunction, do you want your nephew to arrive in disgrace? The Uncles will drain his bank."

The Warden gets up and comes over to me. He takes hold of my dark curls and pulls me to my feet. It hurts my physical me, which is Martha. God knows Arnie, I'm Martha, it seems to me. "Take him back to his quarters," the Warden says to me. "And come back here immediately. I'll try to see you back to your own pattern, but it may be too late. In part, I blame myself. If you must know. So I will try."

Yes, yes, I want to say to him; as I was, dedicated, free; turn me back into myself, I never wanted to be anyone else, and now I don't know if I am anyone at all. The light's gone from his eyes and he doesn't see me, or see anything, does he?

I pick him up and breathe the door out, and go back through the night to his quarters, where the lamp still burns. I'm going to leave him here, where he belongs. Before I go, I pick up the small carving of the murger bird, and take it with me, home to my glass bridge where at the edge of the mirrors the decimals are still clicking perfectly, clicking out known facts; an octagon can be reduced, the planet turns at such a degree on its axis, to see the truth you must have light of some sort, but to see the light you must have darkness of some sort. I can no longer float on the horizon between the two because that horizon has disappeared. I've learned to descend, and to rise, and descend again.

I'm able to revert without help to my own free form, to re-absorb the extra brain tissue. The sun comes up and it's bright. The night comes down and it's dark. I'm becoming somber, and a brilliant student. Even my Uncle says I'll be a good Warden when the time comes.

The Warden goes to conjunction; from the cell banks a nephew is lifted out. The koota lies dreaming of races she has run in the wind. It is our life, and it goes on, like the life of other creatures.

The galaxy is a broad screen upon which sagas and mighty adventures can be cast—or trivial, diminutive stories. Gordon R. Dickson is one of the very few writers who is aware of the true size of our universe, and of the possibilities inherent in this new scale of things. His Emperor has the ring of a true emperor, and behind him we are aware of that star-spanning empire and of the problems it must present. This is a story with a ring of truth to it, and it is a story that moves. Perhaps this is the reason that Mr. Dickson's fellow writers chose this as an award winner: because he is not afraid to entertain us.

CALL HIM LORD

Gordon R. Dickson

He called and commanded me
—Therefore, I knew him;
But later on, failed me; and
—Therefore, *I slew him!*"

"Song of the Shield Bearer"

The sun could not fail in rising over the Kentucky hills, nor could Kyle Arnam in waking. There would be eleven hours and forty minutes of daylight. Kyle rose, dressed, and went out to saddle the gray gelding and the white stallion. He rode the stallion until the first

Nebula Award, Best Novelette 1966

fury was out of the arched and snowy neck; and then led both horses around to tether them outside the kitchen door. Then he went in to breakfast.

The message that had come a week before was beside his plate of bacon and eggs. Teena, his wife, was standing at the breadboard with her back to him. He sat down and began eating, rereading the letter as he ate.

". . . The Prince will be traveling incognito under one of his family titles, as Count Sirii North; and should not be addressed as 'Majesty'. *You will call him 'Lord'* . . ."

"Why does it have to be you?" Teena asked.

He looked up and saw how she stood with her back to him.

"Teena—" he said, sadly.

"Why?"

"My ancestors were bodyguards to his—back in the wars of conquest against the aliens. I've told you that," he said. "My forefathers saved the lives of his, many times when there was no warning—a Rak spaceship would suddenly appear out of nowhere to lock on, even to a flagship. And even an Emperor found himself fighting for his life, hand to hand."

"The aliens are all dead now, and the Emperor's got a hundred other worlds! Why can't his son take his Grand Tour on them? Why does he have to come here to Earth—and you?"

"There's only one Earth."

"And only one you, I suppose?"

He sighed internally and gave up. He had been raised by his father and his uncle after his mother died, and in an argument with Teena he always felt helpless. He got up from the table and went to her, putting his hands on her and gently trying to turn her about. But she resisted.

He sighed inside himself again and turned away to the weapons cabinet. He took out a loaded slug pistol, fitted it into the stubby holster it matched, and clipped the holster to his belt at the left of the buckle, where the hang of his leather jacket would hide it. Then he selected a dark-handled knife with a six-inch blade and bent over to slip it into the sheath inside his boot top. He dropped the cuff of his trouser leg back over the boot top and stood up.

"He's got no right to be here," said Teena fiercely to the breadboard. "Tourists are supposed to be kept to the museum areas and the tourist lodges."

"He's not a tourist. You know that," answered Kyle, patiently. "He's the Emperor's oldest son and his great-grandmother was from Earth. His wife will be, too. Every fourth generation the Imperial line has to marry back into Earth stock. That's the law—still." He put on his leather jacket, sealing it closed only at the bottom to hide the slug-gun holster, half turned to the door—then paused.

"Teena?" he asked.

She did not answer.

"Teena!" he repeated. He stepped to her, put his hands on her shoulders and tried to turn her to face him. Again, she resisted, but this time he was having none of it.

He was not a big man, being of middle height, round-faced, with sloping and unremarkable-looking, if thick, shoulders. But his strength was not ordinary. He could bring the white stallion to its knees with one fist wound in its mane—and no other man had ever been able to do that. He turned her easily to look at him.

"Now, listen to me—" he began. But, before he could finish, all the stiffness went out of her and she clung to him, trembling.

"He'll get you into trouble—I know he will!" she choked, muffledly into his chest. "Kyle, don't go! There's no law making you go!"

He stroked the soft hair of her head, his throat stiff and dry. There was nothing he could say to her. What she was asking was impossible. Ever since the sun had first risen on men and women together, wives had clung to their husbands at times like this, begging for what could not be. And always the men had held them, as Kyle was holding her now—as if understanding could somehow be pressed from one body into the other—and saying nothing, because there was nothing that could be said.

So, Kyle held her for a few moments longer, and then reached behind him to unlock her intertwined fingers at his back, and loosen her arms around him. Then, he went. Looking back through the kitchen window as he rode off on the stallion, leading the gray horse, he saw her standing just where he had left her. Not even crying, but standing with her arms hanging down, her head down, not moving.

He rode away through the forest of the Kentucky hillside. It took him more than two hours to reach the lodge. As he rode down the valleyside toward it, he saw a tall, bearded man, wearing the robes they wore on some of the Younger Worlds, standing at the gateway to the interior courtyard of the rustic, wooded lodge.

When he got close, he saw that the beard was graying and the man was biting his lips. Above a straight, thin nose, the eyes were bloodshot and circled beneath as if from worry or lack of sleep.

"He's in the courtyard," said the gray-bearded man as Kyle rode up. "I'm Montlaven, his tutor. He's ready to go." The darkened eyes looked almost pleadingly up at Kyle.

"Stand clear of the stallion's head," said Kyle. "And take me in to him."

"Not that horse, for him—" said Montlaven, looking distrustfully at the stallion, as he backed away.

"No," said Kyle. "He'll ride the gelding."

"He'll want the white."

"He can't ride the white," said Kyle. "Even if I let him, he couldn't ride this stallion. I'm the only one who can ride him. Take me in."

The tutor turned and led the way into the grassy courtyard, surrounding a swimming pool and looked down upon, on three sides, by the windows of the lodge. In a lounging chair by the pool sat a tall young man in his late teens, with a mane of blond hair, a pair of stuffed saddlebags on the grass beside him. He stood up as Kyle and the tutor came toward him.

"Majesty," said the tutor, as they stopped, "this is Kyle Arnam, your bodyguard for the three days here."

"Good morning, Bodyguard . . . Kyle, I mean." The Prince smiled mischievously. "Light, then. And I'll mount."

"You ride the gelding, Lord," said Kyle.

The Prince stared at him, tilted back his handsome head, and laughed.

"I can ride, man!" he said. "I ride well."

"Not this horse, Lord," said Kyle, dispassionately. "No one rides this horse, but me."

The eyes flashed wide, the laugh faded—then returned.

"What can I do?" The wide shoulders shrugged. "I give in—always I give in. Well, almost always." He grinned up at Kyle, his lips thinned, but frank. "All right."

He turned to the gelding—and with a sudden leap was in the saddle. The gelding snorted and plunged at the shock; then steadied as the young man's long fingers tightened expertly on the reins and the fingers of the other hand patted a gray neck. The Prince raised his eyebrows, looking over at Kyle, but Kyle sat stolidly.

"I take it you're armed good Kyle?" the Prince said slyly. "You'll protect me against the natives if they run wild?"

"Your life is in my hands, Lord," said Kyle. He unsealed the leather jacket at the bottom and let it fall open to show the slug pistol in its holster for a moment. Then he resealed the jacket again at the bottom.

"Will—" The tutor put his hand on the young man's knee. "Don't be reckless, boy. This is Earth and the people here don't have rank and custom like we do. Think before you—"

"Oh, cut it out, Monty!" snapped the Prince. "I'll be just as incognito, just as humble, as archaic and independent as the rest of them. You think I've no memory! Anyway, it's only for three days or so until my Imperial father joins me. Now, let me go!"

He jerked away, turned to lean forward in the saddle, and abruptly put the gelding into a bolt for the gate. He disappeared through it, and Kyle drew hard on the stallion's reins as the big white horse danced and tried to follow.

"Give me his saddlebags," said Kyle.

The tutor bent and passed them up. Kyle made them fast on top of his own, across the stallion's withers. Looking down, he saw there were tears in the bearded man's eyes.

"He's a fine boy. You'll see. You'll know he is!" Montlaven's face, upturned, was mutely pleading.

"I know he comes from a fine family," said Kyle, slowly. "I'll do my best for him." And he rode off out of the gateway after the gelding.

When he came out of the gate, the Prince was nowhere in sight. But it was simple enough for Kyle to follow, by dinted brown earth and crushed grass, the marks of the gelding's path. This brought him at last through some pines to a grassy open slope where the Prince sat looking skyward through a single-lens box.

When Kyle came up, the Prince lowered the instrument and, without a word, passed it over. Kyle put it to his eye and looked skyward. There was the whir of the tracking unit and one of Earth's three orbiting power stations swam into the field of vision of the lens.

"Give it back," said the Prince.

"I couldn't get a look at it earlier," went on the young man as Kyle handed the lens to him. "And I wanted to. It's a rather expensive present, you know—it and the other two like it—from our Imperial treasury. Just to keep your planet from drifting into another ice age. And what do we get for it?"

"Earth, Lord," answered Kyle. "As it was before men went out to the stars."

"Oh, the museum areas could be maintained with one station and a half-million caretakers," said the Prince. "It's the other two stations and you billion or so free-loaders I'm talking about. I'll have to look into it when I'm Emperor. Shall we ride?"

"If you wish, Lord." Kyle picked up the reins of the stallion and the two horses with their riders moved off across the slope.

". . . And one more thing," said the Prince, as they entered the farther belt of pine trees. "I don't want you to be misled—I'm really very fond of old Monty, back there. It's just that I wasn't really planning to come here at all—*Look at me, Bodyguard!*"

Kyle turned to see the blue eyes that ran in the Imperial family blazing at him. Then, unexpectedly, they softened. The Prince laughed.

"You don't scare easily, do you, Bodyguard . . . Kyle, I mean?" he said. "I think I like you after all. But look at me when I talk."

"Yes, Lord."

"That's my good Kyle. Now, I was explaining to you that I'd never actually planned to come here on my Grand Tour at all. I didn't see any point in visiting this dusty old museum world of yours with people still trying to live like they lived in the Dark Ages. But—my Imperial father talked me into it."

"Your father, Lord?" asked Kyle.

"Yes, he bribed me, you might say," said the Prince thoughtfully. "He was supposed to meet me here for these three days. Now, he's messaged there's been a slight delay—but that doesn't matter. The point is, he belongs to the school of old men who still think your Earth is something precious and vital. Now, I happen to like and admire my father, Kyle. You approve of that?"

"Yes, Lord."

"I thought you would. Yes, he's the one man in the human race I look up to. And to please him, I'm making this Earth trip. And to please him—only to please *him,* Kyle—I'm going to be an easy Prince for you to conduct around to your natural wonders and watering spots and whatever. Now, you understand me—and how this trip is going to go. Don't you?" He stared at Kyle.

"I understand," said Kyle.

"That's fine," said the Prince, smiling once more. "So now you can start telling me all about these trees and birds and animals so that I can memorize their names and please my father when he shows up. What are those little birds I've been seeing under the trees—brown on top and whitish underneath? Like that one—there!"

"That's a Veery, Lord," said Kyle. "A bird of the deep woods and silent places. Listen—" He reached out a hand to the gelding's bridle and brought both horses to a halt. In the sudden silence, off to their right they could hear a silver bird-voice, rising and falling, in a descending series of crescendos and diminuendos, that softened at last into silence. For a moment after the song was ended the Prince sat staring at Kyle, then seemed to shake himself back to life.

"Interesting," he said. He lifted the reins Kyle had let go and the horses moved forward again. "Tell me more."

For more than three hours, as the sun rose toward noon, they rode through the wooded hills, with Kyle identifying bird and animal, insect, tree and rock. And for three hours the Prince listened—his attention flashing and momentary, but intense. But when the sun was overhead that intensity flagged.

"That's enough," he said. "Aren't we going to stop for lunch? Kyle, aren't there any towns around here?"

"Yes, Lord," said Kyle. "We've passed several."

"Several?" The Prince stared at him. "Why haven't we come into one before now? Where are you taking me?"

"Nowhere, Lord," said Kyle. "You lead the way. I only follow."

"I?" said the Prince. For the first time he seemed to become aware that he had been keeping the gelding's head always in advance of the stallion. "Of course. But now it's time to eat."

"Yes, Lord," said Kyle. "This way."

He turned the stallion's head down the slope of the hill they were crossing and the Prince turned the gelding after him.

"And now listen," said the Prince, as he caught up. "Tell me I've got it all right." And to Kyle's astonishment, he began to repeat, almost word for word, everything that Kyle had said. "Is it all there? Everything you told me?"

"Perfectly, Lord," said Kyle. The Prince looked slyly at him.

"Could you do that, Kyle?"

"Yes," said Kyle. "But these are things I've known all my life."

"You see?" The Prince smiled. "That's the difference between us, good Kyle. You spend your life learning something—I spend a few hours and I know as much about it as you do."

"Not as much, Lord," said Kyle, slowly.

The Prince blinked at him, then jerked his hand dismissingly, and half-angrily, as if he were throwing something aside.

"What little else there is probably doesn't count," he said.

They rode down the slope and through a winding valley and came out at a small village. As they rode clear of the surrounding trees a sound of music came to their ears.

"What's that?" The Prince stood up in his stirrups. "Why, there's dancing going on, over there."

"A beer garden, Lord. And it's Saturday—a holiday here."

"Good. We'll go there to eat."

They rode around to the beer garden and found tables back away from the dance floor. A pretty, young waitress came and they ordered, the Prince smiling sunnily at her until she smiled back—then hurried off as if in mild confusion. The Prince ate hungrily when the food came and drank a stein and a half of brown beer, while Kyle ate more lightly and drank coffee.

"That's better," said the Prince, sitting back at last. "I had an appetite . . . Look there, Kyle! Look, there are five, six . . . seven drifter platforms parked over there. Then you don't all ride horses?"

"No," said Kyle. "It's as each man wishes."

"But if you have drifter platforms, why not other civilized things?"

"Some things fit, some don't, Lord," answered Kyle. The Prince laughed.

"You mean you try to make civilization fit this old-fashioned life of yours, here?" he said. "Isn't that the wrong way around—" He broke off. "What's that they're playing now? I like that. I'll bet I could do that dance." He stood up. "In fact, I think I will."

He paused, looking down at Kyle.

"Aren't you going to warn me against it?" he asked.

"No, Lord," said Kyle. "What you do is your own affair."

The young man turned away abruptly. The waitress who had served them was passing, only a few tables away. The Prince went after her and caught up with her by the dance floor railing. Kyle could see the girl protesting—but the Prince hung over her, looking down from his tall height, smiling. Shortly, she had taken off her apron and was out on the dance floor with him, showing him the steps of the dance. It was a polka.

The Prince learned with fantastic quickness. Soon, he was swinging the waitress around with the rest of the dancers, his foot stamping on the turns, his white teeth gleaming. Finally the number ended and the members of the band put down their instruments and began to leave the stand.

The Prince, with the girl trying to hold him back, walked over to the band leader. Kyle got up quickly from his table and started toward the floor.

The band leader was shaking his head. He turned abruptly and slowly walked away. The Prince started after him, but the girl took hold of his arm, saying something urgent to him.

He brushed her aside and she stumbled a little. A busboy among the tables on the far side of the dance floor, not much older than the Prince and nearly as tall, put down his tray and vaulted the railing onto the polished hardwood. He came up behind the Prince and took hold of his arm, swinging him around.

". . . Can't do that here." Kyle heard him say, as Kyle came up. The Prince struck out like a panther—like a trained boxer—with three quick lefts in succession into the face of the busboy, the Prince's shoulder bobbing, the weight of his body in behind each blow.

The busboy went down. Kyle, reaching the Prince, herded him away through a side gap in the railing. The young man's face was white with rage. People were swarming onto the dance floor.

"Who was that? What's his name?" demanded the Prince, between his teeth. "He put his hand on me! Did you see that? *He put his hand on me!*"

"You knocked him out," said Kyle. "What more do you want?"

"He manhandled me—*me!*" snapped the Prince. "I want to find out who he is!" He caught hold of the bar to which the horses were tied, refusing to be pushed farther. "He'll learn to lay hands on a future Emperor!"

"No one will tell you his name," said Kyle. And the cold note in his voice finally seemed to reach through to the Prince and sober him. He stared at Kyle.

"Including you?" he demanded at last.

"Including me, Lord," said Kyle.

The Prince stared a moment longer, then swung away. He turned, jerked loose the reins of the gelding and swung into the saddle. He rode off. Kyle mounted and followed.

They rode in silence into the forest. After a while, the Prince spoke without turning his head.

"And you call yourself a bodyguard," he said, finally.

"Your life is in my hands, Lord," said Kyle. The Prince turned a grim face to look at him.

"Only my life?" said the Prince. "As long as they don't kill me, they can do what they want? Is that what you mean?"

Kyle met his gaze steadily.

"Pretty much so, Lord," he said.

The Prince spoke with an ugly note in his voice.

"I don't think I like you, after all, Kyle," he said. "I don't think I like you at all."

"I'm not here with you to be liked, Lord," said Kyle.

"Perhaps not," said the Prince, thickly. "But I know *your* name!"

They rode on in continued silence for perhaps another half hour. But then gradually the angry hunch went out of the young man's shoulders and the tightness out of his jaw. After a while he began to sing to himself, a song in a language Kyle did not know; and as he sang, his cheerfulness seemed to return. Shortly, he spoke to Kyle, as if there had never been anything but pleasant moments between them.

Mammoth Cave was close and the Prince asked to visit it. They went there and spent some time going through the cave. After that they rode their horses up along the left bank of the Green River. The Prince seemed to have forgotten all about the incident at the beer garden and be out to charm everyone they met. As the sun was at last westering toward the dinner hour, they came finally to a small hamlet back from the river, with a roadside inn mirrored in an artificial lake beside it, and guarded by oak and pine trees behind.

"This looks good," said the Prince. "We'll stay overnight here, Kyle."

"If you wish, Lord," said Kyle.

They halted, and Kyle took the horses around to the stable, then entered the inn to find the Prince already in the small bar off the dining room, drinking beer and charming the waitress. This waitress was younger than the one at the beer garden had been; a little girl with soft, loose hair and round brown eyes that showed their delight in the attention of the tall, good-looking, young man.

"Yes," said the Prince to Kyle, looking out of the corners of the Imperial blue eyes at him, after the waitress had gone to get Kyle his coffee, "This is the very place."

"The very place?" said Kyle.

"For me to get to know the people better—what did you think, good Kyle?" said the Prince and laughed at him. "I'll observe the people here and you can explain them—won't that be good?"

Kyle gazed at him, thoughtfully.

"I'll tell you whatever I can, Lord," he said.

They drank—the Prince his beer, and Kyle his coffee—and went in a little later to the dining room for dinner. The Prince, as he had promised at the bar, was full of questions about what he saw—and what he did not see.

". . . But why go on living in the past, all of you here?" he asked Kyle. "A museum world is one thing. But a museum people—" he broke off to smile and speak to the little, soft-haired waitress, who had somehow been diverted from the bar to wait upon their dining-room table.

"Not a museum people, Lord," said Kyle. "A living people. The only way to keep a race and a culture preserved is to keep it alive. So we go on in our own way, here on Earth, as a living example for the Younger Worlds to check themselves against."

"Fascinating . . ." murmured the Prince; but his eyes had wandered off to follow the waitress, who was glowing and looking back at him from across the now-busy dining room.

"Not fascinating. Necessary, Lord," said Kyle. But he did not believe the younger man had heard him.

After dinner, they moved back to the bar. And the Prince, after questioning Kyle a little longer, moved up to continue his researches among the other people standing at the bar. Kyle watched for a little while. Then, feeling it was safe to do so, slipped out to have another look at the horses and to ask the innkeeper to arrange a saddle lunch put up for them the next day.

When he returned, the Prince was not to be seen.

Kyle sat down at a table to wait; but the Prince did not return. A cold, hard knot of uneasiness began to grow below Kyle's breastbone. A sudden pang of alarm sent him swiftly back out to check the horses. But they were cropping peacefully in their stalls. The stallion whickered, low-voiced, as Kyle looked in on him, and turned his white head to look back at Kyle.

"Easy, boy," said Kyle and returned to the inn to find the innkeeper.

But the innkeeper had no idea where the Prince might have gone.

". . . If the horses aren't taken, he's not far," the innkeeper said. "There's no trouble he can get into around here. Maybe he went for a walk in the woods. I'll leave word for the night staff to keep an eye out for him when he comes in. Where'll you be?"

"In the bar until it closes—then, my room," said Kyle.

He went back to the bar to wait, and took a booth near an open window. Time went by and gradually the number of other customers began to dwindle. Above the ranked bottles, the bar clock showed nearly midnight. Suddenly, through the window, Kyle heard a distant scream of equine fury from the stables.

He got up and went out quickly. In the darkness outside, he ran to the stables and burst in. There in the feeble illumination of the stable's night lighting, he saw the Prince, pale-faced, clumsily saddling the gelding in the center aisle between the stalls. The door to the stallion's stall was open. The Prince looked away as Kyle came in.

Kyle took three swift steps to the open door and looked in. The stallion was still tied, but his ears were back, his eyes rolling, and a saddle lay tumbled and dropped on the stable floor beside him.

"Saddle up," said the Prince thickly from the aisle. "We're leaving." Kyle turned to look at him.

"We've got rooms at the inn here," he said.

"Never mind. We're riding. I need to clear my head." The young man got the gelding's cinch tight, dropped the stirrups and swung heavily up into the saddle. Without waiting for Kyle, he rode out of the stable into the night.

"So, boy . . ." said Kyle soothingly to the stallion. Hastily he untied the big white horse, saddled him, and set out after the Prince. In the darkness, there was no way of ground-tracking the gelding; but he leaned forward and blew into the ear of the stallion. The surprised horse neighed in protest and the whinny of the gelding came back from the darkness of the slope up ahead and over to Kyle's right. He rode in that direction.

He caught the Prince on the crown of the hill. The young man was walking the gelding, reins loose, and singing under his breath—

the same song in an unknown language he had sung earlier. But, now as he saw Kyle, he grinned loosely and began to sing with more emphasis. For the first time Kyle caught the overtones of something mocking and lusty about the incomprehensible words. Understanding broke suddenly in him.

"The girl!" he said. "The little waitress. Where is she?"

The grin vanished from the Prince's face, then came slowly back again. The grin laughed at Kyle.

"Why, where d'you think?" The words slurred on the Prince's tongue and Kyle, riding close, smelled the beer heavy on the young man's breath. "In her room, sleeping and happy. Honored . . . though she doesn't know it . . . by an Emperor's son. And expecting to find me there in the morning. But I won't be. Will we, good Kyle?"

"Why did you do it, Lord?" asked Kyle, quietly.

"Why?" The Prince peered at him, a little drunkenly in the moonlight. "Kyle, my father has four sons. I've got three younger brothers. But I'm the one who's going to be Emperor; and Emperors don't answer questions."

Kyle said nothing. The Prince peered at him. They rode on together for several minutes in silence.

"All right, I'll tell you why," said the Prince, more loudly, after a while as if the pause had been only momentary. "It's because you're not *my* bodyguard, Kyle. You see, I've seen through you. I know whose bodyguard you are. You're *theirs!*"

Kyle's jaw tightened. But the darkness hid his reaction.

"All right—" The Prince gestured loosely, disturbing his balance in the saddle. "That's all right. Have it your way. I don't mind. So, we'll play points. There was that lout at the beer garden who put his hands on me. But no one would tell me his name, you said. All right, you managed to bodyguard him. One point for you. But you didn't manage to bodyguard the girl at the inn back there. One point for me. Who's going to win, good Kyle?"

Kyle took a deep breath.

"Lord," he said, "some day it'll be your duty to marry a woman from Earth—"

The Prince interrupted him with a laugh, and this time there was an ugly note in it.

"You flatter yourselves," he said. His voice thickened. "That's the trouble with you—all you Earth people—you flatter yourselves."

They rode on in silence. Kyle said nothing more, but kept the head of the stallion close to the shoulder of the gelding, watching the young man closely. For a little while the Prince seemed to doze. His head sank on his chest and he let the gelding wander. Then, after a while, his head began to come up again, his automatic horseman's fingers tightened on the reins, and he lifted his head to stare around in the moonlight.

"I want a drink," he said. His voice was no longer thick, but it was flat and uncheerful. "Take me where we can get some beer, Kyle."

Kyle took a deep breath.

"Yes, Lord," he said.

He turned the stallion's head to the right and the gelding followed. They went up over a hill and down to the edge of a lake. The dark water sparkled in the moonlight and the farther shore was lost in the night. Lights shone through the trees around the curve of the shore.

"There, Lord," said Kyle. "It's a fishing resort, with a bar."

They rode around the shore to it. It was a low, casual building, angled to face the shore; a dock ran out from it, to which fishing boats were tethered, bobbing slightly on the black water. Light gleamed through the windows as they hitched their horses and went to the door.

The barroom they stepped into was wide and bare. A long bar faced them with several planked fish on the wall behind it. Below the fish were three bartenders—the one in the center, middle-aged, and wearing an air of authority with his apron. The other two were young and muscular. The customers, mostly men, scattered at the square tables and standing at the bar wore rough working clothes, or equally casual vacationers' garb.

The Prince sat down at a table back from the bar and Kyle sat down with him. When the waitress came they ordered beer and coffee, and the Prince half-emptied his stein the moment it was brought to him. As soon as it was completely empty, he signaled the waitress again.

"Another," he said. This time, he smiled at the waitress when she brought his stein back. But she was a woman in her thirties, pleased but not overwhelmed by his attention. She smiled lightly back and moved off to return to the bar where she had been talking to two men her own age, one fairly tall, the other shorter, bullet-headed and fleshy.

The Prince drank. As he put his stein down, he seemed to become aware of Kyle, and turned to look at him.

"I suppose," said the Prince, "you think I'm drunk?"

"Not yet," said Kyle.

"No," said the Prince, "that's right. Not yet. But perhaps I'm going to be. And if I decide I am, who's going to stop me?"

"No one, Lord."

"That's right," the young man said, "that's right." He drank deliberately from his stein until it was empty, and then signaled the waitress for another. A spot of color was beginning to show over each of his high cheekbones. "When you're on a miserable little world with miserable little people . . . hello, Bright Eyes!" he interrupted himself as the waitress brought his beer. She laughed and went back to her friends. ". . . You have to amuse yourself any way you can," he wound up.

He laughed to himself.

"When I think how my father, and Monty—everybody—used to talk this planet up to me—" he glanced aside at Kyle. "Do you know at one time I was actually scared—well, not scared exactly, nothing scares me . . . say *concerned*—about maybe having to come here, some day?" He laughed again. "Concerned that I wouldn't measure up to you Earth people! Kyle, have you ever been to any of the Younger Worlds?"

"No," said Kyle.

"I thought not. Let me tell you, good Kyle, the worst of the people there are bigger, and better-looking and smarter, and everything than anyone I've seen here. And I, Kyle, I—the Emperor-to-be—am better than any of them. So, guess how all you here look to me?"

He stared at Kyle, waiting. "Well, answer me, good Kyle. Tell me the truth. That's an order."

"It's not up to you to judge, Lord," said Kyle.

"Not—? Not up to me?" The blue eyes blazed. "*I'm* going to be Emperor!"

"It's not up to any one man, Lord," said Kyle. "Emperor or not. An Emperor's needed, as the symbol that can hold a hundred worlds together. But the real need of the race is to survive. It took nearly a million years to evolve a survival-type intelligence here on Earth. And out on the newer worlds people are bound to change. If something gets lost out there, some necessary element lost out of the race, there needs to be a pool of original genetic material here to replace it."

The Prince's lips grew wide in a savage grin.

"Oh, good, Kyle—good!" he said. "Very good. Only, I've heard all that before. Only, I don't believe it. You see—I've seen you people, now. And you don't outclass us, out on the Younger Worlds. *We* outclass *you*. We've gone on and got better, while you stayed still. And you know it."

The young man laughed softly, almost in Kyle's face.

"All you've been afraid of, is that we'd find out. And I have." He laughed again. "I've had a look at you; and now I know. I'm bigger, better and braver than any man in this room—and you know why? Not just because I'm the son of the Emperor, but because it's born in me! Body, brains and everything else! I can do what I want here, and no one on this planet is good enough to stop me. Watch."

He stood up, suddenly.

"Now, I want that waitress to get drunk with me," he said. "And this time I'm telling you in advance. Are you going to try and stop me?"

Kyle looked up at him. Their eyes met.

"No, Lord," he said. "It's not my job to stop you."

The Prince laughed.

"I thought so," he said. He swung away and walked between the tables toward the bar and the waitress, still in conversation with the two men. The Prince came up to the bar on the far side of the waitress and ordered a new stein of beer from the middle-aged bartender. When it was given to him, he took it, turned around, and rested his elbows on the bar, leaning back against it. He spoke to the waitress, interrupting the taller of the two men.

"I've been wanting to talk to you," Kyle heard him say.

The waitress, a little surprised, looked around at him. She smiled, recognizing him—a little flattered by the directness of his approach, a little appreciative of his clean good looks, a little tolerant of his youth.

"*You* don't mind, do you?" said the Prince, looking past her to the bigger of the two men, the one who had just been talking. The other stared back, and their eyes met without shifting for several seconds. Abruptly, angrily, the man shrugged, and turned about with his back hunched against them.

"You see?" said the Prince, smiling back at the waitress. "He knows I'm the one you ought to be talking to, instead of—"

"All right, sonny. Just a minute."

It was the shorter, bullet-headed man, interrupting. The Prince turned to look down at him with a fleeting expression of surprise. But the bullet-headed man was already turning to his taller friend and putting a hand on his arm.

"Come on back, Ben," the shorter man was saying. "The kid's a little drunk, is all." He turned back to the Prince. "You shove off now," he said. "Clara's with us."

The Prince stared at him blankly. The stare was so fixed that the shorter man had started to turn away, back to his friend and the waitress, when the Prince seemed to wake.

"Just a minute—" he said, in his turn.

He reached out a hand to one of the fleshy shoulders below the bullet head. The man turned back, knocking the hand calmly away. Then, just as calmly, he picked up the Prince's full stein of beer from the bar and threw it in the young man's face.

"Get lost," he said, unexcitedly.

The Prince stood for a second, with the beer dripping from his face. Then, without even stopping to wipe his eyes clear, he threw the beautifully trained left hand he had demonstrated at the beer garden.

But the shorter man, as Kyle had known from the first moment of seeing him, was not like the busboy the Prince had decisioned so neatly. This man was thirty pounds heavier, fifteen years more experienced, and by build and nature a natural bar fighter. He had not stood there waiting to be hit, but had already ducked and gone forward to throw his thick arms around the Prince's body. The young man's punch bounced harmlessly off the round head, and both bodies hit the floor, rolling in among the chair and table legs.

Kyle was already more than halfway to the bar and the three bartenders were already leaping the wooden hurdle that walled them off. The taller friend of the bullet-headed man, hovering over the two bodies, his eyes glittering, had his boot drawn back ready to drive the point of it into the Prince's kidneys. Kyle's forearm took him economically like a bar of iron across the tanned throat.

He stumbled backwards choking. Kyle stood still, hands open and down, glancing at the middle-aged bartender.

"All right," said the bartender. "But don't do anything more." He turned to the two younger bartenders. "All right. Haul him off!"

The pair of younger, aproned men bent down and came up with the bullet-headed man expertly handlocked between them. The man made one surging effort to break loose, and then stood still.

"Let me at him," he said.

"Not in here," said the older bartender. "Take it outside."

Between the tables, the Prince staggered unsteadily to his feet. His face was streaming blood from a cut on his forehead, but what could be seen of it was white as a drowning man's. His eyes went to Kyle, standing beside him; and he opened his mouth—but what came out sounded like something between a sob and a curse.

"All right," said the middle-aged bartender again. "Outside, both of you. Settle it out there."

The men in the room had packed around the little space by the bar. The Prince looked about and for the first time seemed to see the human wall hemming him in. His gaze wobbled to meet Kyle's.

"Outside . . . ?" he said, chokingly.

"You aren't staying in here," said the older bartender, answering for Kyle. "I saw it. You started the whole thing. Now, settle it any way you want—but you're both going outside. Now! Get moving!"

He pushed at the Prince, but the Prince resisted, clutching at Kyle's leather jacket with one hand.

"Kyle—."

"I'm sorry, Lord," said Kyle. "I can't help. It's your fight."

"Let's get out of here," said the bullet-headed man.

The Prince stared around at them as if they were some strange set of beings he had never known to exist before.

"No . . ." he said.

He let go of Kyle's jacket. Unexpectedly, his hand darted in towards Kyle's belly holster and came out holding the slug pistol.

"Stand back!" he said, his voice high-toned. "Don't try to touch me!"

His voice broke on the last words. There was a strange sound, half grunt, half moan, from the crowd; and it swayed back from him. Manager, bartenders, watchers—all but Kyle and the bullet-headed man drew back.

"You dirty slob . . ." said the bullet-headed man, distinctly. "I knew you didn't have the guts."

"Shut up!" The Prince's voice was high and cracking. "Shut up! Don't any of you try to come after me!"

He began backing away toward the front door of the bar. The room watched in silence, even Kyle standing still. As he backed, the Prince's back straightened. He hefted the gun in his hand. When he reached the door he paused to wipe the blood from his eyes with his left sleeve, and his smeared face looked with a first touch of regained arrogance at them.

"Swine!" he said.

He opened the door and backed out, closing it behind him. Kyle took one step that put him facing the bullet-headed man. Their eyes met and he could see the other recognizing the fighter in him, as he had earlier recognized it in the bullet-headed man.

"Don't come after us," said Kyle.

The bullet-headed man did not answer. But no answer was needed. He stood still.

Kyle turned, ran to the door, stood on one side of it and flicked it open. Nothing happened; and he slipped through, dodging to his right at once, out of the line of any shot aimed at the opening door.

But no shot came. For a moment he was blind in the night darkness, then his eyes began to adjust. He went by sight, feel and memory toward the hitching rack. By the time he got there, he was beginning to see.

The Prince was untying the gelding and getting ready to mount.

"Lord," said Kyle.

The Prince let go of the saddle for a moment and turned to look over his shoulder at him.

"Get away from me," said the Prince, thickly.

"Lord," said Kyle, low-voiced and pleading, "you lost your head in there. Anyone might do that. But don't make it worse, now. Give me back the gun, Lord."

"Give you the gun?"

The young man stared at him—and then he laughed.

"Give *you* the gun?" he said again. "So you can let someone beat me up some more? So you can not-guard me with it?"

"Lord," said Kyle, "please. For your own sake—give me back the gun."

"Get out of here," said the Prince, thickly, turning back to mount the gelding. "Clear out before I put a slug in you."

Kyle drew a slow, sad breath. He stepped forward and tapped the Prince on the shoulder.

"Turn around, Lord," he said.

"I warned you—" shouted the Prince, turning.

He came around as Kyle stooped, and the slug pistol flashed in his hand from the light of the bar windows. Kyle, bent over, was lifting the cuff of his trouser leg and closing his fingers on the hilt of the knife in his boot sheath. He moved simply, skillfully, and with a speed nearly double that of the young man, striking up into the chest before him until the hand holding the knife jarred against the cloth covering flesh and bone.

It was a sudden, hard-driven, swiftly merciful blow. The blade struck upwards between the ribs lying open to an underhanded thrust, plunging deep into the heart. The Prince grunted with the impact driving the air from his lungs; and he was dead as Kyle caught his slumping body in leather-jacketed arms.

Kyle lifted the tall body across the saddle of the gelding and tied it there. He hunted on the dark ground for the fallen pistol and returned it to his holster. Then, he mounted the stallion and, leading the gelding with its burden, started the long ride back.

Dawn was graying the sky when at last he topped the hill overlooking the lodge where he had picked up the Prince almost twenty-four hours before. He rode down towards the courtyard gate.

A tall figure, indistinct in the pre-dawn light, was waiting inside the courtyard as Kyle came through the gate; and it came running to meet him as he rode toward it. It was the tutor, Montlaven, and he was weeping as he ran to the gelding and began to fumble at the cords that tied the body in place.

"I'm sorry . . ." Kyle heard himself saying; and was dully shocked by the deadness and remoteness of his voice. "There was no choice. You can read it all in my report tomorrow morning–"

He broke off. Another, even taller figure had appeared in the doorway of the lodge giving on the courtyard. As Kyle turned towards it, this second figure descended the few steps to the grass and came to him.

"Lord–" said Kyle. He looked down into features like those of the Prince, but older, under graying hair. This man did not weep like the tutor, but his face was set like iron.

"What happened, Kyle?" he said.

"Lord," said Kyle, "you'll have my report in the morning . . ."

"I want to know," said the tall man. Kyle's throat was dry and stiff. He swallowed but swallowing did not ease it.

"Lord," he said, "you have three other sons. One of them will make an Emperor to hold the worlds together."

"What did he do? Whom did he hurt? Tell me!" The tall man's voice cracked almost as his son's voice had cracked in the bar.

"Nothing. No one," said Kyle, stiff-throated. "He hit a boy not much older than himself. He drank too much. He may have got a girl in trouble. It was nothing he did to anyone else. It was only a fault against himself." He swallowed. "Wait until tomorrow, Lord, and read my report."

"*No!*" The tall man caught at Kyle's saddle horn with a grip that checked even the white stallion from moving. "Your family and mine have been tied together by this for three hundred years. What was the flaw in my son to make him fail his test, back here on Earth? *I want to know!*"

Kyle's throat ached and was dry as ashes.

"Lord," he answered, "he was a coward."

The hand dropped from his saddle horn as if struck down by a sudden strengthlessness. And the Emperor of a hundred worlds fell back like a beggar, spurned in the dust.

Kyle lifted his reins and rode out of the gate, into the forest away on the hillside. The dawn was breaking.

Allegorical short stories are about as out of style these days as the political poem or pamphlet, and who is to say that the world is a better place as a result? Yet, as we have already noted, there is more than a hint of allegory in the best science fiction. Mr. Smith's story is both brief and entertaining—so that his allegory can only be accepted as a happy bonus.

IN THE IMAGICON

George Henry Smith

Dandor leaned back on the warm silk of the lounge and stretched, letting his eyes wander up to the high ceiling of his palace and then drop down to the blonde who knelt at his feet. She was putting the finishing touches on his carefully manicured toenails while the voluptuous brunette with the mobile hips and the full red mouth leaned forward to pop another grape into his mouth.

He studied the blonde, whose name was Cecily, and thought about the other service she had performed for him last night. That had been nice . . . very nice. But today he felt bored with her, just as he was bored with the brunette whose name he couldn't remember at the moment, and with the cuddly redheaded twins and with . . .

Dandor yawned. Why were they all so damn worshipful and always so eager to please?

It was almost, he thought with a wry grin, as though they were products of his imagination, or rather—and he almost laughed aloud —of that greatest of all man's inventions, the Imagicon.

"There now, don't they look nice?" Cecily said, sitting back to admire his finished pedicure with pride.

Dandor looked at the ten shining objects of her gaze and grimaced. It made him feel pretty silly.

Then Cecily made him feel even sillier by leaning over and kissing his right foot with passionate red lips. "Oh, Dandor! Dandor, I love you so much," she murmured.

Dandor resisted the temptation to use one of his newly pampered feet to give her a healthy kick on her round little bottom. He resisted it because even at times like this, when his life with these women began to seem unreal, he tried to be as kind as possible to them. Even when their worship and adoration threatened to bore him to death, he tried to be kind.

So instead of kicking Cecily, he yawned.

The effect was almost the same. Her blue eyes widened in fear, and the brunette raised wide eyes from the grape she was peeling, her lips starting to tremble.

"You . . . you're going to leave us, aren't you?" Cecily asked.

He yawned again and patted her head absentmindedly. "Just for a little while, darling."

"Oh, Dandor!" the brunette wailed. "Don't you love us?"

"Of course I do, but—"

"Dandor, please don't go," Cecily begged. "We'll do anything to make you happy!"

"I know," he said, getting to his feet and stretching. "You're both very sweet. But somehow I just feel drawn to—"

"Please stay," the brunette pleaded, falling at his feet. "We'll have a party with champagne. Any kind of pleasure you desire. We'll go get the other girls . . . I'll dance for you . . ."

"I'm sorry, Daphne," he said, finally remembering her name, "but you girls are beginning to seem unreal to me. And when that happens, I must go."

"But—" Cecily was crying so hard she could hardly get the words out—"when you leave us . . . it's a-almost . . . as th-though we were . . . turned off."

Her words saddened him a little because in a way it was true. When he left it was almost like turning them off. But true or not, he couldn't do anything about it because he felt himself being drawn irresistibly toward that other world.

He took one last look around at the incredible luxury of his palatial palace, at the beauty of his women and at the warm sun shining through the windows, and then he was gone.

The first thing he heard when he came out of the Imagicon was the howling of the wind and the first thing he felt was the numbing cold.

The next thing that assaulted his ears was the rasping screech of his wife's voice. "So you finally came out of it, did you?" Nona was yelling. "It's about time, you good-for-nothing little runt!"

So he was really back on Nestrond, back on the coldest hell of a colonial world in any universe. He had often thought that he would never return. But here he was . . . back on Nestrond and back with Nona.

"You've been gone long enough!" Nona said. She was a big, rawboned woman with stringy black hair, a broad, flat face with thin lips and uneven, yellowish teeth.

God but she's ugly, he thought as he stared at her. Beside her, Cecily and the others are goddesses.

"It's a good thing you got back 'cause the ice wolves is actin' up and we need frozen ice moss for the fire and . . ."

Dandor just stood there and listened as she went on with the long list of chores that needed doing. Why, he wondered, didn't she get one of her boy friends from down at the mines to do these things? He knew without being told that her lovers had been around while he was "gone." Nona was as faithless as she was ugly. And since there were twenty men to every woman on this planet, she had plenty of opportunity.

". . . and the cattleshed needs a new roof," she finished. When he didn't answer immediately, she thrust her face close to his. "Did you hear me? I said there's things to be done!"

"Yes, I heard you," he said.

"Then don't stand there like an idiot. Sit down and eat your breakfast and then get out and get to work!"

Breakfast was a thick, greasy piece of rancid pork and a bowl of lukewarm grits. Dandor choked on it but finally forced it down. Then he put on his thermal suit and furs and started for the door.

"Here, stupid!" Nona said, picking up a face mask from a pile of litter on the table and flinging it at him. "You want to freeze your nose off?"

He slapped the mask on quickly so she wouldn't see the anger on his face, opened the door and plunged out. The wind hit him in the face, hurling jagged ice crystals against his mask. Nestrond! My God, why Nestrond? He thought longingly of the comparative warmth of the cabin as he stared out at the bleak landscape. He thought of the black box that was the Imagicon. It sat in the one clear corner of the cabin and was the only way back to . . .

But no, he couldn't go back yet. There were too many things to be done here. So with an axe over his shoulder, he started across the frozen waste to the ancient peat bog where they cut their fuel.

All morning long, with the wind raging at him and the bitter cold making every breath an aching torment in his chest, he cut and stacked the frozen peat. Then when the pale yellow sun peeked through the clouds of ice crystals for a moment and he saw it was almost directly overhead, he tied up a large bundle of the brick-like slabs and hoisted it onto his shoulder for the trip back to the miserable huts of Nestrond.

Nona slapped a bowl of thin soup and a piece of stale bread down in front of him and called it lunch. He ate in silence and then went out behind the cabin to spend the afternoon digging the new cesspool.

This made the work of the morning seem like a rest cure. The ground had been frozen since Nestrond first started to roll around its inadequate sun. By evening, his back and legs and thighs ached tormentingly. With only a foot of ground excavated, he had to give up when night fell and staggered back toward the cabin with only one thought in mind . . . sleep.

The howl that wrenched him from his first troubled slumber seemed to come from the deepest pits of hell.

"Wha . . . what's that?" he asked.

"Ice wolves, you fool!" Nona screeched. "They're after the cattle-shed! Get out there and stop them!"

Dandor staggered to his feet and fumbled for his clothes as another howl rent the night. He reached for his laser rifle while Nona yelled again. "Hurry up! Those things can rip logs off a shed like it was kindlin'."

He was out the door then with flashlight in one hand and rifle in the other. He saw them at once. There were two of the six-legged terrors. One of them was raised up on its four back legs, its massive jaws ripping at the timber of the shed. Dandor could hear the terrified bellow of the cattle inside.

He ploughed through the snow toward the creature. It heard him and turned fiery red eyes in his direction. It kept on slashing at the logs for a second and then whirled and came at him in great leaping bounds.

Caught by surprise, he had no time to drop the flashlight and lift the laser rifle to fringe position. He had to fire from the hip and the beam caught the monster in the shoulder.

It wasn't good enough. He sidestepped as the huge body hurtled past him and then blasted its head off. Then he almost died himself as the decapitated thing went slithering through the snow, spurting blood everywhere. He almost died because for a split second he had forgotten its mate.

He remembered only when the creature struck him from behind and sent him sprawling on the frozen ground. The monstrous beast was on top of him and he screamed as a claw ripped flesh away from his thigh and the powerful jaws moved toward his throat.

The flashlight had been flung from his hand but the real rifle was still resting in its sling attached to his shoulder. He found the trigger and fired at full power. The laser beam tore off a leg and haunch of the ice wolf, and it fell away from him as he blasted it again. Then blackness closed in over him.

When he came to, he was lying on the table in the cabin. Nona and a strange man were bending over him.

"Well, you got yourself in a pretty mess this time!" Nona said as his eyes opened.

"That leg is going to have to come off," the stranger said.

"Are you a doctor?" Dandor asked in a husky croak.

"Only one this side of Alpha Centaury," the man said.

"The pain . . . can't you give me something for the pain?"

"I gave you the last morphine I had. Back on Earth we might have saved that leg, but here—" He made a helpless gesture.

White-hot flame seemed to envelop the slashed leg. Dandor winced and then saw the half smile on Nona's lips as she said, "With no more morphine or anything else, cutting off that leg is gonna hurt like hell, ain't it, Doc?"

"I got some whiskey in my car," the doctor said. "I'll go get it."

He went hobbling off, and Nona leaned over Dandor and looked into his eyes. "It's really gonna hurt, sweetie. It's gonna hurt like it hurt me all those times when you went off and left me. When you went off in your black box."

"No, Nona, no! It didn't hurt you. You're not—" He almost said she wasn't capable of being hurt. But he stopped, because he didn't know for sure if that were true.

"With only one leg, you're not gonna be able to get in that damn thing by yourself," she said. "You're gonna have to stay here and be nice to me."

"Nona!! No, you don't understand!" He started to plead with her, but then the doctor was back with a quart of whiskey and his black bag.

"Here, drink this fast," the man said, handing Dandor the bottle.

He drank deeply and quickly. But it didn't help much.

As the doctor cut and sawed, Dandor was sure his screams would burst his skull. At times he wondered why his curses didn't snap the straps that held him down or drive off the two tormentors bending over him.

"Well, I guess that's it," the doctor was saying when the agony dragged him up into consciousness again. "We're gonna have to cauterize this stump or he'll bleed to death. I ain't got nuthin' but fire to do it with either. Come help me heat up the poker, woman."

Dandor came fully awake as he caught the over-the-shoulder look Nona gave him and saw her eyes dart toward the Imagicon. It was almost as though she had said aloud, "You'll belong to me now . . . only to me. There won't be no more of that goin' off."

But she couldn't! How could she? Through the haze of morphine, alcohol and pain, Dandor tried to ask himself . . . why should she treat him this way? He couldn't think of any answer.

And as they hurried off to prepare the cauterizing iron for the bloody stump of his leg, the black coffin-like shape of the Imagicon filled his eyes and his mind.

If the pain hadn't already been more than reason could bear, he wouldn't have had the courage to roll off the table and begin crawling toward the black box, leaving a trail of blood behind him. The black box. Somehow he knew it represented a surcease from pain, a promise of ultimate safety.

He reached it without their being aware of his actions, and by making a supreme effort, he pulled himself up high enough to press his palm against the sensor that identified him instantly and was the only thing in this or any other universe that could open it.

He collapsed, more dead than alive, into the Imagicon and it closed silently over him.

Then there was a bright, warm world around him, and bright young faces above him.

"Oh, Dandor, darling! Darling," Cecily cried, putting her soft, warm arms around him.

"Sweetheart, you've come back!" Daphne whispered.

"We're so happy to see you!" the redheaded Terri murmured.

"We're so happy to see you!" her twin, Jerri, repeated.

"And I'm the happiest of all!" Dandor assured them, gazing down at his leg . . . at his perfectly whole, intact leg which felt no pain whatever. "Thank God! Thank God, I'm back!"

The Imagicon had worked! It had worked once again! It had taken him to the world of imagination and back again to reality . . . to wonderful, wonderful reality!

Dandor sat up and looked around at his own warm, marvelous world. It was the world of Earth in 22300, the world a hundred years after The Plague. The Plague which had attacked the male genes and reduced the male population to a few thousand and made each man the center of an eager and worshipful harem of women.

Many of the surviving men had not been able to stand the strain. Too many years of adoration, too many years of having everything and every woman they wanted had proved too much for them.

Then there had come the Imagicon, the invention that made any world a man desired seem absolutely real. Some men had used it to create even more exotic and wonderful worlds than the one they lived in, but that had been only more of a good thing and had made them more dissatisfied than ever.

Dandor had been wise. With his Imagicon, he had created an entirely different kind of world . . . a world of cold and terror called Nestrond. Dandor had known a great truth.

What good was paradise without something to compare it to? Without a taste of hell from time to time, how could a man appreciate heaven?

The science fiction writers of this world are resolutely different—from mankind and from each other—except that Philip K. Dick is more different. He goes his own way, writing his own kind of book, irrespective of changing moods and styles, true unto himself and his own inner vision. He produces steadily, but never badly, and won a well-deserved Hugo for his "Man in the High Castle." Here he is at his deep-probing best, keeping the reader on the run, exploring levels of consciousness and worrying—but worrying well—the SF worrying-tooth of "what is *reality?"*

WE CAN REMEMBER IT FOR YOU WHOLESALE

Philip K. Dick

He awoke—and wanted Mars. The valleys, he thought. What would it be like to trudge among them? Great and greater yet: the dream grew as he became fully conscious, the dream and the yearning. He could almost feel the enveloping presence of the other world, which only Government agents and high officials had seen. A clerk like himself? Not likely.

"Are you getting up or not?" his wife Kirsten asked drowsily, with her usual hint of fierce crossness. "If you are, push the hot coffee button on the darn stove."

"Okay," Douglas Quail said, and made his way barefoot from the bedroom of their conapt to the kitchen. There, having dutifully pressed the hot coffee button, he seated himself at the kitchen table, brought out a yellow, small tin of fine Dean Swift snuff. He inhaled briskly, and the Beau Nash mixture stung his nose, burned the roof of his mouth. But still he inhaled; it woke him up and allowed his dreams, his nocturnal desires and random wishes, to condense into a semblance of rationality.

I will go, he said to himself. Before I die I'll see Mars.

It was, of course, impossible, and he knew this even as he dreamed. But the daylight, the mundane noise of his wife now brushing her hair before the bedroom mirror—everything conspired to remind him of what he was. A miserable little salaried employee, he said to himself with bitterness. Kirsten reminded him of this at least once a day and he did not blame her; it was a wife's job to bring her husband down to Earth. Down to Earth, he thought, and laughed. The figure of speech in this was literally apt.

"What are you sniggering about?" his wife asked as she swept into the kitchen, her long busy-pink robe wagging after her. "A dream, I bet. You're always full of them."

"Yes," he said, and gazed out the kitchen window at the hovercars and traffic runnels, and all the little energetic people hurrying to work. In a little while he would be among them. As always.

"I'll bet it has to do with some woman," Kirsten said witheringly.

"No," he said. "A god. The god of war. He has wonderful craters with every kind of plant-life growing deep down in them."

"Listen." Kirsten crouched down beside him and spoke earnestly, the harsh quality momentarily gone from her voice. "The bottom of the ocean—*our* ocean is much more, an infinity of times more beautiful. You know that; everyone knows that. Rent an artificial gill-outfit for both of us, take a week off from work, and we can descend and live down there at one of those year-round aquatic resorts. And in addition—" She broke off. "You're not listening. You should be. Here is something a lot better than that compulsion, that obsession you have about Mars, and you don't even listen!" Her voice rose piercingly. "God in heaven, you're doomed, Doug! What's going to become of you?"

"I'm going to work," he said, rising to his feet, his breakfast forgotten. "That's what's going to become of me."

She eyed him. "You're getting worse. More fanatical every day. Where's it going to lead?"

"To Mars," he said, and opened the door to the closet to get down a fresh shirt to wear to work.

Having descended from the taxi Douglas Quail slowly walked across three densely-populated foot runnels and to the modern, attractively inviting doorway. There he halted, impeding mid-morning traffic, and with caution read the shifting-color neon sign. He had, in the past, scrutinized this sign before . . . but never had he come so close. This was very different; what he did now was something else. Something which sooner or later had to happen.

REKAL, INCORPORATED

Was this the answer? After all, an illusion, no matter how convincing, remained nothing more than an illusion. At least objectively. But subjectively—quite the opposite entirely.

And anyhow he had an appointment. Within the next five minutes.

Taking a deep breath of mildly smog-infested Chicago air, he walked through the dazzling poly-chromatic shimmer of the doorway and up to the receptionist's counter.

The nicely-articulated blonde at the counter, bare-bosomed and tidy, said pleasantly, "Good morning, Mr. Quail."

"Yes," he said. "I'm here to see about a Rekal course. As I guess you know."

"Not 'rekal' but *re*call," the receptionist corrected him. She picked up the receiver of the vidphone by her smooth elbow and said into it, "Mr. Douglas Quail is here, Mr. McClane. May he come inside, now? Or is it too soon?"

"Giz wetwa wum-wum wamp," the phone mumbled.

"Yes, Mr. Quail," she said. "You may go on in; Mr. McClane is expecting you." As he started off uncertainly she called after him, "Room D, Mr. Quail. To your right."

After a frustrating but brief moment of being lost he found the proper room. The door hung open and inside, at a big genuine walnut desk, sat a genial-looking man, middle-aged, wearing the latest Martian frog-pelt gray suit; his attire alone would have told Quail that he had come to the right person.

"Sit down, Douglas," McClane said, waving his plump hand toward a chair which faced the desk. "So you want to have gone to Mars. Very good."

Quail seated himself, feeling tense. "I'm not so sure this is worth the fee," he said. "It costs a lot and as far as I can see I really get nothing." Costs almost as much as going, he thought.

"You get tangible proof of your trip," McClane disagreed emphatically. "All the proof you'll need. Here; I'll show you." He dug within a drawer of his impressive desk. "Ticket stub." Reaching into a manila folder he produced a small square of embossed cardboard. "It proves you went—and returned. Postcards." He laid out four franked picture 3-D full-color postcards in a neatly-arranged row on the desk for Quail to see. "Film. Shots you took of local sights on Mars with a rented movie camera." To Quail he displayed those, too. "Plus the names of people you met, two hundred poscreds worth of souvenirs, which will arrive—from Mars—within the following month. And passport, certificates listing the shots you received. And more." He glanced up keenly at Quail. "You'll know you went, all right," he said. "You won't remember us, won't remember me or ever having been here. It'll be a real trip in your mind; we guarantee that. A full two weeks of recall; every last piddling detail. Remember this: if at any time you doubt that you really took an extensive trip to Mars you can return here and get a full refund. You see?"

"But I didn't go," Quail said. "I won't have gone, no matter what proofs you provide me with." He took a deep, unsteady breath. "And I never was a secret agent with Interplan." It seemed impossible to him that Rekal, Incorporated's extra-factual memory implant would do its job—despite what he had heard people say.

"Mr. Quail," McClane said patiently. "As you explained in your letter to us, you have no chance, no possibility in the slightest, of ever actually getting to Mars; you can't afford it, and what is much more important, you could never qualify as an undercover agent for Interplan or anybody else. This is the only way you can achieve your, ahem, life-long dream; am I not correct, sir? You can't be this; you can't actually do this." He chuckled. "But you can *have been* and *have done*. We see to that. And our fee is reasonable; no hidden charges." He smiled encouragingly.

"Is an extra-factual memory that convincing?" Quail asked.

"More than the real thing, sir. Had you really gone to Mars as an Interplan agent, you would by now have forgotten a great deal; our analysis of true-mem systems—authentic recollections of major events in a person's life—shows that a variety of details are very quickly lost to the person. Forever. Part of the package we offer you is such deep implantation of recall that nothing is forgotten. The packet which is fed to you while you're comatose is the creation of trained experts, men who have spent years on Mars; in every case we verify details down to the last iota. And you've picked a rather easy extra-factual system; had you picked Pluto or wanted to be Emperor of the Inner Planet Alliance we'd have much more difficulty . . . and the charges would be considerably greater."

Reaching into his coat for his wallet, Quail said, "Okay. It's been my life-long ambition and I can see I'll never really do it. So I guess I'll have to settle for this."

"Don't think of it that way," McClane said severely. "You're not accepting second-best. The actual memory, with all its vagueness, omissions and ellipses, not to say distortions—that's second-best." He accepted the money and pressed a button on his desk. "All right, Mr. Quail," he said, as the door of his office opened and two burly men swiftly entered. "You're on your way to Mars as a secret agent." He rose, came over to shake Quail's nervous, moist hand. "Or rather, you have been on your way. This afternoon at four-thirty you will, um, arrive back here on Terra; a cab will leave you off at your conapt and as I say you will never remember seeing me or coming here; you won't, in fact, even remember having heard of our existence."

His mouth dry with nervousness, Quail followed the two technicians from the office; what happened next depended on them.

Will I actually believe I've been on Mars? he wondered. That I managed to fulfill my lifetime ambition? He had a strange, lingering intuition that something would go wrong. But just what—he did not know.

He would have to wait to find out.

The intercom on McClane's desk, which connected him with the work area of the firm, buzzed and a voice said, "Mr. Quail is under sedation now, sir. Do you want to supervise this one, or shall we go ahead?"

"It's routine," McClane observed. "You may go ahead, Lowe; I don't think you'll run into any trouble." Programming an artificial memory of a trip to another planet—with or without the added fillip of being a secret agent—showed up on the firm's work-schedule with monotonous regularity. In one month, he calculated wryly, we must do twenty of these . . . ersatz interplanetary travel has become our bread and butter.

"Whatever you say, Mr. McClane," Lowe's voice came, and thereupon the intercom shut off.

Going to the vault section in the chamber behind his office, McClane searched about for a Three packet—trip to Mars—and a Sixty-two packet: secret Interplan spy. Finding the two packets, he returned with them to his desk, seated himself comfortably, poured out the contents—merchandise which would be planted in Quail's conapt while the lab technicians busied themselves installing the false memory.

A one-poscred sneaky-pete side arm, McClane reflected; that's the largest item. Sets us back financially the most. Then a pellet-sized transmitter, which could be swallowed if the agent were caught. Code book that astonishingly resembled the real thing . . . the firm's models were highly accurate: based, whenever possible, on actual U.S. military issue. Odd bits which made no intrinsic sense but which would be woven into the warp and woof of Quail's imaginary trip, would coincide with his memory: half an ancient silver fifty cent piece, several quotations from John Donne's sermons written incorrectly, each on a separate piece of transparent tissue-thin paper, several match folders from bars on Mars, a stainless steel spoon engraved PROPERTY OF DOME-MARS NATIONAL KIBBUZIM, a wire tapping coil which—

The intercom buzzed. "Mr. McClane, I'm sorry to bother you but something rather ominous has come up. Maybe it would be better if you were in here after all. Quail is already under sedation; he reacted well to the narkidrine; he's completely unconscious and receptive. But—"

"I'll be in." Sensing trouble, McClane left his office; a moment later he emerged in the work area.

On a hygienic bed lay Douglas Quail, breathing slowly and regularly, his eyes virtually shut; he seemed dimly—but only dimly—aware of the two technicians and now McClane himself.

"There's no space to insert false memory-patterns?" McClane felt irritation. "Merely drop out two work weeks; he's employed as a clerk at the West Coast Emigration Bureau, which is a government agency, so he undoubtedly has or had two weeks vacation within the last year. That ought to do it." Petty details annoyed him. And always would.

"Our problem," Lowe said sharply, "is something quite different." He bent over the bed, said to Quail, "Tell Mr. McClane what you told us." To McClane he said, "Listen closely."

The gray-green eyes of the man lying supine in the bed focussed on McClane's face. The eyes, he observed uneasily, had become hard; they had a polished, inorganic quality, like semi-precious tumbled stones. He was not sure that he liked what he saw; the brilliance was too cold. "What do you want now?" Quail said harshly. "You've broken my cover. Get out of here before I take you all apart." He studied McClane. "Especially you," he continued. "You're in charge of this counter-operation."

Lowe said, "How long were you on Mars?"

"One month," Quail said gratingly.

"And your purpose there?" Lowe demanded.

The meager lips twisted; Quail eyed him and did not speak. At last, drawling the words out so that they dripped with hostility, he said, "Agent for Interplan. As I already told you. Don't you record everything that's said? Play your vid-aud tape back for your boss and leave me alone." He shut his eyes, then; the hard brilliance ceased. McClane felt, instantly, a rushing splurge of relief.

Lowe said quietly, "This is a tough man, Mr. McClane."

"He won't be," McClane said, "after we arrange for him to lose his memory-chain again. He'll be as meek as before." To Quail he said, "So *this* is why you wanted to go to Mars so terribly badly."

Without opening his eyes Quail said, "I never wanted to go to Mars. I was assigned it—they handed it to me and there I was:

stuck. Oh yeah, I admit I was curious about it; who wouldn't be?" Again he opened his eyes and surveyed the three of them, McClane in particular. "Quite a truth drug you've got here; it brought up things I had absolutely no memory of." He pondered. "I wonder about Kirsten," he said, half to himself. "Could she be in on it? An Interplan contact keeping an eye on me . . . to be certain I didn't regain my memory? No wonder she's been so derisive about my wanting to go there." Faintly, he smiled; the smile—one of understanding—disappeared almost at once.

McClane said, "Please believe me, Mr. Quail; we stumbled onto this entirely by accident. In the work we do—"

"I believe you," Quail said. He seemed tired, now; the drug was continuing to pull him under, deeper and deeper. "Where did I say I'd been?" he murmured. "Mars? Hard to remember—I know I'd like to see it; so would everybody else. But me—" His voice trailed off. "Just a clerk, a nothing clerk."

Straightening up, Lowe said to his superior, "He wants a false memory implanted that corresponds to a trip he actually took. And a false reason which is the real reason. He's telling the truth; he's a long way down in the narkidrine. The trip is very vivid in his mind—at least under sedation. But apparently he doesn't recall it otherwise. Someone, probably at a government military-sciences lab, erased his conscious memories; all he knew was that going to Mars meant something special to him, and so did being a secret agent. They couldn't erase that; it's not a memory but a desire, undoubtedly the same one that motivated him to volunteer for the assignment in the first place."

The other technician, Keeler, said to McClane, "What do we do? Graft a false memory-pattern over the real memory? There's no telling what the results would be; he might remember some of the genuine trip, and the confusion might bring on a psychotic interlude. He'd have to hold two opposite premises in his mind simultaneously: that he went to Mars and that he didn't. That he's a genuine agent for Interplan and he's not, that it's spurious. I think we ought to revive him without any false memory implantation and send him out of here; this is hot."

"Agreed," McClane said. A thought came to him. "Can you predict what he'll remember when he comes out of sedation?"

"Impossible to tell," Lowe said. "He probably will have some dim, diffuse memory of his actual trip, now. And he'd probably be in grave doubt as to its validity; he'd probably decide our programming slipped a gear-tooth. And he'd remember coming here; that wouldn't be erased—unless you want it erased."

"The less we mess with this man," McClane said, "the better I like it. This is nothing for us to fool around with; we've been foolish enough to—or unlucky enough to—uncover a genuine Interplan spy who has a cover so perfect that up to now even he didn't know what he was—or rather is." The sooner they washed their hands of the man calling himself Douglas Quail the better.

"Are you going to plant packets Three and Sixty-two in his conapt?" Lowe said.

"No," McClane said. "And we're going to return half his fee."

"'Half'! Why half?"

McClane said lamely, "It seems to be a good compromise."

As the cab carried him back to his conapt at the residential end of Chicago, Douglas Quail said to himself, It's sure good to be back on Terra.

Already the month-long period on Mars had begun to waver in his memory; he had only an image of profound gaping craters, an ever-present ancient erosion of hills, of vitality, of motion itself. A world of dust where little happened, where a good part of the day was spent checking and rechecking one's portable oxygen source. And then the life forms, the unassuming and modest gray-brown cacti and maw-worms.

As a matter of fact he had brought back several moribund examples of Martian fauna; he had smuggled them through customs. After all, they posed no menace; they couldn't survive in Earth's heavy atmosphere.

Reaching into his coat pocket he rummaged for the container of Martian maw-worms—

And found an envelope instead.

Lifting it out he discovered, to his perplexity, that it contained five hundred and seventy poscreds, in 'cred bills of low denomination.

Where'd I get this? he asked himself. Didn't I spend every 'cred I had on my trip?

With the money came a slip of paper marked: *one-half fee ret'd. By McClane*. And then the date. Today's date.

"Recall," he said aloud.

"Recall what, sir or madam?" the robot driver of the cab inquired respectfully.

"Do you have a phone book?" Quail demanded.

"Certainly, sir or madam." A slot opened; from it slid a microtape phone book for Cook County.

"It's spelled oddly," Quail said as he leafed through the pages of the yellow section. He felt fear, then; abiding fear. "Here it is," he said. "Take me there, to Rekal, Incorporated. I've changed my mind; I don't want to go home."

"Yes sir, or madam, as the case may be," the driver said. A moment later the cab was zipping back in the opposite direction.

"May I make use of your phone?" he asked.

"Be my guest," the robot driver said. And presented a shiny new emperor 3-D color phone to him.

He dialed his own conapt. And after a pause found himself confronted by a miniature but chillingly realistic image of Kirsten on the small screen. "I've been to Mars," he said to her.

"You're drunk." Her lips writhed scornfully. "Or worse."

"'S god's truth."

"When?" she demanded.

"I don't know." He felt confused. "A simulated trip, I think. By means of one of those artificial or extra-factual or whatever it is memory places. It didn't take."

Kirsten said witheringly, "You *are* drunk." And broke the connection at her end. He hung up, then, feeling his face flush. Always the same tone, he said hotly to himself. Always the retort, as if she knows everything and I know nothing. What a marriage. Keerist, he thought dismally.

A moment later the cab stopped at the curb before a modern,

very attractive little pink building, over which a shifting, polychromatic neon sign read: REKAL, INCORPORATED.

The receptionist, chic and bare from the waist up, started in surprise, then gained masterful control of herself. "Oh hello Mr. Quail," she said nervously. "H-how are you? Did you forget something?"

"The rest of my fee back," he said.

More composed now the receptionist said, "Fee? I think you are mistaken, Mr. Quail. You were here discussing the feasibility of an extrafactual trip for you, but—" She shrugged her smooth pale shoulders. "As I understand it, no trip was taken."

Quail said, "I remember everything, miss. My letter to Rekal, Incorporated, which started this whole business off. I remember my arrival here, my visit with Mr. McClane. Then the two lab technicians taking me in tow and administering a drug to put me out." No wonder the firm had returned half his fee. The false memory of his "trip to Mars" hadn't taken—at least not entirely, not as he had been assured.

"Mr. Quail," the girl said, "although you are a minor clerk you are a good-looking man and it spoils your features to become angry. If it would make you feel any better, I might, ahem, let you take me out . . ."

He felt furious, then. "I remember you," he said savagely. "For instance the fact that your breasts are sprayed blue; that stuck in my mind. And I remember Mr. McClane's promise that if I remembered my visit to Rekal, Incorporated I'd receive my money back in full. Where is Mr. McClane?"

After a delay—probably as long as they could manage—he found himself once more seated facing the imposing walnut desk, exactly as he had been an hour or so earlier in the day.

"Some technique you have," Quail said sardonically. His disappointment—and resentment—were enormous, by now. "My so-called 'memory' of a trip to Mars as an undercover agent for Interplan is hazy and vague and shot full of contradictions. And I clearly remember my dealings here with you people. I ought to take this to the Better Business Bureau." He was burning angry, at this point; his sense of being cheated had overwhelmed him, had destroyed his customary aversion to participating in a public squabble.

Looking morose, as well as cautious, McClane said, "We capitulate, Quail. We'll refund the balance of your fee. I fully concede the fact that we did absolutely nothing for you." His tone was resigned.

Quail said accusingly, "You didn't even provide me with the various artifacts that you claimed would 'prove' to me I had been on Mars. All that song-and-dance you went into—it hasn't materialized into a damn thing. Not even a ticket stub. Nor postcards. Nor passport. Nor proof of immunization shots. Nor—"

"Listen, Quail," McClane said. "Suppose I told you—" He broke off. "Let it go." He pressed a button on his intercom. "Shirley, will you disburse five hundred and seventy more 'creds in the form of a cashier's check made out to Douglas Quail? Thank you." He released the button, then glared at Quail.

Presently the check appeared; the receptionist placed it before McClane and once more vanished out of sight, leaving the two men alone, still facing each other across the surface of the massive walnut desk.

"Let me give you a word of advice," McClane said as he signed the check and passed it over. "Don't discuss your, ahem, recent trip to Mars with anyone."

"What trip?"

"Well, that's the thing." Doggedly, McClane said, "The trip you partially remember. Act as if you don't remember; pretend it never took place. Don't ask me why; just take my advice: it'll be better for all of us." He had begun to perspire. Freely. "Now, Mr. Quail, I have other business, other clients to see." He rose, showed Quail to the door.

Quail said, as he opened the door, "A firm that turns out such bad work shouldn't have any clients at all." He shut the door behind him.

On the way home in the cab Quail pondered the wording of his letter of complaint to the Better Business Bureau, Terra Division. As soon as he could get to his typewriter he'd get started; it was clearly his duty to warn other people away from Rekal, Incorporated.

When he got back to his conapt he seated himself before his Hermes Rocket portable, opened the drawers and rummaged for carbon paper—and noticed a small, familiar box. A box which he had carefully filled on Mars with Martian fauna and later smuggled through customs.

Opening the box he saw, to his disbelief, six dead maw-worms and several varieties of the unicellular life on which the Martian worms fed. The protozoa were dried-up, dusty, but he recognized them; it had taken him an entire day picking among the vast dark alien boulders to find them. A wonderful, illuminated journey of discovery.

But I didn't go to Mars, he realized.

Yet on the other hand—

Kirsten appeared at the doorway to the room, an armload of pale brown groceries gripped. "Why are you home in the middle of the day?" Her voice, in an eternity of sameness, was accusing.

"*Did I go to Mars?*" he asked her. "You would know."

"No, of course you didn't go to Mars; *you* would know that, I would think. Aren't you always bleating about going?"

He said, "By God, I think I went." After a pause he added, "And simultaneously I think I didn't go."

"Make up your mind."

"How can I?" He gestured. "I have both memory-tracks grafted inside my head; one is real and one isn't but I can't tell which is which. Why can't I rely on you? They haven't tinkered with you." She could do this much for him at least—even if she never did anything else.

Kirsten said in a level, controlled voice, "Doug, if you don't pull yourself together, we're through. I'm going to leave you."

"I'm in trouble." His voice came out husky and coarse. And shaking. "Probably I'm heading into a psychotic episode; I hope not, but—maybe that's it. It would explain everything, anyhow."

Setting down the bag of groceries, Kirsten stalked to the closet. "I was not kidding," she said to him quietly. She brought out a coat, got it on, walked back to the door of the conapt. "I'll phone you one of these days soon," she said tonelessly. "This is goodbye, Doug. I hope you pull out of this eventually; I really pray you do. For your sake."

"Wait," he said desperately. "Just tell me and make it absolute;

I did go or I didn't—tell me which one." But they may have altered your memory-track also, he realized.

The door closed. His wife had left. Finally!

A voice behind him said, "Well, that's that. Now put up your hands, Quail. And also please turn around and face this way."

He turned, instinctively, without raising his hands.

The man who faced him wore the plum uniform of the Interplan Police Agency, and his gun appeared to be UN issue. And, for some odd reason, he seemed familiar to Quail; familiar in a blurred, distorted fashion which he could not pin down. So, jerkily, he raised his hands.

"You remember," the policeman said, "your trip to Mars. We know all your actions today and all your thoughts—in particular your very important thoughts on the trip home from Rekal, Incorporated." He explained, "We have a telep-transmitter wired within your skull; it keeps us constantly informed."

A telepathic transmitter; use of a living plasma that had been discovered on Luna. He shuddered with self-aversion. The thing lived inside him, within his own brain, feeding, listening, feeding. But the Interplan police used them; that had come out even in the homeopapes. So this was probably true, dismal as it was.

"Why me?" Quail said huskily. What had he done—or thought? And what did this have to do with Rekal, Incorporated?

"Fundamentally," the Interplan cop said, "this has nothing to do with Rekal; it's between you and us." He tapped his right ear. "I'm still picking up your mentational processes by way of your cephalic transmitter." In the man's ear Quail saw a small white-plastic plug. "So I have to warn you: anything you think may be held against you." He smiled. "Not that it matters now; you've already thought and spoken yourself into oblivion. What's annoying is the fact that under narkidrine at Rekal, Incorporated you told them, their technicians and the owner, Mr. McClane, about your trip; where you went, for whom, some of what you did. They're very frightened. They wish they had never laid eyes on you." He added reflectively, "They're right."

Quail said, "I never made any trip. It's a false memory-chain improperly planted in me by McClane's technicians." But then he thought of the box, in his desk drawer, containing the Martian life forms. And the trouble and hardship he had had gathering them. The memory seemed real. And the box of life forms; that certainly was real. Unless McClane had planted it. Perhaps this was one of the "proofs" which McClane had talked glibly about.

The memory of my trip to Mars, he thought, doesn't convince me—but unfortunately it has convinced the Interplan Police Agency. They think I really went to Mars and they think I at least partially realize it.

"We not only know you went to Mars," the Interplan cop agreed, in answer to his thoughts, "but we know that you now remember enough to be difficult for us. And there's no use expunging your conscious memory of all this, because if we do you'll simply show up at Rekal, Incorporated again and start over. And we can't do anything about McClane and his operation because we have no jurisdiction over anyone except our own people. Anyhow, McClane hasn't committed any crime." He eyed Quail. "Nor, technically, have you. You didn't go to Rekal, Incorporated with the idea of regaining your memory; you went, as we realize, for the usual reason people go there—a love by plain, dull people for adventure." He added, "Unfortunately you're not plain, not dull, and you've already had too much excitement; the last thing in the universe you needed was a course from Rekal, Incorporated. Nothing could have been more lethal for you or for us. And, for that matter, for McClane."

Quail said, "Why is it 'difficult' for you if I remember my trip—my alleged trip—and what I did there?"

"Because," the Interplan harness bull said, "what you did is not in accord with our great white all-protecting father public image. You did, for us, what we never do. As you'll presently remember—thanks to narkidrine. That box of dead worms and algae has been sitting in your desk drawer for six months, ever since you got back. And at no time have you shown the slightest curiosity about it. We didn't even know you had it until you remembered it on your way home from Rekal; then we came here on the double to look for it." He added, unnecessarily, "Without any luck; there wasn't enough time."

A second Interplan cop joined the first one; the two briefly conferred. Meanwhile, Quail thought rapidly. He did remember more, now; the cop had been right about narkidrine. They—Interplan—probably used it themselves. Probably? He knew darn well they did; he had seen them putting a prisoner on it. Where would *that* be? Somewhere on Terra? More likely Luna, he decided, viewing the image rising from his highly defective—but rapidly less so—memory.

And he remembered something else. Their reason for sending him to Mars; the job he had done.

No wonder they had expunged his memory.

"Oh god," the first of the two Interplan cops said, breaking off his conversation with his companion. Obviously, he had picked up Quail's thoughts. "Well, this is a far worse problem, now; as bad as it can get." He walked toward Quail, again covering him with his gun. "We've got to kill you," he said. "And right away."

Nervously, his fellow officer said, "Why right away? Can't we simply cart him off to Interplan New York and let them—"

"*He* knows why it has to be right away," the first cop said; he too looked nervous, now, but Quail realized that it was for an entirely different reason. His memory had been brought back almost entirely, now. And he fully understood the officer's tension.

"On Mars," Quail said hoarsely, "I killed a man. After getting past fifteen bodyguards. Some armed with sneaky-pete guns, the way you are." He had been trained, by Interplan, over a five year period to be an assassin. A professional killer. He knew ways to take out armed adversaries . . . such as these two officers; and the one with the ear-receiver knew it, too.

If he moved swiftly enough—

The gun fired. But he had already moved to one side, and at the same time he chopped down the gun-carrying officer. In an instant he had possession of the gun and was covering the other, confused, officer.

"Picked my thoughts up," Quail said, panting for breath. "He knew what I was going to do, but I did it anyhow."

Half sitting up, the injured officer grated, "He won't use that gun on you, Sam; I pick that up, too. He knows he's finished, and he knows we know it, too. Come on, Quail." Laboriously, grunting with pain, he got shakily to his feet. He held out his hand. "The gun," he said to Quail. "You can't use it, and if you turn it over to me I'll guarantee not to kill you; you'll be given a hearing, and someone higher up in Interplan will decide, not me. Maybe they can erase your memory once more; I don't know. But you know the thing I was going to kill you for; I couldn't keep you from remembering it. So my reason for wanting to kill you is in a sense past."

Quail, clutching the gun, bolted from the conapt, sprinted for the elevator. If you follow me, he thought, I'll kill you. So don't. He jabbed at the elevator button and, a moment later, the doors slid back.

The police hadn't followed him. Obviously they had picked up his terse, tense thoughts and had decided not to take the chance.

With him inside the elevator descended. He had gotten away—for a time. But what next? Where could he go?

The elevator reached the ground floor; a moment later Quail had joined the mob of peds hurrying along the runnels. His head ached and he felt sick. But at least he had evaded death; they had come very close to shooting him on the spot, back in his own conapt.

And they probably will again, he decided. When they find me. And with this transmitter inside me, that won't take too long.

Ironically, he had gotten exactly what he had asked Rekal, Incorporated for. Adventure, peril, Interplan police at work, a secret and dangerous trip to Mars in which his life was at stake—everything he had wanted as a false memory.

The advantages of it being a memory—and nothing more—could now be appreciated.

On a park bench, alone, he sat dully watching a flock of perts: a semi-bird imported from Mars' two moons, capable of soaring flight, even against Earth's huge gravity.

Maybe I can find my way back to Mars, he pondered. But then what? It would be worse on Mars; the political organization whose leader he had assassinated would spot him the moment he stepped from the ship; he would have Interplan and *them* after him, there.

Can you hear me thinking? he wondered. Easy avenue to paranoia; sitting here alone he felt them tuning in on him, monitoring, recording, discussing . . . he shivered, rose to his feet, walked aimlessly, his hands deep in his pockets. No matter where I go, he realized. You'll always be with me. As long as I have this device inside my head.

I'll make a deal with you, he thought to himself—and to them. Can't you imprint a false-memory template on me again, as you did before, that I lived an average, routine life, never went to Mars? Never saw an Interplan uniform up close and never handled a gun?

A voice inside his brain answered, "As has been carefully explained to you: that would not be enough."

Astonished, he halted.

"We formerly communicated with you in this manner," the voice continued. "When you were operating in the field, on Mars. It's been months since we've done it; we assumed, in fact, that we'd never have to do so again. Where are you?"

"Walking," Quail said, "to my death." By your officers' guns, he added as an afterthought. "How can you be sure it wouldn't be enough?" he demanded. "Don't the Rekal techniques work?"

"As we said. If you're given a set of standard, average memories you get—restless. You'd inevitably seek out Rekal or one of its competitors again. We can't go through this a second time."

"Suppose," Quail said, "once my authentic memories have been cancelled, something more vital than standard memories are implanted. Something which would act to satisfy my craving," he said. "That's been proved; that's probably why you initially hired me. But you ought to be able to come up with something else—something equal. I was the richest man on Terra but I finally gave all my money to educational foundations. Or I was a famous deep-space explorer. Anything of that sort; wouldn't one of those do?"

Silence.

"Try it," he said desperately. "Get some of your top-notch military psychiatrists; explore my mind. Find out what my most expansive daydream is." He tried to think. "Women," he said. "Thousands of them, like Don Juan had. An interplanetary playboy—a mistress in every city on Earth, Luna and Mars. Only I gave that up, out of exhaustion. Please," he begged. "Try it."

"You'd voluntarily surrender, then?" the voice inside his head asked. "If we agreed to arrange such a solution? *If* it's possible?"

After an interval of hesitation he said, "Yes." I'll take the risk, he said to himself. That you don't simply kill me.

"You make the first move," the voice said presently. "Turn yourself over to us. And we'll investigate that line of possibility. If we can't do it, however, if your authentic memories begin to crop up again as they've done at this time, then—" There was silence and then the voice finished, "We'll have to destroy you. As you must understand. Well, Quail, you still want to try?"

"Yes," he said. Because the alternative was death now—and for certain. At least this way he had a chance, slim as it was.

"You present yourself at our main barracks in New York," the voice of the Interplan cop resumed. "At 580 Fifth Avenue, floor twelve. Once you've surrendered yourself we'll have our psychiatrists begin on you; we'll have personality-profile tests made. We'll attempt to determine your absolute, ultimate fantasy wish—and then we'll bring you back to Rekal, Incorporated, here; get them in on it, fulfilling that wish in vicarious surrogate retrospection. And—good luck. We do owe you something; you acted as a capable instrument for us." The voice lacked malice; if anything, they—the organization—felt sympathy toward him.

"Thanks," Quail said. And began searching for a robot cab.

"Mr. Quail," the stern-faced, elderly Interplan psychiatrist said, "you possess a most interesting wish-fulfillment dream fantasy. Probably nothing such as you consciously entertain or suppose. This is commonly the way; I hope it won't upset you too much to hear about it."

The senior ranking Interplan officer present said briskly, "He better not be too much upset to hear about it, not if he expects not to get shot."

"Unlike the fantasy of wanting to be an Interplan undercover agent," the psychiatrist continued, "which, being relatively speaking a product of maturity, had a certain plausibility to it, this production is a grotesque dream of your childhood; it is no wonder you fail to recall it. Your fantasy is this: you are nine years old, walking alone down a rustic lane. An unfamiliar variety of space vessel from another star system lands directly in front of you. No one on Earth but you, Mr. Quail, sees it. The creatures within are very small and helpless, somewhat on the order of field mice, although they are attempting to invade Earth; tens of thousands of other such ships will soon be on their way, when this advance party gives the go-ahead signal."

"And I suppose I stop them," Quail said, experiencing a mixture of amusement and disgust. "Single-handed I wipe them out. Probably by stepping on them with my foot."

"No," the psychiatrist said patiently. "You halt the invasion, but not by destroying them. Instead, you show them kindness and mercy, even though by telepathy—their mode of communication—you know why they have come. They have never seen such humane traits exhibited by any sentient organism, and to show their appreciation they make a covenant with you."

Quail said, "They won't invade Earth as long as I'm alive."

"Exactly." To the Interplan officer the psychiatrist said, "You can see it does fit his personality, despite his feigned scorn."

"So by merely existing," Quail said, feeling a growing pleasure, "by simply being alive, I keep Earth safe from alien rule. I'm in effect, then, the most important person on Terra. Without lifting a finger."

"Yes indeed, sir," the psychiatrist said. "And this is bedrock in your psyche; this is a life-long childhood fantasy. Which, without depth and drug therapy, you never would have recalled. But it has always existed in you; it went underneath, but never ceased."

To McClane, who sat intently listening, the senior police official said, "Can you implant an extra-factual memory pattern that extreme in him?"

"We get handed every possible type of wish-fantasy there is," McClane said. "Frankly, I've heard a lot worse than this. Certainly we can handle it. Twenty-four hours from now he won't just *wish* he'd saved Earth; he'll devoutly believe it really happened."

The senior police official said, "You can start the job, then. In preparation we've already once again erased the memory in him of his trip to Mars."

Quail said, "What trip to Mars?"

No one answered him, so, reluctantly, he shelved the question.

And anyhow a police vehicle had now put in its appearance; he, McClane and the senior police officer crowded into it, and presently they were on their way to Chicago and Rekal, Incorporated.

"You had better make no errors this time," the police officer said to heavy-set, nervous-looking McClane.

"I can't see what could go wrong," McClane mumbled, perspiring. "This has nothing to do with Mars or Interplan. Single-handedly stopping an invasion of Earth from another star-system." He shook his head at that. "Wow, what a kid dreams up. And by pious virtue, too; not by force. It's sort of quaint." He dabbed at his forehead with a large linen pocket handkerchief.

Nobody said anything.

"In fact," McClane said, "it's touching."

"But arrogant," the police official said starkly. "Inasmuch as when he dies the invasion will resume. No wonder he doesn't recall it; it's the most grandiose fantasy I ever ran across." He eyed Quail with disapproval. "And to think we put this man on our payroll."

When they reached Rekal, Incorporated the receptionist, Shirley, met them breathlessly in the outer office. "Welcome back, Mr. Quail," she fluttered, her melon-shaped breasts—today painted an incandescent orange—bobbing with agitation. "I'm sorry everything worked out so badly before; I'm sure this time it'll go better."

Still repeatedly dabbing at his shiny forehead with his neatly-folded Irish linen handkerchief, McClane said, "It better." Moving with rapidity he rounded up Lowe and Keeler, escorted them and Douglas Quail to the work area, and then, with Shirley and the senior police officer, returned to his familiar office. To wait.

"Do we have a packet made up for this, Mr. McClane?" Shirley asked, bumping against him in her agitation, then coloring modestly.

"I think we do." He tried to recall; then gave up and consulted the formal chart. "A combination," he decided aloud, "of packets Eighty-one, Twenty, and Six." From the vault section of the chamber behind his desk he fished out the appropriate packets, carried them to his desk for inspection. "From Eighty-one," he explained, "a magic healing rod given him—the client in question, this time Mr. Quail—by the race of beings from another system. A token of their gratitude."

"Does it work?" the police officer asked curiously.

"It did once," McClane explained. "But he, ahem, you see, used it up years ago, healing right and left. Now it's only a memento. But he remembers it working spectacularly." He chuckled, then opened packet Twenty. "Document from the UN Secretary General thanking him for saving Earth; this isn't precisely appropriate, because part of Quail's fantasy is that no one knows of the invasion except himself, but for the sake of verisimilitude we'll throw it in." He inspected packet Six, then. What came from this? He couldn't recall; frowning, he dug into the plastic bag as Shirley and the Interplan police officer watched intently.

"Writing," Shirley said. "In a funny language."

"This tells who they were," McClane said, "and where they came from. Including a detailed star map logging their flight here and the system of origin. Of course it's in *their* script, so he can't read it. But he remembers them reading it to him in his own tongue." He placed the three artifacts in the center of the desk. "These should be taken to Quail's conapt," he said to the police officer. "So that when he gets home he'll find them. And it'll confirm his fantasy. SOP—standard operating procedure." He chuckled apprehensively, wondering how matters were going with Lowe and Keeler.

The intercom buzzed. "Mr. McClane, I'm sorry to bother you." It was Lowe's voice; he froze as he recognized it, froze and became mute. "But something's come up. Maybe it would be better if you came in here and supervised. Like before, Quail reacted well to the narkidrine; he's unconscious, relaxed and receptive. But—"

McClane sprinted for the work area.

On a hygienic bed Douglas Quail lay breathing slowly and regularly, eyes half-shut, dimly conscious of those around him.

"We started interrogating him," Lowe said, white-faced. "To find out exactly when to place the fantasy-memory of him single-handedly having saved Earth. And strangely enough—"

"They told me not to tell," Douglas Quail mumbled in a dull drug-saturated voice. "That was the agreement. I wasn't even supposed to remember. But how could I forget an event like that?"

I guess it would be hard, McClane reflected. But you did—until now.

"They even gave me a scroll," Quail mumbled, "of gratitude. I have it hidden in my conapt; I'll show it to you."

To the Interplan officer who had followed after him, McClane said, "Well, I offer the suggestion that you better not kill him. If you do they'll return."

"They also gave me a magic invisible destroying rod," Quail mumbled, eyes totally shut, now. "That's how I killed that man on Mars you sent me to take out. It's in my drawer along with the box of Martian maw-worms and dried-up plant life."

Wordlessly, the Interplan officer turned and stalked from the work area.

I might as well put those packets of proof-artifacts away, McClane said to himself resignedly. He walked, step by step, back to his office. Including the citation from the UN Secretary General. After all—

The real one probably would not be long in coming.

One of the editors of this volume does not know that this story is going into it. There has been collusion in high places. The President of SFWA, Damon Knight, and the other editor have overruled in advance any complaints that Brian W. Aldiss might make. This story was one of three that tied for the Best Short Story award and is, in its own right, a fine piece of fiction. Here is art, in the interweaving of idea and dialog, and here is something vital being said about the human condition. It has earned its place in this book.

H.H.

MAN IN HIS TIME

Brian W. Aldiss

His absence

Janet Westermark sat watching the three men in the office: the administrator who was about to go out of her life, the behaviourist who was about to come into it, and the husband whose life ran parallel to but insulated from her own.

She was not the only one playing a watching game. The behaviourist, whose name was Clement Stackpole, sat hunched in his chair with his ugly strong hands clasped round his knee, thrusting his intelligent and simian face forward, the better to regard his new subject, Jack Westermark.

The administrator of the Mental Research Hospital spoke in a lively and engaged way. Typically, it was only Jack Westermark who seemed absent from the scene.

Your particular problem, restless

His hands upon his lap lay still, but he himself was restless, though the restlessness seemed directed. It was as if he were in another room with other people, Janet thought. She saw that he caught her eye when in fact she was not entirely looking at him, and by the time she returned the glance, he was gone, withdrawn.

"Although Mr. Stackpole has not dealt before with your particular problem," the administrator was saying, "he has had plenty of field experience. I know——"

"I'm sure we won't," Westermark said, folding his hands and nodding his head slightly.

Smoothly, the administrator made a pencilled note of the remark, scribbled the precise time beside it, and continued, "I know Mr. Stackpole is too modest to say this, but he is a great man for working in with people——"

"If you feel it's necessary," Westermark said. "Though I've seen enough of your equipment for a while."

The pencil moved, the smooth voice proceeded. "Good. A great man for working in with people, and I'm sure you and Mr. Westermark will soon find you are glad to have him around. Remember, he's there to help both of you."

Janet smiled, and said from the island of her chair, trying to smile at him and Stackpole, "I'm sure that everything will work——" She was interrupted by her husband, who rose to his feet, letting his hands drop to his sides and saying, turning slightly to address thin air, "Do you mind if I say good-bye to Nurse Simmons?"

Her voice no longer wavered

"Everything will be all right, I'm sure," she said hastily. And Stackpole nodded at her, conspiratorially agreeing to see her point of view.

"We'll all get on fine, Janet," he said. She was in the swift process of digesting that unexpected use of her Christian name, and the administrator was also giving her the sort of encouraging smile so many people had fed her since Westermark was pulled out of the ocean off Casablanca, when her husband, still having his lonely conversation with the air, said, "Of course, I should have remembered."

His right hand went half way to his forehead—or his heart? Janet wondered—and then dropped, as he added, "Perhaps she'll come round and see us some time." Now he turned and was smiling faintly at another vacant space with just the faintest nod of his head, as if slightly cajoling. "You'd like that, wouldn't you, Janet?"

She moved her head, instinctively trying to bring her eyes into his gaze as she replied vaguely, "Of course, darling." Her voice no longer wavered when she addressed his absent attention.

There was sunlight through which they could see each other

There was sunlight in one corner of the room, coming through the windows of a bay angled towards the sun. For a moment she caught, as she rose to her feet, her husband's profile with the sunlight behind it. It was thin and withdrawn. Intelligent: she had always thought him over-burdened with his intelligence, but now there was a lost look there, and she thought of the words of a psychiatrist who had been called in on the case earlier: "You must understand that the waking brain is perpetually lapped by the unconscious."

Lapped by the unconscious

Fighting the words away, she said, addressing the smile of the administrator—that smile which must have advanced his career so much—"You've helped me a lot. I couldn't have got through these months without you. Now we'd better go."

She heard herself chopping her words, fearing Westermark would talk across them, as he did: "Thank you for your help. If you find anything . . ."

Stackpole walked modestly over to Janet as the administrator rose and said, "Well, don't either of you forget us if you're in any kind of trouble."

"I'm sure we won't."

"And, Jack, we'd like you to come back here to visit us once a month for a personal check-up. Don't want to waste all our expensive equipment, you know, and you are our star—er, patient." He smiled rather tightly as he said it, glancing at the paper on his desk to check Westermark's answer. Westermark's back was already turned on him, Westermark was already walking slowly to the door, Westermark had said his good-byes, perched out on the lonely eminence of his existence.

Janet looked helplessly, before she could guard against it, at the administrator and Stackpole. She hated it that they were too professional to take note of what seemed her husband's breach of conduct. Stackpole looked kindly in a monkey way and took her arm with one of his thick hands.

"Shall we be off then? My car's waiting outside."

Not saying anything, nodding, thinking, and consulting watches

She nodded, not saying anything, thinking only, without the need of the administrator's notes to think it, "Oh yes, this was when he said, 'Do you mind if I say good-bye to Nurse'—who's-it?—Simpson?" She was learning to follow her husband's footprints across the broken path of conversation. He was now out in the corridor, the door swinging to behind him, and to empty air the administrator was saying, "It's her day off today."

"You're good on your cues," she said, feeling the hand tighten on her arm. She politely brushed his fingers away, horrid Stackpole, trying to recall what had gone only four minutes before. Jack had said something to her; she couldn't remember, didn't speak, avoided eyes, put out her hand and shook the administrator's firmly.

"Thanks," she said.

"Au revoir to both of you," he replied firmly, glancing swiftly: watch, notes, her, the door. "Of course," he said. "If we find anything at all. We are very hopeful. . . ."

He adjusted his tie, looking at the watch again.

"Your husband has gone now, Mrs. Westermark," he said, his manner softening. He walked towards the door with her and added,

"You have been wonderfully brave, and I do realise—we all realise—that you will have to go on being wonderful. With time, it should be easier for you; doesn't Shakespeare say in Hamlet that 'Use almost can change the stamp of nature'? May I suggest that you follow Stackpole's and my example and keep a little notebook and a strict check on the time?"

They saw her tiny hesitation, stood about her, two men round a personable woman, not entirely innocent of relish. Stackpole cleared his throat, smiled, said, "He can so easily feel cut off you know. It's essential that you of all people answer his questions, or he will feel cut off."

Always a pace ahead

"The children?" she asked.

"Let's see you and Jack well settled in at home again, say for a fortnight or so," the administrator said, "before we think about having the children back to see him."

"That way's better for them and Jack *and* you, Janet," Stackpole said. 'Don't be glib,' she thought; 'consolation I need, God knows, but that's too facile.' She turned her face away, fearing it looked too vulnerable these days.

In the corridor, the administrator said, as valediction, "I'm sure Grandma's spoiling them terribly, Mrs. Westermark, but worrying won't mend it, as the old saw says."

She smiled at him and walked quickly away, a pace ahead of Stackpole.

Westermark sat in the back of the car outside the administrative block. She climbed in beside him. As she did so, he jerked violently back in his seat.

"Darling, what is it?" she asked. He said nothing.

Stackpole had not emerged from the building, evidently having a last word with the administrator. Janet took the moment to lean over and kiss her husband's cheek, aware as she did so that a phantom wife had already, from his viewpoint, done so. His response was a phantom to her.

"The countryside looks green," he said. His eyes were flickering over the grey concrete block opposite.

"Yes," she said.

Stackpole came bustling down the steps, apologising as he opened the car door, settled in. He let the clutch back too fast and they shot forward. Janet saw then the reason for Westermark's jerking backwards a short while before. Now the acceleration caught him again; his body was rolled helplessly back. As they drove along, he set one hand fiercely on the side grip, for his sway was not properly counterbalancing the movement of the car.

Once outside the grounds of the institute, they were in the country, still under a mid-August day.

His theories

Westermark, by concentrating, could bring himself to conform to some of the laws of the time continuum he had left. When the car he was in climbed up his drive (familiar, yet strange with the rhododendrons unclipped and no signs of children) and stopped by the front door, he sat in his seat for three and a half minutes before venturing to open his door. Then he climbed out and stood on the gravel, frowning down at it. Was it as real as ever, as material? Was there a slight glaze on it?—as if something shone through from the interior of the earth, shone through all things? Or was it that there was a screen between him and everything else? It was important to decide between the two theories, for he had to live under the discipline of one. What he hoped to prove was that the permeation theory was correct; that way he was merely one of the factors comprising the functioning universe, together with the rest of humanity. By the glaze theory, he was isolated not only from the rest of humanity but from the entire cosmos (except Mars?). It was early days yet; he had a deal of thinking to do, and new ideas would undoubtedly emerge after observation and cogitation. Emotion must not decide the issue; he must be detached. Revolutionary theories could well emerge from this—suffering.

He could see his wife by him, standing off in case they happened embarrassingly or painfully to collide. He smiled thinly at her through her glaze. He said, "I am, but I'd prefer not to talk." He stepped towards the house, noting the slippery feel of gravel that would not move under his tread until the world caught up. He said, "I've every respect for *The Guardian,* but I'd prefer not to talk at present."

Famous Astronaut Returns Home

As the party arrived, a man waited in the porch for them, ambushing Westermark's return home with a deprecatory smile. Hesitant but business-like, he came forward and looked interrogatively at the three people who had emerged from the car.

"Excuse me, you are Captain Jack Westermark, aren't you?"

He stood aside as Westermark seemed to make straight for him. "I'm the psychology correspondent for *The Guardian,* if I might intrude for a moment."

Westermark's mother had opened the front door and stood there smiling welcome at him, one hand nervously up to her grey hair. Her son walked past her. The newspaper man stared after him.

Janet told him apologetically, "You'll have to excuse us. My husband did reply to you, but he's really not prepared to meet people yet."

"*When* did he reply, Mrs. Westermark? Before he heard what I had to say?"

"Well, naturally not—but his life stream. . . . I'm sorry, I can't explain."

"He really is living ahead of time, isn't he? Will you spare me a minute to tell me how you feel now the first shock is over?"

"You really must excuse me," Janet said, brushing past him. As she followed her husband into the house, she heard Stackpole say, "Actually, I read *The Guardian,* and perhaps I could help you. The Institute has given me the job of remaining with Captain Westermark. My name's Clement Stackpole—you may know my book, *Persistent Human Relations,* Methuen. But you must not say that Westermark is living ahead of time. That's quite incorrect. What you can say is that some of his psychological and physiological processes have somehow been transposed forward——"

"Ass!" she exclaimed to herself. She had paused by the threshold to catch some of his words. Now she whisked in.

Talk hanging in the air among the long watches of supper

Supper that evening had its discomforts, although Janet Westermark and her mother-in-law achieved an air of melancholy gaiety by bringing two Scandinavian candelabra, relics of a Copenhagen holiday, onto the table and surprising the two men with a gay-looking hors d'œuvre. But the conversation was mainly like the hors d'œuvre, Janet thought: little tempting isolated bits of talk, not nourishing.

Mrs. Westermark senior had not yet got the hang of talking to her son, and confined her remarks to Janet, though she looked towards Jack often enough. "How are the children?" he asked her. Flustered by the knowledge that he was waiting a long while for her answer, she replied rather incoherently and dropped her knife.

To relieve the tension, Janet was cooking up a remark on the character of the administrator at the Mental Research Hospital, when Westermark said, "Then he is at once thoughtful and literate. Commendable and rare in men of his type. I got the impression, as you evidently did, that he was as interested in his job as in advancement. I suppose one might say one even *liked* him. But you know him better, Stackpole; what do you think of him?"

Crumbling bread to cover his ignorance of whom they were supposed to be conversing, Stackpole said, "Oh, I don't know; it's hard to say really," spinning out time, pretending not to squint at his watch.

"The administrator was quite a charmer, didn't you think, Jack?" Janet remarked—perhaps helping Stackpole as much as Jack.

"He looks as if he might make a slow bowler," Westermark said, with an intonation that suggested he was agreeing with something as yet unsaid.

"Oh, *him*!" Stackpole said. "Yes, he seems a satisfactory sort of chap on the whole."

"He quoted Shakespeare to me and thoughtfully told me where the quotation came from," Janet said.

"No thank you, Mother," Westermark said.

"I don't have much to do with him," Stackpole continued. "Though I have played cricket with him a time or two. He makes quite a good slow bowler."

"Are you really?" Westermark exclaimed.

That stopped them. Jack's mother looked helplessly about, caught her son's glazed eye, said, covering up, "Do have some more sauce, Jack, dear," recalled she had already had her answer, almost let her knife slide again, gave up trying to eat.

"I'm a batsman, myself," Stackpole said, as if bringing an old pneumatic drill to the new silence. When no answer came, he doggedly went on, expounding on the game, the pleasure of it. Janet sat and watched, a shade perplexed that she was admiring Stackpole's performance and wondering at her slight perplexity; then she decided that she had made up her mind to dislike Stackpole, and immediately dissolved the resolution. Was he not on their side? And even the strong hairy hands became a little more acceptable when you thought of them gripping the rubber of a bat handle; and the broad shoulders swinging. . . . She closed her eyes momentarily, and tried to concentrate on what he was saying.

A batsman himself

Later, she met Stackpole on the upper landing. He had a small cigar in his mouth, she had two pillows in her arms. He stood in her way.

"Can I help at all, Janet?"

"I'm only making up a bed, Mr. Stackpole."

"Are you not sleeping in with your husband?"

"He would like to be on his own for a night or two, Mr. Stackpole. I shall sleep in the children's room for the time being."

"Then please permit me to carry the pillows for you. And do please call me Clem. All my friends do."

Trying to be pleasanter, to unfreeze, to recall that Jack was not moving her out of the bedroom permanently, she said, "I'm sorry. It's just that we once had a terrier called Clem." But it did not sound as she had wished it to do.

He put the pillows on Peter's blue bed, switched on the bedside lamp, and sat on the edge of the bed, clutching his cigar and puffing at it.

"This may be a bit embarrassing, but there's something I feel I should say to you, Janet." He did not look at her. She brought him an ashtray and stood by him.

"We feel your husband's mental health may be endangered, although I hasten to assure you that he shows no signs of losing his mental equilibrium beyond what we may call an inordinate absorption in phenomena—and even there, we cannot say, of course we can't, that his absorption is any greater than one might expect. Except in the totally unprecedented circumstances, I mean. We must talk about this in the next few days."

She waited for him to go on, not unamused by the play with the cigar. Then he looked straight up at her and said, "Frankly, Mrs. Westermark, we think it would help your husband if you could have sexual relations with him."

A little taken aback, she said, "Can you imagine——" Correcting herself, she said, "That is for my husband to say. I am not unapproachable."

She saw he had caught her slip. Playing a very straight bat, he said, "I'm sure you're not, Mrs. Westermark."

With the light out, living, she lay in Peter's bed

She lay in Peter's bed with the light out. Certainly she wanted him: pretty badly, now she allowed herself to dwell on it. During the long months of the Mars expedition, while she had stayed at home and he had got farther from home, while he actually had existence on that other planet, she had been chaste. She had looked after the children and driven round the countryside and enjoyed writing those articles for women's magazines and being interviewed on TV when the ship was reported to have left Mars on its homeward journey. She had been, in part, dormant.

Then came the news, kept from her at first, that there was confusion in communicating with the returning ship. A sensational tabloid broke the secrecy by declaring that the nine-man crew had all gone mad. And the ship had overshot its landing area, crashing into the Atlantic. Her first reaction had been a purely selfish one—no, not selfish, but from the self: He'll never lie with me again. And infinite love and sorrow.

At his rescue, the only survivor, miraculously unmaimed, her hope had revived. Since then, it had remained embalmed, as he was embalmed in time. She tried to visualise love as it would be now, with everything happening first to him, before she had begun to—— With his movement of pleasure even before she—— No, it wasn't possible! But of course it was, if they worked it out first intellectually; then if she just lay flat. . . . But what she was trying to visualise, all she could visualise, was not love-making, merely a formal prostration to the exigencies of glands and time flow.

She sat up in bed, longing for movement, freedom. She jumped out and opened the lower window; there was still a tang of cigar smoke in the dark room.

If they worked it out intellectually

Within a couple of days, they had fallen into routine. It was as if the calm weather, perpetuating mildness, aided them. They had to be careful to move slowly through doors, keeping to the left, so as not to bump into each other—a tray of drinks was dropped before they agreed on that. They devised simple knocking systems before using the bathroom. They conversed in bulletins that did not ask questions unless questions were necessary. They walked slightly apart. In short, they made detours round each other's lives.

"It's really quite easy as long as one is careful," Mrs. Westermark senior said to Janet. "And dear Jack is *so* patient!"

"I even get the feeling he likes the situation."

"Oh, my dear, how could he *like* such an unfortunate predicament?"

"Mother, you realise how we all exist together, don't you? No, it sounds too terrible—I daren't say it."

"Now don't you start getting silly ideas. You've been very brave, and this is not the time for us to be getting upset, just as things are going well. If you have any worries, you must tell Clem. That's what he's here for."

"I know."

"Well then."

She saw Jack walk in the garden. As she looked, he glanced up, smiled, said something to himself, stretched out a hand, withdrew it, and went, still smiling, to sit on one end of the seat on the lawn. Touched, Janet hurried over to the french windows, to go and join him.

She paused. Already, she saw ahead, saw her sequence of actions, for Jack had already sketched them into the future. She would go onto the lawn, call his name, smile, and walk over to him when he smiled back. Then they would stroll together to the seat and sit down, one at each end.

The knowledge drained all spontaneity from her. She might have been working a treadmill, for what she was about to do had already been done as far as Jack was concerned, with his head's start in time. Then if she did not go, if she mutinied, turned back to the discussion of the day's chores with her mother-in-law. . . . That left Jack mouthing like a fool on the lawn, indulging in a fantasy there was no penetrating. Let him do that, let Stackpole see; then they could drop this theory about Jack's being ahead of time and would have to treat him for a more normal sort of hallucinatory insanity. He would be safe in Clem's hands.

But Jack's actions proved that she would go out there. It was insane for her not to go out there. Insane? To disobey a law of the universe was impossible, not insane. Jack was not disobeying—he had simply tumbled over a law that nobody knew was there before the first expedition to Mars; certainly they had discovered something more momentous than anyone had expected, and more unforeseen. And she had lost—— No, she hadn't lost yet! She ran out onto the lawn, calling to him, letting the action quell the confusion in her mind.

And in the repeated event there was concealed a little freshness, for she remembered how his smile, glimpsed through the window, had held a special warmth, as if he sought to reassure her. What had he said? That was lost. She walked over to the seat and sat beside him.

He had been saving a remark for the statutory and unvarying time lapse.

"Don't worry, Janet," he said. "It could be worse."

"How?" she asked, but he was already answering: "We could be a day apart. 3.3077 minutes at least allows us a measure of communication."

"It's wonderful how philosophical you are about it," she said. She was alarmed at the sarcasm in her tone.

"Shall we have a talk together now?"

"Jack, I've been wanting to have a private talk with you for some time."

"I?"

The tall beeches that sheltered the garden on the north side were so still that she thought, "They will look exactly the same for him as for me."

He delivered a bulletin, looking at his watch. His wrists were thin. He appeared frailer than he had done when they left hospital. "I am aware, my darling, how painful this must be for you. We are both isolated from the other by this amazing shift of temporal function, but at least I have the consolation of experiencing the new phenomenon, whereas you—"

"I?"

Talking of interstellar distances

"I was going to say that you are stuck with the same old world all of mankind has always known, but I suppose you don't see it that way." Evidently a remark of hers had caught up with him, for he added inconsequentially, "I've wanted a private talk with you."

Janet bit off something she was going to say, for he raised a finger irritably and said, "Please time your statements, so that we do not talk at cross purposes. Confine what you have to say to essentials.

Really, darling, I'm surprised you don't do as Clem suggests, and make notes of what is said at what time."

"That—I just wanted—we can't act as if we were a board meeting. I want to know your feelings, how you are, what you are thinking, so that I can help you, so that eventually you will be able to live a normal life again."

He was timing it so that he answered almost at once, "I am not suffering from any mental illness, and I have completely recovered my physical health after the crash. There is no reason to foresee that my perceptions will ever lapse back into phase with yours. They have remained an unfluctuating 3.3077 minutes ahead of terrestrial time ever since our ship left the surface of Mars."

He paused. She thought, 'It is now about 11.03 by my watch, and there is so much I long to say. But it's 11.06 and a bit by *his* time, and he already knows I can't say anything. It's such an effort of endurance, talking across this three and a bit minutes; we might just as well be talking across an interstellar distance.'

Evidently he too had lost the thread of the exercise, for he smiled and stretched out a hand, holding it in the air. Janet looked round. Clem Stackpole was coming out towards them with a tray full of drinks. He set it carefully down on the lawn, and picked up a martini, the stem of which he slipped between Jack's fingers.

"Cheers!" he said, smiling, and, "Here's your tipple," giving Janet her gin and tonic. He had brought himself a bottle of pale ale.

"Can you make my position clearer to Janet, Clem? She does *not* seem to understand it yet."

Angrily, she turned to the behaviourist. "This was meant to be a private talk, Mr. Stackpole, between my husband and myself."

"Sorry you're not getting on too well, then. Perhaps I can help sort you out a bit. It is difficult, I know."

3.3077

Powerfully, he wrenched the top off the beer bottle and poured the liquid into the glass. Sipping, he said, "We have always been used to the idea that everything moves forward in time at the same rate. We speak of the course of time, presuming it only has one rate of flow. We've assumed, too, that anything living on another planet in any other part of our universe might have the same rate of flow. In other words, although we've long been accustomed to some oddities of time, thanks to relativity theories, we have accustomed ourselves, perhaps, to certain errors of thinking. Now we're going to have to think differently. You follow me."

"Perfectly."

"The universe is by no means the simple box our predecessors imagined. It may be that each planet is encased in its own time field, just as it is in its own gravitational field. From the evidence, it seems that Mars's time field is 3.3077 minutes ahead of ours on Earth. We deduce this from the fact that your husband and the eight other men with him on Mars experienced no sensation of temporal difference among themselves, and were unaware that anything was untoward until they were away from Mars and attempted to get into communication again with Earth, when the temporal discrepancy at once showed up. Your husband is still living in Mars time. Unfortunately, the other members of the crew did not survive the crash; but we can be sure that if they did, they too would suffer from the same effect. That's clear, isn't it?"

"Entirely. But I still cannot see why this effect, if it is as you say—"

"It's not what *I* say, Janet, but the conclusion arrived at by much cleverer men than I." He smiled as he said that, adding parenthetically, "Not that we don't develop and even alter our conclusions every day."

"Then why was a similar effect not noticed when the Russians and Americans returned from the moon?"

"We don't know. There's so much we don't know. We *surmise* that because the moon is a satellite of Earth's, and thus within its gravitational field, there is no temporal discrepancy. But until we have more data, until we can explore further, we know so little, and can only speculate so much. It's like trying to estimate the runs of an entire innings when only one over has been bowled. After the expedition gets back from Venus, we shall be in a much better position to start theorising."

"*What* expedition to Venus?" she asked, shocked.

"It may not leave for a year yet, but they're speeding up the programme. That will bring us really invaluable data."

Future time with its uses and abuses

She started to say, "But after this surely they won't be fool enough——" Then she stopped. She knew they would be fool enough. She thought of Peter saying, "I'm going to be a spaceman too. *I* want to be the first man on Saturn!"

The men were looking at their watches. Westermark transferred his gaze to the gravel to say, "This figure of 3.3077 is surely not a universal constant. It may vary—I think it will vary—from planetary body to planetary body. My private opinion is that it is bound to be connected with solar activity in some way. If that is so, then we may find that the men returning from Venus will be perceiving on a continuum slightly in arrears of Earth time."

He stood up suddenly, looking dismayed, the absorption gone from his face.

"That's a point that hadn't occurred to me," Stackpole said, making a note. "If the expedition to Venus is primed with these points beforehand, we should have no trouble about organising their return. Ultimately, this confusion will be sorted out, and I've no doubt that it will eventually vastly enrich the culture of mankind. The possibilities are of such enormity that . . ."

"It's awful! You're all crazy!" Janet exclaimed. She jumped up and hurried off towards the house.

Or then again

Jack began to move after her towards the house. By his watch, which showed Earth time, it was 11.18 and twelve seconds; he thought, not the first time, that he would invest in another watch, which would be strapped to his right wrist and show Martian time. No, the one on his left wrist should show Martian time, for that was the wrist he principally consulted and the time by which he lived, even when going through the business of communicating with the earth-bound human race.

He realised he was now moving ahead of Janet, by her reckoning. It would be interesting to have someone ahead of *him* in perception; then he would wish to converse, would want to go to the labour of it. Although it would rob him of the sensation that he was perpetually first in the universe, first everywhere, with everything dewy in that strange light—Marslight! He'd call it that, till he had it classified, the romantic vision preceding the scientific, with a touch of the grand permissible before the steadying discipline closed in. Or then again, suppose they were wrong in their theories, and the perceptual effect was some freak of the long space journey itself; supposing time were quantal. . . . Supposing *all* time were quantal. After all, ageing was a matter of steps, not a smooth progress, for much of the inorganic world as for the organic.

Now he was standing quite still on the lawn. The glaze was coming through the grass, making it look brittle, almost tingeing each blade with a tiny spectrum of light. If his perceptual time were further ahead than it was now, would the Marslight be stronger, the Earth more translucent? How beautiful it would look! After a longer star journey one would return to a cobweb of a world, centuries behind one in perceptual time, a mere embodiment of light, a prism. Hungrily, he visualised it. But they needed more knowledge.

Suddenly he thought, 'If I could get on the Venus expedition! If the Institute's right, I'd be perhaps six, say five and a half—no, one can't say—but I'd be ahead of Venerean time. I *must* go. I'd be valuable to them. I only have to volunteer, surely.'

He did not notice Stackpole touch his arm in cordial fashion and go past him into the house. He stood looking at the ground and through it, to the stoney vales of Mars and the unguessable landscapes of Venus.

The figures move

Janet had consented to ride into town with Stackpole. He was collecting his cricket shoes, which had been restudded; she thought she might buy a roll of film for her camera. The children would like photos of her and Daddy together. Standing together.

As the car ran beside trees, their shadows flickered red and green before her vision. Stackpole held the wheel very capably, whistling under his breath. Strangely, she did not resent a habit she would normally have found irksome, taking it as a sign that he was not entirely at his ease.

"I have an awful feeling you now understand my husband better than I do," she said.

He did not deny it. "Why do you feel that?"

"I believe he does not mind the terrible isolation he must be experiencing."

"He's a brave man."

Westermark had been home a week now. Janet saw that each day they were more removed from each other, as he spoke less and stood frequently as still as a statue, gazing at the ground raptly. She thought of something she had once been afraid to utter aloud to her mother-in-law; but with Clem Stackpole she was safer.

"You know why we manage to exist in comparative harmony," she said. He was slowing the car, half-looking at her. "We only manage to exist by banishing all events from our lives, all children, all seasons. Otherwise we'd be faced at every moment with the knowledge of how much at odds we really are."

Catching the note in her voice, Stackpole said soothingly, "You are every bit as brave as he is, Janet."

"Damn being brave. What I can't bear is—nothing!"

Seeing the sign by the side of the road, Stackpole glanced into his driving mirror and changed gear. The road was deserted in front as well as behind. He whistled through his teeth again, and Janet felt compelled to go on talking.

"We've already interfered with time too much—all of us, I mean. Time is a European invention. Goodness knows how mixed up in it we are going to get if—well, if this goes on." She was irritated by the lack of her usual coherence.

As Stackpole spoke next, he was pulling the car into a lay-by, stopping it by overhanging bushes. He turned to her, smiling tolerantly. "Time was God's invention, if you believe in God, as I prefer to do. We observe it, tame it, exploit it where possible."

"Exploit it!"

"You mustn't think of the future as if we were all wading knee deep in treacle or something." He laughed briefly, resting his hands on the steering wheel. "What lovely weather it is! I was wondering —on Sunday I'm playing cricket over in the village. Would you like to come and watch the match? And perhaps we could have tea somewhere afterwards."

All events, all children, all seasons

She had a letter next morning from Jane, her five-year-old daughter, and it made her think. All the letter said was: "Dear Mummy, Thank you for the dollies. With love from Jane," but Janet knew the labour that had gone into the inch-high letters. How long could she bear to leave the children away from their home and her care?

As soon as the thought emerged, she recalled that during the previous evening she had told herself nebulously that if there was going to be 'anything' with Stackpole, it was as well the children would be out of the way—purely, she now realised, for her convenience and for Stackpole's. She had not thought then about the children; she had thought about Stackpole who, despite the unexpected delicacy he had shown, was not a man she cared for.

'And another intolerably immoral thought,' she muttered unhappily to the empty room, 'what alternative have I to Stackpole?'

She knew Westermark was in his study. It was a cold day, too cold and damp for him to make his daily parade round the garden. She knew he was sinking deeper into isolation, she longed to help, she feared to sacrifice herself to that isolation, longed to stay outside it, in life. Dropping the letter, she held her head in her hands, closing her eyes as in the curved bone of her skull she heard all her possible courses of action jar together, future lifelines that annihilated each other.

As Janet stood transfixed, Westermark's mother came into the room.

"I was looking for you," she said. "You're so unhappy, my dear, aren't you?"

"Mother, people always try and hide from others how they suffer. Does everyone do it?"

"You don't have to hide it from me—chiefly, I suppose, because you can't."

"But I don't know how much *you* suffer, and it ought to work both ways. Why do we do this awful covering up? What are we afraid of—pity or derision?"

"Help, perhaps."

"Help! Perhaps you're right. . . . That's a disconcerting thought."

They stood there staring at each other, until the older woman said, awkwardly, "We don't often talk like this, Janet."

"No." She wanted to say more. To a stranger in a train, perhaps she would have done; here, she could not deliver.

Seeing nothing more was to be said on that subject, Mrs. Westermark said, "I was going to tell you, Janet, that I thought perhaps it would be better if the children didn't come back here while things are as they are. If you want to go and see them and stay with them at your parents' house, I can look after Jack and Mr. Stackpole for a week. I don't think Jack wants to see them."

"That's very kind, Mother. I'll see. I promised Clem—well, I told Mr. Stackpole that perhaps I'd go and watch him play cricket tomorrow afternoon. It's not important, of course, but I did say—anyhow, I might drive over and see the children on Monday, if you could hold the fort."

"You've still plenty of time if you feel like going today. I'm sure Mr. Stackpole will understand your maternal feelings."

"I'd prefer to leave it till Monday," Janet said—a little distantly, for she suspected now the motive behind her mother-in-law's suggestion.

Where the Scientific American *did not reach*

Jack Westermark put down the *Scientific American* and stared at the table top. With his right hand, he felt the beat of his heart. In the magazine was an article about him, illustrated with photographs of him taken at the Research Hospital. This thoughtful article was far removed from the sensational pieces that had appeared elsewhere, the shallow things that referred to him as The Man That Has Done More Than Einstein To Wreck Our Cosmic Picture; and for that very reason it was the more startling, and presented some aspects of the matter that Westermark himself had not considered.

As he thought over its conclusions, he rested from the effort of reading terrestrial books, and Stackpole sat by the fire, smoking a cigar and waiting to take Westermark's dictation. Even reading a magazine represented a feat in space-time, a collaboration, a conspiracy. Stackpole turned the pages at timed intervals, Westermark read when they lay flat. He was unable to turn them when, in their own narrow continuum, they were not being turned; to his fingers, they lay under the jelly-like glaze, that visual hallucination that represented an unconquerable cosmic inertia.

The inertia gave a special shine to the surface of the table as he stared into it and probed into his own mind to determine the truths of the *Scientific American* article.

The writer of the article began by considering the facts and observing that they tended to point towards the existence of 'local times' throughout the universe; and that if this were so, a new explanation might be forthcoming for the recession of the galaxies and different estimates arrived at for the age of the universe (and of course for its complexity). He then proceeded to deal with the problem that vexed other writers on the subject; namely, why, if Westermark lost Earth time on Mars, he had not reciprocally lost Mars time back on Earth. This, more than anything, pointed to the fact that 'local times' were not purely mechanistic but to some extent at least a psycho-biological function.

In the table top, Westermark saw himself being asked to travel again to Mars, to take part in a second expedition to those continents of russet sand where the fabric of space-time was in some mysterious and insuperable fashion 3.3077 minutes ahead of Earth norm. Would his interior clock leap forward again? What then of the sheen on things earthly? And what would be the effect of gradually drawing away from the iron laws under which, since its scampering pleistocene infancy, humankind had lived?

Impatiently he thrust his mind forward to imagine the day when Earth harboured many local times, gleaned from voyages across the vacancies of space; those vacancies lay across time, too, and that little-understood concept (McTaggart had denied its external reality, hadn't he?) would come to lie within the grasp of man's understanding. Wasn't that the ultimate secret, to be able to understand the flux in which existence is staged, as a dream is staged in the primitive reaches of the mind?

And—— But—— Would not that day bring the annihilation of Earth's local time? That was what he had started. It could only mean that 'local time' was not a product of planetary elements; there the writer of the *Scientific American* article had not dared to go far enough; local time was entirely a product of the psyche. That dark innermost thing that could keep accurate time even while a man lay unconscious was a mere provincial; but it could be educated to be a citizen of the universe. He saw that he was the first of a new race, unimaginable in the wildest mind a few months previously. He was independent of the enemy that, more than Death, menaced contemporary man: Time. Locked within him was an entirely new potential. Superman had arrived.

Painfully, Superman stirred in his seat. He sat so wrapt for so long that his limbs grew stiff and dead without his noticing it.

Universal thoughts may occur if one times carefully enough one's circumbendibus about a given table

"Dictation," he said, and waited impatiently until the command had penetrated backwards to the limbo by the fire where Stackpole sat. What he had to say was so terribly important—yet it had to wait on these people. . . .

As was his custom, he rose and began to walk round the table, speaking in phrases quickly delivered. This was to be the testament to the new way of life. . . .

"Consciousness is not expendable but concurrent. . . . There may have been many time nodes at the beginning of the human race. . . . The mentally deranged often revert to different time rates. For some, a day seems to stretch on for ever. . . . We know by experience that for children time is seen in the convex mirror of consciousness, enlarged and distorted beyond its focal point. . . ." He was momentarily irritated by the scared face of his wife appearing outside the study window, but he brushed it away and continued.

". . . its focal point. . . . Yet man in his ignorance has persisted in pretending time was some sort of uni-directional flow, and homogenous at that . . . despite the evidence to the contrary. . . . Our conception of ourselves—no, this erroneous conception has become a basic life assumption. . . ."

Daughters of daughters

Westermark's mother was not given to metaphysical speculation, but as she was leaving the room, she turned and said to her daughter-in-law, "You know what I sometimes think? Jack is so strange, I wonder at nights if men and women aren't getting more and more apart in thought and in their ways with every generation—you know, almost like separate species. My generation made a great attempt to bring the two sexes together in equality and all the rest, but it seems to have come to nothing."

"Jack will get better." Janet could hear the lack of confidence in her own voice.

"I thought the same thing—about men and women getting wider apart I mean—when my husband was killed."

Suddenly all Janet's sympathy was gone. She had recognised a familiar topic drifting onto the scene, knew well the careful tone that ironed away all self-pity as her mother-in-law said, "Bob was dedicated to speed, you know. That was what killed him really, not the fool backing into the road in front of him."

"No blame was attached to your husband," Janet said. "You should try not to let it worry you still."

"You see the connection though. . . . This progress thing. Bob so crazy to get round the next bend first, and now Jack. . . . Oh well, there's nothing a woman can do."

She closed the door behind her. Absently, Janet picked up the message from the next generation of women: "Thank you for the dollies."

The resolves and the sudden risks involved

He was their father. Perhaps Jane and Peter should come back, despite the risks involved. Anxiously, Janet stood there, moving herself with a sudden resolve to tackle Jack straight away. He was so irritable, so unapproachable, but at least she could observe how busy he was before interrupting him.

As she slipped into the side hall and made for the back door, she heard her mother-in-law call her. "Just a minute!" she answered.

The sun had broken through, sucking moisture from the damp garden. It was now unmistakably autumn. She rounded the corner of the house, stepped round the rose bed, and looked into her husband's study.

Shaken, she saw he leaned half over the table. His hands were over his face, blood ran between his fingers and dripped onto an open magazine on the table top. She was aware of Stackpole sitting indifferently beside the electric fire.

She gave a small cry and ran round the house again, to be met at the back door by Mrs. Westermark.

"Oh, I was just—— Janet, what is it?"

"Jack, Mother! He's had a stroke or something terrible!"

"But how do you know?"

"Quick, we must phone the hospital—I must go to him."

Mrs. Westermark took Janet's arm. "Perhaps we'd better leave it to Mr. Stackpole, hadn't we? I'm afraid——"

"Mother, we must do what we can. I know we're amateurs. Please let me go."

"No, Janet, we're—it's *their* world. I'm frightened. They'll come if they want us." She was gripping Janet in her fright. Their wild eyes stared momentarily at each other as if seeing something else, and then Janet snatched herself away. "I must go to him," she said.

She hurried down the hall and pushed open the study door. Her husband stood now at the far end of the room by the window, while blood streamed from his nose.

"Jack!" she exclaimed. As she ran towards him, a blow from the empty air struck her on the forehead, so that she staggered aside, falling against a bookcase. A shower of smaller volumes from the upper shelf fell on her and round her. Exclaiming, Stackpole dropped his notebook and ran round the table to her. Even as he went to her aid, he noted the time from his watch: 10.24.

Aid after 10.24 and the tidiness of bed

Westermark's mother appeared in the doorway.

"Stay where you are," Stackpole shouted, "or there will be more trouble! Janet, you see what you've done. Get out of here, will you? Jack, I'm right with you—God knows what you've felt, isolated without aid for three and a third minutes!" Angrily, he went across and stood within arm's length of his patient. He threw his handkerchief down onto the table.

"Mr. Stackpole——" Westermark's mother said tentatively from the door, an arm round Janet's waist.

He looked back over his shoulder only long enough to say, "Get towels! Phone the Research Hospital for an ambulance and tell them to be here right away."

By midday, Westermark was tidily in bed upstairs and the ambulance staff, who had treated him for what after all was only nosebleed, had left. Stackpole, as he turned from closing the front door, eyed the two women.

"I feel it is my duty to warn you," he said heavily, "that another incident such as this might well prove fatal. This time we escaped very lightly. If anything else of this sort happens, I shall feel obliged to recommend to the board that Mr. Westermark is moved back to the hospital."

Current way to define accidents

"He wouldn't want to go," Janet said. "Besides, you are being absurd; it was entirely an accident. Now I wish to go upstairs and see how he is."

"Just before you go, may I point out that what happened was *not* an accident—or not as we generally define accidents, since you saw the results of your interference through the study window before you entered. Where you were to blame——"

"But that's absurd——" both women began at once. Janet went on to say, "I never would have rushed into the room as I did had I not seen through the window that he was in trouble."

"What you saw was the result on your husband of your later interference."

In something like a wail, Westermark's mother said, "I don't understand any of this. What did Janet bump into when she ran in?"

"She ran, Mrs. Westermark, into the spot where her husband had been standing 3.3077 minutes earlier. Surely by now you have grasped this elementary business of time inertia?"

When they both started speaking at once, he stared at them until they stopped and looked at him. Then he said, "We had better go into the living room. Speaking for myself, I would like a drink."

He helped himself, and not until his hand was round a glass of whisky did he say, "Now, without wishing to lecture to you ladies, I think it is high time you both realised that you are not living in the old safe world of classical mechanics ruled over by a god invented by eighteenth-century enlightenment. All that has happened here is perfectly rational, but if you are going to pretend it is beyond your female understandings——"

"Mr. Stackpole," Janet said sharply. "Can you please keep to the point without being insulting? Will you tell me why what happened was not an accident? I understand now that when I looked through the study window I saw my husband suffering from a collision that to him had happened three and something minutes before and to me would not happen for another three and something minutes, but at that moment I was so startled that I forgot——"

"No, no, your figures are wrong. The *total* time lapse is only 3.3077 minutes. When you saw your husband, he had been hit half that time–1.65385 minutes–ago, and there was another 1.65385 minutes to go before you completed the action by bursting into the room and striking him."

"But she *didn't* strike him!" the older woman cried.

Firmly, Stackpole diverted his attention long enough to reply. "She struck him at 10.24 Earthtime, which equals 10.20 plus about

36 seconds Mars or his time, which equals 9.59 or whatever Neptune time, which equals 156 and a half Sirius time. It's a big universe, Mrs. Westermark! You will remain confused as long as you continue to confuse event with time. May I suggest you sit down and have a drink?"

"Leaving aside the figures," Janet said, returning to the attack—loathsome opportunist the man was—"how can you say that what happened was no accident? You are not claiming I injured my husband deliberately, I hope? What you say suggests that I was powerless from the moment I saw him through the window."

"'Leaving aside the figures . . .'" he quoted. "That's where your responsibility lies. What you saw through the window was the result of your act; it was by then inevitable that you should complete it, for it had already been completed."

Through the window, draughts of time blow

"I can't understand!" she clutched her forehead, gratefully accepting a cigarette from her mother-in-law, while shrugging off her consolatory 'Don't try to understand, dear!' "Supposing when I had seen Jack's nose bleeding, I had looked at my watch and thought, 'It's 10.20 or whenever it was, and he may be suffering from my interference, so I'd better not go in,' and I *hadn't* gone in? Would his nose then miraculously have healed?"

"Of course not. You take such a mechanistic view of the universe. Cultivate a mental approach, try and live in your own century! You could not think what you suggest because that is not in your nature: just as it is not in your nature to consult your watch intelligently, just as you always 'leave aside the figures', as you say. No, I'm not being personal; it's all very feminine and appealing in a way. What I'm saying is that if *before* you looked into the window you had been a person to think, 'However I see my husband now, I must recall he has the additional experience of the next 3.3077 minutes', then you could have looked in and seen him unharmed, and you would not have come bursting in as you did."

She drew on her cigarette, baffled and hurt. "You're saying I'm a danger to my own husband."

"*You're* saying that."

"God, how I hate men!" she exclaimed. "You're so bloody logical, so bloody smug!"

He finished his whisky and set the glass down on a table beside her so that he leant close. "You're upset just now," he said.

"Of course I'm upset! What do you think?" She fought a desire to cry or slap his face. She turned to Jack's mother, who gently took her wrist.

"Why don't you go off straight away and stay with the children for the weekend, darling? Come back when you feel like it. Jack will be all right and I can look after him—as much as he wants looking after."

She glanced about the room.

"I will. I'll pack right away. They'll be glad to see me." As she passed Stackpole on the way out, she said bitterly, "At least *they* won't be worrying about the local time on Sirius!"

"They may," said Stackpole, imperturbably from the middle of the room, "have to one day."

All events, all children, all seasons

AFTERWORD

THE YEAR IN SF

I believe that sf attracts the more imaginative, inquiring child, the type who can make a success in the scientific field. God knows we need that type.

Dr. JULES T. SIMON, U. S. Atomic Energy Commission

It was definitely the year of the book in 1966. One speciality book dealer, the F. and S.F. Book Co., informed us that he had to work overtime to fill his orders and that he looked forward to an even better year ahead. There were approximately 319 science fiction books published during this twelve-month period; of this number, seventy-three were hardbound and 241 were paperback books. Doubleday and Company led the hardbound publishers with twenty-six books, and Ace Books topped the other paperback houses with seventy-two titles.

These figures are not entirely accurate; as soon as you look at them closely they begin to shimmer and change. Though the publishers were co-operation itself, it proved immensely difficult to track down all of the publishers. Many of the titles, once discovered, proved to be in that shadowy borderland of "but is it science fiction?". Should we include the *Doc Savage* books from Bantam—even though the editors of Bantam themselves do not consider the bronze man's heroic exploits to be SF? And what about that mysterious paperback firm of Corinth who published 48 titles in 1966 that they dredged up from the old pulps, names to bring a tear to the middle-aged eye: *Phantom Detective, Operator No. 5, Dusty Ayres*? Are they SF? In the light of this, we present the above figures as being about as science-fictional as the works under discussion and, in essence, a partly personal conclusion.

So much for quantity—what about quality? Here we are on firmer ground and, in two men's opinions, the books seemed far superior to the short stories, an observation which we shall examine in some detail in a moment. Perhaps one reason for the superiority of the novel is the remarkable vitality of well-liked works of SF. Some of these books, though beaten to death with critical crowbars, annually assemble their scattered bones and spattered blood and rise from the grave born anew. E. E. Smith, Ph.D. ("Doc" to his friends and fans —and the world, since this is the title his publishers now label him with on their covers) began writing his Lensman saga a longish time ago; the oldest volume was copyrighted in 1937, and he produced a good half million words about his hero before he finished. Pyramid Books have seen fit to bring out a complete edition of all of the volumes this year (*Triplanetary, First Lensman, Galactic Patrol, Gray Lensman, Second Stage Lensman, Children of the Lens*), and they must have their reasons. Perhaps it is possible to agree with the critic who argues that, after the opening sentence, "Two thousand million or so years ago two galaxies were colliding," we are in for six volumes of anticlimax, and, at the same time, to remain fascinated by Doc's work—the longest of the hard-core SF sagas. This was fine stuff in the golden days of our youth, and it still remains fresh in a rather charming and wooden way, and must certainly produce some feeling of satisfaction in the youngsters of today.

Not quite as hoary, but certainly as enduring, is the Foundation series by Isaac Asimov, also a Ph.D., though he misses being referred to as "Doc" on his covers. If anything proves that magazine and paperback readers are essentially two different groups, the publication of this series does. For years beyond counting the Science Fiction Book Club has been enticing new members with the offer of this trilogy for the sum of 10¢. Avon, ignoring this with enthusiastic disdain, have elected to publish *Foundation, Second Foundation,* and *Foundation and Empire* in three volumes in a new edition for a total sum of $1.80. It is to be assumed that they know what they are doing, for they did it also with James Blish's Cities in Flight—the

Okies—series. Once more in *They Shall Have Stars, Life for the Stars, Earthman, Come Home* and *The Triumph of Time* the spindizzies whine and the cities fly off to the far reaches of the galaxy. Heady stuff this, and all three series certainly deserve some place in a scientifictional hall of fame, not only for their intrinsic interest but certainly for their durability.

Good science fiction wears well, that is obvious; though it is immensely difficult to find out in just what ratio new and old books appear. The situation is complex, to say the least. To take an example: one major paperback publisher released twenty-two titles during the year, thirteen of these were new books—and of this number three were first books—while five were reprints of hardbound volumes. The remaining four were reissues of earlier titles. To further confuse the situation, some of the new books were anthologies of previously published stories and the reissues had new covers to entice old readers.

In addition to good old books, a number of good new books were published. We do not pretend impartiality or completeness, other than the complete statement that the following titles impressed and left their mark and memory behind them. The following list is, can only be, partial and partisan.

Who Can Replace a Man? by Brian W. Aldiss (Harcourt, Brace and World) The original English title of this book was *The Best Science Fiction Stories of Brian W. Aldiss,* and that is most descriptive. These stories compare favorably with any written in the English language and are a landmark of some kind in SF which has, for the most part, been long on idea but very short on literary quality. The author has combined both qualities in a number of masterful short stories that can be unconditionally recommended. (Harcourt, Brace and World)

John W. Campbell: *Collected Editorials from Analog;* Selected by Harry Harrison. One of the must-buys of the year. From the shower of sermons rattling from the Astounding-Analog pulpit ever since most of us were lads, Harrison has selected a representative thirty-and-three, some dating back to the forties, all stamped with Campbell's individual brand of coat-trailing sagacity. They stand up surprisingly well as a book. (Doubleday)

John Christopher: *The Ragged Edge.* Great opening chapters. Cotter, like author Christopher, lives on the island of Guernsey. After a bad night, he goes out to find the shattered island is an island no longer; he can now walk to England—which he eventually does. . . . Christopher is an old hand at the convulsed landscape, social as well as geographic, of catastrophe; but here he gets involved in sentimental loose ends. Result: too ragged, too little edge. Damnably readable, for all that! (Simon & Schuster)

William Dexter: *World in Eclipse* and *Children of the Void.* One story in two volumes. The old themes again, threats from aliens, flying saucers, Earth torn out of orbit . . . all terribly unsophisticated and unscientific. But William Dexter writes as if he genuinely enjoyed writing and telling this far-out tale of odd races and odd illusions. He has just the style for it, a rather ponderous, unamazed style, which recalls Fowler Wright. Great fun, if you aren't too blasé. (Paperback Library)

Philip K. Dick: *Now Wait for Last Year.* Not the best Dick, but brilliant by the standards of lesser SF writers. Dick's great theme of the questionable nature of reality, many realities, is one he has examined over and over since he first entered the field; with each novel he comes closer to it, draws forth more insights. This time, it is unhappy Dr. Sweetscent, whose wife Cathy drifts in and out of drugged states, involved with his millionaire boss Ackerman and, through Ackerman, planetary politics. Earth is allied to one repulsive interstellar race against another. Time-travel is involved; so is the suffering world leader, Molinari. Dick is as subtle as ever with complex plots and ramified detail of future worlds. One reason why this is not quite so prime an example of his art may be that in structure it rather closely resembles Dick's masterwork Martian Timeslip. (Doubleday)

Gordon R. Dickson: *No Room for Man.* "Who Am I? What Am I?" asks the blurb, on this retitled reprint of Necromancer. In fact, metaphysics goes out the window in preference for a menace-to-men theme, in this fast-moving Van Vogtian tale, where a guild using Absolute Laws and Magic opposes an intricate technological civilization, and a third force sorts them both out. (Macfadden)

Harry Harrison: *Make Room! Make Room!* A marvelously saddening novel, the most effective warning ever against over-population, and consequently for birth-control. Harrison's story of New York in 1999, crammed with thirty-five million people leading substandard lives, needs no gimmicks or sudden catastrophes, relying on compressed emotion and strong atmospheric detail for its effect. (Doubleday)

Fred Hoyle: *October the First Is Too Late.* A wonderful idea crippled by inadequate handling. Hoyle must be given all the credit for a novel and broad-screen twist on the hoary time travel theme. Here we have different parts of the globe existing in different eras at the same time. We are teased to attention at modern Britain looking with horror across the channel where the First World War is still in progress, but we no sooner face the problem than we are whipped away. If Mr. Hoyle had only worked harder and gone into the detail and extrapolation needed for this kind of book he might very well have written a modern masterpiece. As it is, he writes lyrically for the first time. (Harper & Row)

Daniel Keyes: *Flowers for Algernon.* Remarkable, beautiful, and penetrating novel about the gentle moron who becomes something like the world's greatest genius, and then charts his own descent down into the intellectual depths again. The message is rather schmaltzy: maybe you're a nicer guy as a moron; which may account for its success (as a short story, in translation, as TV drama, as film, now as novel); but for all that, its fine qualities of pity and intelligence make it one of the year's, possibly decade's best. (Harcourt, Brace and World)

John Norman: *Tarnsman of Gor.* Another long Burroughs-like series begins, certain to wow the fans and bore the eggheads. This first dose of the saga of Tarl Cabot on Counter-Earth reveals itself to be decently written and a bit less camp than you might expect. (Ballantine)

Edgar Pangborn: *The Judgment of Eve.* After the Holocaust (jacket blurb's capitalization) again, and well-plowed ground it is. In a most civilized way, Pangborn uses the setting only as a stage for his characters to ask many questions about Life (reviewers' capitalization) and it is to his credit that he manages to sustain interest to the very end. A weak book from a strong writer, yet enjoyable nevertheless. (Simon & Schuster)

Mack Reynolds: *Of Godlike Power.* Another excellent polemical novel by a neglected novelist. In this one, Reynolds has his tone just right. The story of a prophet of a new religion opposed by a cheapskate radio announcer never becomes too stodgy or whimsical and, marvelously, prophet and announcer are credible. So are the new religion, and all the thrusts against our too-fat society. It happens to be fun to read as well as ringing true. (Belmont)

Robert Silverberg: *Needle in a Timestack.* A collection of ten Silverberg stories, Silverberg in a rather thoughtful mood. There's a lot of contemporary point to such stories as "The Pain Peddlars"—when the latent sadism of those medic sagas on the idiot box is not so damned latent—and a sound moral trim to the punishment used by a future society in "To See the Invisible Man". (Ballantine)

E. E. Smith: The Lensman Series: *Triplanetary, First Lensman, Galactic Patrol, Gray Lensman, Second Stage Lensman, Children of the Lens.* It can be argued that, after the opening sentence, "Two thousand million or so years ago two galaxies were colliding," we are in for six volumes of anticlimax, and, at the same time, to remain fascinated by this work—the longest of the hard-core SF sagas. Even if it remains cops and robbers without transcending into Good and Evil, it still stays fresh in its rather charming wooden way, and the various aliens remain more human than the human characters. (Pyramid)

The John Wyndham Omnibus. Contains Wyndham's three best novels, *The Day of the Triffids, The Kraken Wakes, The Chrysalids.* Too little has appeared from the once-prolific Wyndham of late; here's the reason in one unparallelled volume: he is resting adequately on his laurels. The very English method of narration suits the theme of the leisurely magnitude of civilization's fall. (Simon & Schuster)

William F. Temple: *Shoot at the Moon.* Perhaps an SF first, with a Spillane-type wise-cracking tough-guy novel all about rocketships. (Simon & Schuster) While Bill Temple is too nice a guy to be as foul as this exercise demands, he still moves the story along at a nice clip so that it has the readability of a good mystery. This despite the rough and tough characters' startling ability to throw quotes at each other rather than brick bats. "Because I'm in mourning for my life," the heroine declaims, and the hero instantly recognizes it as Masha's line from *The Seagull.* There is a lot more like this, and, surprisingly enough, Pangborn's *The Judgment of Eve* is shot full of the same kind of thing. Perhaps we make too much of a small coincidence, but can it be possible that these are first signs of intellectual awareness, that science fiction is part and parcel of literature and not a form of super-pulp somewhere between the western and the romance?

There is certainly some evidence for this belief. Critical books about SF appear regularly and stay in print. 1966 was a bumper year. Pride of place goes to the MIT *Index to the Science Fiction Magazines, 1957–1965*. This index, of all the stories and all the authors in all the magazines during this period, was published by the university science fiction society who, with fitting justice, used a computer to process the material.

Advent, a speciality publishing house that produces only non-fiction about SF, brought out James Blish's *The Issue at Hand,* a collection of this author's best critical essays. They also published *The Universes of E. E. Smith,* the same "Doc" referred to earlier, by R. Ellik and B. Evans, an unusual volume that is referred to as "a concordance to the Lensman and Skylark novels". Well! A symposium conducted by the American Academy of Arts and Sciences produced *Mumford Utopias and Utopian Thought* (Houghton, Mifflin) which analyses in detail all the aspects of utopias, both in fiction and in practice. The inexhaustible Sam Moskowitz produced two companion volumes, *Seekers of Tomorrow* and *Modern Masterpieces of SF* (World), the latter being an anthology of stories written by the authors who are examined in the former. While the effort is a laudable one, it might be wished that a bit less personal opinion and a shade more accuracy went into this author's work.

On a more scholarly level is Professor H. Bruce Franklin's *Future Perfect:* American Science Fiction of the Nineteenth Century (Oxford University Press). The Professor punctuates his discussion with stories by Hawthorne, Poe, Melville, Bierce, Bellamy, O'Brien, Twain, and others. Some critics have claimed that, in fact, the stories discussed are not science fiction; their readability has also been questioned. But Franklin's contributions repay careful study. He has many insights to offer that illuminate the present. Possibly the humanistic approach of his examples also offers an examplar for today.

Another scholarly fascinator—and rather fun—is I. F. Clarke's *Voices Prophesying War, 1763–1984* (Oxford University Press), English, or Scottish rather, in origin, dealing with the plethora of invasion and rebellion stories that the nineteenth century, especially France, Germany, and Britain, inflicted on itself. Clarke is skilful at showing how the development of a new weapon led to a new attack of nerves and consequently a new attack of invasion SF. Now we are saddled with the parallel theme of alien invasion. The transition point is marked by H. G. Wells's *The War of the Worlds;* Clarke's examination of this epoch-making novel is one of the best things in an extremely useful critical history. Fuller extracts from the scarce works he discusses would have been appreciated; presumably space did not permit this. As compensation, there are a number of prime illustrations from various sources.

Memorial to a great and various man is the collection of essays and stories by C. S. Lewis, edited by Walter Hooper and entitled *Of Other Worlds* (Harcourt, Brace and World). Lewis was born in Queen Victoria's reign. Like remarkably many other Victorians, he invented a fantasy-world at a very early age; his great trilogy, which begins with *Out of the Silent Planet,* has, in its almost obsessive attention to detail, the hallmarks of this sort of water-tight refuge from the real world, plus ironic references to that real world, which characterise Carroll's, the Brontes', and many Victorian painters' fantasy-worlds. The essays included here shed some light on Lewis's methods of creation, and on his breadth of understanding of myth-creating, as well as reminding us that he was a friend of Tolkein's. There is also the interview he gave on science fiction which was first published in *SF Horizons;* two short stories first published in *F&SF;* and two stories, one incomplete, published for the first time.

These are only a few of this year's books: and we are conscious of omitting many novels which have merit (while meritorious regular anthologies like Damon Knight's *Orbit,* Berkley; Wollheim and Carr's *World's Best Science Fiction,* Ace; and Judith Merril's far-ranging *Year's Best SF,* Delacorte, must flourish on their self-continuing reputations). We have found ourselves with no space/time to deal with, for instance, new writer Samuel "Chip" Delany's *BABEL-17* (Ace) or Jimmy Ballard's *The Crystal World* (Farrar Straus), which has already attracted much attention elsewhere. And we have avoided a swarm of novels on the well-tramped theme of alien invasion of Earth, or the well-tramped decks of mighty starships.

Clearly, the science fiction novel is in a lusty state, but what of the short story and the novelette in SF this year? As our duty, and partial pleasure, the undersigned have read a great number of stories to fulfill our editorial obligations. With our towering imaginations, we have no difficulty in imagining these yearly *Nebula* anthologies and the yearly Nebula Award still being handed out in A.D. 2000.

This places us under considerable pressure to discharge honorably our responsibilities as editors. Last year saw the first Awards and the first Anthology. The President of the controlling body, Science Fiction Writers of America, contributed the Introduction, and was concerned with introducing the whole scheme to the public. As the direct result of his, Damon Knight's, hard work, *SFWA,* the Nebula Awards, and the Nebula Anthology, are an established part of the literary scene. But we still have a precedent to establish here. A precedent of responsibility.

SFWA was established to further the interests of science fiction writers everywhere. We do not see how those interests can ultimately be furthered without the interests of the reader being also cared for. We feel that, in certain vital respects, the reader is being neglected.

And this is where our responsibilities come in. As readers as well as writers, we see our loyalties chopped two ways. As editors, we see the twin temptations which will beset all future editors of this series (the editor of the A.D. 2000 volume is probably yet unborn, but his responsibility is waiting for him!); those temptations lie between performing a proper job of work as critics and uttering publicity matter on behalf of Good Old SF.

Both the present editors have devoted and do devote the adolescent and adult years of their lives to science fiction; they contend that this demonstrates sufficiently their love for the medium. They also edit a small irregular journal of criticism, *SF Horizons*. In this journal, they came to a conclusion that they happily pass on here to future Nebula story editors: that the general welfare and good of science fiction is succored only by good science fiction stories. They have long since believed—having reached that mellow age where they are as apt to discuss their waistlines as sex—that high-powered ballyhoo does nothing for an inferior product.

The few beautiful stories garnered and be-laurelled here were retrieved from a decidedly non-vintage year. A danger in any art medium is that it will become victim of its conventions; this danger seems to threaten science fiction. Once-daring assumptions that man might travel through interplanetary space in machines built for the purpose, or visit distant stars powered by a faster-than-light drive, or even step into the past and future in time-machines, are daring no longer. They are clichés. Originally, they had bold and imaginative thinking behind them; now, they merely annihilate thinking.

An example. In one of this year's more popular stories, we came across this passage: "The Antoranite hove close, a Comet class with wicked-looking guns. Her probelight flashed the command to halt. He obeyed. The other went sublight likewise, matched kinetic velocities, and lay at a cautious distance. The radio buzzed."

Such a passage—and there are too many similar passages in this year's stories—can only pretend to sense in a science fiction magazine. It suggests the magazines are living on intellectually unearned income, cannibalising their past. The horrible jingle of "probelight" and "sublight" emphasises the decay of language that always goes hand-in-hand with decay of ideas. There is no science here, no imagination, only a meaningless rehash of what might once have had scientific and imaginative meaning. This trend was all too evident in most of the material we read.

Too many of this year's crop of tales deal in these old clothes. Space ship tales, robot tales, invasion tales . . . these old themes roll forth, clad in dead language. We found carelessnesses like "Xanten presently found a bin containing a number of containers" to downright idiocies like "Three minutes can seem an everlasting half hour." We found old plots; guys still fight over the last oxygen cylinder on Mars.

We found endless thick-headed toughies as heroes, but little characterization. We found numerous coy introductions of sex interest, but no attempts to portray women intelligently and lovingly, except in the beautiful story by a woman which we present here.

Clearly, one has to look for reasons for this curious state of affairs. We were interested to notice that even that elite, the members of SFWA, writers or editors all, voted for some indefensible stories. This gave us the idea that we as a fraternity might perhaps indeed use the fraternity as a way of bettering—not only ourselves—but our standards, that these annual volumes should be a sort of bar or tribunal before which we have to come yearly up to scratch: a public performance in which we must do better than just root for our buddies.

It will not be enough for writers to scrape under the admittedly not-very-exacting standards of the magazines. We are not selling them yard goods, trash instantly exchangeable for cash. We are selling them stories, by God, for real people to read and enjoy, to derive some excitement and enjoyment and maybe help from. Maybe they will also derive some better understanding of the dynamically changing world about them.

But this was the year of the yard goods, with a few honorable exceptions.

We would have liked to include here stories that maybe illuminated the pressing color question, the current political situation, not to mention present scientific developments, or the effects of those developments on art and customs, or the war in Vietnam. We could not; no such story was voted for—or maybe written! The discrepancy between the stories in the magazines and the often challenging and alert editorials was never more remarkable.

The great big wonderful world of Western technology goes on unrolling at the same exhilarating pace; beyond its borders lie more shadowy realms, full of strange factors for sf writers to investigate and extrapolate. Not much has been done about either sphere, this year, although there is always Mack Reynolds. Nor, on the other hand, have we had the benefit of many pure flights of the imagination that turn the mundane world into another and enchanted place. Well, there are always paragons like Jack Vance, and there was Cordwainer Smith. But we are grumbling about the rule, not the exceptions.

Science fiction has had good and bad years before. Why the trouble this year?

More than most of us care to admit, science fiction is influenced by the world around us. It may be fantasy about Earths packed with robots, or starving people, or large green insects that arrived here by "sublight," but the writers themselves have to bow to the more stimulating perils of the here-and-now. That bothersome and endless war in Vietnam may be having its effect.

Would it not be a relief if we had a few stories dealing imaginatively with that situation? It should attract science fiction writers and readers. Robert Heinlein taught us years ago that the old saw about force solving nothing was all nonsense, but here seems to be an interesting exception to his law. Force, in this science fictional case, seems to be solving very little, judging by the military in the de-militarized zone over there.

Sure, there's plenty of *force* in this year's stories! More violence than you could shake an electronic whip at! All too often, when ideas run out, violence is brought in, jaws are broken, mandibles crushed, planets blasted right out of existence, just to round off the plot. Friends, we're getting as bad as television! *Vision* has always been the electric charge we needed from science fiction. Let's hear it for the imagination, eh?

Science fiction appears to be the last viable, exciting and commercially successful market for the short story. While the rewards, on average, are not grand, they are at least fair payment for work done and a showcase for writers. We do not think it right that this showcase has been filled with nothing better than splintered chips from the true cross and machine-made copies of original models. The showcase is not good nor is it bad. It is just there. We writers, and we alone, are responsible for what is placed inside it.

Brian W. Aldiss

Harry Harrison

NEBULA AWARDS 1966

Best Novel: (tie) *Flowers for Algernon* by Daniel Keyes (Harcourt, Brace & World) and *Babel-17* by Samuel R. Delany (Ace Books, Inc.)

Best Novella: "The Last Castle," by Jack Vance (Galaxy, April 1966).

Best Novelette: "Call Him Lord," by Gordon R. Dickson (Analog Science Fiction/Science Fact, May 1966)

Best Short Story: "The Secret Place," by Richard McKenna (ORBIT 1, 1966)

ROLL OF HONOR

"Light of Other Days," by Bob Shaw (Analog Science Fiction/Science Fact, August 1966).

"Who Needs Insurance?" by Robin S. Scott (Analog Science Fiction/Science Fact, April 1966)

"Among the Hairy Earthmen," by R. A. Lafferty (Galaxy, August 1966)

"Day Million," by Frederik Pohl (Rogue, February 1966)

"When I Was Miss Dow," by Sonya Dorman (Galaxy, June 1966)

"In the Imagicon," by George Henry Smith (Galaxy, February 1966)

"We Can Remember It for You Wholesale," by Philip K. Dick (The Magazine of Fantasy and Science Fiction, April 1966)

"Man in His Time," by Brian W. Aldiss ("Who Can Replace a Man?" 1965)

1965 NEBULA AWARDS

Best Novel: *Dune* by Frank Herbert

Best Novella (tie): *The Saliva Tree* by Brian Aldiss and *He Who Shapes* by Roger Zelazny

Best Novelette: *The Doors of His Face, the Lamps of His Mouth* by Roger Zelazny

Best Short Story: *"Repent, Harlequin!" Said the Ticktockman* by Harlan Ellison